THE
MOSUL
LEGACY

THE
MOSUL
LEGACY

CHRISTOPHER LOWERY

Urbane
PUBLICATIONS

urbanepublications.com

First published in Great Britain in 2018 by Urbane Publications Ltd
Suite 3, Brown Europe House, 33/34 Gleaming Wood Drive, Chatham, Kent
ME5 8RZ
Copyright © Christopher Lowery, 2018

A CIP catalogue record for this book is available from the British Library.

ISBN 978-1-911583-92-9
MOBI 978-1-911583-93-6

Design and Typeset by Julie Martin
Cover by Julie Martin

Printed and bound by 4edge UK

urbanepublications.com

To Marjorie, my Beloved Wife of 54 years.

*'The Only Thing Necessary for the Triumph of Evil
is that Good Men Do Nothing.'*

Attrib. to Edmund Burke MP, 18th Century.

PROLOGUE

Mosul, Iraq
June 2014

'*Allahu Akbar*, Allah is Great!'

The man was known as Karl. His face and limbs were burned brown from years in the desert and his features under the spotlight were aquiline and cruel. A livid scar ran across his right cheek, witness to only one of the many wars he'd fought for his cause. He had survived so many battles he'd outlived everyone who had ever borne arms at his side. He was a living legend, and he was on the verge of his greatest triumph.

His cry was taken up and repeated by the hundreds of ISIL jihadists under his command, echoing across the desert surrounding Qaryat al Ashiq, at the junction of Route 47 and Highway One, the western entry road into Mosul, the largest town in northern Iraq. Karl lifted his AK47 assault rifle and fired into the air. A moment later, dozens of pick-up trucks mounted with heavy machine guns and spotlights sped off towards the city in deadly convoys, destroying everything in their path. Each truck held fighters carrying assault rifles and light machine guns, mostly captured from previous battles with the Iraqi army. They blasted their way past the checkpoints and advanced through the suburbs into the heart of the city with virtually no opposition from the military or police contingents.

It was 02:30 in the morning on Wednesday 4th June

2014 and after the fall of Fallujah, the *City of Mosques*, close to Baghdad in central Iraq, it was now Mosul's turn to feel the devastating sting of the jihadists' venom. The previous night, the ISIL military leader, Abu Abdulrahman al-Bilawi, had blown himself up to avoid being captured by the Iraqi police. The police commander, Lieutenant General Mahdi Gharawi, had hoped this would avert an attack on the city. He was wrong.

An ancient Assyrian city, Mosul had achieved a brief moment of fame in July 2003, when Saddam Hussein's sons, Qusay and Uday, were killed there in a gun battle during the allied invasion. The city was the greatest prize ever targeted by ISIL, with a population of 2.5 million citizens – ten times that of Raqqa in Syria, which they captured in 2014 during the civil war against the hated tyrant, Bashar al-Assad. Raqqa was named as the capital of the *Islamic State of Iraq and the Levant* by the self-proclaimed Caliph, Abu Bakr al-Baghdadi. Ever since, it had been a convenient launching pad for incursions into Iraq by ISIL fighters.

Following Karl's simple, bold plan, the jihadists came across Syria's eastern desert and over the border into the ancient lands of Nineveh Plains in Iraq's north-western territory. Their objective was to secure a couple of outlying neighbourhoods, but such was their barbaric, ruthless efficiency and the incompetent and fainthearted lack of resistance from the Iraqi defence forces, they reached the Tigris River, which runs through the centre of Mosul. On the way, they overran several military bases, strengthening their arsenal with the heavy weapons, armoured vehicles and ammunition depots they held.

The Iraqis capitulated before their onslaught and the ISIL fighters captured several key positions in the city.

Karl was astonished at the success of their incursion; instead of the attack being a hit and run, they had established a solid base in the heart of Mosul. Despite having infiltrated hundreds of spies and sleeper cells amongst the population in the months preceding the attack, he'd had no inkling of how ill-prepared and craven their defensive forces were. As the realisation dawned on him, he had an audacious idea, an idea that would change the world's perception of the ISIL jihadist caliphate. That night, he returned to the desert to meet other senior militants to prepare a plan of execution and once again take the Iraqis by surprise.

On June 6th and 7th, ISIL forces attacked the north-west defences, battering the city with mortar fire, shelling and missiles. Then, on the morning of June 8th, with four other commanders, Karl led convoys of four hundred heavily armed fighters in a hundred trucks into Mosul, penetrating all areas of the city. They targeted police stations, the security headquarters and military barracks, executing all those who failed to escape their wrath. The sleeper cells that had been waiting for the attack were activated and carried out selected assassinations of key political and security officials. The city quickly found itself leaderless and a state of anarchy took over. For two more days the ISIL jihadists purged what was left of the forces of order and captured more strategic objectives. They seized industrial and government buildings and infrastructure, including the International Airport with dozens of fighting helicopters. Large numbers of prisoners were released from the jails and immediately took up arms with them.

During this short period of warfare, only six days from Karl's first attack, the Iraqi forces crumbled and fled from the fighting. Thirty thousand soldiers and the same number of police officers left the city. Many of them threw off their uniforms and joined the ISIL troops or dressed as civilians to escape the barbaric death that awaited them. On June 10th, with less than two thousand jihadists, outnumbered thirty to one, ISIL took control of Mosul and all it contained, including the two million citizens who still remained there. As well as seizing a prestigious and strategically situated centre, ISIL acquired millions of US-supplied arms, munitions and vehicles abandoned by the army. The jewel in the crown of the *Caliphate of the Islamic State of Iraq and the Levant* was now Mosul and on 10th June 2014, black flags flew over the city.

By August, the jihadists had extended their rule of terror over 350km on the west side of the Tigris as far as Fallujah. More than thirty thousand Christian families were driven from their homes and ancestral lands, fleeing to Kurdistan, with only the clothes on their backs. This huge expanse of terrain counted hundreds of villages and small towns, as well as the strategic military airport at Qayyarah West, near the oil centre of Qayyarah. It also brought massive revenue from the oilfields in this area and in Kirkuk province to the east. Immediately they were in control; militants secured the oilfields and engineers were sent in to begin operations and ship the crude oil to market. By the following April, when Kirkuk was retaken by the Iraqis, the caliphate had earned $US 450 million from oil shipments.

In Mosul, the ISIL barbarians set about the rounding up and systematic slaughter of Iraqi soldiers, police, security officers, so-called spies and anyone else who was deemed to be a traitor to the jihadist cause. The murderous bloodletting went on for weeks, until thousands of 'enemies of the caliphate' or non-believers had been tortured to death, publicly executed by firing squad, beheaded, burned alive or simply disposed of in such primitively efficient fashions as driving trucks and busloads of men, women and children into the sinkholes found in the desert surrounding the city.

As a senior officer, Karl had a dual role, military planner and infantry commander, and he tried to stay away from the security and espionage services. He did not declare war on civilian men, women or children. His reputation and seniority meant he had never been ordered to participate in the butchery, but he was often ordered to observe. He was sickened by the fact that the bodies of many thousands of civilians were buried just a few kilometres from his command post in Qayyarah. In two nearby villages alone, Khasfa and Hamman al Alil, up to five thousand bodies were disposed of in the sinkholes, many hundreds of metres deep.

The ISIL fighters had pursued their attack with sophisticated weaponry, employed in a devastatingly ruthless annihilation of everything and everyone who stood in their way. A great number of their planners, senior commanders and officers were *Baathists*, ex-officers in Saddam Hussein's security services and army, who had joined up with Al-Qaeda in Iraq and then converted to ISIL. Standing against this well-trained and well-armed fighting machine were only the impotent Iraqi defence forces. Since Obama's withdrawal of US troops in 2011, leaving a political and administrative void behind them, this so-called army had become a disorganised, lazy and corrupt rabble, unfit for purpose.

The superiority of the ISIL leaders, fighters and armoury was enhanced by the most effective and sophisticated weapons ever invented; mobile phones, tablets and the internet. Communication between planners, commanders and senior fighters was devastatingly efficient. On the move, they texted and talked using prepaid, unidentifiable mobile phones, then once established in secure bases they used the internet, coordinating and directing their forces by encrypted emails, *WhatsApp* or their own secure voice messaging network. Once their triumph was assured, internet news services and social media channels like *YouTube* and *Facebook* were used to spread their propaganda around the world. *Tor*, the dark web hidden in the foul underbelly of the internet, was a key tool used to radicalise, enlist and corrupt susceptible people of all nationalities, religions, age and sex, to throw away their lives for the ISIL cause – to rid the world of 'infidels', that is, anyone who didn't agree with them.

Without incompetent Western politicians, oil, mobile communications and the internet, ISIL might never have existed, but it did.

ONE

Mosul, Iraq
February 2015

'They've stopped advancing. Looks like they're digging in to stay.' Karl was speaking to his boss, the latest supreme commander in Mosul. He was on the right bank of the Tigris, the north-western outskirts of the city, on the Nineveh Plains near Highway One, looking through his binoculars at a huge number of Kurdish Peshmerga forces about 3km away. During the past few weeks, they had cut off the ISIL supply route from Raqqa and seized many villages, to take back control of over 500km2 of land in the region between the Syrian border and Mosul. Until that morning they had been advancing alongside the highway towards the city, but they had now stopped near Badush Dam, 8km from the centre.

He breathed a sigh of relief; his spies had been right. They'd told him that Kurdish officials had decided not to move beyond primarily Kurdish areas and retaking the city of Mosul itself was left to the Iraqi Army. They'd also informed him there were five thousand Peshmerga out there and he knew his men could never have stopped them. ISIL had already lost over two hundred fighters in the bloody skirmishes to prevent their advance past this point. Twenty-one senior militants, including his close brother-in-arms, the new ISIL governor of Nineveh province, had been killed. Once again, Karl was one of the only surviving commanders in the sector. Despite receiving reinforcements from other areas, his forces now numbered less than three hundred and they were exhausted from the unrelenting fighting of the last few weeks.

Since January, the Kurds had mounted simultaneous offensives from the northwest, northeast, and southeast. They were supported by air strikes from the *Global Coalition to Counter the Islamic State of Iraq and the Levant,* the US-led coalition forces. The ISIL command had suspected this was the preparatory phase of the well-advertised offensive to retake Mosul. Kurdish forces would cut off their supply routes to the north and the west of the city, while Iraqi forces moved in from the south. Now, if he could believe the other news he'd been given by his informants, that attack was not as imminent as they'd feared. The cowardly Iraqis weren't yet ready to fight for Mosul. They were preoccupied with preventing the jihadists from taking Ramadi, a city of 250,000 inhabitants, west of Baghdad. Once they had secured that city, they would turn their attention to Mosul again. Karl hoped they might get a little respite from the fighting, enough time to plan the defense of their prize possession.

He finished his call and summoned two of his senior fighters, Jabbar and his brother-in-law Sulaiman. He knew both men had been with Saddam Hussein's Imperial Guards before the invasion and had escaped to Europe, returning to Iraq the previous year. Since the taking of Mosul and ISIL's rapid rise in profile, thousands of recruits had joined the jihadist movement, including many ex-Hussein supporters. These counted members of his family and senior security and military officers. It didn't matter to Karl; they hated the Western coalition, they were well trained, brave and clever and they were fighting with him and ISIL needed every experienced warrior it could call on.

'It looks like things will be quieter for a while. The Kurds won't budge until those fucking Iraqi cowards make a move and that's not about to happen. I've been called to Mosul for a meeting of commanders. It's getting very bad there, the coalition is bombing the shit out of the city, softening us up for the end game. We've got to prepare for the next series of attacks, so I'll be gone a few days.'

'What are your orders?' It was Jabbar, the taciturn one, who asked.

'You're in charge while I'm away. I'll be back by the weekend. Get your people sorted and fed and let them relax. There's still a few women in the area, round them up and let the guys have their fill while they can.'

'They need it,' Sulaiman interjected. 'Some of these fighters should be wearing nappies, especially the European kids. They thought they'd come for a vacation and now they're crying and wailing like fucking schoolgirls, shitting in their pants all day. Apart from the Irish, Baki and the other two, I wouldn't be surprised if they pissed off home before long.'

'Give them a woman and make sure they stay. We can't lose any more men, we'll need everyone in Mosul soon. Tell them they'll have a break and we'll be moving back into town any day. Keep them happy.'

He climbed into his truck. 'I'll be back by Saturday. *Allahu Akbar.*'

As always, the two men obeyed Karl's orders to the letter. They liked obeying orders; it gave them a sense of purpose, fulfilment and order, in a chaotic world they had never been able to cope with alone.

That night, after the women, they sat away from the main camp under the stars with Baki and his friends from Belfast. Every few minutes they heard the sound of rockets and Grad missiles passing overhead on their way to Mosul, followed by a distant explosion. Although the Kurds had suspended their ground attack, they were still bombarding the city with everything they had.

'We should pray,' Jabbar said. 'We haven't prayed properly for a long time. We're alive and the battle is over for now. We should thank Allah and praise him.'

The five men kneeled on their blankets and pressed their foreheads to the ground. *SubhanAllah wa biHamdihi,* they chanted together.

They didn't hear the faulty Grad missile that veered from its path and came to earth after only 10km instead of the 18km it was programmed for. The Russian 9M22U rocket delivered a 20-kilo fragmentation warhead at 75km per hour into the middle of the group, creating a crater five metres in diameter and two in depth. Nothing was left of the five men who had been praying there a moment before the bomb landed in their midst. Nothing to show that they had ever existed, that they had been radicalised by false preachers and internet propaganda and had rallied to the ISIL cause, that they had fought bravely and killed dozens of warriors just like themselves, all convinced they were right and the others were wrong. Never having the chance to realise at the end that it was all for nothing, that it was just a deadly game of religion, power and politics, and that their lives were the wagers their leaders were prepared to lose to play the game.

TWO

The studio flat was in a small, shabby apartment building in the Kalk district of Cologne, not far from the mosque. The facade of the building was scarred by primitive graffiti writings and drawings in a mixture of German, English and Arabic – complaints about the massive increase in the Muslim community in the city due to the influx of one million immigrants during the Middle East wars. The most vicious and obscene messages daubed on this and the neighbouring blocks had been added since the sexual attacks against hundreds of women during the New Year's Eve celebrations. Alongside a bright red swastika drawn with blood running down from it was scrawled, *'That bitch Merkel's immigration policy will destroy our country.'*

A battered square table took up most of the room and the man who had rented the place two months ago was lying on a mattress on the floor when the 'ping' of an email arriving on his laptop roused him. The message was on his 'studentpost@web.de' address and said simply, *'My Travel Dossier'*. He opened up the travel agent site offering trips to Australia and New Zealand then entered the coordinates he'd been given by text message on his phone and entered a site in the Dark Web, where he found the next link. A password request came up and he typed in *'redemption16'*. A file containing a PDF document entitled '*Instructions Part One*' was revealed. The second password was '*joyfulday*'. Written in Arabic, the document contained drawings, photographs and diagrams. He didn't download it in case his computer might be interrogated later, but it took a while to print on his clapped-out old printer, then he closed the link. He knew it would be removed within the hour by the sender.

The first eleven pages compared various options, the advantages, disadvantages and risks of each type of process. The last page was a general list of the kind of materials he would need to purchase. There were many everyday items that could be acquired in the local supermarket, but he didn't want to risk attracting attention by buying anything there except food. There would be other less innocuous materials to buy later and he wanted to avoid any unnecessary risks until then. He would give a list of those items to his younger brother, Jamil, to purchase. He was only twelve and looked like an angel.

By many standards, Ibrahim bin Omar al-Ahmad was not much more than a boy himself. In January he had celebrated his twentieth birthday at a pizza restaurant with Jamil and their six-year-old sister, Fatima. They didn't live with him but with his mother, a few streets away. He mostly saw Jamil at the mosque since he had moved out of their mother's flat, but he came from time to time when he wanted to talk, and he often brought Fatima. They were the only reasons he was still living in this filthy country full of corrupt German infidels. He hadn't informed his brother of his plan; the boy was still struggling to come to terms with the Imam's preaching, but Ibrahim was sure he would soon see the light, especially after the event he was planning. He would become a hero, a martyr to the cause, and Jamil would be proud of him.

It was coming up to noon and he heard through the open window the sound of the *muezzin* from the nearby mosque calling him to worship. Ibrahim washed his feet then unfolded his prayer mat and laid the frayed fabric on the floor, kneeling on it to make his *Dhuhr* midday supplication. Afterwards he sat at the table with a slice of cold pizza and a carton of orange juice. Before turning his attention to the instructions file, he opened up another shadow site, a clandestine 'News Agency', sponsored by ISIL. To cleanse his mind of his surroundings, Ibrahim watched a video posted a couple of months before by his brothers in arms. He had seen it many times before. The first part showed the mass execution of over seven hundred Shia prison inmates in Mosul, Iraq, by firing squads using truck-mounted Russian NSV heavy machine guns. This exploit was a show of 'security cleansing' after ISIL's capture of the city in June 2014.

Ibrahim's father, an ISIL officer fighting under his original Iraqi name of Abu bin al Khattab, had been killed there the following year. His obsession with secrecy and self-effacement was the reason that the German authorities had never taken any interest in his family. He had left Cologne for Copenhagen in 2014, arrived in Iraq via Istanbul, then fought for over a year and sacrificed his life for ISIL, all without fanfare or recognition. His family had been told of his death by the Imam Mohammad. No one else knew he was no longer in Germany, let alone dead in a besieged, condemned city, his body probably buried beneath tons of rubble along with thousands of other men, women and children, all martyrs to the glory of Allah.

Ibrahim knelt and chanted *SubhanAllah wa biHamdihi,* several times, praising Allah and remembering his father's glorious martyrdom.

He went back to his laptop to watch the second part of the film. This featured a series of huge detonations as ISIL explosives specialists demolished the two-thousand-year-old Arch of Triumph, in Palmyra, Syria. A thrill of power and achievement flooded through his body as the series of ear-splitting explosions gradually reduced each part of the ancient edifice to rubble, leaving only a few remnants of the entrance arch still standing, resembling, as it now was, a broken doorway into a lost civilisation. The noise and destruction were so deeply erotic and sensual that he had an erection and had to masturbate to calm himself down. As always, he felt ashamed at his lack of mental discipline and swore it wouldn't happen again.

He replayed the second part of the video again, revelling in this demonstration of pure, unrestrained power and intent. A demonstration that had been seen and understood by every nation on earth, testifying to the inevitable destitution of the corrupt civilisations that would soon be removed by the Islamist movement. He pondered on this vicarious revenge, regretting once again he hadn't joined the group of friends who had left for

Turkey, en route to Iraq, six months before. Since they had received news of his father's death, he had thought of nothing else but to go over to avenge him.

Ibrahim had never been close to his mother but idolised his father, known by everyone as Jabbar, a name which described his character; a tough, determined and resourceful man who, in 2003, somehow managed to save his pregnant wife and seven-year-old son from the Iraqi death trap and find a way to safety in Europe. Germany, with its disbelieving infidel people, was no substitute for their country, but at least it wasn't the UK or US, the treacherous conspirators who had invaded their homeland and murdered many of their friends and family.

He had not been a committed Islamist until, deprived of the father he had admired and respected, the lost and lonely teenager had sought consolation and advice in the mosque. Imam Mohammad had easily converted him into a committed ISIL believer, ready to follow his father's example and offer his life to their crusade. This was a cause of huge friction between him and his mother. She had lost her husband in what she thought was a senseless adventure; a meaningless gesture, flying off to die in a country which was no longer his own, a country where coalition forces and its own army were murdering its citizens with indiscriminate shelling and bombing. Another anonymous death to add to the hundreds of thousands of unnamed victims.

She implored Ibrahim not to become part of those horrible statistics, but he was adamant. His father's brilliant career and his family's life had been destroyed by the murderous US-European alliance that had stolen his country and forced him to flee with them like a cowardly criminal. All this had been done in the name of 'liberation' and invented threats of potential attacks with 'weapons of mass destruction' which didn't even exist. The Imam had explained to him that the invasion of Iraq had only two objectives; to satisfy the bloodlust of the US' and UK's megalomaniac politicians and to steal their most precious resource, their oil, leaving its 23 million citizens with nothing but war, ruin and starvation, and leaving his family in a foreign country surrounded by people they hated. His mother didn't understand what had happened, but now he did, and he would make them pay. He would travel the same road as his father and, if necessary, suffer the same fate.

Then it seemed his plans had been thwarted by Allah. His mother suffered a serious heart attack and couldn't work; he had felt guilty and obliged to stay to help look after his brother and sister. For six months he worked at two menial jobs to pay the rent on their flat, foregoing his plans for the sake of his family. But now his mother's health was improving and she was able to work again, things were going to change. Now it was his turn to strike out at the non-believers, to show that though he wasn't in the front line of attack, he was fighting for his beliefs, fighting for and with his brothers in ISIL. Through the Imam's preaching, Allah had revealed to him a different plan and two months ago he'd moved out of the family's flat with this new, deadly purpose in mind. His patience had not been in vain; his glorious project was worth the delay. He took up the instruction manual and started reading and making notes, learning new skills.

Ash Shurta Neighbourhood, Mosul, Iraq

'We can't take this any longer. The children are having awful nightmares, it's too much to expect them to see this slaughter day after day, week after week. They can't cope with it anymore and neither can we.' Hema Al-Douri took her husband by the shoulders, gazing up imploringly into his eyes, tears pouring down her cheeks.

Faqir looked at the face of the woman he had fallen in love with twenty years before. She was still the loveliest person he'd ever known, but the strain of living under the ISIL rule was showing; today, she seemed to have aged by ten years.

Earlier that week, members of the Mosul Battalion, the secret resistance group, had attacked a truck carrying six ISIL fighters with rifle fire, killing or injuring them, before disappearing into the bowels of the city. Although most of the supporters of the movement dared only to spray the letter 'M', meaning *Muqawama* – Resistance – on the walls of buildings, this was one of the rare attempts at retaliation, all resulting in the same penalty, the callous murder of more residents of the city. That morning, the couple and their family had been forced to witness twenty innocent civilians being tortured to death by flame throwers in an unsuccessful attempt to identify the culprits.

'I'm worried about the girls,' she went on, her voice breaking with sobs. 'Even with those awful *niqabs* they have to wear, these ISIL creatures can still see they're young and beautiful. They get molested every time we walk along the street by some stinking pervert. Today I had to stop Malik from pushing the man away. He's going to get into trouble, he'll be whipped or shot if his temper gets the better of him.'

Faqir put his arms around her, searching for something positive to say. 'Be thankful he hasn't had the idea of joining the Battalion,' he spoke in a whisper, even pronouncing the name was punishable by death.

She went on, 'And it's not just the children. I saw Rana at the market, she's going crazy. Her parents have been rounded up with some other older people and put in the cells. They're starting to grab them to be used as human shields or suicide bombers when the street fighting starts here.'

For the first time, Faqir silently thanked God that he and his wife had only one surviving parent, her mother, Hadiya, who lived with them and their four children in two of the bedrooms of their small hotel-restaurant near the university on Mosul's left bank. The university was now an ISIL headquarters and training facility and Faqir's premises no longer functioned as a public facility. The other bedrooms and the dining room served as a dosshouse for fifty fighters and they were expected to provide meals twice a day for them and any other militants who called in. Even after Hussein's downfall, they had scraped a living; for several years US troops had regularly mingled with local customers and life had been bearable, but after the 2014 ISIL invasion, their business was destroyed.

The Al-Douri family were Christians, the only

reason for their survival under the ISIL doctrine being the restaurant they owned. In July 2014, just after the occupation, like all Christians, they had received an ultimatum from the new regime; *convert to Islam or be executed or pay a 'protection tax'* (known as jiziya), *to avoid the death sentence.* Faqir had managed to barter his restaurant business as payment of the tax. The premises were large and his family managed the restaurant well; the jihadists needed to eat and sleep so it suited them to spare their lives. When he had originally made the deal, a rate per night and per meal had been agreed, but it was now over a year since they'd seen a dinar in payment and his hard-earned savings were gradually dwindling away.

In the meantime, like every building in the area, the hotel was slowly but surely being destroyed by the escalating coalition attacks on the city. Every morning, the streets around the university were littered with bodies and body parts, either from the night-time US air attacks or the collateral damage of the terrorist's own indiscriminate rockets and mortar bombing. Once the Iraqi forces entered Mosul, it would be hand-to-hand fighting and Rana's parents and hundreds or even thousands like them would just be cannon fodder. And with or without his restaurant, as Christians, he and his family would not be spared.

The couple were blessed with twin sons, sixteen years old, and girls of fourteen and thirteen. Until now, because of the facility of the restaurant premises, the jihadists had left them alone, although they were called out regularly, like that morning, to witness beatings and executions in the nearby square. Men, women, children and anyone who was considered to have disobeyed the ultra-strict mockery of Shariah law imposed by the caliphate's bullies. *In the end, we'll be just another example of their pathological dogma,* he realised.

Hema was saying tearfully, 'The kids are so unhappy and frustrated, squabbling amongst themselves and with us, hiding from the bombs and those evil people who can't wait for us to be killed, or to transgress some stupid rule so they can beat or execute us. When it's safe to go outside, they never see their friends, there's no point, they're not allowed to laugh or have fun.' She wiped her eyes. 'They're surrounded by death and destruction that children shouldn't have to witness, just waiting and wondering if it will ever be over and they can live a normal life again. The boys won't take it much longer, one day they'll do something to defy these monsters and we'll all suffer, more than we already do.'

Looking bleakly at him, she said, 'We both know how it will end. We're amongst the few Christians still alive here and when the terrorists are facing defeat, we'll be the first to be sacrificed. They'll take our daughters as sex slaves and send our sons out with rifles, so they'll be killed by the Iraqis and we'll be used as suicide bombers or something more dreadful.' She broke down in tears again, sobbing desperately. 'We've got to get away from this place before it's too late to save our family.'

He held her close. 'I know, we should have taken our chance when there were still visas to be had. I've been concentrating on surviving and so far, it's worked, but you're right, if we stay, it's finished, there'll be no survival for us. But there's still a chance we can get away, we've got some cash put aside, enough to buy our way out and survive for a while, if we're careful. I've heard some names, guys who can get documents and help people like us to escape. I'm going to get in touch, to find a way out as soon as we possibly can.'

She wiped her eyes. 'You promise?' When he nodded gravely, being a pragmatic woman, she asked, 'Is England still your first choice?'

'There's no other sensible option. It's the only language we speak reasonably well and the English are the most welcoming people in the world. You loved it there.' He was referring to the trip they'd taken to London for their honeymoon, in 1998, before Hussein's relations with the Western powers broke down completely. They had kept up their language practice, often speaking English with their children, to relieve the constant feeling of being trapped in a Muslim world inhabited by fear and claustrophobia.

'If we can get into Turkey, I'm sure we can make it to Europe, there's thousands of people who've done it.' He spoke convincingly, but he knew that Turkey had suspended issuing visas to Iraqis earlier that year and without them, he didn't know how he'd get his family across the border. He needed documents and he needed a guide to have any chance of getting safely out of Mosul and across the border. If they did make it, then the only feasible routes were through Greece and across the Aegean to Italy, or by 'The Balkan Route', through Bulgaria and Romania to the Germanic states in northern Europe.

'There has to be a way around the visa problem,

I know refugees are still getting through the Turkish border. I'll find people to help us to do the same.' He had a sudden feeling of panic when he uttered the word, 'refugees'. *That's what we'll become, homeless refugees at the mercy of everyone who wants to take advantage of us. But it can't be worse than what will happen to us here.* He kissed Hema's brow, 'Stop worrying. I promise I'll find a solution.'

'Be careful, don't take any risks, or you'll make things worse. We need to find someone very soon, someone we can trust, who won't be suspected.'

Faqir knew Hema was right, but he would have to take risks, whether he liked it or not, or they would never get away from the Mosul death trap.

THREE

'Hello big brother, how are things?'

'All the better when I hear from you, little brother,' Ibrahim laughed, as he always did when he spoke to Jamil. The boy was a ray of sunshine in an otherwise miserable, dreary, boring town, a town he intended to wake up to the reality of the world outside very soon.

'Are we going to the park on Saturday?'

'That's a silly question. You're off school, the forecast is good, and you and Fatima need some sunshine and fresh air, so of course we're going.'

'Cool. I'll tell her, she's already asking what you'll get her for her birthday, but I haven't said anything.'

They talked for a few minutes and after promising to pick them up on Saturday at ten, Ibrahim put away his mobile with confused emotions. He knew he would miss his brother and sister after the event, and they would be sad too, but it was a sacrifice he had to make. It was too late to back out and his duty to his father's memory was paramount. He had to follow his example, whatever the price, and afterwards Jamil would be so proud of him that he would quickly forget his sadness.

Ibrahim was not part of a cell; he had no partners in his project. Using the Imam as a conduit and his father's reputation as a bargaining chip, he had made contact via the shadow internet with a high-ranking member of ISIL and put his proposal forward. An ISIL operative met Ibrahim in Essen and he passed the test, even though he imposed his own conditions:

They must never contact him without his instigation. He would initiate all contact and would work to his own timetable.

He insisted on acting as a lone operative. There was an existing cell in Cologne, but he knew the leader, Ahmad, in his opinion an arrogant idiot, blinded by ideology and incapable of organising a walk in the park.

They offered him instructions, a PayPal account (in the name of Klaus Ritterman, with a Berlin address) *and a new, apparently unbreakable 'Encryption App'.* He accepted these contributions, without any conditions attached.

Ibrahim wanted both the risk and the opportunity of fame and martyrdom to be his alone and because of his father's reputation, his conditions had been transmitted to a higher authority. An Emir, the ISIL commander who would manage him from Iraq, contacted him a few days later to confirm their acceptance and set up the internet procedure. His job at a friend's car repair garage provided him with the money he needed, but the *PayPal* account was useful to make untraceable payments. Now, only the internet and his brother's help were required to prepare and execute his plan. *Inshallah! If Allah wills it.*

After printing out the first set of instructions, Ibrahim had studied the various options in detail before he made his final choice; the manufacture of TATP,

Triacetone Triperoxide. He shivered with fear and anticipation when he went back onto the shadow site to request part two, with its list of specific requirements. There were six more pages and drawings with numerous warnings, written in red capitals and illustrated by bloody photographs of previous accidents. He ignored the warnings and looked at the complete itemised list of requirements. The banal supermarket items were listed first, and the cosmetics and chemical purchases were at the bottom of the page, marked in yellow. He cut the list in half; the top part he would give to Jamil on Saturday and the rest of the items he would buy himself from the pharmacy and hardware store.

There had been a lot of noise recently on the websites he visited. He knew something was going to happen, something in Europe, but he didn't know what or where. Selfishly he hoped he could launch his attack before anyone else – show the way, execute the next *Charlie Hebdo* or *Paris Massacre* event, but on German soil. Show the world that no European country was safe from retribution, ISIL style.

Then on the morning of Tuesday 22 March, he switched on the TV and stared in amazement and dismay at the screen; reports and images of the attacks by gunmen and suicide bombers on Zaventem international airport and the Maelbeek metro station in Brussels, close to several European Union institutions. The almost simultaneous attacks killed thirty-two people and injured scores more. Like the *Paris Massacre*, the Belgian event was breath-taking in its planning, execution and results. He checked every other channel; they were all showing the same thing, *The Brussels Bombings* it had been named. The murderous images were being transmitted around the globe, to every country on the planet. It was an historic event.

Ibrahim felt strangely dejected. His own project had suddenly become a pathetic effort by comparison. How could he hope, single-handed, to compete with such a powerful statement of intent? That evening he went to listen to the Imam, who said something that resonated in his mind. Mohammad applauded the massacre and announced, *'Paris and Brussels were historic steps in the march towards our liberation and world ascendance. But each was only one step of many. A single step which will be followed by many more until all those steps become a stampede from which the infidels will flee. Each of us must take our own step. It is our duty to Allah.'*

On his knees, Ibrahim understood the significance of the Imam's words. Every action against the West was a historic event, however small and trivial it might appear. Each successful act in itself was a moment of triumph, a tiny spotlight of fame for the perpetrator and another tiny chink in the armour of the infidel. The accumulation of all these acts, however paltry individually, would inevitably outweigh the strength of the opposition.

As forecast, Saturday morning was sunny, and he took Jamil and Fatima to the park and bought them fruit drinks and sweets. His cousin, Hassan, came with them. He was a year older than Ibrahim and the only other remaining member of his mother's family in Germany. Hassan's own mother, Ibrahim's aunt, had died on the boat trip from Iraq to Greece, then he was orphaned when their fathers had died fighting together in Mosul. He was making his way from Hamburg to stay with an uncle in Munich and had borrowed Ibrahim's bed in the room he had shared with Jamil, staying for a few weeks and making a small but welcome contribution to the rent. Unlike Ibrahim, Hassan detested the ISIL movement, and he had told him nothing of his plan, but they tolerated each other for the sake of family.

They went to the shopping mall where he gave Jamil some cash and the top half of the shopping list before sending him into the supermarket. In the toy store he chose a gift for his sister's seventh birthday that coming weekend, then walked around the pharmacy and the DIY store with Hassan, attempting to look innocuous, talking about redecorating his flat, looking for the products on his list. Step by step, Ibrahim's project was taking shape.

Mosul, Iraq

'We've lost Abu Furqan, he was killed by a rocket shell in Qayyara. Probably from a howitzer at that US base in Makhmur. They're moving west, towards El Nasr where we've got all those vehicles stored. We can't afford to lose them. Get back there and take over immediately.'

The man called Karl was in the chemistry laboratory of Mosul University, the buildings chosen for ISIL's headquarters in the city. Despite the perpetual shelling and bombing of the city, a large part of the campus was still standing, including the lab and many of its store rooms. A team of scientists, explosives experts and engineers, had been working for over a year, developing bombs and other weapons from the large stocks of materials hidden away in the well-equipped premises. They had already succeeded in concocting several new types of explosive devices, as well as training a team of unqualified militants to build them. Over the past few months, the lab had become a manufacturing plant, producing increasing quantities of deadly weapons to be used against ISIL's perceived enemies, military and civilian alike. Roadside bombs, suicide vests, handheld and rocket propelled grenades, all ideally suited to urban fighting, were being churned out of the university as if it were a factory assembly line.

The previous week the campus had been evacuated when a coalition-led air attack blitzed the buildings, killing five workers, but the chemistry lab was left more or less intact. Karl had been pulled away from his post of south-west Mosul field commander to inspect and advise on the situation to see when they could reopen their manufacturing line; the military council wanted to see them back in production ASAP. Now, on the orders of his boss, Salam Abd Shabib al-Jbouri, the supreme commander of Mosul, he had to drop that assignment to return to his day job at Qayyarah. *Another typical day of total chaos*, he said to himself.

He checked the time; it was 8:00 am. 'Why do you think it was a US rocket?'

'It's almost thirty k's away from their lines. Those Iraqi clowns couldn't hit a mosque at twenty paces. Get moving, now.'

Karl's motorbike was parked outside the lab and he sped along University Highway then south on Highway One at 120 km/h, thinking about the commander's message. The dead man, Abu Furqan al-Misry, was someone he detested. Like Karl, he was an ISIL commander, but also a notorious executioner who revelled in finding new and ever more gruesome ways to dispatch his victims. In Karl's opinion, he wasn't a true ISIL believer; the only thing he believed in was sadistic murder and the caliphate gave him ample opportunity to practise it. His latest triumph had been three hundred Iraqis mowed down by truck-mounted heavy machine guns in the city the previous month, condemned for whatever crime he'd invented on the spur of the moment to satisfy his bloodlust. *It's no wonder US soldiers are firing rocket-assisted shells at us, I'd be doing the same.*

At ten o'clock, he ran into the warehouse that housed the Qayyarah headquarters. The sound of exploding shells rang out constantly around the village. 'What's the situation?'

His latest second-in-command, Qadir, had been with him for only a week, since his predecessor had died in the university air attack. He couldn't remember how many adjutants he'd outlived over the years, but it wasn't something that bothered him any longer. If they were useful while they were alive, that was all that mattered.

'The Iraqis crossed the river at daybreak and they've taken Garmandi, Kudila and Khurburdan. We lost ten men and the rest fell back to Al-Nasr and we're holding it for now.' Al-Nasr was a village about 20 kilometres south east of Qayyara, where ISIL had a large number of booby-trapped jeeps and lorries stored, the vehicles al-Jbouri had mentioned. Part of the defence armaments they'd need when the inevitable fight for Mosul itself would occur.

'They're shelling us here from Al-Nasr? Who's feeding you the info? How many troops?'

'Nissam called a half hour ago. Around a thousand Iraqis. Says the Kurds didn't show up, thanks to Allah, they're still sitting on their arses in Makhmur.'

'So how did we lose those villages against a thousand spineless, shit-scared Iraqis?'

'Coordinated air strikes, and the Americans at that new base are firing rocket-assisted shells. Even the Iraqis are brave when the Americans are firing missiles at us.'

'What about Al-Nasr and the vehicles? What do we have there to hold it?'

'Mortars, machine guns and about two hundred men. There's a dozen with suicide vests taking the Iraqis out. And now the aircraft are gone they're up shit creek. Nissam said they've fallen back to regroup.'

'So the pressure's off for the minute, *alhamd lilah*. I'll go when I've had a coffee. By the way, I heard al-Misry was killed?'

'He'd just arrived here, said he'd heard two of our guys had been seen retreating from the fight when we attacked the US base last week. He'd come to arrest them and take them back to Mosul for execution. He got in his jeep to drive to Al-Nasr ...'

'And Allah or the Americans decided otherwise,' Karl laughed. 'I don't know which to thank. Have you had much evidence of them here?'

'They're firing to support the Iraqi sorties, but every now and then they send a couple of shells in our direction, just to prove they can. No harm so far, except Commander al-Misry.' Qadir kept a straight face and went to get a coffee for his boss.

Karl arrived in Al-Nasr at eleven-thirty and ran into the disused schoolhouse where Nissam Bukhari, his Pakistani communications officer, was speaking on the phone while tending a wounded man, binding up his leg. It looked like the man's knee had been shot off and he didn't give the leg much chance, but he just acknowledged the men and went to the window with his binoculars. He peered through the blanket of dense smoke that hung around the village. *That's the Americans firing smoke bombs to blind us, so the Iraqis can sneak up like the cowardly shits they are.* He panned across the scene, squinting though the lenses, and made out some of his men shooting from the protection of the burned-out buildings that stood on the outskirts of the village. Other fighters manned rocket launchers on the square in front of them, and heavy machine guns mounted on trucks parked at the sides of buildings were firing continuously.

Bukhari had finished bandaging the man's leg and Karl called him over to the window. Iraqi rockets and shells from the US howitzers were falling continuously and the cacophony of noise from their own mortars and rocket launchers was deafening.

'How many men have we lost?' he shouted.

'About twenty, that's counting six suicide bombers, but the Iraqis have regrouped and they're starting a pincer movement. I gave the supreme commander the same information. That was him on the phone from Mosul.'

'Did you tell him I just arrived?'

'Sure, but he didn't want to talk to you.'

Karl thought about this for a split second. 'So he told you something he didn't want to tell me. What did he say?

'We have to hold Al-Nasr and save the vehicle park at any cost. *Any man who retreats will be executed, if he's still alive.*'

'He's a hell of a strategic thinker. Right, he's just ordered me back here as the commander on the spot, so ignore what he said and listen to me, I take full responsibility, OK?'

'What do you want me to do?'

'Are there any Iraqis or Americans on the west side of the village?'

'No, they're attacking from the east.'

'OK, we're going to do two things. First, get as many vehicles as possible out and on the way back to Qayyarah, we'll lose a few on the road, but we'll save a lot. Then get our fighters to evacuate the village. Set up firing positions two k's to the west and sit and wait.'

'I don't understand, the supreme commander said ...'

'He said *anyone who retreats*. We're not retreating, we're regrouping to the west of the village. From there we cover the vehicles as they leave and we wait.'

'What happens to Al-Nasr?'

'We leave a few suiciders here and let the Iraqis take it from the east, then we shell the shit out of them from the west. They'll be sitting ducks. We'll take it back again when they go running off with their balls hanging out their mouths. Come on, let's get them moving.'

•••

Karl got back to his Qayyarah headquarters at ten o'clock that night. His strategy had been partly successful. The Iraqis had taken over the village at midday and his remaining two hundred men had pounded them with shells, mortar rockets and heavy machine guns all afternoon, until they'd fled back to Kudila, leaving two dozen bodies behind, including six killed by suicide vest wearers. The bad news was that a group of Kurdish Peshmerga soldiers had advanced with them and, being made of sterner stuff, had held their positions. There was a stand-off for several hours, each side shelling the other, before the Iraqis slowly came back to the village to join the Kurds.

His decision had saved about thirty booby-trapped vehicles and one hundred men, but the same number had been killed in the battles and El-Nasr was now on the list of lost causes. By defying the supreme commander's orders, he'd protected half of his men from a certain death, but it was a bitter pill to swallow. To make it worse, during the fighting he'd received a call from Qadir. While he and his men had waited to the west of the highway, the Iraqis had sent an artillery unit to the north, past Al-Nasr, and heavily shelled their headquarters in Qayyarah before retreating back towards Makhmur.

He arrived back to mourn the loss of twenty-five more of his brothers-in-arms, including men he had fought with since taking Mosul, men for whom he would gladly have given his own life. Then a call from the supreme commander informed him that Iraqi military aircraft had targeted their missile development plant in al-Hawijah,

100 kilometres south east of Makhmur, with the loss of thirty-five more fighters. Karl was not a mathematician, but he knew how few fighters ISIL really had, and he knew that number was becoming perilously low.

During the next couple of weeks, Karl received more bad news. In early April, a force of Kurdish Yazidis, natives of the Sinjar mountains in north-western Iraq, fighting alongside Iraqi tribal warriors, took control of the territory between Sinjar and the Syrian border. A simultaneous airstrike by RAF and US bombers destroyed a bridge over the Tigris which was the main entry into the safer north-western zone in Mosul. This combined attack effectively cut off key supply lines from Raqqa by Route 47 and Highway One, ironically, the route taken by Karl's forces when they stormed Mosul in 2014. Then Iraqi forces attacked the city of Hit, near Ramadi, releasing fifteen hundred civilian prisoners from the underground jail. Hit was one of the few remaining towns still held by ISIL in the Baghdad area and it looked like it would soon be lost.

FOUR

Ash Shurta Neighbourhood, Mosul, Iraq
April 2016

'This morning I was talking to Aziz, that Tunisian fighter who sleeps here.'

Hema put a finger to her lips, went to make sure the bedroom door was firmly closed, then nodded to her husband.

Faqir went on, 'He told me they've suffered some massive defeats in the last couple of weeks.'

'Why were you talking to him? He might be a spy, trying to catch you out saying something that'll get us into trouble. I don't trust any of those people, especially the non-Iraqis, they're just paid mercenaries, they don't have any allegiance to anybody or anything except money.'

'It was your cousin, Zamir, who told me I should speak to him. He says he's helped some people get away from Mosul and he doesn't ask for a fortune.'

'Did you talk to him about us, our plans?'

'Not yet, I wanted to discuss it with you first. But he told me they've lost hundreds of fighters this month. There was a big offensive against Al Nasr and the Iraqis and Peshmerga fighters took the town and ISIL lost about fifty men. Apparently, they've retaken a lot more villages around Mosul and Aziz says they've lost another two or three hundred fighters.'

'So the Iraqis are preparing to enter the city?'

'That's what he and everyone else is saying. He thinks they're only weeks away from an all-out offensive.'

She thought for a moment. 'You want to hire this Tunisian to help us get out?'

'Hema, we don't have any other options, he's the only one. I've spent the last two weeks asking around and he's the only name I've been given with any kind of recommendation. I think he likes you and the children, he's always been polite with us, not like most of those ignorant pigs who stay here. That's probably why he was telling me how bad things are, to make us realise it's time to leave. He knows we're Christians and what'll happen to us if we don't get out.'

'What about the things we need to be able to leave?'

'It's all in hand. I'll have everything in a week at most.' He put his arms around her, looking down into her eyes. 'You told me to find a way to get out and I've done everything I could to prepare for it. Now it's up to you to decide if you're ready or not.'

'Are you sure we can trust this Aziz?'

'No. But if we pay him, he has as much to lose as we do if we get caught. I think we either have to trust him or stay here and suffer the consequences.'

She gave a deep sigh. 'You're right, we don't have any alternative. It's time to take a decision, for our children's sake. Kneel down with me and we'll say a prayer to ask the Lord to help and protect us on this step into the unknown.'

Hamam Alil, Iraq
'How long can we hold out in Qayyara?'

The speaker was Karl's boss, Salam Abd Shabib al-Jbouri, the supreme commander of Mosul. He'd come down to visit a group of warehouses and disused factories on the outskirts of Hamam Alil, a town situated mid-way between Mosul and the ISIL south-western headquarters at Qayyara. The constant barrage of firing from the US firebase at Makhmur and allied air support had emboldened the Iraqi troops and together with Peshmerga forces, they were moving closer towards the Qayyarah base. If they established a bridgehead across the river, the south-western HQ would have to be pulled back towards Mosul.

'We could hold out until we get annihilated, that would take the infidels a while, but it would cost us five hundred fighters. An orderly move would take three months. We need to make sure we don't leave anything valuable behind, equipment, paperwork, information, it has to be done well. This place is perfect, we can move the chemicals facility, the explosives factory, the admin, the training unit, everything, and we can sleep at least five hundred men.'

'Come with me.' Al-Jbouri led him outside, where a bodyguard of a dozen men were deployed with assault rifles and machine guns. They looked to the south through their binoculars. 'You can see for 20 kilometres here. Look, a dozen oil wells within striking distance of the Iraqis and there's forty more we can't see. That's the problem. As long as we've got them under pressure from Qayyarah, we can keep the pumps working. The minute we pull back we lose our oil supplies and a shitload of revenue.'

'I'm not talking about pulling our fighters back, we can move the HQ here and still keep a strong force down there. It's a key location and I wouldn't recommend abandoning it unless it was a completely lost cause. But there's a lot of functions we can relocate and handle here much more safely and productively. It's hard to manufacture explosives when the sirens are going every half hour and rockets are blowing your balls off.'

'That's smart, you're right, we should move the operations but not the fighters. If we leave a strong attack force they won't have to be concerned about protecting any installations. Get it done, as quick as you can. This is also a great place to set up a radar monitoring facility for the whole area.' Al-Jbouri turned in a circle. 'Almost 360 degrees visibility. What the fuck's that?' he said, pointing away into the distance.

Karl sighted his glasses. A puff of smoke was visible off to the east, and he could see the faint dots of vehicles on the track across the desert from Highway One. 'Visitors,' he said, 'and I don't think they're coming for coffee. Back inside, now!' As he pulled al-Jbouri towards the door, the ground in front of them erupted and an ear-splitting explosion blew the men off their feet, smashing them into the wall of the warehouse.

It was several moments before Karl shook the concussion from his head. His left hand was numb and he held it up in front of his face. Two of his fingers were missing and blood was pouring onto the ground. He tore a strip from his shirt, wrapped it round in a fist to slow the bleeding then crawled to his knees and looked about him. There were body parts all over the place and the supreme commander was lying three metres from him, not moving. Several of the guards were unhurt and already shooting at four vehicles which were almost upon them, filled with US and Peshmerga soldiers, firing machine guns and automatic rifles into the group.

'Grenades!' Karl called. He crawled over to his boss's body, lying in a pool of blood, one of his arms missing and a grievous wound to his chest and shoulder. Karl checked his pulse although he could see from the lifeless eyes that the man, Salam Abd Shabib al-Jbouri, Supreme Commander of ISIL forces in Mosul, was dead. He picked up an assault rifle and emptied the magazine at the lead truck as it came level with them, while one of his men hurled an RGD-5 Russian-made hand grenade. The grenade bounced off the windscreen and fell at the driver's feet, blowing off both of his legs. The driverless vehicle careened madly across the path of the jeeps, preventing the allied soldiers from shooting accurately. They drove frantically through the hail of bullets from Karl's men then turned south and headed off back towards Highway One. The remaining occupants of the damaged truck didn't survive for long.

Mosul, Iraq

'This is no coincidence; some treacherous bastard's been talking.' Karl was at a meeting with the four heads of the Islamic State's Military Council, where he'd just given a report on the previous day's death of the Mosul supreme commander. He'd had his hand sewn up at a field hospital before returning, preferring a surgeon he knew and trusted to some untrained quack in the city. Fortunately, he was right-handed, so still able to eat and fight without too much of a problem.

When there was no response, he said, 'Look, on Sunday, our brother Imad was blown up by a missile from a single RAF fighter. He was going into Salam Hospital for treatment to his burn wounds. The plane came overhead, fired one missile, then left.' Karl was referring to one of his closest friends, Imad Khalim Afar, like him a senior commander and advisor to the council. 'Then yesterday, al-Jbouri comes down to meet me at Hamam Alil, where he's never set foot before, and a four-vehicle hit squad arrives from nowhere and blows us away. I was lucky, but they almost got rid of three of our most senior commanders in two days. Don't tell me it was an accident they found us just like that, in the right place at the right time.'

'We already came to the same conclusion, but we'll never find out who it is.' The speaker was the council's Chief of Staff, Abu al-Qasim Ibn Khaldun. 'They've got informers inside our troops and we've got them in theirs, it was one of your own contacts who alerted us to that US firebase. You know better than most that's the nature of war, loyalty and treachery. Anyway, there's no time to waste on impossible tasks, we've lost our Mosul supreme commander and we need a replacement. Farooq has proposed your name and we've all agreed.' They all looked expectantly at him.

Karl climbed the stairs to the apartment in the old town he'd managed to temporarily commandeer when the old couple who rented it had been taken to prison to be used as hostages or suicide bombers. He didn't approve of the practice, but he couldn't influence it, so he ignored it, like more and more of the ISIL traits he was coming to despise. He'd taken over the two-roomed flat the day before, welcoming the luxury of sleeping in a proper bed for a while. He figured he'd earned a spell of comfort after the time he'd had recently.

His woman was in the kitchen, bare-headed, her fair hair tied back in a ponytail. She hated wearing the *niqab* indoors and he didn't mind; she was an attractive woman and he liked looking at her. 'I've made a stew, like we used to have at home. There's no beef to be had, so I used chicken. It's late, sit at the table and I'll bring it.' They spoke English together, since she understood a little Arabic, but like many Europeans found it difficult to speak.

She put a dish in front of him. 'How's your hand?'

'It stings a bit, but it'll be OK.'

'I'll bathe it and change the bandage after supper.'

They ate the thick stew with spoons, the silence broken from time to time by the muted sound of explosions from coalition aircraft bombing the northern and eastern parts of the city. She knew he was going through a tough period and left him to his thoughts; he wasn't a great talker at the best of times. She'd been with him now for over a year, a long time in ISIL terms. He was almost twice her age, but they got along fairly well so long as she knew when to watch her mouth. He liked strong women, provided they remembered who was the boss, otherwise they deserved a beating. She knew the other women were jealous of her; he was brave and clever; his reputation spoke for itself and she was proud he'd chosen her after her previous man had been killed.

'This is good.' He finally broke the silence. 'Is there some more?'

She fetched another dish and said, 'How was it at the meeting?'

He was quiet for a while, then, 'They wanted to make me Mosul supreme commander.'

'Sure, and that's a marvellous thing. What did you say?'

'You know what I think about those top commanders, but I didn't tell them what shit-heaps they've become. I told them it's a great offer which I would be honoured to accept, but it's beyond my humble abilities. I'm a fighter, planner and advisor, not an administrator. I want to stay with my men in Qayyarah, fight with them, share their successes, their failures, their pain. But most of all, when I die, I want to die alongside them, brothers to the end.'

This was one of the longest speeches she'd heard from him and it sent a shiver up her spine. 'I doubt they wouldn't be happy with that.'

'The guy who's happy is Abdullah. He got promoted and now he's my boss. He's a total arsehole and he probably hates my guts because I turned the job down and he was their second choice. But he might leave me alone in Qayyarah, he'll have enough trouble with everything else that's going on around here. Things are not going well; the allied forces are getting their act together and we're losing territory and men every day.'

He finished his stew and she cleaned and dressed

his hand. 'Come and lie down. You can forget your problems for a little while.' She led him to the bedroom, undressed him and lay down beside him, stroking his body. He didn't respond, and she realised he'd fallen asleep. *Things must be bad,* she thought. *I wonder how long we've got?*

By the end of the month, ISIL were to suffer their worst losses since 2014. To the north of Mosul, the villages of Khorsabad, Nawara and Barima were lost, together with Khayata, Mahana and Khardanas in the south. In Mosul itself, more disasters followed quickly after, when the Turkish government authorised coalition airstrikes on their own consulate building which was now an ISIL command post, then a training headquarters near the Grand Mosque was wiped out. In all, almost one thousand fighters were lost in the month of April. The mathematics were looking worse and worse.

FIVE

It took Ibrahim five weeks to construct the device, working whenever he wasn't at the garage or with his family. He visited the shadow site as little as possible and always by carefully disguised enquiries to the travel company. He assumed that the encryption app was doing its work, but he didn't care that much.

Jamil bought most of the materials he needed – their mother was back to work, so he had free time between school to run errands for him. The boy had no idea what he was planning and Ibrahim intended to keep it that way. '*Children should not be party to important information*,' the Imam had ordained, and he was always right. The tiny bathroom had now become a workshop and the door was closed and locked whenever anyone was in the flat, which apart from his brother and sister was seldom. He didn't invite his cousin and had confided to Jamil only that he was working on an important project which would bring his family recognition and honour. When he went out, he hid everything in the bathroom and disposed of the remnants of the materials he had used in various rubbish bins along the streets he walked, visiting a series of different stores on each occasion.

The acetone came from several branches of a DIY chain, the hair bleach for the hydrogen peroxide from cosmetics stores and hairdressers, and the sulphuric acid from the garage where he worked. He went online and found a portable toaster, powered by four AA batteries. It was extremely thin and small but would create enough heat to detonate the TATP. He paid 22 euros for the toaster by *PayPal* and had it delivered to his mother's flat. In practice, he found that the TATP was not as unstable or sensitive as he had expected and slowly but surely, he got the hang of the oxidation procedure and the production and storage of the explosive material.

When he wasn't sweating over the conversion of the chemicals, he was following happenings on the battered little TV set in the flat and online. It seemed that everyone had become involved in Iraq; Shia Muslim groups, Syrians and Kurdish Peshmerga killing his brothers as well as the Iraqi independence fighters. Ibrahim was confused. *Who is really fighting who? Whose side is anyone on?* He asked himself. But when he walked along every evening to the mosque to listen to the regular 'information sessions' from Imam Mohammad, it all became clear to him again. It didn't matter who was fighting whom. There was only one enemy; the infidels, the non-believers, the non-Muslims. They were the enemies of ISIL and had to be destroyed.

By the end of April, Ibrahim managed to prepare enough of the crystalline powder to fill eight polythene food storage boxes. Bought by Jamil, they were 20 centimetres long and 10 wide and deep, fitting exactly into the carton that had housed his little sister's birthday present; a folding red scooter, which she'd been delighted to receive. He fastened the end flaps closed with duct tape and opened up the front panel, so he could place the storage boxes flat into the carton. The rigid material would protect the powder from accidental knocks which might cause the unstable substance to detonate, but it would burst and expel the shrapnel inside with deadly force.

At the nearest Vodafone store, he bought two prepaid SIM cards and put them into two old Nokia mobile phones he'd salvaged from his mother's flat. They had a vibrate function which worked perfectly, and he set them up with the password he always used, to avoid memorising or writing down new ones. He wired one up as per the diagram then connected it to the portable toaster, attached to a bunch of matches with a rubber band. When he called the number from his own mobile, the vibrator wheel spun around, closing the circuit to the batteries that heated the toaster. It took eight seconds for the matches to burst into flame. He expected the delay would be even less for the TATP.

According to the instructions, the outward pressure created by the explosion would be one and a half tons per square inch, on a par with TNT. The bolts and nails packed under, around and on top of the device would be blown out with such force and speed that anyone within a radius of twenty metres would be literally shredded to pieces.

The phones had an alarm function which he could have used, but he wanted to set the explosion off himself, in real time, not hiding behind a remote detonation like a coward. And a pre-set alarm could go wrong if he was delayed or it could fail to trigger the detonation. He would take the device and detonate it at the place and time of his choosing. This was his moment and he would make the most of it. The world would learn of Ibrahim bin Omar al-Ahmad. His step towards the stampede would not go unnoticed.

He had already reconnoitred a number of options for his target and decided on the time and place. On Monday, May 2nd, after the Labour Day weekend, he would detonate his bomb at the *Haus und Heim* department store in the town centre near the markets, museums, railway station and hotels full of Western tourists. It was two kilometres walk across the *Deutzer Brücke* bridge from his flat. He had bought a plastic shopping bag with the store logo to carry the carton in, so he would look like just another shopper. He calculated the combined weight of the device and metal projectiles at about 12 kilos and he had done two trial runs with that same weight in the bag to test his plan. There were security staff at the main doors, so he couldn't enter at street level, but the car park was under the building and was also used by the public. A staircase went down from the street to the first underground level, where the pay machines were located. A bank of shopping trolleys stood near the machines. He pushed a trolley in with the shopping bag inside, went up to the ground floor supermarket in the lift and entered without being noticed.

Two escalators were situated directly above each other, going from the supermarket to the furniture department on the third level. The floors were linked by an open central shaft between them. If he left the shopping trolley by the bottom of the escalator the blast would go out both laterally, destroying the supermarket, and vertically up the open shaft, causing more death and destruction on the other two floors. He would stand at the side of the escalator to make the deadly call, waiting for the maximum number of shoppers to arrive and imagining the explosion and chaos he'd cause, just by pressing a button on a mobile phone.

He disconnected the detonator phone from the toaster and following the very last instruction, he programmed it to vibrate only when it was called by the trigger phone. The predetermined number would eliminate the chance of any accidental calls setting off the device. He tried the number from his own phone and from the trigger phone to ensure it would only respond to the latter. When he was sure that nothing could go wrong, he plugged both phones into their chargers to ensure the batteries would not let him down. Satisfied with his work, he burned the sheets of instructions and other notes he'd made, anything that could possibly help the inevitable investigation after his death. *My death*, he said to himself. *My death, a worthy sacrifice in a sacred cause.*

He placed the empty carton flat on the table and made a bed of metal shrapnel on the bottom with some of the screws, nails and bolts he had collected from the garage in small quantities, day by day. Carefully, almost without breathing, he laid the storage boxes with their deadly contents onto the metal bed. The flat was quite cold, but he was sweating by the time he had them laid in place. It was Thursday evening and time to go to the mosque to listen to Imam Mohammad, cleanse his mind, and prepare himself for the execution of his glorious plan. *Inshallah.*

SIX

Ash Shurta Neighbourhood, Mosul, Iraq
April 2016

'It's fixed for Tuesday, the 3rd of May. He'll come for us at 10:00 pm. Sunrise is at five o'clock, so we'll have seven hours to cover twenty kilometres, that should be enough. We can only take what we can carry, it's a lot of walking.' Faqir Al-Douri took a sip of tea and rubbed his eyes wearily; it had been a long and tiring day. It was late at night and the children were already asleep in the bedroom they shared with Hema's mother. The other rooms were full of ISIL fighters and the couple were in their room whispering quietly.

'I'm really scared about this. Are you certain we can trust him?'

He shook his head. 'There's no way we can be sure, Hema, but he's our only hope, we just have to pray he's for real.'

They were talking about the man who'd agreed to take them from Mosul to Batnaya, a village north of Mosul. Their guide was Aziz al-Safar, the ISIL militant from Tunisia who had been sleeping and eating in the restaurant for the past year and had become friendly with the family. For 1,000 euros, 500 up front and the balance on leaving them near the Kurdish defence lines, he would lead them through the no man's land between the two towns.

'He told me he was one of the team that planted the

mines alongside the road, so he can keep us clear of them. I believe him.'

'What happens after that?' She shivered, 'If we make it through.'

'We walk up the road to Telskuf. We'll run into a Peshmerga unit on the way, Aziz says there's a big encampment there and they're patrolling all the time. When they see we're civilians with women and kids, they'll take us to their camp and we're well on the way to the Turkish border.'

'That's assuming we can get out of the camp, they must have thousands of refugees there, what makes us so special?'

'Aziz gave me a name. A guy at the Department of Health delegation in the camp. He's used him before. He had two brothers in Mosul, one was executed by ISIL and the other's in prison. He escaped, and he helps people to get to the Turkish border.'

She shuddered, 'What a dreadful reason for helping people. But I'm sure he doesn't do it for free?'

'It should cost another 1,000 euros, but we'll be out of the camp almost as soon as we get in.'

'What about the border? You're sure we'll get through with those visas you bought?'

Faqir took the documents from their hiding place. 'Here, look. These visas are genuine, the paper, the stamps, the signatures, everything. We've already missed the 60-day validity since they stopped issuing them in February, so I got them dated 28th January, it looks less suspicious. They're exactly what you'd get from the visa office in Erbil at the time. They're valid up to the end of

March, so when we arrive at the border they'll be only a month out of date. Our passports are all in order and I'm certain we can get the immigration people to bend the rules a bit and let us through if we show that we can fly to Istanbul and leave the country within a few days. Until February you could arrive at the border without a visa and get one stamped as you went through.'

'You mean you think they can be bribed to let us through.'

'It'll probably take some money, but it won't be a lot. You know how these policemen are, they're paid so little, 500 euros is a fortune for them.'

'That's the next problem – money. Do we have sufficient put aside?'

'I haven't had any luck in trying to collect those old debts, nobody's got any cash to spare and if they have, they're hiding it. We've got a bit less than we had when we closed the restaurant, a little over fifty thousand. We'll have to be careful, but if there's not too many surprises, it should get us through. I'll buy enough Turkish lira for the local expenses, it won't be much. And when we get to the UK, don't forget I've got a signature on my father's old account at Lloyds. We'll be in better shape once we're there.'

'Yes, of course, but I was just thinking ...' she said quietly.

He recognised the tone of voice; Hema was worried about something. 'What is it?'

'You shouldn't keep all that cash on you, in case something happens. We should split it between us so if we lose a part, we should still have enough to make it.'

He kissed her on the cheek, 'You're right, as usual. We'll split it four ways, between you, me and the boys. Happy with that?'

'It makes sense, that'll be about twelve thousand each and you keep the Turkish Lira for the local expenses.' She sighed, 'And that's just one of the risks we'll face. England seems so far away. I don't know how we're ever going to make it.'

'Listen, Hema, once we get to Istanbul, it doesn't matter where we go. It's just a question of which border we can get through and we've got a choice of two, Greece or Bulgaria. Just rely on me and don't worry. I'll make sure nothing bad happens to us.'

Faqir was a lot less confident than he sounded. He'd spent the last few weeks talking to everyone he thought might be helpful, gleaning information about the options available to escape to Europe, hopefully without giving away their plan. He quickly discounted any route that required a sea voyage; everyone knew that at least four thousand migrants had perished in the Mediterranean and on its beaches during the previous year. He wouldn't risk putting the lives of his family into the hands of corrupt, murderous people-smugglers with boats that couldn't stay afloat. That left the overland route through the Balkans, a long and dangerous journey through ever more inhospitable borders to Austria, Hungary or Germany, depending on the political whim of the day, or more likely the exchange of money – a life for a bribe.

Hema interrupted his thoughts, 'God willing. I'll have to start sorting things out for the journey. We'll need to buy two more backpacks for the girls, they can't carry suitcases. Now that I think seriously about it, we're going to need a lot of things.'

'Make a list and I'll try to find them. There's still a few black-market traders around. I'll start tomorrow.'

'When are we going to tell the children and my mother? They have to be prepared for such a dangerous journey.'

'Let's leave it as late as possible, we don't want to risk anyone saying something. A couple of days before at the most.'

'All right, in the middle of next week, but it's not going to be easy. However bad it's become, this place is all they've ever known.'

'Don't worry, Hema, the kids are smart enough to see it's the only sensible solution. Your mother might not be so easy to convince.'

Faqir put his arm around his wife's shoulders and smiled confidently, but he knew this would be a journey into the unknown, with no guarantee of success. As she had said, God willing.

Mosul, Iraq

'That bastard Abdullah has really got it in for me.' Karl was in the apartment in Mosul old town, where he'd come for a night's comfort with his woman.

'What's happened now?'

'He's taking me away from Qayyarah.'

'You won't be south-west field commander anymore?'

'Not just that. He's not moving operations to Hamam Alil like I recommended. If Qayyarah falls, the whole south-western administration will collapse.'

'And why would anyone be stupid enough to do such a thing?'

'Two reasons. He hates me and it's his way of making up for his own incompetence. The military council's taking it out on him and he's taking it out on me, simple logic.'

'But if they think he's so feckin' useless, why don't they get rid of him? Everyone knows he's an arsehole, it wouldn't be a surprise. They might offer you the job again, stranger things have happened.'

'It doesn't work like that. They'll put pressure on him until he cracks or gets killed then they'll replace him. I turned them down, so they don't give a shit what happens to me now.'

'Has he given you a new job?'

He laughed cynically. 'When I tell you, you won't believe it.' She just looked at him and he said, 'I'm his new number two in Mosul.'

She thought for a moment. 'So we can keep this flat?'

SEVEN

Ibrahim was up at seven-thirty on Monday, May 2nd. The barely discernible sunrise came at eight o'clock in a cloudy, rainy sky and he said his morning *Fajr* prayer then ate a breakfast of fruit he'd bought at the *Haus und Heim* supermarket the previous Friday. He had gone at eleven-thirty to check that nothing had changed, that nothing would go wrong with his plan. The supermarket had been busy, hundreds of shoppers milling around him, unaware of the power that he, Ibrahim bin Omar al-Ahmad, an apparently insignificant youth, now possessed and that would be unleashed in a few days. The store was closed on Saturday and Sunday for the Labour Day weekend and he knew Monday would be even busier and his attack could be more than just a tiny step towards the stampede. *It could be another Paris or Brussels Massacre*, he thought to himself. He just had to place the trolley in the right spot and pray that the blast worked in the way he had calculated.

He moved the package carefully out of the bathroom then showered and scrubbed his body so hard it was painful. Then he towelled dry his unruly mop of curls and shaved as close as he could with his electric razor. For this memorable day, he dressed in a white shirt and a pair of torn denim jeans he'd been keeping for the moment. The two phones were fully charged. He didn't yet switch them on but opened his laptop and watched the latest events posted on YouTube. The Shia militia were now launching rockets at the Iraqi city of Fallujah, where his friends were fighting, and again he envied the possibility that they might become martyrs to their cause. The other news he found was hilarious, describing how the Paris bombers had been travelling in and around Europe on fake passports for several months. *These stupid, naïve Europeans*, he thought to himself. *Do they really think we're as incompetent as they are?*

His laptop showed it was almost ten-thirty. He closed it and placed it beside the phones on the kitchen bench; he would take it with him so it would be destroyed with his own phone in the explosion and they couldn't be searched for evidence. Placing the carton on the table, he switched on the trigger phone and reconnected it to the toaster, gently placing them together in one of the polythene boxes. He fitted the lids on the boxes and packed the remaining shrapnel around and on top of them, until they were tightly held together by the blanket of metal. Sheets of tissue paper he packed in layers all around the contents; the paper would shred and it wouldn't diminish the blast. The front panel fitted tightly over the contents, so nothing would dislodge as he carried it. After fastening the carton tightly with more duct tape so that it was virtually hermetically sealed, he laid the shopping bag flat beside it and slid the carton gently in. Lifting it as gently as he would a baby, he put it by the door. Last, he put his passport and ID card into his jeans pocket. *No need to leave anything to help them.*

He was kneeling and silently praying to prepare his

mind for the attack when his own mobile rang. It was his mother; she sounded panicky. 'Ibrahim, you must come home for me.' Her voice was trembling and breathless.

'What's happened?'

'I have terrible chest pains and I can hardly breathe. It's another heart attack coming on. I have to get to the hospital.' His mother spoke very little German and was terrified of the administrative procedures in the country.

'I'll call an ambulance. Hassan can go with you.' His cousin was still staying at his mother's flat. Ibrahim was convinced he would never leave, she looked after him too well.

'He's not here. He's coming with Jamil and Fatima to see you.'

'I'll arrange the ambulance then call him and send them back.'

'They haven't got their phones. Jamil can't find his and Hassan said his needed fixing. He left it here in the apartment.'

He could hear her breathing, rapid and struggled. 'Are the pains very bad?'

'Like the first attack. I can hardly breathe.'

He looked at his watch. It was only 10:45 and the hospital was not far away from her apartment. 'I'll take you. I'll call an ambulance now and be there when it arrives.'

'May Allah bless you my son.'

Ibrahim called the hospital's emergency hotline and quickly explained his mother's condition. The woman said an ambulance would be at her apartment in a few minutes. He confirmed the address then carefully put the shopping bag back in the bathroom and locked the door, shoving the key in his pocket. He grabbed his wallet and phone and ran out of the apartment. His bike had been stolen the previous week, so he sprinted off on foot towards his mother's flat.

Jamil arrived at his apartment with Fatima and their cousin an hour after he left. Hassan had offered them breakfast on the way and they had stopped at a pastry shop to have sugared doughnuts and orange juice. When no one answered his ring, he opened the door with his spare key. The living room was empty and, as usual, the bathroom door was locked.

'He must have just gone out.' Jamil saw the Nokia phone on the kitchen bench beside Ibrahim's laptop. 'That's not his phone. It looks like an old one he's using again. He'll have his other one with him. I'll call him.'

He guessed the password for the Nokia; it was the same as his own and their mother's. They all used the same code in case of emergencies, but he couldn't remember Ibrahim's number. There were no numbers in the phone at all, neither in the *Contacts* nor the *Favourites*. He looked in the list of recent calls; there was only one number, listed four times. He pressed the number.

Ibrahim was walking back from the hospital. His mother had suffered another heart attack in the ambulance and was unconscious when they arrived at A&E. The young female doctor had come out after a few minutes to call him in to see her. She was lying on a clean white sheet on a trolley; a drip feed was plugged into her arm; her eyes were closed. She wasn't breathing and she looked rested and peaceful, more like her age of forty-three years than he had ever seen before. The young woman left him alone and he knelt on the floor and offered up prayers for his mother and father. *Now they are together again with Allah, blessed be his name.*

After a few minutes, the doctor came back. She remembered the family from his mother's previous visits and knew he had a young brother and sister. 'There's nothing you can do here. Go home and look after your family, they'll need you there,' she told him. 'We'll call as soon as the necessary paperwork has been done.'

He walked slowly away in a daze, heading back to his apartment. As he approached his street an ambulance screamed by, followed by a fire engine, both with their sirens blaring. Now he could see black smoke billowing up over the rooftops.

He ran to the corner, keeping himself out of sight, and looked across at his apartment building. The side of the ground floor facade was almost gone, a gaping hole where the window had been, with bricks and debris lying in front of it. He suddenly felt sick, remembering his mother's words, 'Hassan's coming with Jamil and Fatima to see you.'

Please, Mighty Allah, he prayed, *don't let it be Jamil and Fatima, they're innocent children, you must spare them, I beg you.* But deep in his heart he was sure they must have caused the blast and been killed by it. A fire engine and two ambulances stood in front of the entrance and police cars blocked off the roads on each side. The firemen were hosing the flames that still flickered from inside his apartment. A tent was being erected over the yard and two policemen were cordoning off the area with red and white tape, around the building and across the two streets. A tall blonde man in plain clothes who seemed to be in charge of the operation was giving instructions.

Residents from the other five flats stood in front of the entrance. They looked dazed and frightened as the police and ambulance staff helped them into the ambulances. He tried to remember who else lived in the building, but he had never become friendly with anyone. There were only three adults and four children there, so it looked as if a lot of them had been out. Not that he cared about that. His remaining family were probably dead.

Instead of taking a 'tiny step towards the stampede', he was sure he had killed the only two persons left in the world that he truly loved. Tears ran down his cheeks for the first time since he was a child. Even when he'd heard of his father's death he hadn't cried. He'd felt proud; his father was remembered as a hero and a martyr, as he'd wanted to be. Now he'd be remembered as just a bungling amateur who had not only failed to carry out his attack but had murdered his siblings into the bargain. He knew his entire family was now gone. He was alone.

Ibrahim walked back up the street, towards the tram stop, his mind whirling, trying to focus on what to do next. Whether to stay, or if he fled; how to get away, where to go, what to do about his family. His mother was lying dead in the hospital and it was his duty, his *muhima*, to look after her burial, but the police would soon be looking for him if they found out he hadn't been killed in the blast. If he stayed, he could do nothing for her; he'd be arrested. The same applied to his brother and sister, the state would have to look after their funerals or safety, whatever had happened to them. There was nothing he could do, no one he could help if he was caught by the police.

He made up his mind, praying silently. *'Forgive me, mother, Jamil, Fatima. I will always love you and pray for you, but I can't stay here and be arrested. You and my father are now together with Allah, may he look after you and bless you in his kingdom. SubhanAllah wa biHamdihi.*

He gathered his thoughts; the *Hauptbahnhof,* the central railway station, was ten minutes away on the *VRS* tram and he had his *KölnCard* free pass in his wallet. He could buy a train ticket with the PayPal account, there was still plenty of credit left. Counting the money in his wallet as he walked, he had 165 euros. *That won't last me long.* He stopped, concentrating, remembering. It would take some time before the police made the connection. It was worth taking the risk. He strode quickly along the street towards his mother's flat, it was just five minutes away.

There was no one to be seen near the building and Ibrahim let himself into the second- floor apartment where she lived, *had lived,* he reminded himself. Fighting back his tears, he went into his old bedroom where Hassan and Jamil had been sleeping. Jamil's bed was tidy and clean but the other was unmade, strewn with books and papers. Clothes littered the floor by the bed, making it look like what it was, a temporary refuge. On the floor was a black hooded jumper and he put it on over his white shirt. It fitted loosely; he zipped it up and put the hood over his head so it hid his mop of curly hair and shadowed his face.

Lying on the bed were a German passport and ID card in the name of Hassan Al-Balawi. Like Ibrahim, he had qualified for dual nationality when he was fifteen, after eight years of residency. He looked at the photographs, suddenly realising that no one knew Hassan had probably been with Jamil and Fatima that morning. Remembering that there was nothing he could do to help him or his brother and sister. *If he is dead, they'll think his body is mine. I have to think of my own survival now; I can take his place, pretend to be him if anyone asks.* He had his own passport and ID card in his pocket but knew he couldn't risk using either. His cousin was about the same height and a little heavier, but the resemblance ended there. Anything more than a casual examination would lead to questions which he wasn't able to answer. But though he didn't think he needed any ID unless he left the Schengen zone, the documents might come in handy. He shoved them into the pocket of the hoodie then looked around the room for any other giveaway signs that Hassan had stayed there, but saw nothing except the clothes and books, which could have belonged to anyone.

He remembered his mother saying Hassan's phone needed fixing and searched the apartment, but it was nowhere to be found. He called the number from his own mobile, but it didn't answer, Jamil's number gave the same result. Ibrahim checked the time; he was starting to feel panicky. *There's no connection with me, if they're here, I'll just have to leave them.* Then he realised his phone could be traced and he switched it off and removed the SIM to be sure. *Careful,* he thought, *a dead man can't make phone calls.*

He went to the kitchen and put a stool by the counter to stand on. On the top shelf was a tin marked *Zucker*, Sugar, containing almost 4,000 euros, what remained of the money his father had left them when he went off to his death. His mother and family didn't need it anymore and it would last him at least six months if he was careful. Now he had money, ID documents and a mobile phone. He could get out of Germany and go into hiding in a new country, but where? He'd decide when he looked at the departure schedule at the train station. It didn't really matter, anywhere but Cologne would do for now.

EIGHT

Cologne, Germany,
May 2016

'We are treating this explosion as a suspicious incident. That's all I can say for the moment.' After one of the shortest interviews on record, *Polizeioberkommissar,* Police Senior Commissioner, Major Max Kellerman of the *Landeskriminalamt,* the State Criminal Police Office, walked away from the TV camera in the street and re-joined the two local police officers in the entrance hall of the apartment building. Kellerman had been a forensic and technical support officer in Department Six of the North Rhine-Westphalia Police Force for seven years. His areas of expertise were explosions and fire damage, and this was his first TV appearance. He was happier when he was managing his team of behind-the-scenes technicians and handing the results over to the public relations people, although his tall, athletic figure and blonde Germanic good looks would have been the envy of many a celebrity.

Normally stationed at the State Investigation Bureau (SIB) in Düsseldorf, the previous month Kellerman had been named as liaison officer with the newly formed '*BFE+, Beweissicherungs- und Festnahmeeinheit plus*', Evidence Collection and Arrest Unit plus. The new agency, with fifty agents, had been created after the terrorist atrocities in France and was located at the federal police's Blumenberg base near Berlin. Pending enlistment of further men, liaison arrangements had been made with other forces around the country and Kellerman had been nominated by the SIB in Düsseldorf.

When the blast occurred, Max was at the headquarters of the Cologne Police Department in Kalk, giving lectures to the local constabulary on his specialist subjects. During a hurried call with his director, he was instructed to assist the police in their investigation and had arrived at the site within twenty minutes of the blast. The local officers had no knowledge of explosives or explosions and welcomed his command. He immediately ordered the erection of a tent against the outside wall and over the yard with tape and crime scene notices around the site. There were body parts lying around and one of the officers was so overcome he had to be replaced. A news crew from Köln.tv and from the local radio station were on the scene, waiting for someone to make a statement, so he had obliged in the shortest possible fashion.

'Bloody media coverage,' he said to the two men. 'These days, everybody knows everything and understands nothing. I don't want anyone talking to them again until we have some idea of what the hell happened here. Right, let's get started. Call the photographer and pathologists over and don't let them walk anywhere without my say-so.'

By mid-afternoon, the team confirmed that the remains of three victims in the debris were of one male adult and a young boy and girl. The blast had occurred in the bathroom and had blown away the door then ripped out across the kitchen with such force that the window and surrounding brickwork were demolished. Other pieces of material evidence were bits of a laptop, two mobile phones, and remnants of polythene boxes and burned cardboard. The floor inside the studio was covered with screws, nails and bolts, 'primitive shrapnel', as Kellerman called it. Sifting through the wreckage would no doubt produce further useful evidence, but he was already convinced that this had been a bomb-making process which had gone wrong.

Max gave instructions to the policemen and pathologists to send the remains of the laptop to the SIB lab in Düsseldorf and to continue their forensic procedures, then returned to police headquarters for news. Questioning of the other residents had resulted in very little information. They had seldom seen the young man who rented the flat and didn't know his name. A young boy and girl were seen occasionally, but no one knew who they were. The flat was rented in the name of Ahmed Mahmoudi, a local garage owner, but the premises were deserted and a notice on the door read, 'Closed for the holiday weekend'. There was no one at Mahmoudi's apartment and he wasn't answering his mobile phone. Kellerman had been given an office at the station and had started drawing up a chart, an incident board, to try to patch together the pieces of information as they came in, but by nightfall, he was no nearer to discovering who the victims or the flat residents were and he wasn't happy.

The TV stations were still following the story every hour on the news bulletins and he authorised Sergeant Hans-Pieter Riechter, the local police chief, to give a short interview confirming that there were three victims of the explosion, but no details would be released until after the post mortem and further investigation. He used the favourite words from the police phrase book, 'we are pursuing several lines of enquiry', which everyone understood to mean, 'we have no idea what happened'. It was too late for the national morning papers and all they had was footage of a blasted wall and a one-line statement from him. They were interviewing residents of nearby buildings but since no one knew anything, the news time allotted to the event diminished.

The remains of the three bodies were transported to the mortuary and the following day, Tuesday, Kellerman received a preliminary report from the DNA tests and post mortems. The results confirmed that they were all members of the same family, probably two brothers and a sister. The dental and medical examinations estimated the ages of the males as twelve and twenty-one and the girl as six years old. They had all died from burns and major trauma inflicted by a powerful blast and a virtual bombardment of metal projectiles. The pathologists calculated the strength of the blast as equivalent to a massive charge of TNT, but no traces of that explosive were present.

There was as yet no report from the SIB lab specialist who was trying to recover information from the laptop's hard drive; there wasn't much of it left. He had, however, received the report on the two mobiles. One of them was totally destroyed and the SIM seemed to have disintegrated. *That's the detonator phone*, he knew immediately. The SIM from the other phone could still be read. It was a Vodafone prepaid SIM with only one number on it. *That's the signal phone.* He updated his chart with everything he'd learned and the connections between each piece of information, but there were still many missing links. *Why are there no personal mobiles? With three bodies, there should be at least one or two more mobiles.*

He returned to the apartment and spent the morning directing the forensic work which was still in progress, but first indications showed that it was probably a material he knew well, *triacetone triperoxide,* TATP. It was often referred to as the 'Mother of Satan' by terrorists who had reason to fear its power and instability. All of this information would turn out to be extremely accurate, but it was of no practical use to him until he could identify the victims and the perpetrator. He was becoming very frustrated.

Max emailed the report to his director in Düsseldorf and to *BFE+,* and called them to discuss the problem of identification and the follow-up that would be required. Since he was already in Cologne and deeply involved in the assignment, they agreed he should stay there at least until the three bodies had been identified and the investigation plan established with the appropriate police departments. Kellerman agreed to schedule a TV press conference to keep the media happy and appeal for help in identifying the victims, but he wasn't convinced it would be useful. He advised the reception at his hotel that he would be staying for an indefinite period, then called his partner, Monika Schellinger, to break the news that he wouldn't be seeing her for a while. Neither of them was very happy with the situation.

Mosul, Iraq

'I've got to go out late tonight. That shithead Abdullah's blaming me for El Nasr, the coalition attack around Qayyarah and the loss of the oilfields. It seems I'm solely responsible for the destruction of the caliphate in Iraq. He's giving me every crappy assignment he can think of.' It was 6:00 pm and Karl had returned early to the apartment.

'What is it this time?'

'A ground reconnaissance up beside the Badush Dam. It's nothing special, just seeing what the Kurds have been up to recently. A complete waste of time, since we've got drones that can do a better job. Don't worry about me, it's nothing to be concerned about.'

'Isn't that a bit close to their camp?'

'Don't be stupid woman, it's kilometres away. Now fix me something to eat, then I'll grab a few hours of sleep before I leave.'

She went into the kitchen to heat up a can of soup. Although she liked nothing better than a good argument, it was best not to say anything when he was in this mood. But she wasn't happy with the assignment.

Near Batnaya, North Mosul

'Another kilometre that's all, and we reach the road from Batnaya to Telskuff. Then it's an easy walk up the road for six or seven kilometres to the Kurdish encampment.' Faqir and his family were tired; they'd followed Aziz al-Safar from Mosul, past Tall Kayf, heading towards the northern limit of the ISIL-controlled territory, often hiking in a continuous zigzag with only the occasional flash of his torch to show them the terrain, making the 20 km journey feel more like 30. It was 2:00 am and their bags were becoming heavier and heavier until they seemed to weigh a ton.

The sandy, rocky surface was unrelenting, hard and uneven, straining their untrained muscles. It was a cool night; the sky was cloudy and there was no moonlight, just the occasional flashes from rockets and missiles whistling over their heads on their way to Mosul. This was a mixed blessing, since they were virtually invisible in the gloom but had difficulty in seeing where they were treading. Hadiya, Hema's sixty-five-year-old mother, didn't complain at all but was leaning heavily on Faqir's arm, weighing him down as they navigated the circuitous path made by their guide.

Aziz hadn't lied to them – his knowledge of the heavily mined terrain had prevented them from being blowing up, but in the gloom, they had seen the bodies of many others who hadn't had a guide to help them. Faqir had counted almost fifty during the journey; the jihadists left the bodies rotting to dissuade other attempts to flee. Even though the children had been forced to attend many executions and had seen sights in Mosul which no child should have to witness, he tried to steer them past the corpses that lay near the craters caused by the exploded mines. They held handkerchiefs to their noses to prevent them from retching at the putrid stink from the cadavers.

After another ten minutes of walking, Aziz said, 'This is it. You're a hundred metres from the road, straight ahead. Turn right and you reach Telskuff in less than two hours.'

'We'll stop and sit for a moment.' Faqir put down the backpack and case he was carrying. 'We need a few minutes rest and some water.' The guide passed a bottle and they gratefully swallowed the now warm liquid. Each of them, apart from Hadiya, had a backpack and a bag, while he and his sons were also lugging suitcases. They sat on the gravelly sand for a while, catching their breath and stretching their cramped sinews.

'You can give me the second payment now, I've kept my promise. You're right next to the road, safe and sound.'

'Alright. I've got it here. Another 500 euros. Just take us to the roadside please, we're all still terrified of stepping on a mine in the dark.'

Picking up their bags, they followed him until they were standing on an asphalt road, firm and flat beneath their feet. Looking south, towards Mosul, they could make out the flashes of explosions, courtesy of the coalition aircraft and the Kurdish rocket launchers fulfilling their night duties.

Faqir opened his money belt and took out some folded notes. 'Here's your money. Thanks Aziz, you were true to your word.'

Aziz flashed his torch onto the bills. 'Thanks. May Allah be with you on your journey.'

'*Tawaquf hunak*. Stop there, don't move,' a voice called from the darkness on the north side of the road and a flashlight illuminated the group.

Faqir's family froze with fear as Aziz reached for his pistol and the voice said, 'If you do that, you're all dead.'

A man appeared behind the dim beam of light. He was carrying an assault rifle.

The guide recognised him. 'Karl, what are you doing here?'

'The question is, why are you here, Aziz? Although that seems pretty obvious with this family from Mosul.' He quickly flashed his torch across their faces. 'I know you, you've got the restaurant beside the university.'

'And I know you, Commander. I'm Faqir and you have honoured me several times by visiting our humble premises.' Al-Douri was trembling with fear, not for himself, but for his family. After the careful preparations and the long, dangerous hike across the desert, apparently to safety, the shock of this senior ISIL officer appearing out of nowhere was almost too much for them. The women and girls began to sob, crying out in their fear. Hema put her arms around their shoulders, pulling them to her. She looked worriedly at her sons, afraid they'd make a foolish move and risk their lives.

'Quiet! Tell your family to keep quiet, there are Peshmerga around here.'

He hushed them, 'I'm sorry Commander, they're frightened of what you might do to us.'

'Why are you trying to escape?'

'We're Christians and we know what will happen when Mosul is in danger of falling.' He went down on his knees. 'Please spare us, sir. We've done nothing wrong except to try to find a new life for our children. We've lived for two years under the ISIL government, never breaking any rules, not even minor transgressions. But we've lost almost everything, my restaurant, my parents and my wife's father, all lost since ISIL took Mosul. Please be merciful and let us have this last chance.'

Tears ran down his cheeks as he said, 'If you must make someone pay for this, it can only be me. It was my idea, I'm the head of the family and I'm responsible. Please take my life and spare my family, I beg of you, Commander.'

At this, Hema let out a cry. 'Don't hurt him, sir. He's a good man, he's never done anything to hurt anyone, he doesn't deserve to die, not for loving his family and wanting them to be safe.'

Karl said nothing for a moment, then, 'How much did you pay this man?'

Aziz spoke up. 'They gave me a thousand euros, here,' he held out the notes Faqir had just given him. 'There's five hundred, half, you can keep it.'

When Karl said nothing, he pulled out the rest of the money. 'Take it all, a thousand euros. I promise I'll never do anything like this again and I'll never speak of what happened this night.'

Karl took the money and shoved it in his pocket. 'Get up,' he said to the kneeling man.

Faqir could hardly get to his feet, he was trembling with fear. He shut his eyes, waiting for the shot that would end his life but might save his loved ones.

Karl shone his torch onto the faces of each of the family. The daughters, who had thrown off their *niqabs* during the hike, were beautiful young women who would make fine wives, like their mother. The sons would grow up to be tall and brave like their father, if he spared them. He saw the fear and terror in their eyes as he looked silently at them in the flashlight.

'You and your family take your bags and get out of here. Don't come back this way or I'll shoot you all. If you're lucky, the Kurds might take pity on you, if you're not, they'll kill you. I don't care one way or the other, but I don't want your deaths on my conscience. Now go, before I change my mind.'

The family grabbed their bags and Faqir led them up the road to the north, the fear revitalising their weary limbs as they strode off into the darkness, towards Telskuff and another unknown danger. A few moments later, they heard a single shot, then the sound of a motorcycle riding away towards Mosul. They didn't turn to see what had occurred, they thanked God for a miracle.

NINE

It was Wednesday before any kind of a breakthrough occurred. Major Kellerman had talked to the media on Tuesday evening, confirming that the explosion had 'most likely' been caused by an explosive device and it had resulted in the deaths of a young man, a boy and a girl, probably of the same family, but the investigation was ongoing and no further information was available. The address of the apartment and a hotline number were broadcast but nothing came of it apart from twenty-seven unhelpful calls.

At ten o'clock on Wednesday morning, he was waiting impatiently with Sergeant Riechter and a uniformed driver at the garage when Mahmoudi, the owner, arrived with his son in his battered Mercedes. They had just driven back from a weekend of sailing at the Hook of Holland, hence the non-response from his mobile. Kellerman asked him only about the lease on the apartment, waiting to see what his reaction would be.

'He's the son of Fakhriya, a woman I know, Iraqis, like me. I took him on a couple of years ago. Good mechanic. He wanted to get a flat of his own, but he didn't have any references, it's not easy for young people now. Then his father died, so I signed the lease for him. He's an honest kid, what's happened, why are the police here?'

Kellerman explained about the explosion and the

three bodies, nothing more, still watching for any slip-up. Mahmoudi was distraught at the news. 'It must be Ibrahim and his brother and sister. *Ya 'iilhi!*' he cried, 'Oh my God! What kind of explosion? Does their mother know, where is she? How did it happen?'

Twenty minutes later, Kellerman and Riechter were knocking on the door of Fakhriya bin Omar al-Ahmad's apartment and the garage owner was on his way to the police station to make a statement. Max was convinced Mahmoudi knew nothing about the matter and time was slipping away. He needed some concrete information about Ibrahim bin Omar al-Ahmad and he needed it quickly. There was no reply and they could hear nothing from inside. He authorised Riechter to force the door. The apartment was empty and the dirty dishes in the kitchen suggested it had been for some time. One bedroom was obviously used by the mother and daughter and the other by the two sons. A photograph in the living room showed a woman of about fifty posing with a young man, a teenage boy and a young girl. The date on the picture was December 20th, 2015.

The house phone in the kitchen was flashing. Kellerman picked it up and listened to the four messages. They were all from the General Hospital in Kalk, asking to speak to Ibrahim to discuss the arrangements for his mother's funeral. While Riechter continued searching the flat, he called the number back and was put through to the doctor in A&E who had received Fakhriya on Monday. She recounted everything that had occurred and told him she sent Ibrahim home after his mother passed away.

'What time was that?'

He heard the rustle of papers, then, 'She was recorded dead at 11:22.'

'And Ibrahim left straight away?'

'He prayed for a few minutes then I sent him to be with his brother and sister.'

'And it was him who called the ambulance, and he came with her?'

'That's right. They were here within a half hour of him calling. I've met him before, he's a nice young man. Fakhriya was very ill earlier this year and he looked after his brother and sister.'

Kellerman thanked the doctor, 'Someone from the station will see to the arrangements as soon as possible.'

He looked at the recent call list. The last call at 10:45 was labelled, 'Ibrahim, mob'. *So, she called him to take her to the hospital and he then called for the ambulance and went to meet it at her flat.* He quickly calculated in his head. The blast had been at almost exactly 11:45. Ibrahim's flat would have to be not more than a fifteen-minute walk from the hospital for him to get back so quickly. He looked at a map on his phone; the hospital was only a kilometre from the flat. *And his brother and sister would have to arrive there with him or be waiting for him for the timing to work,* he realised.

He was still trying to envisage the fatal scenario when Riechter came into the kitchen. 'Nothing unusual here, only a mobile. It was on a shelf in the living room and the SIM had been taken out, I put it back and it's working.'

'No other phones?'

Riechter shook his head.

'Same as at the other apartment, I don't understand this lack of phones. Whose is it?'

'I don't know, the answering service just gives the number, no name, but there's been a lot of calls to a Munich number, listed as Kamir. The last one was on Sunday morning at 09:30.'

'We'll send it to be analysed in Düsseldorf when we get back, they can get blood out of a stone. In the meantime, try calling the Munich number, see what you can find out.'

Kellerman wandered about the flat, trying to put the events together in his mind. *Ibrahim's building a bomb in his flat. With his sister and brother there? Doesn't sound reasonable. He takes his mother to the hospital and she dies. He gets back to the flat, depressed and unstable and blows the place up and kills the rest of his family. And all this happens in the space of one hour? Impossible.*

'The phone belongs to Ibrahim's cousin, Hassan al-Balawi.' Riechter had finished his phone call and was reading his notes. 'His mother and Fakhriya were sisters, but he's an orphan now. Kamir is Hassan's uncle, his father's brother. Apparently, he was on his way to stay with him, but he's been living here for several weeks. He called Kamir on Sunday morning to tell him he was going to leave for Munich this week. That's all he knows.'

'Why the hell didn't he call the hotline? It's been running for the last few days, he must have seen it.'

'I asked him that. He's been in bed with flu, hasn't seen the TV for days.'

Max assimilated this news for a moment. He still

couldn't make sense of it; he needed more information and there wasn't anything more to find out here.

'You can drive me back to headquarters. Lock the place up and leave the driver here until we get someone over to put no-entry tape across the door and interview the other residents, not that I think there'll be much to find out. Set up a press announcement when we get back and get this photo of al-Ahmad boosted up as much as possible. We'll put out another TV request with the photo, asking for Hassan or anyone with any information to contact us on the hotline.'

As they drove back to HQ, he called his boss in Düsseldorf and brought him up to date. 'Can you get Munich to send someone around to the uncle's place? Someone who can interrogate him properly. And tell them to get a photo of Hassan, he's bound to have one, then scan it to me. I'll give a press conference tonight and post it on the TV request with Ibrahim's. Düsseldorf can also find his mobile phone number and put a trace on it. He must have had a personal phone and there were none at the scene, or at the mother's place, so someone's got it and if it's on we can find them. We know one of them is still in circulation, I just can't figure out which one for the moment.'

'OK, I'll get everyone moving, but you know you can't use the photos without barring them. We can't publish untouched photos or full names without getting top brass authorisation and they won't give it until we have proof positive. You'll have to settle for the censored versions. Sorry, but don't blame me. That's the bloody privacy laws for you, designed to make our job impossible instead of just difficult.'

In his office, Kellerman updated his wall chart and called his liaison officer at *BFE+* in Berlin, who confirmed the restriction. Despite his protestations, he was obliged to make his press conference with bars pasted across the faces of the two photos and refer to the men as Ibrahim b O a-A and Hassan A-B. The censorship of the photos was doubly misleading, because it hid the fact that Hassan had a strong hooked nose, whereas Ibrahim's features were softer, more feminine. The only obvious difference that could be seen was Ibrahim's curly hair and his cousin's shaved head. *And we know how quickly that can change*, he said to himself.

The next morning, he bought the UK Daily Telegraph, which showed the uncensored photos of the two men with their names in full. Other European papers had the same information, but not many Germans bought other European newspapers.

'How bloody stupid is that?' he said to Sergeant Riechter.

TEN

Frankfurt, Germany
May 2016

Ibrahim had bought a cheap pair of sunglasses at a shop near the station, which together with the hoodie, kept him unnoticed on the trip to Frankfurt. Once there, he walked around near the station and found the *Berliner ApartmentHaus,* a run-down aparthotel on Esslinger Strasse. It looked like the building had been acquired for redevelopment; the upper floors were boarded up and on a ground floor window was a sign; *Rooms to Let – €20- per night. VAT included.* An anonymous apartment room would be a safe harbour until he could think clearly again. In a supermarket he purchased a backpack, a few clothes, a cheap razor and some toilet items. Next, he went to the nearest Vodafone store, bought a prepaid data SIM and paid up 40 euros of credit for 500 minutes of European calls and the same number of megabytes. He had his mobile with its contact list, but it was switched off. He couldn't risk using it in Germany; he knew it would be traced, and he couldn't function without a phone. He hadn't eaten all day; he was starving and went into a Kentucky Fried Chicken outlet along the street.

It was after six by the time he went into the aparthotel. It was still light outside and he was wearing sunglasses and the hood of the jerkin over his head. The pathetic disguise wasn't necessary. The check-in clerk behind the counter was old and sounded Eastern European, with a pock-marked face and long, filthy hair hanging to his shoulders. He must have been watching a TV show on the screen behind the desk because he didn't bother to look up, just grunted *'Ja'* to Ibrahim's request for a room and slapped a registration form down on the counter. He was about to complete it with a false name when the reality of his new status struck home at the man's demand, *'ID bitte?'* He stepped back nervously; the man's breath stank of alcohol and his voice was slurred. Handing over Hassan's ID card with trembling fingers, he prepared himself for a reaction. The clerk didn't look at it; he made a photocopy, shoved it into a plastic file with several others and handed it back. Ibrahim completed the form with an indeterminate scrawl and put a 20 euro note on the counter. The man pushed a key across the counter, slurring, 'Thirteen, along the corridor,' then fixed his gaze back on the screen in front of him.

Ibrahim wondered where the copy would end up. *Probably at some government immigration or tourist department.* At the thought of Hassan's details being disclosed to the authorities his mind ran riot with fear. He realised he was trembling and sweating and walked quickly along the corridor. Closing the door, he fell into a chair by the bed, breathing heavily, his eyes closed. After a while, he pulled himself together; *I'd better get used to this*, he realised. *Ibrahim is dead and gone. My name is now Hassan Al-Balawi.*

He looked up the contact list in his phone and wrote down the few numbers he thought he might need, then replaced the SIM with the prepaid one and entered the contact numbers. Although in the circumstances it was too dangerous to contact anyone at all, now he had an anonymous mobile with a few useful numbers, he felt better. Later that evening he was dozing on the bed when there was a knock at the door. He jumped up with fright. *The police have seen through the swap. They're here to arrest me. It's over.* He pulled up the hoodie and went to the door. The corridor was almost pitch black, but he recognised the pock-marked man from the desk swaying in the doorway.

He showed him a black baseball cap. 'Is this yours?' He sounded and smelled worse than before. 'It was on the floor.'

Ibrahim almost fainted with relief. He muttered, '*Nein, danke*', and shut the door in the man's face. He hardly slept that night. The events in Cologne had almost shattered his faith and he felt vulnerable and discarded, even suicidal, drained of all emotion. He couldn't understand why Allah had dealt with him so cruelly, destroying his family when he was about to make the ultimate sacrifice; to give up his life in the name of his beliefs.

The next morning, Ibrahim, now Hassan, walked a few streets away from the aparthotel to a newspaper stand with the morning papers stacked in racks. He casually picked up the *Frankfurter Allgemeine* and glanced at the front page. A photograph of the hole in the wall of his building was in the middle of the page with the heading, *Suspicious Explosion in Kalk Apartment.* Keeping his head down, he counted out 2,70 € and went straight back to his room to find out what the article had to say.

He scoured the text, frantically looking for any evidence of identification or incrimination. A policeman from Düsseldorf called Commissioner Max Kellerman was in charge of the case, but had commented only that it was a suspicious explosion. He breathed a sigh of relief when he saw that nothing at all was known about him, his family or what had happened. *Maybe they were not at the flat, they're not dead. Iirda' allah alaqwia', please mighty Allah, let them be alive.*

Ibrahim stayed for two days in the apartment with the blinds almost closed, performing his prayers, asking for guidance, and offering to make any penance for his mistake. He didn't try to find a mosque in case his description had been circulated but went out early each morning to buy food and soft drinks and a newspaper. He timed his outings to coincide with the cleaning woman's perfunctory visits and the desk clerk's hours, which seemed to be 10:00 am to 10:00 pm. He met no one else on his comings and goings, but he knew from sounds he could hear through the flimsy apartment doors as he passed that a few were occupied. There was no television in his room and the set in the reception area was never on, since the clerk seemed to spend all of his time glued to his own screen. He didn't want to make himself conspicuous by asking him to switch on the TV and went out at eight each evening to watch the news in a café along the street.

On the Tuesday evening news, he watched the press conference and Max Kellerman announcing, 'The blast was most likely caused by an explosive device and it resulted in the deaths of a young man, a boy and a girl, probably of the same family.'

Ibrahim shook as if he'd been struck by a lightning bolt. *So, it's true. I've killed my family. Allah yahmini, may Allah protect me. My innocent brother and sister are dead, because of my vanity and stupidity.* He walked back to the aparthotel in a daze, trembling with emotion, tears running down his face. In his room, he knelt down and prayed to Allah for forgiveness and for the souls of his lost family.

After a long while, he lay on the bed, dreadful images running through his mind as he tried to think clearly, about his situation, his options, if there were any. He had recognised the speaker on the TV, it was the blonde man he'd seen directing the police at the apartment on Monday morning. He shivered when he realised he'd been only metres away from this man who was now in charge of hunting him down. *Now, I'm a fugitive, a murderer on the run from the German Police.* Eventually, his mind switched off and he fell into a troubled sleep.

The Wednesday morning paper had the same photo of the explosion, with the text of Kellerman's press conference. Ibrahim realised they still had no positive identification of the victims or of himself. *They don't know I'm alive, but it won't take them long to work it out, and when they do, they'll be looking for me.* Even though there was no information on TV, the police must have information they were keeping to themselves. He knew it was too dangerous to stay any longer in the same place or risk showing Hassan's ID again, he had to get away and find an anonymous place to stay for a while where no ID was needed, and no one would see him come and go.

He pushed his few items into the backpack, put the hoodie and sunglasses on, and went along the dark empty corridor to reception. Again, the desk clerk didn't bother to look up when he said he was checking out. He placed the key on the counter and stepped quickly out the door. At the station he decided to move further to the south. He bought a ticket for Stuttgart from a machine on the platform.

Domiz II Refugee Camp, Duhok, Iraq

'Can I speak to Faisal? I have a message from his brother in Mosul.'

After leaving Karl and Aziz, Faqir and his family had trudged up the Telskuff road for another ninety minutes until they reached a checkpoint manned by Kurdish guards. There had obviously been a large number of escapees from the city, since the system was quite efficient. After checking their documents, the guards hurried them through to the encampment, where they were bundled into a truck and driven straight to the Domiz II refugee camp, about 20 km away in the Dohuk Governorate of Iraqi Kurdistan. Even at that early hour the 'processing' staff were on duty, but there were few other arrivals and their registration forms were quickly completed. The officer proudly informed them that the camp held about seven thousand persons and was one of five refugee compounds with a total capacity of over 100,000. They were given a map of the property and vouchers to buy food at a market situated at the southeast corner. Then they finally managed to get a few hours of sleep in a large, noisy communal tent with several other families, mostly Syrians.

Later that morning, the family walked around the camp. It was a massive, sprawling, dirty expanse of tents, like a huge camping site, but with two profound and almost unnerving differences from Mosul, the lack of noise and aggression. There was no constant sound of aircraft or explosions, no bodies lying around on the ground, no patrolling security guards with guns, no armed fighters pushing their way through the pedestrians or driving madly about in jeeps or trucks. By comparison it seemed to be reasonably well organised and efficient. The woman in the food market told them it was managed by the IRC, the International Rescue Committee, and the Duhok Department of Health, part of the local Kurd governate.

Although they knew that behind every face there was probably a dreadful history of suffering and loss, the camp was buzzing with crowds of seemingly ordinary people doing ordinary things and as far as he could see, it looked fairly clean and tidy. Outside every tent there were groups of parents standing or sitting on the ground, talking, smoking and watching their children playing football, running noisily around, or riding bicycles up and down the alleyways.

Hema looked around at the normality of the scene. 'It reminds me a little bit of Mosul in the days before ISIL. You remember, when the town was thriving and noisy? It was a real social centre; the people were still full of optimism and belief in the future.'

'I know what you mean,' he said sadly. 'Before ISIL, before they destroyed our lives and our children's future.'

'We're out now,' Hamid, the studious son, said. 'We've got a chance to make a new future. Thanks to you, father.' His brother and sisters voiced their agreement.

Faqir looked fondly at his family. 'You're right. We've got to make the most of this chance, your mother and I won't let you down.'

There was a good mobile signal and he could use the one phone they'd managed to hold onto. The ISIL security spies had confiscated every mobile they could find in Mosul, until there were very few left in the city. The remaining residents who still had one used it only at night, in the darkness of their homes, to contact their loved ones and find out what dreadful things were happening in their city of which they were unaware. Mobile phones were also the prize assets of the *Muqawama* resistance fighters, who coordinated attacks using the mobile network.

He called one of his friends to find out what had happened after their escape. The man answered in a whisper and when he realised who was calling, cut the call without another word. Faqir understood that nothing had changed; the security officers were probably investigating anyone who might have been involved in their flight. The ISIL commander, Karl, might have said nothing to avoid incriminating himself, but their absence from the hotel would soon be noticed. He decided to make no more calls; the less people knew about their escape, the safer they and their friends would remain. He said nothing to Hema, she had enough to worry about without the fate of the friends they'd left behind.

It was now Wednesday afternoon and he was in the office of the DOH, while his family waited outside. The place was in chaos. Crowds of shouting, crying, angry and frustrated Syrian and Iraqi refugees were pushing, jostling and fighting to get to the counter and there was at least the same number outside trying to get into the room. There were three officials on duty, attempting to cope with at least one hundred angry complainants. It had taken an hour for him to elbow his way through the mob until he was finally face to face with a short Kurdish civil servant with an eye patch and unpleasant breath.

'Is that right, a message from his brother?' The man looked him up and down suspiciously. 'Well it'll have to wait, he's not here. His wife's sick and he's taken time off.' He looked impatiently past Faqir at the queue of people all the way outside the door. 'Next,' he called out.

Lying in his camp bed that night, Faqir cursed his luck. They'd missed Faisal by a couple of days and now they were stuck in this Kurdish camp for who knew how long. He'd been despondent when the DOH officer had given him the news, but he knew he couldn't afford to confide the real reason for his request; it was too dangerous and could condemn them all to a lifetime in refugee camps. He'd thanked the man and walked out as if it was of no importance, hoping he would forget about his visit before he had to come back.

Hema had taken the news well, 'It's not too bad here. We can manage a short time, after all, we managed to survive two years of ISIL. Don't worry, we've just been delayed, not stopped.'

His plan had been to get out immediately and enter Turkey via Ibrahim Khalil, the famous Iraq-Turkey border crossing, about 60 km away. He didn't want his family to become another statistic in the international refugee rescue scheme. He wanted to move on quickly into Turkey then get to Istanbul, adjacent to both Bulgaria and Greece, both member countries of the European Union. Once there, he was confident they could cross Europe and safely reach their final destination. He'd checked the entire route online and knew that transport in Turkey was inexpensive; the air fares, local transport and other expenses would not exceed 1,000 euros. He still had over ten thousand in cash, and Hema and the boys twelve and a half each. By using trains and buses for the rest of their journey, he figured his family of seven could get to the UK with enough to spare. Now he'd just have to be patient until Faisal returned, and he could negotiate the next step.

ELEVEN

'He's in Frankfurt!' Sergeant Riechter strode excitedly into Max Kellerman's office. 'We've just received Tuesday's hotel registration reports and Hassan Al-Balawi's at the *Berliner ApartmentHaus,* near Frankfurt station.' He threw a scanned copy of Hassan's ID card on the desk. 'He's been there since Monday, but the name just came up on the system this morning.'

'Fantastic! Is he still there?'

'We'll soon know, the local sergeant's on his way now with two cops.'

It was Thursday morning and Kellerman was sifting through the phone call messages they'd received since last night's TV announcement. None of them told him anything more than he already knew from the Munich agent they'd sent to interview Hassan's uncle. The agent was a professional interrogator and he'd dug out a lot of revealing and relevant information. It turned out that the fathers of both Ibrahim and Hassan were officers in Hussein's Imperial Guard and had escaped to Germany after the US invasion, settling in Cologne and Munich. The search Kellerman had instigated in the police and intelligence department files showed nothing about them at all; they'd managed to stay invisible for the last thirteen years. However, what was much more relevant to the Cologne event was that, according to Kamir, both men had been killed, fighting for ISIL in Iraq the previous year.

Max wondered how they could have escaped unnoticed for so long, given the amount of resources the government was pumping into the counter-terrorist offensive. *Not worth wasting time on that question*, he thought to himself. *The point is, both cousins had ISIL fathers. Now, which one built the bomb and which one is still alive?*

The first question was answered by the report he received from the SIB lab. They had managed to recover a few chunks of data, very few, from the remains of the hard drive. But there were some personal emails from 'ibrahimomar@hotmail.com' and pieces of a sequence of messages from a 'studentpost@web.de' address to a travel company site. The lab had also identified a video showing the beheading of prisoners in Palmyra. The clincher was that the travel company site no longer existed; it had been taken down two months ago. *That's it!* He thumped the desk. *The laptop definitely belonged to Ibrahim and everything points to him being an ISIL follower like his father and uncle.* He now had no doubt that Ibrahim built the bomb. *But did Hassan help him?* He wondered.

Armed with this new information, Max asked for another analysis, using DNA from Fakhriya to identify whether the dead man was Ibrahim, her son and brother of the two children, or her sister's son, Hassan. The answer was inconclusive; the mother's DNA was similar in all the tests, but without a sample from the father, further work was required to be certain that they were completely identical. The explosive material had been definitively identified as TATP and he was still following the theory that both men had been building the bomb and one of them had been killed in an accidental detonation, but he didn't know which one had died and which one was at large.

The spooks in Düsseldorf had also found Ibrahim's mobile phone details. He'd had a Vodafone contract for a couple of months, *probably since he'd left his mother's flat and started his jihadist career*. The phone hadn't been used since Monday and unless he made or received calls they couldn't trace it. On a whim, Max called the number. *You never know, he could be tired and sloppy and I could get lucky*. The automatic reply voice told him the phone was switched off or out of range and couldn't be reached. *Par for the course*, he murmured and closed his phone.

Max had been about to organise another press conference with the still barred photos, but now, if they had found Hassan, he wouldn't need to do it. It also occurred to him that such a rapid success would not do his career any harm at all. Maybe he should get used to the media appearances; his superiors seemed to spend most of their time posing for the cameras. He asked Riechter, 'Did you send the pics to Frankfurt so they can ID him?'

'I sent them both, to be on the safe side. I'm assuming someone will recognise one and know if he's staying there. I told the local cops not to alert him, they'll call me for instructions when they know who's who.'

Max sent an update off to his contact at *BFE+*. *Spread the good news,* he figured.

Fifteen minutes later, Riechter came back in, looking glum. 'We're out of luck, Max. There's nobody there who can identify him.'

'That's impossible. He must have registered at reception. What the hell's the problem?'

'That's exactly the problem. The receptionist who checked him in is an alcoholic and the night duty guy found him passed out behind the desk when he went in for his shift the next day. The computer was on a porn channel and the browser showed he'd been looking at it all day long. They kicked him out when he sobered up and don't know where he is. I've put an all points out for him, but when these low-life shits go to ground, they're impossible to find. In the meantime, Hassan's room has been vacated. He's not there and the bed hasn't been slept in. He must have left yesterday sometime during the day. There's only a cleaning woman and a check-in clerk in the place, it's basically just a doss house, and nobody else has seen him at all. I'm sure he's long gone by now, seems like a smart kid.'

'What about CCTV?'

'There's one at the check-in desk. They're looking at it now, so we might have some luck there.'

'*Scheisse*! It's day four and we still don't know if it's Ibrahim or Hassan we're looking for.'

'Don't you think you're overcomplicating things, Max? Why would Ibrahim be travelling with Hassan's ID? They don't look at all like each other. I just don't buy it.'

'Maybe, but why would Hassan be running if he's got nothing to do with the bomb? We know that Ibrahim built it, but Hassan could have been his accomplice. And it makes no difference, whoever's running is hiding from something and is a highly dangerous suspect. Until we've got a definite ID, I'm keeping our options open. We'll put out an all points alert to the train stations, airports and border guards and give another press conference with the useless barred photos and last known whereabouts in Frankfurt and see what it turns up. He has to eat and sleep somewhere and someone's bound to see him and that's when we'll get him.'

Kellerman sounded confident, but he had a bad feeling that they'd just missed their best chance. He added the latest information to his ever-expanding wall chart; like a jigsaw puzzle, it was now full of pieces, but he couldn't work out what the final picture would look like.

Stuttgart, Germany

Ibrahim had a choice of trains and chose the slow one with a connection at Frankfurt South. He wasn't in a particular hurry and the ticket was only 21 euros and for another 5 euros it had Wi-Fi. The trip took two hours and he spent most of the time looking up apartment rentals in Stuttgart. He avoided *Airbnb* and other accommodation websites and looked for offers from private individuals. When he had found a half dozen, he went to the lavatory to call the owners and discuss the arrangements. The fourth conversation suited him perfectly; the studio flat was immediately available at 25 euros per night. Anna, the elderly owner, was in Austria looking after her sister, who was recuperating from an operation. She expected to be there at least two months and needed to cover the monthly costs of her home. Anna had no internet connection and didn't want to go through an agency, so her sister had placed the ad for her. She wanted a trustworthy person to look after her ground floor apartment who paid in advance, expected no service, and could pick up the keys when she told them how and where.

It was a dream situation for Ibrahim. He described himself as a student who was travelling around Germany to write a travel book about its cities. After a long and laborious conversation, he offered to pay 600 euros up front for a month's rental. When he hinted he might stay longer, she accepted the offer. He gave her a fake name and address in Hamburg and took note of her bank details. Then he transferred the amount from the PayPal account which left about a thousand available.

He spent the night in a youth hostel where they asked for no ID and when Anna contacted her bank the next morning, Thursday, the money was there, so she called him with the address, the entry code to the building and the details of where the key was hidden. Ibrahim bought enough groceries for a week and an hour later, while Max Kellerman started looking for him in Frankfurt, he went to ground in Anna's flat in Stuttgart.

TWELVE

Qayyarah, Iraq
May 2016

'They're preparing an assault on the airfield. What are your instructions?'

'What's the timeline?'

'Early next week.'

'Fuck, I thought we had more time than that. You should have found out earlier.'

Karl had gone down to Qayyarah to meet one of his last remaining spies from the Iraqi Army base in Makhmur. The man had informed him that an Iraqi-US attack on Qayyarah Airfield West in Nineveh province was being prepared. The airfield had been an Iraqi Air Force base before it was captured by ISIL in the aftermath of the Mosul occupation. He was now speaking on an encrypted phone to Abdullah, who, he assumed, was in the university campus in Mosul. Apart from the university building, which had been in use right through the occupation, the senior officers were now seldom assembled in the same place. The targets of the allied air attacks were more and more specific and accurate, and he knew this information could only come from inside Mosul. Despite the dreadful menu of torture and death offered to informers, real or imaginary, there was no doubt from the targeted bombing that their numbers were increasing as the fall of the city became more and more inevitable.

Since he had been given the job, Abdullah seemed determined to make Karl pay for the humiliation of being second choice, but his comment was lost on him. They had known for weeks that this would happen and whether it was yesterday, today or tomorrow, it changed nothing in the equation. The defence of the airfield should not even be considered. It would cost the lives of countless fighters and in the end, would be fruitless. The Iraqi Army never attacked now unless there was no possibility of their forces losing. They had been preparing this assault for several weeks and would come with twenty or thirty times the number of soldiers that ISIL could afford to send. It would be a suicide mission and would only serve to create more deserters and informers. Morale was already at an all-time low and the loss of more fighters in the defence of an airfield from which they had no planes to fly would be just another straw on the camel's back.

'What's your assessment?'

Now Karl knew he would be the scapegoat for whatever happened the next day. This man only asked for advice to avoid responsibility for the consequences. A couple of weeks previously, four of his fellow commanders had been executed for deserting their posts during a battle on the eastern outskirts of the city. He knew they had been forced to fall back when an Iraqi battalion decimated their position with mortar and rocket fire. It was a simple choice of die here or live to fight another day but, like his predecessor, his superior obviously believed that dying was a better option than winning. He knew he was damned whatever response he gave.

In that case I prefer to be damned for saving some men to do something useful than for sacrificing them uselessly. On the phone he heard a series of explosions; the allies were obviously bombing the university again and he waited, vaguely hoping his boss would become a statistic in the Mosul death toll, then he heard Abdullah say, 'I'm waiting for an answer.'

'We need our men here, to defend the city,' he replied. 'Qayyarah West will be lost whatever we do. The Iraqis are sending thousands of troops and we stand no chance of success. The airport is of no use to us at all and we shouldn't spend another life on trying to keep it. It's your decision, but my advice is to evacuate our men and bring them back here to fight the real battle, the battle for Mosul. I was one of those who took the city two years ago and it was the greatest success we have ever had, more important even than Raqqa. We must devote all our resources to keeping it for as long as possible, even if we fail in the end, *la samah alllah*, God forbid.'

'This would leave the Iraqis to take back the airfield without any resistance. Our reputation will suffer.'

Karl didn't reply. He'd given his opinion, now the commander had to take a decision.

There was silence for a few moments, then, 'Send a messenger. Evacuate immediately.' The phone went dead.

Cologne, Germany

'More than thirty calls and still nothing to follow up. Nobody's seen them, nobody's heard from them, nothing. It's like these guys never existed.'

It was Friday morning and Kellerman's press conference

and TV appeal for information on both men had gone out the previous night and was still being repeated on the hourly news channels. For the first time Max stated that the two men were dangerous and wanted in connection with a possible terrorist act in which three people had died. He didn't reveal that they had no idea who was on the run; it would be confusing and make the police look incompetent. He also didn't divulge that the fathers had been killed in Iraq fighting for ISIL. *BFE+* had warned him to keep it quiet for the moment as it would put every department in the German security services under scrutiny and wouldn't change the situation.

Unfortunately, the footage from the CCTV at the desk of the Frankfurt hotel was totally inconclusive. Every shot showed a man in a hooded jerkin with his head down and no possibility of identifying whether it was Ibrahim or Hassan. *Riechter was right*, he reflected, *seems like a smart kid*. His constant demands to have the photographs uncensored had been ignored and he knew they were not good enough to make identification easy. He vainly hoped the constant TV bombardment might bring a miracle, but so far, they hadn't had a valid sighting from anywhere or anyone. They'd received a number of calls from shocked friends or acquaintances; people who knew either Ibrahim or Hassan and had nothing but good things to say about them, but no information. A few reported sightings were quickly discarded as attention-seeking screwballs and the fact remained that whoever was on the loose, Ibrahim or Hassan, he had disappeared, at least for the time being, and time was not on Kellerman's side.

Max called his liaison officer at *BFE+* in Berlin to report, not that there was anything worth reporting. 'This will go off the boil very quickly,' he said. 'The media attention span is less than a chicken's and if they don't get something new, they'll drop the story in a couple of days. We've got nothing to tell them and the privacy problem is really screwing up our appeals, so I'm frankly not optimistic, unless the guy, whoever he is, makes a mistake. I think it's unlikely he's still in Frankfurt and he won't go back to Cologne, so it's probably no longer useful for me to stay here. I suggest we take three steps to try to maintain some momentum in the investigation. We should circulate the dossier through the Atlas Network sharing programme to our colleagues in neighbouring countries, France, Benelux, etc, so they've got as much, or as little information as us. And we do the same thing with Interpol. Last time I talked to them they told me they've got over six thousand terrorist cases to follow up, so I doubt that'll produce anything, but we've got to try every option. And I think we should hold another TV press conference and offer a reward for a genuine sighting which leads to an arrest.'

Commissioner Max Kellerman folded up his incident wall chart and went home to Düsseldorf that weekend, his tail between his legs. He was still waiting for the final DNA report to reveal which man was dead and which was on the run. It was a complicated test; the lab was overworked and there were many other priorities, equal to or greater than his, so he would have to be patient, and if it did provide an identity, they still had to find him and that was proving impossible. The top brass had authorised a reward of 50,000 euros which he would announce in his press conference that evening in a last attempt to keep the public's interest in the case, but he knew that without any more information to catch their attention it wouldn't hold very long. Max was not happy with the situation, but there was nothing he could do until something beyond his control occurred, and they might just get lucky. Monika was pleased to have him home and that was at least a small consolation.

THIRTEEN

Domiz II Refugee Camp, Duhok, Iraq
May 2016

'He's still not here and we don't know when he'll be back.'

Faqir and his family had now been in the camp for a week and this was the third time he'd enquired after Faisal. To come so often to the DOH desk was inviting suspicion, but he was now desperate to find the man whose name had been given to him by their guide, Aziz. Fortunately, it was a different officer and he'd told him they were friends and he was concerned about his wife's health. He'd spoken quietly and calmly to avoid being noticed by the other refugees crowding around him, but inside the Iraqi was panicking. He knew his family couldn't withstand much longer in this dreadful place.

After their initial pleasant surprise at the apparent organisation, efficiency and discipline of the camp, the first night revealed the horrors that lay beneath the calm surface. They were awoken in the middle of the night by horrific screams from outside. It sounded as if someone was being murdered.

Hema and the children gathered nervously around him, 'What's happening?'

A voice in Arabic from the other side of the tent answered, 'It's a fight. Probably drug dealers, the place is full of them.' In the gloom, a middle-aged Arab man wearing a thawb approached them. 'It's an ideal business opportunity, this place. Everybody's got a little money and nothing to do, it's a perfect set-up for the dealers.'

'Why don't the authorities clamp down on it? This is a government centre, they should be able to control what goes on.'

He laughed. 'You really think they care what happens to refugees? They're probably hoping we'll all kill each other and solve their problem for them.'

Faqir pulled his family close. *What have I got us into?* He asked himself. *It's no better than Mosul. How am I going to keep them safe for a week in a place like this?* Then, *what if Faisal can't get us out and we're stuck here forever?*

When the shouting and screaming finally stopped, they went back to their camp beds. The others were soon asleep, still tired after their journey, but Faqir lay awake for hours, his mind in turmoil, wondering what the future held in store for them, praying that he could find a way out, that the risks they'd already run weren't to be in vain.

Since then, the same thing had happened every night and on a couple of occasions they heard gunshots and the sirens of police cars and ambulances in the distance. The next morning, they learned that several people had been killed in the violence, but no one knew who, and no one cared. Stories of robbery, rape, violence and murder were commonplace and Faqir forbade his family to go outside without him and they never ventured out after dark. He found a length of solid wood which he fashioned into a club and carried whenever they left the tent. It would probably not protect them if they were attacked, but it made him feel less vulnerable. The camp was a hellhole, full of desperate victims of war who had lost their homes and everything they possessed, even their identities. Life was cheap and they had to get out, or they would end up like those unknown victims.

Faqir hid his disappointment as well as he could, 'Thanks, if you hear from him, please say that Faqir, Aziz's friend from Mosul, was asking after him.' He walked out of the office to find his family. *Please God, don't leave us in this place much longer. We won't survive it.*

Düsseldorf, Germany

'I'm convinced it's Ibrahim who's on the run, using Hassan's ID. Why would he use his own when he knows every policeman in Germany is out looking for him? It makes no sense to flash your own ID, so he's somehow got hold of his cousin's to create some confusion. I also don't believe either of them would be working with the bomb when the children were there, so it had to be an accident. And, the clincher is, the timing's too tight for it to have been Ibrahim when he got back from the hospital, I've checked it myself and it doesn't work. The most likely scenario is that while he was looking after his mother, his family came to his flat with Hassan and accidently caused the explosion. Maybe we should go along with his game, cause some confusion, just like he's doing with us – pretend we have proof that it was he who escaped and see what it brings. If he thinks we know Hassan was killed in the explosion and he's on the run, he might get nervous. That's the only way we'll get him, if he makes a mistake. Otherwise we stand no chance after all this time.'

Max Kellerman was sitting with his boss, Lieutenant Eric Schuster, in his office at the State Investigation Bureau in Düsseldorf. On the wall behind them was the chart he'd started in Cologne and was updating with the sparse pieces of information that had come through since he'd left. Despite the massive manhunt that had gone on all over the country, there had been only two developments since the fiasco in Frankfurt and neither was positive. CCTV footage had been recovered from the railway station in Cologne and from the train to Frankfurt, showing a man in a hoodie, who was probably the escaped survivor, but like the hotel video it was impossible to identify him. Similarly unhelpful footage had been found at Frankfurt station where several men wearing hoodies had bought tickets from the platform machines that morning, but finding which one was the fugitive and which of the eleven hundred trains that leave per day he had taken from the busiest station in Germany had proved impossible.

The second development was deeply disappointing; the final results of the DNA tests had come through and were inconclusive. All the victims had similar DNA and none of them were identical. Since the mothers were sisters, without samples from at least one of the fathers or from Hassan's mother, there was no way of proving whose remains were recovered from the explosion. Max was frustrated; he was certain it was Hassan who was killed, but so far there was no evidence to prove it. It was possible that he was involved with the project, but Max's instinct was that he wouldn't have had the children with him if that was the case. Once again, his deduction was perfectly accurate, but it didn't lead him anywhere.

The two men were now arguing about what to do with this information. Schuster wanted to follow the standard procedure of announcing that the DNA tests had confirmed that all three victims were related, but the identity of the escaped survivor was still unknown and once again putting out an appeal with both photographs. He was sure he could get approval to show the uncensored pictures now that they had the DNA results.

Max didn't agree. 'If it's Ibrahim, he must be holed up somewhere where he can't be found, otherwise we'd have him by now. He might still be in Germany or he could be in a different country. Without border controls, we have no idea. We already showed both pictures for two weeks without any result whatsoever.' Schuster started to interrupt but he cut him off. 'I know the photos were barred, but it was probably good enough to make a sighting, with all the publicity that surrounded the explosion. In my opinion, showing two photos is worse than showing none. It causes confusion and the public can't be expected to remember two faces when most of the time they can't even remember one. And to be out of sight for two weeks he's either well disguised or found a great hiding place. Either way, by now he's thinking we've lost him. His confidence will be high and he's likely to make a mistake. If we announce that we know it's him and show his picture again, unbarred, he might start running again and someone could spot him.'

'That's against all official procedures. Berlin will never

go along with it. The public needs to be aware that there's a dangerous killer out there and it could be one of two men. It's our duty to inform them, if something happens we could be in serious shit.'

As usual, Schuster's worrying more about his own liability than about catching Ibrahim, Max registered. 'Eric, if it's Ibrahim, and I'm absolutely certain it is, our duty is to get him and stop him from harming anyone else. How we do it is our decision and it doesn't mean we don't warn the public.'

'So, what do you suggest?'

'That we put out an announcement that we've now established through DNA tests that it was Ibrahim who was building a bomb and his cousin and family were killed in an accidental explosion. We are searching him, he's a dangerous terrorist, travelling with his cousin's ID. We still offer the fifty thousand reward and appeal for information, with only his unbarred photograph and both their full names. We tell Interpol and the other security services what we're doing and everyone will be on the lookout for Ibrahim, as per his photo, travelling as Hassan. That way, we're warning the public that there's a dangerous man who needs to be caught, we're eliminating the confusion of the two photos and Ibrahim will believe we have proof and the manhunt is for him.'

'And what if it's actually Hassan who's on the run and it's Ibrahim who's in the morgue?'

'I don't buy that and it doesn't really make any difference, because we're giving both names and whoever shows the ID card, it has Hassan's photo and name. Listen, I'm thinking of what happened in Spain last year. We put out a shitload of warnings and photos about Dieter Fuchs and Franck Müller, the suspected Hamburg arsonists, and achieved absolutely nothing. Two months after we dropped Müller's photo and went with only Fuchs's, he screwed up in Malaga, a really stupid mistake that he wouldn't normally have made. Somebody recognised him and we nabbed him.'

'I can't approve this, Max, I'm just not convinced. I'll put it to our Division Chief and tell him what your theory is, even though I don't go along with it. He can talk to *BFE+* and take it to the top brass if he thinks it'll fly. I'll get back to you in time to make an announcement tonight one way or the other. I don't promise anything, but let's see what they say.'

FOURTEEN

Ibrahim had been in the apartment for two weeks, feeling more relaxed and confident with each passing day. He slept a lot during the first days, catching up on the stress of the intensive pressure in Kalk, going outside only when necessary. He prayed three times a day for forgiveness for the deaths of Jamil and Fatima, which gradually assuaged the deep feelings of guilt that had racked him.

The apartment was on the ground floor near the entrance door and so far, he had encountered only a few of the other residents coming out and going in. Each time, he turned away as if he'd mistaken the address or forgotten something. Wearing his sunglasses and hoodie, he made certain they had no chance of seeing his face. To be even more sure, he'd now let his beard grow into a substantial bush and he looked nothing like the photo. The reward offered by the blonde policeman had made him fret for a few days, but the photographs of Hassan and himself were so unrecognisable that after a while he decided he had little to worry about so long as he was vigilant.

He watched the TV news every morning and evening and bought the daily newspaper, scouring it from beginning to end. By the second week there was no further mention of the event or the manhunt neither on TV or in the papers. As more time passed and the publicity about the Cologne explosion died, he was sure no one would recognise him. He knew he was going to have to move on again some time, but he wasn't yet ready to venture away from what had become a safe and anonymous bolthole.

Then, almost three weeks after the blast, he was a TV and front-page news celebrity again. An announcement was made that the intelligence services had been unable to positively identify the man's body from their forensic examinations and subsequent DNA analysis. The three bodies found in the flat were Jamil, Fatima and either himself or his cousin. The search was continuing for them both, Hassan Al-Balawi or Ibrahim bin Omar al-Ahmad, shown with unbarred photos, travelling with Hassan's ID. The public was again offered a fifty thousand Euro reward for any information that might assist the continued investigation.

I wish them well, he thought to himself. Unless they arrested the Imam Mohammad, there was nobody who knew anything about him. With his newly grown beard, it would take a very sharp observer to identify him and he was sure there was now very little interest in a story that had taken place three weeks ago almost four hundred kilometres away. He felt a rush of adrenalin and for a moment a feeling of pride that he'd successfully escaped capture in an international manhunt.

Ibrahim spent a couple of days enjoying his newly found feeling of freedom; the weather was dry and he walked around the city like a tourist. He went to the zoo, visited the historic sights and strolled through the parks.

He still wore his disguise but was gradually losing the paranoia he'd felt about being recognised. During this euphoric period, his mind kept returning to the failed bomb attempt, his family's deaths and his failure to prove himself a worthy ISIL warrior. He still went down on his knees three times a day to pray that somehow Allah would find a way for him to take at least one tiny step to achieve his destiny, to avenge his family's deaths and follow in his father's footsteps as a martyr to his cause. *Help me to find a way I can prove myself, please Allah, help me find a way.*

On May 17th, he was listlessly watching an episode of a German soap opera when a news flash came across the bottom of the screen; *Over 300 killed or injured in Baghdad Bombings.* He switched to a news channel to see the report, stating that a series of eight separate bomb attacks in Baghdad market places had decimated the local population. ISIL had claimed responsibility and he had no doubt they had carried it out.

Once again, Ibrahim felt both admiration and envy for this successful blow against the establishment. Despite the so-called liberation of the Iraqi capital by the coalition forces, freedom fighters had succeeded in achieving what he hadn't been permitted to achieve, another step towards the stampede that the Imam Mohammad had described to him. *There has to be a way I can follow this example, a way I can fulfil my destiny.* He thought through the last few weeks, after the misfortune that had ruined his perfect plan and killed his siblings. *But I escaped, I'm still free*, and the crucial point, he realised, was *they don't know who is still alive.*

Ibrahim realised his mission might be compromised, but it was not destroyed.

'Thanks to Allah,' he said out loud, beginning to understand that perhaps there was after all some reason for the sacrifice of his family. He became even more determined to make up for his mistake, to try again to prove himself in the eyes of his fellow fighters and take his vengeance on the infidels. *Who can help me, who can I trust?* He pondered, then it dawned on him. *There's only one person in the world.* It was 8:00 pm, after the evening service at the mosque. *Mohammad will be eating his supper*, he thought.

On the spur of the moment, he called the Imam, avoiding using his name and saying only, 'Jabbar's son'. Mohammad was incredulous. *'Al-Hamd lillah!'* he chanted several times before he could be calmed down. Like everyone else he'd been convinced that Ibrahim had perished in the blast. He quickly saw the advantage of his new situation and promised to pass the information on.

It's not over, Ibrahim told himself. *With Allah's help, I can still follow in my father's footsteps and make amends for the deaths of my brother and sister. Inshallah.*

Domiz II Refugee Camp, Duhok, Iraq

'You'll have to talk to the IRC representative.' The fat, balding officer in the scruffy, badly-fitting uniform looked around the overflowing room impatiently. You're registered here at Domiz now, so there's nothing I can do.'

It was Thursday 19th May, and Faisal was finally back in the DOH office. After enquiring after his wife's health, Faqir had asked him about moving on from the camp. As always, he kept his voice down, speaking quietly and respectfully, ensuring no one in the crowded office could hear him, trying not to show his anxiety and fear. Desperately hoping he could find a way out of this nightmare before one of his sons or daughters suffered the same fate as so many victims since they arrived.

The previous night had been as bad as anything they'd experienced in Mosul. For two hours the sound of a battle raging outside their tent had kept them awake, Hema and the children huddled in a heap with him on the floor, terrified to make a sound and become a part of whatever was happening. At 5:00 am, they'd been called out by the guards and questioned about what they'd witnessed. Four bodies were lying under blood-soaked covers and a woman was being carried away on a stretcher, alive or dead they couldn't tell. An ambulance was driving off with other bodies, they didn't know how many. They learned that the woman had been attacked and raped at knife-point and the fight had been between her family and a gang of drug dealers. It didn't look as if anyone had survived the battle and it was now just a question of ticking boxes and filling in forms.

After answering 'no' to a list of pointless questions, Faqir had walked directly along to the DOH office, queuing for two hours before it opened, praying that Aziz's contact had returned and that he might be the solution to their ghastly predicament. Now, unlikely as it seemed, the unkempt man in front of him was probably their only lifeline out of this place. He forced himself to remain calm and think clearly. If he talked to the IRC it would become a game of shuttlecock with the Kurds; he and his family would be bounced back and forwards between them and no one would ever take a decision, they would be stuck there until they died there.

'Where are our registration records?' he asked.

'When did you arrive?'

'Two weeks ago. Early in the morning of Wednesday the 4th.'

'Then they've either been transmitted to the central IRC network or they're in our computer system ready to be sent. I've told you, there's nothing I can do, so don't waste any more of my time.'

Faqir said quietly, 'If you could locate them, they might just get erased and no one would know any different. Aziz told me you have a score to settle with the Mosul barbarians, so do we, we're on the same side.'

'I don't know what you're talking about,' he was speaking more quietly now.

'How much would that cost, if it was possible?' He opened his tunic and showed a wad of bills from his pocket, knowing he was taking a risk, but he had no choice. He hardly dared to breathe, waiting for the man to take a decision.

Faisal looked around the chaotic room; no one was paying attention to them. 'Come here.' He went into a cubicle next to the counter. 'You would leave immediately for Zakho?'

'If you know someone who can drive us, we could be out of here in a half hour.'

'How many?'

'Seven.'

'The paperwork is a hundred each and the driver five more.'

'A thousand for everything. Five hundred to you and five to the driver.'

Faisal paused. The noise from the office was getting worse; his colleagues would be looking for him. 'OK, Give me the five hundred. Go to the main gates and wait until a white truck pulls up. The driver's name is Khalid.'

Faqir and his family waited nervously near the gate, well away from the guards. 'Was I a fool?' he said to Hema. 'I can't prove I gave him the money. What if he does nothing, or even reports me for trying to bribe him?'

She squeezed his hand, 'You did the best you could. Let's hope he's an honest crook.'

Hamid spoke up. 'I suppose it doesn't matter if he never erases the files. The camp's in Iraq, so we haven't officially registered in any other country yet.'

'Good point. If this works, we'll still be invisible.'

A few minutes later, a white truck pulled up beside them. 'Khalid?' Faqir asked when he leaned out the window.

'Get in.' The man opened up the rear doors, revealing boxes and sacks of groceries, vegetables and fruit piled up in rows. Many of them were stamped with the IRC initials. They loaded their bags and climbed inside, where there was just space for them to sit on the filthy floor. 'Where's the money?' he asked. Faqir handed him another wad of euros. 'Make no noise at all,' he said, then closed the doors and locked them inside.

After bouncing around for a while in the truck, Malik, the impetuous son, asked quietly, 'Why do you think he's driving a lorry full of food away from the camp and not towards it?'

Mosul, Iraq

'This could be interesting. I want you to follow it up. Keep me informed if anything comes of it.' Abdullah Abdulrafi, supreme commander of Mosul forces and Karl's immediate boss, handed him a dossier of emails and print-outs.

As his second in command, Karl spent most of his time in the city now. He missed the field action he'd been used to in Qayyarah and he missed his men, those who were still around. He knew they missed him too. On his last visit, Qadir, his ex-number two, had come up to him in desperation, begging him to come back. He knew Saad, his replacement, a Saudi who was a sycophantic supporter of Abdullah and equally incompetent. His doctrine was also the same; never make a strategic retreat, keep getting your men killed until you have none left to fight. Many of Karl's best fighters, old friends, had been lost in unnecessary skirmishes and futile defence of worthless terrain, while the Iraqis, with US support, had run rings around them on their way to their remaining oilfields. But Karl was trapped in the city and he knew he would never get out alive.

It was a month since he'd taken up his new post and he was already sickened by it. In Qayyarah he'd avoided the hate-filled cruelty that ISIL now espoused, but in Mosul he couldn't escape it. The previous day he'd been obliged to watch yet another mass execution in the old town. Sixty-five civilians, men and women, including office employees, university students and manual workers, all accused of consorting with spies and anti-security contacts, were made to kneel in the street, then were shot in the head. Their names were posted outside the morgue, so their loved ones could retrieve the bodies to try to have them buried in one of the overflowing cemeteries. Another ninety civilians were arrested and herded into the filthy, rat-infested dungeons on various spurious charges, including lack of cooperation with the security agencies, shaved beards and carrying mobile phones. Karl had never seen Abdullah looking so happy.

He found no time to look at the file until he returned to the flat that evening. While the woman was preparing their meal, he started reading. His attention was immediately grabbed when he recognised the name on the first line of the background page, *Ibrahim bin Omar al-Ahmad. This is Jabbar's son,* he realised. *He's in Germany and he's a believer.* Reading on, he became engrossed in the story of the failed attack in Cologne and the subsequent futile manhunt for the perpetrator. He had heard nothing about the attempted attack, but that wasn't surprising; he concentrated on news items which were useful to him and this hadn't been, at the time. *He's ready to make a second attempt,* he realised, *it looks like the first one almost worked.* He remembered the commander who had handled Ibrahim previously. The man was long gone, killed in an air strike in eastern

Mosul. *He was al-Jbouri's number two in Mosul*, he recalled. *That's not very promising.*

'What's that you're reading?' the woman asked.

'A contact in Germany,' he answered cautiously. 'Could be an opportunity for an attack over there, you never know. I'll follow it up and see if it comes to anything. Is my meal ready?'

After eating, Karl studied the file thoroughly, an idea beginning to form in his mind. He was tired of cleaning up after Abdullah – he needed a project of his own. He found the mobile number in the file then composed a short text message. *Let's see if there's anything in this*, he said to himself, as he pressed send.

FIFTEEN

Ibrahim Khalil Iraq-Turkey Border Crossing, near Zakho, Iraq
May 2016

'Where is the senior officer?' Faqir asked for the fourth or fifth time. It was after 7:00 pm and he had already spent two hours trying to convince the immigration official to accept his expired visas. Khalid, the truck driver, had dropped them off at a town called Saru Kani, then continued on what they assumed was his black market run to sell the stolen, much-needed foodstuffs from Domiz II refugee camp. Their situation was too precarious to intervene, and they set off at a slow march towards the border crossing, still hours away. On the way they passed an inn and stopped to have a snack and some strong Turkish coffee.

His family were now sitting on the sidewalk outside the office, along with dozens of other refugees whose papers weren't in order. He'd been arguing with the man intermittently, when he wasn't stamping valid visas for other travellers who passed through quickly and efficiently.

'What's going on?' A tall, bearded Turkish officer walked into the office.

The official stood to attention. 'He's trying to get his family through on expired visas. I'm sure they're fakes, it wouldn't be the first time.'

'Let me see.' The officer examined the visas and passports then went outside to look at Faqir's family.

'Why are you a month late in presenting these passes?' he asked.

'It's hell in Mosul, sir. My parents and my wife's father were killed in an airstrike in March, just before we were due to leave Mosul. It's an administrative nightmare and by the time we got everything sorted out, the passes had expired and the office in Erbil wasn't issuing new ones.' Faqir's story was partially true. The officer had no way of confirming that his parents and father-in law had indeed been killed by a coalition missile, but it was in 2015, not 2016.

'So you had visas for the whole family, all ten of you?' The man was as smart as he looked.

'Just a moment, please.' Faqir went outside and fished in his backpack, returning with three more documents. 'These are their visas, but they never lived to use them.'

'Hmm. They're exactly the same date stamp, you got them all together.'

'That's right, sir. I didn't keep the receipt because I wasn't expecting to be delayed, especially for such a tragic reason.'

'Ask your wife to come in here.'

The officer repeated the same questions to Hema, who replied tearfully to confirm Faqir's story. 'We have to get to Istanbul,' she finished, 'our lives in Mosul are over. Apart from my mother and our children, most of our family have been lost and I don't know what will happen to the others when it's discovered we've left.' At this, she broke into a flood of tears and Faqir put his arm around her shoulders.

'How do you expect to get there?'

Faqir had anticipated this question. When they had stopped at the roadside inn on the way, he said to Hema. 'I have to risk a little money to get through the border. Do you trust me?'

'It depends how much and what it's for.'

'We have to convince the immigration people that we don't intend to stay in Turkey, they'll be more inclined to let us through. The best way is to have our plane tickets for Istanbul to show them we're honest and serious.'

'How can we do that?'

'I've got the Turkish Airlines site on my mobile. There's lots of flights from Batman to Istanbul. I can buy the tickets online and pay with the last of the money in our business account. They'll cost about 120 euros each and there's still over a thousand in the bank.'

'That money will be lost in any case, so you're not really risking anything.'

'Exactly. Shall I book them for tomorrow?'

'That's taking a chance. Book them for the day after, in case anything goes wrong.'

'Nothing's going to go wrong, but you're right as usual. Better safe than sorry.'

Now, he showed the officer his mobile. 'Here's the confirmation for our tickets. You can see, we're not refugees, we've got money and tickets and want to make our way to Europe, where we have family living.'

The confirmation was for seven adult tickets on a Turkish Airlines flight from Batman to Istanbul at 2:00 pm on Saturday 21st May, in two days.

'You're planning was good, you've included some time for delays. Where will you go from there?'

Faqir replied, 'Either Greece or Bulgaria, then to northern Europe.'

'Wait a moment.' He took the official aside and they talked for several minutes, then he came over. 'I'm not convinced you'll make it because those countries are tightening their borders every day. But you've got young children and I don't want to stand in your way, so I'll issue you with visas for one month only, time to get to Istanbul and out of Turkey, if you can. If you're still here after that, you'll all go into a refugee camp and I can't guarantee what will happen to you. Or, you can still turn around and go back into Iraq, what is your decision?'

Hema grabbed her husband's arm. She suddenly felt faint with the relief of hearing those words.

He reached out to shake the officer's hand. 'Thank you, sir, thank you from all my family. We will never forget your kindness.'

'Thank the Lord above you thought of everything my darling. But I thought that telling the officer we have family in Europe was a bit risky. He might have asked who and where.'

It was close to midnight and they were sitting in a ten-seater minibus, on the 100 km trip from the border to Siirt, where they would get a bus to the airport at Batman, a further 60 km away. Faqir was in the front next to the driver, Bahri, a wizened little Kurdish man with a straggly beard, while his family were squeezed into the seats behind.

'I had a few answers ready, but I'm glad he didn't interrogate me any further on it, or we might have been in trouble. And it was good that we had the airline bookings, I think that persuaded him. But my research wasn't thorough enough – I stupidly thought there was still a bus service from Silopi, but it was cancelled after they stopped issuing visas, I should have thought of that. We've got to get to Batman by Saturday or we lose the tickets.' Faqir had expected to pay less than 100 euros for public transport and instead was obliged to negotiate with the taxi driver to take them at a price of 50 euros per head. 'Another three hundred and fifty gone,' he said worriedly. 'I can't afford to make any more mistakes like that.'

'You're too hard on yourself,' she answered. 'We didn't have to bribe the officer, so that makes up for it.'

After something to eat at the *kafe* beside the border post, they set off at 10:00 pm and although there was little traffic, the drive was extremely slow. This stretch of the road to Siirt was narrow, winding and pitch black; Bahri had his headlights on, but most of the few cars that passed them were unlit. He calculated the journey would take another two hours, if they made it safely. The bus to Batman was at nine in the morning, so they would be able to sleep at the bus station. Their flight wasn't until the next day, so they had time to spare, or so he thought.

Stuttgart, Germany

Ibrahim was watching TV when he heard the 'ping' of a message arriving on his phone. It was 10:00 pm on the night after he'd called the Imam, Mohammad. The text said, *'Throw away your SIM and buy a prepaid one with minimum usage. Confirm back to this phone.'* The message came from a number with a 040-dialling code, which he found was Romania.

He went down on his knees and pressed his forehead to the floor. *Allah has listened to me. He has found a way for me to fulfil my destiny and find vengeance.* When he finally fell asleep, his dreams were full of images of battles, executions and explosions. The next morning, on awakening, he knew this was the first day of the rest of his life, a new life, another chance to achieve a glorious martyrdom.

SIXTEEN

Near Şirnak, en route to Batman Airport, Turkey
May 2016

For a moment, Faqir imagined he was back in Mosul when the sound of gunshots woke him from an exhausted sleep.

'Get down everyone,' the driver shouted. 'On the floor.'

'What's going on?' Hema's heart started pounding with fear. The vehicle was veering from side to side on the road and through the dirty back window they could see motor bike lights. She pulled her mother down onto the floor and shouted to the children to do the same. They lay fearfully on the filthy matting, hardly daring to breathe, not daring to imagine what had gone wrong now.

'Robbers, trying to stop us,' the driver shouted. 'There's gangs of them on the roads around Şırnak, looking for taxis with wealthy passengers.'

'Stay down all of you. Don't move.' In the front seat, Faqir lowered himself as far as he could. Frantically, he pulled out his mobile phone. 'What's the emergency number, I'll call for help?'

'Not from here, you can't. There's no connection.'

His heart sank when he saw there was no signal. 'So what do we do?'

'We've just got to try to outrun them.'

He looked at the time, 'We must be more than an hour from Siirt. We can't outrun motorbikes for that long.'

Bahri's eyes were fixed on the dark road ahead. 'There's a petrol station outside Çakırsöğüt, about two kilometres from here. We can make it there if we're lucky.'

Now they could hear the sound of bullets smashing against the back of the vehicle. '*Iilhi*, My God,' Hema cried out. 'They're trying to kill us.' The bus was suddenly filled with the crying and wailing of the women. Putting her arms around her mother's shaking frame, she called out, 'Hamid, Malik, keep your sisters close to you.'

Faqir squinted around the back of his seat. He could see there were two bikes, each with two riders and one of them was accelerating to get level with the bus. 'Watch out, they're splitting up,' he warned the driver.

The leading bike came alongside and the passenger aimed his gun at the front tyre. He shot twice then the bike accelerated away from them. The women screamed in fear as the bus swerved violently across the road onto a sandy verge with a ditch running alongside. Bahri was standing on the brake, desperately gripping the steering wheel to stop the vehicle from turning over. Faqir grabbed the wheel to help him and to brace himself for the upcoming shock. Amid the stench of burning rubber, the bus screeched to a halt with its left front wheel in the ditch and the passengers thrown chaotically around inside. For a moment there was silence, then the women's cries resumed, as they saw the lights of the motor bikes draw up beside them. Faqir tried to open the passenger door, but it was jammed. As he climbed over to the back seats to help his family, he saw Bahri push open his door and run off into the darkness.

Both bikes shone their lights onto the bus as someone

pulled back the door. They couldn't see the others behind the lights, but the man was wearing a balaclava. He looked very young.

'Out, everyone,' he shouted in Arabic, waving a short-barrelled rifle at them.

Faqir helped his family from the vehicle. His mother-in-law, Hadiya, had hurt her knee in the crash and he held her, his arm around her shoulders, feeling the silent sobs that wracked her frail body. Hema and the girls were weeping and shaking with fear and he saw that Malik was clenching his fists, ready for a fight.

'They're women and children,' he said. 'Don't hurt them, they've done nothing against you. We're just refugees from Mosul, trying to escape the war.'

The man ignored him, pushing the gun into his face. 'Give me your money, all of it.'

He put his hand up to ward off the gun and reached for the remaining bills in his pocket, held the money out, trying to control his trembling hand. 'This is all we've got left. We gave the rest to pay for this bus and now we can't get to Batman, we're stuck in the middle of nowhere, with nothing.'

'Bullshit. You're in a taxi, so you must have money.' He raised his gun. 'The old woman goes first, then the others, one by one, until you give it to me.' He pulled the trigger.

Faqir heard the gasp of Hadiya's breath and felt the impact of the bullet as it hit her chest. As if in a dream, he heard Hema cry, 'MAMA!', as her head fell forward against his arm. He realised the blood was soaking into his shirt and slowly and carefully he laid the lifeless body down on the ground at his feet. Hema cried again, a long, anguished wail, as she kneeled on the bare sandy surface, cradling her mother's face in her hands. The two boys took their hysterical sisters and turned them away from the scene, trying to calm them down.

He looked down at her body, lying on the dusty, sandy ground, the familiar, loving face now expressionless, her life snuffed out as easily as a candle's flame. Tears sprang to his eyes and he wept helplessly at the senseless slaughter. *This is my fault, I should have just given him the money.*

A car without lights drove slowly past them towards Çakırsöğüt and through his tears Faqir saw the driver looking out the window at the scene. He lifted his arm listlessly to signal to him, but when the man realised what was happening, he put his foot down and sped away.

The gunman pointed his weapon at Hema's head. 'She's next. Where's the money?'

'No, wait. Here, take it and leave us.' He unwrapped his money belt and threw it at the man, praying he wouldn't search the others.

He took the bills out and started counting, then looked up as the road was suddenly lit by the lights of a car coming from the direction of Şırnak. Throwing the empty pouch on the ground, he shouted, 'OK, come on guys. Out of here.'

Faqir felt an overwhelming sense of hopelessness and failure as he watched the two motorcycles roar off back towards Şırnak. The car drove past without slowing down and darkness and silence enveloped them again. The children came and knelt with their mother, weeping and praying for their lost grandmother. After a while, he helped Hema to her feet and wrapped his arms around her and his family. *What in God's name have we done to deserve this nightmare? And how are we going to manage without that money?* He asked himself.

SEVENTEEN

Düsseldorf, Germany
May 2016

'We have no idea where he is. He's been off the radar since he left the aparthotel and disappeared in Frankfurt.' Max Kellerman moved uncomfortably in his chair. It was Friday, 20th May, three weeks since the explosion in Kalk, and he was distinctly embarrassed by his lack of progress.

'So, it seems your theory about him dropping his guard or getting nervous hasn't worked.' Eric Schuster seemed to be enjoying himself. Despite a flurry of calls and a couple of incorrect identifications following the announcement of the reward, nothing material had transpired. Whichever of the two suspects had survived remained at large and the combined forces of the EU national police, security and the Atlas EU anti-terrorist collaboration, plus Interpol, hadn't been able to lift the veil of invisibility that he seemed to have hidden behind.

'We know this is a waiting game where one side or the other will finally run out of patience. The guy must still be in Europe, almost certainly in the Schengen zone, because we'd have had a passport alert if he'd tried to cross to a non-Schengen country. The immigration controls at those borders are a lot more stringent than they were and there's virtually no chance he could have got out. We have to be patient, alert and ready to take advantage of the first mistake he makes, and it's bound to happen.'

Internally, Max was cursing the lack of inter-European immigration controls. He was certain that if Germany still had border guards, they would have had their man a long time ago. But there was nothing he could do about it and complaining about Schengen would label him as a non-EU supporter which would certainly not help his career.

Schuster said, 'Well. I'm sorry, Max, but the guys at the top are saying we're becoming a laughing stock in the EU security back rooms and they don't like it. We'll make one more announcement and if we get nowhere, we'll have to review the situation and decide what to do next, if anything.' He paused, looking embarrassed.

'What is it? You can tell me. Am I off the case?'

'It's not just that. They need a scapegoat and they've chosen you. You won't be demoted, I've made sure of that, you're too good a man to lose. But there'll be no more TV celebrity stuff for you, you'll be back at the desk job again. That's the best I could manage under the circumstances.'

Max wished he could find something constructive to say, but he couldn't. He didn't want to admit it, but he had thoroughly enjoyed his moment in the spotlight. *Well, now it's over, unless a miracle occurs.* He gave a wan smile and went back to his desk, back to his paperwork, hoping for the impossible to happen. He left the Kalk chart on the wall behind him, just in case this wasn't the end of the story.

Stuttgart, Germany

Ibrahim went to a mobile phone store and reluctantly replaced the Vodafone SIM, which still had 20 euros credit on it, with a 15-euro T-Mobile SIM. He texted the number back then, understanding the procedure, he bought SIMs from two other shops in the neighbourhood. He now had three SIMs to interchange after each call.

That afternoon, a man who identified himself only as Karl, called and asked him several questions in Arabic. Most of them were obviously to check on his real identity; his parent's names, his place and date of birth, details of his uncle, his brother and sister, other questions that only he could answer and which must have been gleaned from his father's dossier. Finally, the man seemed satisfied. He informed him that his previous contact was 'no longer with the company' and he would be his manager now, if he qualified for any further activity.

He said, 'I have some more questions for you. Choose your words carefully when you answer.' Ibrahim waited in silence.

'Did you make the machine?'

'Yes.'

'How long did it take?'

'Five or six weeks.'

'Why did it break?'

'My cousin or brother must have disturbed it when I had to go to the hospital with my mother.'

'So, it worked as required but was broken by an accident?'

'Yes.'

'Could you make it again?'

'Yes.'

'Do you have money?'

'Enough for six months.'

'Can you drive?'

'Yes, but I don't have my licence.'

'What papers do you have?'

'I don't understand. Papers?'

'To travel.'

'I have my cousin's ID card. We were the same age.'

'Can you be recognised?'

'I don't think so. I wear a hoodie and sunglasses and I grew a beard.'

The Emir seemed satisfied. He told Ibrahim he would get back to him when he'd considered how he could be used. Then he asked, 'Do you have a computer?'

'No, it was broken.'

'Do you have enough money to buy another?'

'I can find a cheap one quickly.'

'Get one and let me know your email address when we speak again. And don't forget to change the SIM after every call.'

'I understand. I'll do it every time.'

'Good. Remember, always keep your head down when there might be a camera nearby.' The man rang off.

Ibrahim went to an electronics shop and bought a notebook for less than 300 euros. He paid cash; there was still five hundred left on the PayPal account, but he wanted to keep it in case of an emergency. While the shop owner, a Moroccan immigrant, loaded it with illegal copies of the basic software he'd need, he sat and read with the newspaper hiding his face. He was still cautious about being identified, although he knew the risk was virtually zero after all this time and his disguise had helped to avoid any chance of recognition. He was ready for the next step.

Mosul, Iraq

'We have to get out of this flat.'

'Sure, and you're not serious?'

'It's not my decision, it's Abdullah's.'

'Shit! Why's that bastard throwing us out? It's the only comfortable place I've been in since I came to this crap country.'

'Two reasons. He hates the sight of me and would do anything to screw up my life. And he says he needs it for someone more important. We've got to be out by tomorrow.' Karl didn't look her in the eyes in case she realised he wasn't telling the truth.

'Someone more important? And isn't that a likely story? Fuck him, the son of a bitch. Where will we go? I was talking to that Russian girl, Ekaterina, today and she said there's no flats to be had.'

Karl knew that it wasn't just the comfort of the apartment she would miss; it was the feeling of pride of being one up on the other women. She loved her position as 'wife' of the legendary commander and the respect she earned from the others. She had earned the right to have a 'nom de guerre', a warrior's name, but had never taken one; being with Karl was enough. He had first noticed her in February 2015, fighting alongside her previous man in the great battle with the Kurdish

Peshmerga forces when they had retaken the north-western lands on the Nineveh Plains. Seeing her firing a Kalashnikov assault rifle like the fighting men around her, he admired both her bravery and looks and envied the man she was with. After he was killed by a missile strike, Karl had taken her as his woman, a great honor for her and a great comfort for him. Despite his renown as one of the liberators of Mosul, he'd been without a companion for several months, until he met her.

She'd been with him for over a year and he felt sad to do this to her, but he couldn't avoid it. It had to be done. 'Who's she with? Where are they staying?' he asked casually.

'She was with that Turkish fella, Emrah. He was killed in the El Nasr attack. Now she's on her own, staying in the Beirut Hotel in the Hayy Ar Rabi district, beside the park.'

'Go over and see if there's space there for us. It's not a bad area, less air attacks because of all the civilians still there. If there's room, we'll go tomorrow.'

EIGHTEEN

It was 10:30 am on Saturday when Faqir and his family stepped off the Metro Turizm bus from Siirt. They had taken the first and only connection which left at 9:00 am, on time.

After watching their attackers disappear into the darkness, the family prayed together and consoled each other until they could cope with the death of Mama Hadiya. Faqir was guilt-ridden and frantic with worry that more bandits would come along and attack them in their vulnerable state. He tried desperately to plan some kind of solution to their predicament. Their only security was the minibus itself, and he climbed back in to take stock of the crash. Bahri had left the keys in the ignition when he ran off and the engine started without a problem. With Hema at the wheel, the others tried vainly to push the vehicle out of the ditch. It was too heavy to move forwards or in reverse gear.

During their efforts, several cars passed and Malik finally managed to flag one of them down, an Iraqi who agreed to take someone to the service station at Çakırsöğüt. Faqir and Malik would go with their good Samaritan to organise a rescue mission, while the others stayed in the bus. They sadly laid Hadiya's body on a blanket in the boot space and Hema, the girls and Hamid locked themselves in the bus. It wasn't a secure solution, but the only one available for them until the others returned.

It took only five minutes to reach the all-night station and their driver dropped them off and drove away, refusing the few notes that Faqir offered him. The employee spoke Arabic and they were explaining the dreadful events of the night when a sweating, filthy Bahri walked in the door.

'You fucking cowardly traitor, leaving us there to die. You killed my grandma.' Malik grabbed him, screaming abuse, punching and kicking the little man, knocking him to the floor.

The driver scrambled away from the punches and kicks. 'I came here for help,' he shouted. 'I've walked two kilometres in the dark to get help.'

'It's OK, Malik, let him talk.' Faqir pulled his son away. 'What kind of help?'

'They've got a pick-up truck here. There's always accidents on this piece of road. We can fix the bus and get to Siirt in a few hours.'

'He's lying to save his skin, the murderous little bastard.'

'Is it true?' Faqir asked the employee, who seemed to be enjoying the show.

'It's behind the building, in good condition. He's right, we use it a lot.'

'How much will it cost?'

'Depends what needs to be done.'

Bahri entered into a staccato discussion in Turkish with the assistant, bargaining over a price, then, switching back to Arabic, he said, '200 euros to pull the bus out and change the tyre. That's if there's no damage to the wheel.'

'How quickly can you come?'

He looked at the time; it was eleven-thirty. 'It's a slow night, there's been hardly anybody here except you. I can shut the place up for an hour, that should be enough if the damage isn't too serious.'

They were back at the minibus within fifteen minutes, to find their family still safely inside. Forty minutes later, the vehicle was back on the road with the spare tyre fitted and the wing and bumper more or less hammered back into shape. Everything seemed to be working. Hema ensured her mother's body was properly protected and the family climbed back inside.

'Here's my hundred.' Faqir handed the last of his euros over to the garage attendant.

'I said two hundred?'

He opened the passenger door to climb in. 'Bahri will pay half. It's his bus you've repaired and I paid him three hundred and fifty. He can afford it.'

The driver hesitated for a moment then reluctantly peeled off the notes and handed them over.

As the bus twisted and turned on its way to Siirt, Hema and the children talked quietly together, reminiscing about Hadiya, swapping stories, remembering happy events, when life in Mosul had been almost normal, before ISIL came. Faqir was quiet, his mind in turmoil, blaming himself for the attack and his mother-in-law's murder, wishing he'd handed over the money immediately.

Then he started worrying about money again. There had been almost 10,000 euros in the money belt he'd handed over. Hema and the boys still had 12,500 euros they'd each started with, so thanks to her foresight, they'd lost less than a quarter of their money, but it was a fortune, one they couldn't afford to lose and couldn't replace. He saw the others had fallen asleep now and closed his eyes, but sleep wouldn't come.

They parked the minibus in the centre of Siirt and slept in the vehicle. Bahri stayed with them, he said it was a gesture of regret for what had happened, but Faqir was sure he was afraid of being attacked if he drove back at night. The parking lot was surrounded by residential buildings where they felt safe and they managed to get a few hours of uncomfortable sleep. Hema was emotionally exhausted and thankfully, slept soundly until the traffic noise woke them at seven. Then they breakfasted on Turkish pastries and strong coffee at a café before confronting the reality of their situation.

Siirt was a smart, busy city of over 100,000 inhabitants and they quickly found the town hall where friendly, concerned staff directed them to a funeral home near the Mezarlik Cemetery, to arrange the burial. Bahri drove off in his battered minibus; despite the awful circumstances of their trip, he had proved to be a decent person and had restored some of their faith in human nature. Then they prayed over Hadiya's body and bade her a tearful farewell; her dream of finding a safe, quiet place to enjoy her last years with her family had quickly been destroyed. Faqir paid the funeral director and they made their way back into the city centre.

The daily bus to Batman had left that morning, so they

spent the rest of the day walking around the city, trying to get over the traumatic events of the night and getting to grips with their situation. Faqir spent as little money as possible and they stayed that night in a cheap hostel near the bus station.

Before going to bed, he had taken Hema aside. 'We need to reorganise the cash between us.'

'Maybe it's better for you not to have any, you're the first person those gunmen asked.'

'I know, but it worked out as the best arrangement. Once they got my money belt, they thought it was all we had, so they left you and the kids alone.'

They compromised, Faqir keeping 7,000 euros in his money belt and Hema and their two sons 10,000 each, hidden in their clothing. *But thank God,* he told himself, *we've paid for the flights. We'll have to manage somehow. Inshallah.*

Stuttgart, Germany

On Saturday, the day after their first conversation, Karl rang again. After ensuring Ibrahim now had a functioning laptop, he switched to English. His first question was, 'Do you speak this language?'

'I can read, write and speak quite well.' Ibrahim had spent five years at *Hauptschule,* secondary school, in Cologne, where the compulsory second language was English. He liked the language and still had a good mastery of it.

The Emir was pleased. 'What about Italian?' He asked. This time the answer was no.

Giving a disappointed grunt, he asked, 'What is your

email address?' After noting it down, he instructed Ibrahim to buy an Italian phrase book, make his way immediately to Milan, find an anonymous lodging, send a text when he got there and then be patient. He had a plan for him, an ambitious plan.

NINETEEN

Karl was dead on his feet after an exhausting discussion with the members of the Military Council. The deputy head of the Security Council was also present, and the subject was the treatment of refugees. He knew each of the men well and had talked to them individually about the problem whenever he got the chance. On this occasion, they had deigned to meet him as a council, the downside being that his boss, Abdullah, was also invited.

In his mind, it was a straightforward matter of resources and logistics. The present rule was to prevent civilians leaving the city and if they were caught while attempting to flee, to publicly execute them. He didn't agree with either of these policies and tried his best to convince the councillors that they were self-defeating, time-consuming and wasteful.

The incident with the café owner and his family out at Batnaya had crystallised and hardened his opinions on the subject. After seeing the desperation and terror on their faces, he'd felt obliged to spare them. If he hadn't, they'd have either been executed by Abdullah's squad, or most likely killed as the situation in the city deteriorated. He sympathised with them for wanting to flee what he saw had become a city of death. A place where human life was now so trivial, so inconsequential, that what had become important was not whether you executed people for transgressing some meaningless dogma, but how you executed them. How many more gruesome, sadistic ways of killing civilians or soldiers alike were still to be invented before Mosul was retaken?

The caliphate's multi-layered security and intelligence agency for Syria and Iraq was headquartered in the city. Named *Amniya*, literally, 'Security', the organisation was under the control of Ayad Hamil al-Jumaili, an ex-Saddam Hussein intelligence officer from Fallujah. The agency had six-branches, each occupied with a different aspect of security, from high level spying and intelligence activities to *Hisba*, a vice squad which paid informers as young as twelve to report on their neighbour's transgressions, so they could be publicly punished. During the two-year period of continued war, strife, starvation and sadistic repression, 1.5 million inhabitants had fled the city to escape ISIL's barbaric rule.

And Karl knew it would never improve, only get worse. As time ran out on the jihadists' occupation of Mosul, the threat to the civilians' lives would increase, from the ever more desperate ISIL leaders, from the intensifying coalition airstrikes and from the bloody fighting that would invade the residential areas when the coalition troops stormed into the city.

'Who wouldn't want to save their family from such a fate?' he'd pleaded. 'If they have a chance to escape from an almost certain death and they have sufficient money to rebuild their lives in a new place, it must be Allah's will to give them the chance to do so.'

Karl was a complex man with his own well-defined sense of right and wrong, which often defied logic.

Although he sympathised with civilians trying to escape, he had no time for ISIL fighters who helped them. He saw no conflict between his humanitarian act of kindness in letting Faqir's family go and then executing the militant who had been paid to help them and confiscating the money he'd received.

'Next, there's the problem of our manpower resources. Every time we catch anyone trying to run, we arrest them, prosecute them, parade them through the city, then execute them in a public exhibition. That means we're wasting thousands of hours of our men's time on unproductive duties. They should be fighting our battles outside the city against the enemies who can hurt us, not inside against people who can do nothing to harm us.'

He'd talked about the problems of governing a city which still counted over a million inhabitants. 'To be truthful, it would make more sense if we encouraged people to leave Mosul, instead of trying to keep them here. They consume food and precious energy resources, oil, electricity, water; we need security officers, prisons, mortuaries and cemeteries to keep them under control or execute them and they bring us virtually nothing in return, no substantial taxes or productive contributions of any kind. What's more, they hate us and try to hurt us. Look at the increase in the numbers of *Muqawama* resistance fighters. If they hate us so much, let them go. They'll be happier, and we'll be more efficient, surrounded only by true believers who behave and live according to our doctrine.'

The discussion went on for two hours and as he'd expected, proved to be a complete waste of time. At one point, Abdullah suggested that he should be arrested for sedition. 'He's proposing policies and concepts which go against the very basic principles of our caliphate. If he talks like this in front of you council members, what is he saying to our fighting men?'

Karl knew he was skating on very thin ice, but the truth was that after twenty years of fighting for causes which he had espoused when he was a young man, his mind was being invaded by doubts. When he looked around at the despoliation and defilement that the ISIL leaders had wrought in Syria and Iraq – the cities, towns, villages, holy places of worship, ancient monuments, the centuries of human achievement that they had obliterated without a second thought and the tens of thousands of innocent people murdered for the same doctrine – he had more and more difficulty in understanding the motives of the caliphate. Were they trying to build something, a new order as he'd always wanted to believe? Or were they intent solely on destroying everything that didn't mirror their rigid, uncompromising beliefs and desire to convert the world to their dogma?

Because of his popularity and legendary reputation, Karl was listened to respectfully for two hours, then ignored. He left the meeting, convinced that the downfall of ISIL was in the best possible hands – their own. They had captured Mosul in a glorious display of bloodthirsty bravado. It looked like they would lose it, along with the many other prizes so boldly won, in the same way.

He finally arrived back at the Beirut Hotel where he and his woman were now squatting. She was with several militants in what remained of the downstairs bar, drinking beer from cases they'd found in the cellar. He didn't approve of drinking alcohol, but many of the fighters were from countries and religions which paid no attention to Muslim practices, so he said nothing and accepted a coke.

She kissed him and put her arm possessively around his shoulders. 'This is Ekaterina, the girl I told you about.'

'Hi, Karl, nice to meet you.' She was tall and willowy, quite attractive and spoke English with a thick Russian accent.

'I knew your guy, Emrah, he was a brave fighter. I'm sorry you lost him.'

She gave him a wry smile. 'I only knew him for a month, same as the one before. Maybe I bring them bad luck.'

'Fighters make their own luck and it's not always good,' he said.

She nodded her head and said nothing. He asked, 'Can I get you another beer?'

His woman looked at him in surprise as he went to fetch the drink. *He never does anything without a reason*, she thought to herself. *What's going on?*

They sat with Ekaterina for a while until she said, 'I'm tired, I'd better get some sleep. I'll maybe see you in the morning.'

'We'll go down with you, I'm shattered as well.' Karl stood up, took them both by the arm and walked them down the stairwell to the corridor with conference rooms where the camp beds were laid out in rows. Ekaterina stopped at one near the entrance.

'*Num jydaan*, sleep well,' he said and they continued

on to their beds. 'Seems like a decent woman,' he murmured, seemingly unaware of the dagger looks being thrown at him by his partner.

Istanbul, Republic of Turkey

The Turkish Airlines flight from Batman was delayed for three hours and it was seven on Saturday evening when they arrived at Istanbul's Atatürk airport. Much to Faqir's relief, the temporary visas they'd received at the border allowed the family to board and disembark the plane without problems. They found the pick-up point for the Havatas bus to take them into the city; it was easier than carrying luggage on the metro, and they were in the centre of the city by eight-thirty. His family needed a decent night's rest; they were all exhausted by the trip and the trauma of Hadiya's death. The area was full of cheap hotels and hostels and they spent the night at the Atlantic Motel.

After their traumatic journey, Hema insisted they should do nothing at all on Sunday but settle themselves on the beach for the day with a picnic. The weather was dry and warm; they slept, talked and played games like any normal family, even testing the cool waters of the Sea of Marmara. Gradually they began the process of putting behind them the sad memories of the last few days. Faqir tried to relax and enjoy the time with his family, but his mind kept returning to the tasks that lay in store for Monday. Somehow, he had to convince either the Bulgarian or the Greek consulate to issue visas for his family to cross into their country. *I managed to persuade the Turkish official,* he told himself, *I can do it again.* But he knew the nearer they got to Europe, the more difficult it would become.

On Monday morning, he had a moment of panic when he discovered the consulates were closed for the day on account of some obscure Turkish holiday. Somehow, he managed to keep his emotions in check as he took his family on a walking tour around the historic city. Listening to their lively chatter, as always, he was full of admiration for Hema's ability to help everyone cope with their changed situation, focussing on their future and slowly putting the past behind them. It would take a long time before she could reconcile herself to the death of her mother, but she gave no sign of her grief, laughing and enjoying these precious moments with her children.

That night, Faqir couldn't get to sleep, fretting alternately about obtaining the precious visas they needed and conserving their fast dwindling cash reserve.

Aware that he was awake and worrying, Hema leaned across and kissed him fondly. 'Well done, my love. Thanks to you, we've got this far. You'll find a way to get us through to Europe. Go to sleep and stop worrying.'

TWENTY

Milan, Italy
May 2016

Ibrahim bin Omar al-Ahmad was sitting on the terrace of a café in Milan. It was early and he was having a breakfast of doughnuts and orange juice. For a moment he thought of his brother and sister, then he closed his mind to the memory and concentrated on his last call with Karl, the ISIL commander who was now his boss. The early stages in the trip from Cologne had been a series of miserable days of desolate fear, loss and loneliness until in Stuttgart, miraculously, he had finally found a new sense of belonging, of purpose and potential fulfilment.

The day after being instructed to go to Milan, Ibrahim had texted Anna that he was leaving her apartment. He felt a sense of sadness, as he had when he'd left his mother's flat in Kalk. It had been a safe place, where he'd been able to sort out his muddled emotions and find a new opportunity, a new path to follow, one he was sure would finally lead him to a glorious martyrdom, like his father's.

He locked up the flat, left the key in its hiding place and went to the station to buy a ticket to Munich in southern Germany. After all the time that had passed, he was no longer concerned about being noticeable or remembered; that was ancient history, unless he had to show ID. Nevertheless, he remembered to look down at the ground whenever there might be a CCTV camera around. With his hoodie and beard it was virtually impossible to see his face. From Munich he took a train across the Austrian border to Innsbruck without any passport control. He decided he loved the Schengen Agreement; it meant he could travel throughout Europe without any ID whatsoever. He remembered how the Paris bombers had done that for months whilst the incompetent, naïve Europeans waited for them to arrive in Paris and blow it up. *Watch out,* he said to himself, *it's going to happen again.*

In Innsbruck he checked into a youth hostel near the station where they didn't ask him for identification. He spoke only English and studied the Italian phrase book he'd bought at Stuttgart railway station, learning a few basic words of the language to help him avoid difficult conversations which might betray him. Apart from anything else the book was quite a good camouflage and had a useful map of Europe folded in the back which helped to mitigate his ignorance of European geography.

At the hostel, he met a group of young people of several nationalities and languages who were taking a bus the next day across the border into Italy. For 20 euros he booked himself a seat on the bus and arrived safely in Verona, once again without arousing any questions. A ninety-minute train ride then brought him to Milan and its four million inhabitants, where he could disappear into the vast sprawl of the city.

The streets were full of aparthotels where a room cost less than 30 euros a night and he still had more than three thousand. He chose *Hosteleria Costa* which had a studio with Wi-Fi available on the ground floor and the manager asked for cash and no ID papers. His first action was to buy three Italian SIMs for his phone and send a text message to Karl, confirming that he was on holiday in Italy. Now, he was enjoying his breakfast, studying his Italian phrase book and waiting for his Emir to contact him again.

Istanbul, Republic of Turkey

Faqir had looked up the addresses of the Greek and Bulgarian Consulates. The former was just a fifteen-minute walk from the motel, near Taksim Square, whereas the Bulgarian office was in Ulus, about 5 km away. He decided to go there first then come back to see the Greeks, if necessary. Following directions from the receptionist, he went off to catch the bus, leaving Hema and the children to visit Sultanahmet, the historic centre of Istanbul, then they planned to meet for lunch. He expected the consulates to be busy and he'd have to wait, then enter into long and complicated discussions, but he was optimistic he could convince one or the other to help his family. He was wrong on both counts.

The Bulgarian Consulate was in a residential area populated by tower blocks painted in several shades of orange, like giant plastic models. An attractive U-shaped, three-storey building in a walled enclosure, it had a security barrier outside and a guard. Faqir had problems communicating with the man, who spoke no Arabic or English. After repeating 'visa' many times and showing his passport, he finally let him through the security gate and he was met by a woman at the door of the consulate building. She let him into the hall and asked him his business. It was a short conversation.

When he showed his Iraqi passport and Turkish visa, she was astonished. 'I don't understand how you obtained that visa. Turkey is not supposed to issue them to refugees from Iraq or Syria, it undermines the whole agreement they've made with the EU.'

At this, Faqir's mind was invaded by fearful doubts. *What if she calls the police and has us arrested, or she confiscates the visas? We'll be stuck here in Turkey for God knows how long.* He pleaded with the woman, trying to convince her that his family were not refugees; they had resources and relatives in Europe and they simply wanted to make their way through Bulgaria to get there.

Finally, she said, 'I'll let you keep the Turkish visa, although I have the right to confiscate it for improper issue. But I cannot issue visas for your family to enter my country, even if you hoped to travel straight through. We have thousands of asylum seekers already and our borders are blocked with queues of refugees. Now that it looks as if Hungary will close its border with Serbia, it's going to be much worse. Frankly, your chances of getting into northern Europe are non-existent. To issue visas to you would be highly improper and I could lose my job.' She ignored his demands to see her superior and the guard came to escort him out of the compound. Shoulders slumped, invaded by a feeling of failure and hopelessness, he walked despondently back to the bus stop, thinking, *now the Greeks are our only hope. Let's pray they are more understanding.*

At eleven-thirty, Faqir rang the bell of the beautiful, old, granite built three-storey residence that housed the Greek Consulate. It was in a busy street near Taksim Square, stuck cheek by jowl between commercial properties, shops and offices. The guard sent him to the visa section on the second floor of the building where the attendant ushered him into a room with large windows looking over a busy square. There were only two other people in the waiting room, a tall, distinguished-looking man who looked about seventy, wearing a striped linen jacket, white shirt and trousers, sitting next to a well-dressed woman, who appeared to be his wife.

The man looked up from his newspaper. '*Günaydın,*' he said politely in Turkish.

Faqir saw he was reading the International Herald Tribune and replied, 'Good morning.' He felt embarrassed and untidy in his shabby, travel-stained clothes and sat on the other side of the room. To avoid their glances, he studied the view from the window. It was a vibrant, busy scene, full of shoppers, beggars, tourists and with red trams running in and out of the square.

The man looked up again and said, 'It shouldn't be long, there's no one in there and we're just waiting for our papers to be signed by the consul.'

'Thank you. Please excuse my appearance, I've been travelling with my family for the last few days.' He gestured at his unkempt clothing. The couple nodded and smiled without saying anything.

A few minutes later, he was called into the office of the assistant consul, a Greek man of about sixty, with a mane of white hair and an abundant beard.

'Can we speak Arabic or English, please?' he replied when the man began to question him in Turkish. They continued in English and Faqir soon realised he'd underestimated the problems ahead for him and his family.

After fifteen minutes of showing documents, arguing, suggesting, pleading and finally begging, the official said, 'Mr Al-Douri, there are tens of thousands of refugees living in my country and more arriving illegally every day. Since the ISIL conflagration we don't know how many Iraqis and Syrians have ended up here in Istanbul and are trying, like you, to get to Greece. I'm sorry, but I'm not allowed to issue visas to you or to anyone else in your position. And since the Turkish agreement with the EU was made last March, even if you manage somehow to get to Greece, they'll probably send you back here. On the other hand, if you stay in Turkey, your visas will expire in a month and you'll become illegal immigrants. Then, if you get picked up by the police, you'll end up in a refugee camp and I would not recommend that to anyone.'

Faqir had never felt so helpless and foolish in his life. He had gambled everything his family possessed on getting into Europe – money, home, even their lives, one of which had already been taken – and he had lost his gamble. They were stuck in Turkey, a country of 80 million inhabitants whose language none of them spoke and where almost 10 million were unemployed. Neither he nor his children would ever find a job, and the pitiful amount of money they had left would be gone in a matter of months. They would end up like millions of poor desperate souls, either homeless, begging in the streets, or in some filthy, rat-infested, dangerous hellhole of a camp, regretting every single day that he had risked everything on such an impossible dream.

The official apologised again that he could do nothing to help and went to open the door. Faqir collected up his papers and staggered out of the office, his mind in turmoil, his hopes shattered.

TWENTY-ONE

Istanbul, Republic of Turkey
May 2016

Faqir stumbled out of the assistant consul's office, his shoulders stooped, tears in his eyes and his face pale with despair.

'Are you OK? Why don't you sit here for a moment?' The man in the linen jacket took his arm and led him to a chair.

He sat down, his head in his hands and the woman took a bottle of water from her bag and handed it to him. 'Take a sip, you don't look well at all.'

He swallowed a mouthful, then wiped his eyes. 'Thank you, that's better. I'll be alright, I just need to rest a moment.'

After a moment, the man said, 'I'm Paddy Carr and this is my wife, Nancy. We're from England.'

'How do you do? I'm Faqir Al-Douri, from Mosul.'

'Are you having visa problems? A lot of your people are.'

Five minutes later, Faqir had unburdened his soul to the couple, the story of their disastrous flight from Mosul, the deaths and losses incurred on the journey and the road block that Istanbul had become.

'So, what are you going to do? You can't go back to Iraq, that's certain death, and you can't stay in Turkey after your visas expire.' Nancy put her hand on his arm sympathetically.

At that moment, a woman came into the room. 'Sorry to keep you waiting, Sir Patrick, here are your employees' visas with the renewal stamps. And this is the permit for your boat departure.'

Carr examined the papers then thanked her in fluent Turkish, 'You've been most efficient, we appreciate it very much.'

She shook their hands, 'It was a privilege to meet you both. Travel safely.'

At Faqir's questioning look, he explained, 'Our boat's in the West Istanbul Marina, we've been here for a month and we're planning to leave this week. Just getting our paperwork updated to avoid any problems. Sorry, Faqir, I shouldn't have said that, didn't mean to be thoughtless.'

'What a ridiculous situation.' His wife frowned. 'We're getting all the permits we need for our staff and Faqir and his family can't even get visas to leave the country.'

Carr looked at his watch. 'It's after midday. Why don't you join us for an early lunch and think about this a bit more? Where's your family?'

Half an hour later, they were sitting on the shaded roof terrace of the Café Napoli pizza house, with views of the Bosporus over the city skyline.

Carr ordered soft drinks and Hema said, 'How did you learn to speak Turkish so fluently?'

'I worked for the embassy in Ankara for several years. It's a good way to learn languages.'

'You worked for them, Sir Patrick, or they worked for you?' she responded.

He laughed modestly and Nancy intervened, 'Tell us

about the situation in Mosul. At home we get some TV and newspaper headlines about Iraq, but there's never much about what it's like for the Iraqis living under the ISIL regime. How bad was it?'

'It's worse than the worst thing you can imagine. Like hell must be, I think.' Hamid, the studious son, spoke for the first time. 'Have you ever walked out your front door and found dead bodies and arms and legs lying in the road, or seen somebody get his head cut off with a sword, right in front of you in the marketplace? And the smell ...'

His father cut him off, 'That's enough, Hamid, it's not the thing to talk about at the table.'

'It's alright, serves me right for asking,' she grimaced, 'I'm sorry, Hamid, we have no idea what's really happening there, but it must be dreadful. It's the same in Syria, except the government there seems to be as bad as ISIL. But let's not talk about it now, what are we going to eat?'

'That's right, time for lunch.' Carr patted his wife's hand; she'd always been a better diplomat than him.

The food was delicious and his family ate ravenously, but Faqir had no appetite at all. His mind was consumed by their predicament, formulating and rejecting idea after idea, only to come back to the same problem; they had no papers and without them they were trapped in Turkey.

Sir Patrick ordered coffees and Hamid took his siblings off to do some sightseeing, Hema's warnings ringing in their ears.

'You don't have to worry about them here in Taksim,

they seem like very sensible kids,' Nancy said. 'You're very lucky, after what they've been through, it's a miracle they're so normal.'

'You're right. They've survived a lot of miracles, we all have. What Hamid said is true, every day in Mosul was worse than the one before.' Faqir took his wife's hand. 'And they suffered more than us, their childhood was stolen away from them. Ordinary things that we take for granted, like going to school with their friends, watching TV, having a game of football, it was all banned by those barbarians. They were so unhappy and frightened of what would happen to them and to us, it affected everything in our lives. It was hard to keep them from rebelling and putting us all in more danger.'

Hema nodded in agreement. 'Hamid wants to be a doctor and Malik an engineer, but apart from their religious madness and propaganda, there hasn't been any schooling in Mosul since ISIL came. They both study whenever they can, the girls do as well, mainly on the internet and with us, whatever we can teach them, but they were so frustrated and angry at missing out on a proper education. Since we left, they've been much better, happier and more relaxed, getting along with each other and looking forward to a better life, learning to live like normal citizens again.'

A tear came to her eye, 'We've already lost my mother on the journey and we don't know how the rest of us will survive, but our family is stronger and closer than it was in Mosul.' She wiped her eyes and Nancy patted her arm and gave a wistful smile. 'Do you have children back in England?'

She exchanged glances with Paddy, 'Unfortunately not, there's just the two of us now, making the most of our retirement.'

Hema sensed there was something unsaid behind the glance and her answer so she changed the subject, 'Now we're praying to God for another miracle, to somehow find a way to get to Europe.'

'You're Christians?' Carr said, surprised.

'You're probably wondering how we survived for so long in Mosul.' Faqir explained the story of the 'conversion, death or tax' ultimatum and how he'd used his restaurant to barter their lives and faith.

'Very ingenious.' He nodded approvingly. 'I don't think there are many people who have faced such impossible situations and found a way to surmount them. Well done, Faqir, you should be proud of what you've achieved so far.'

He breathed a deep, sad sigh. 'Thank you, but now we have to face the facts, we've come as far as we can get. Our journey ends here.' Hema squeezed his hand, incapable of saying anything without breaking into tears.

'Hang on, there's usually a solution to every problem, some are more difficult to find than others, that's all. The problem here is actually quite simple, how do we get you to Europe?' He drank the remains of his coffee. 'We know from experience it can't be done officially.'

His words hung in the air and Nancy gave him a knowing look.

Mosul, Iraq

'Where were you last night?'

'I told you, woman. I had a meeting at the university.'

'Well, wouldn't you know I checked and there was no meeting last night. It's a bit funny, because Ekaterina wasn't around either.' She stood in front of him, her hands on her hips, a cynical smile on her face.

Karl had endured one of the worst days of his time in Mosul. Now using the airfield at Qayyarah as a base, the coalition forces, comprising thousands of Peshmerga and Iraqi fighters, supported by US and UK air support, had launched a twin-pronged attack on the surrounding region. By evening, a heavily populated area from the southern perimeter of Qayyarah to the east and north-east, up to Ajhala, had been liberated from ISIL control. Dozens of militants were killed and hundreds of Iraqi civilians held by the jihadists were released. Hundreds more terrorists were caught in the trap, on the wrong side of the Tigris, unable to re-join their bases in Mosul or Qayyarah, or find a way to refuge in Syria. Just as importantly, five of the oil wells still in the jihadists' hands had been overrun. The Military Council were calling for people's heads, and so was his boss, Abdullah.

Now he had another problem; the Irish woman was looking at him contemptuously, waiting for an answer. He hesitated, thinking of the timetable he had worked out in his mind. 'You're right. I was with the Russian girl.'

He flinched as she slapped him across the face. 'To be sure, I knew it from your look. You didn't have the feckin' guts to tell me in person, I had to find out from one of the other women.'

He grabbed her hand angrily. 'It's not your business

who I fuck. You've been with me for a year and it's been good for both of us, but that doesn't mean we'll be together forever, or even for much longer. The chances are we'll both be killed when Mosul falls and I intend to make the most of that time.'

He watched the conflicting emotions on her face as she digested this news. She was an intelligent woman and he knew she'd understand his message.

'It's that bad is it? So, ISIL is going to lose its Iraq caliphate and we're all going to be what those American movies call "collateral damage". Thanks for being honest with me, but that's a feckin' shame, to be sure.'

She went to her bed and he saw she'd already packed her scant belongings. 'I'll be moving out, make way for Ekaterina. Good luck, Karl, it's been really great.' Fighting back the tears, she walked out of the room and along the corridor to where the unattached women slept. There was a bed vacant and she threw her things on it then lay down and wept quietly.

Karl watched her go, forcing himself to say nothing, to behave like an ISIL senior commander, showing no emotion. But he didn't feel that way, not at all.

TWENTY-TWO

'This is Tony Miller, the skipper of the Lady Claire.' Faqir shook hands with the small, wiry man of about fifty, in a white tee-shirt and shorts. His shaved head and body were so sunburned he could have passed as an African without a second glance.

'Hi Faqir, how's it going?' he said, with a noticeable Australian accent.

After lunch the previous day, Sir Patrick and Lady Carr had spent another hour with Faqir and Hema at the café Napoli. They moved to a quiet table at the edge of the terrace, where no one would overhear their conversation, discussing various ideas that had occurred to the diplomat during their meal. Finally, Carr invited Faqir to visit his boat the following morning to meet Tony and examine each option carefully and realistically. The Al-Douri family had spent another night at the Atlantic Motel, and Hema was now escorting their children around the Grand Bazaar and some of Istanbul's other unique treasures.

The Iraqi was looking around him in disbelief at the incredible size and opulence of the forty-metre, two-ton vessel. The ambassador had given him a quick tour of the boat, an unforgettable experience for him, never having been on a ship of any kind in his life. Above them were two more decks, with the cockpit on the top, and below them, the engine room which harboured twin 7,000 HP inboard MTU diesel engines, capable of a top speed of 40 km/hour. The living areas and two double state rooms were on the bottom deck, with three more on the deck above, enough accommodation for all of them, especially on the short trip Carr had in mind.

They sat at a glass-topped table on the back deck of the yacht and the skipper gave a fascinating and humorous account of his life, once again, quite foreign to Faqir's experience, limited as it was to Iraq. His father was an assistant consul with the Australian Foreign Office and had married a Turkish girl when assigned to the embassy in Ankara, where Tony and his sister were born. He was recalled to Canberra when they were infants and Tony spent most of his childhood and youth there, in Perth and in Sydney, following his father's various career moves and then his own love for everything to do with the sea. He travelled the world for a while, working on freighters and cruise ships then returned to Turkey in his twenties and, thanks to his dual nationality and facility for languages, was employed by the Coast Guard Command in Istanbul.

For twenty years he slowly progressed through the ranks until a chance meeting with Sir Patrick Carr at an official function. A month later, Paddy invited him to captain the Lady Claire. His Turkish wife, Esra, became chef and housekeeper and the Miller family was ensconced in the magnificent surroundings of the Carr's mansion on the sea.

Tony knew the waters around the Greek and Turkish coasts like the back of his hand and his exposure to the problems of drug smuggling and clandestine immigration had taught him a lot more besides. He wasn't at all surprised at the topic of discussion and was obviously moved by the plight of the Iraqi family. As he listened to the man, Faqir's previous despondency gradually changed to optimism. He dared to believe they might get out of their seemingly impossible situation; he didn't know how and he didn't know to where, but he started to believe it was possible.

'There's something you need to know, Faqir. You won't be aware of it because you've been travelling, and I only got wind of it when it was confirmed last night.'

He stiffened, immediately concerned by Sir Patrick's tone. 'What is it?'

'The Hungarians have announced they're going to modify their immigration policy legislation with Serbia. They're being inundated by refugees and it's causing serious disagreements over the EU's stated policy. Viktor Orban's government is closing the door to refugees and migrants requesting asylum. I don't know when it's going to be introduced, but I'm sure they'll start taking action immediately. There are over a thousand refugees waiting on the Serbian side and already they're allowing only fifteen through each day. Anyone apprehended in Hungary within 8 km of the Serbian border will be sent back there for processing.'

The Iraqi's heart sank. 'The woman at the Bulgarian embassy said something about that. So, even if we could get into Serbia there's no way from there into Western Europe?'

'That's what we're going to look at now. Serbia hasn't

yet responded to this news and it'll take a little while before they take any action of their own, so we need to act quickly. I've been thinking about a few different scenarios, but Tony's the man to put meat on the bones. Ideas are only as good as the plan of execution and that's where he's the expert.'

The Australian laid out a large-scale navigation map and several charts of the waters and mainland to the west of Istanbul; the Sea of Marmara linked to the Dardanelles, the narrow Straights that led into the Aegean and the southern coast of Greece. Sir Patrick showed them what he had in mind – a clever, but potentially dangerous route to save the Al-Douri family from destitution in Turkey. Then Tony looked at the individual maps of the bordering countries and the various routes to Europe, all now to be officially closed, since the EU-Turkey agreement and Hungary's new stance. Faqir held his breath as the Australian looked closely at the danger points, assessing if and how they could carry off the ambassador's audacious plan.

After examining the charts and maps for what seemed an eternity, he announced, 'For the first part, we need a local man, a country guy from around the border.'

'And for the rest?'

'I'll need to make some calls, but I think I can resurrect a few contacts.'

'So, you think we can do it. Right,' Carr stood up, 'I'll make some calls of my own. Give us a few days, between us we should manage to get it sorted, it can't be that difficult.'

Milan, Italy

The prepaid phone rang while Ibrahim was praying. There were only two people who knew his latest number and it couldn't be Imam Mohammad, since he was on the same time zone and he'd be praying too.

'Hello Karl,' he answered in Arabic. 'What news?' He was feeling bright and cheerful, fully recovered from the desperation and fear that had plagued him in Germany. After three days in Milan he was sold on Italy; the people, food, sunshine and the light-hearted ambience that pervaded the streets, the shops, trams and buses; everywhere he went, he just loved the place. The phrase book had been useful too. His English was improving more than his Italian, but he was trying to learn the soft, lilting romantic language of the country. He could utter a few phrases and was enjoying the new experience.

The man's voice was sharp and impersonal. 'Where are you?'

Ibrahim immediately felt guilty. *I am not here to have a good time*, he reminded himself. 'In a small aparthotel in Milan, unseen.' He waited nervously for his reaction.

'Is your computer functioning?'

'Yes.'

'Good. Check it every day for a message from "Christian".'

Ibrahim was shocked by the code name, but he knew that ISIL broke the rules when they needed to. That was why they would be triumphant in their fight for supremacy.

'Do you have materials to write?'

He grabbed some paper and a pencil. 'I'm ready.'

'You must make your way to Palermo in Sicily by May 28th. It's an island in the Mediterranean, in the very south of Italy.'

'That's in three days, I'll have to leave right away.'

Karl ignored the interruption. 'There is a hostel there called *Accogliente Ostello*. He spelled out the name. It's not expensive. They will have a room for Ali el Zafar with two beds. That's the name you must use from now on.'

'Excuse me sir. Why do I need two beds?'

'Because we have decided you will have a partner in your next mission. Two of you can work better and more quickly than one alone.'

Ibrahim was thunderstruck. He blurted out, 'But I don't need a partner. I told this to my previous Emir and he let me work alone.'

'And you failed in your attempt. We are sending someone who has fought in the real fight for supremacy, on the battleground. A true believer and fierce fighter. Speak no more about it, it is decided. You must be at the hostel by Saturday and your partner will arrive with all necessary instructions for your mission. Understood?'

Ibrahim was silent for a long moment. Deep inside he knew the Emir was right. His 'partner' in Cologne had been his young brother, who had unknowingly helped him to acquire the materials he needed. But it had gone terribly wrong because he hadn't revealed his plan. If he was to right that dreadful wrong and succeed this time maybe he did need a partner. In any event, he didn't have a choice in the matter.

Finally, he answered, 'Understood.'

'Good. You will travel by local trains as before to a place called Reggio Calabria in the south of Italy. There is a ferry boat to Messina and you can get from there to Palermo by train or bus. It should take you two days at the most.'

Ibrahim scribbled the details down. 'Is my mission to be accomplished there?'

'No. You will travel together to the final destination.'

'How will I know when my partner will arrive?'

'You will receive the information just before their arrival.'

'Can you tell me more about him?'

'You will have time to find out about each other when you meet. Do you have money?'

'Yes, enough for six months.'

'Good. I have no more time now. Is everything clear?'

'Everything is clear.'

'Read my instructions many times to memorise them, then burn the paper and travel only with your memory. Throw away the SIM.'

The line went dead.

TWENTY-THREE

Mosul, Iraq
May 2016

The man called Karl put his phone down and went to look out the aperture in the wall where there had once been a window. He was on the ground floor of a hospital in a central sector of Mosul. It was the only remaining complete floor; the three top levels had already been destroyed and his theory was that the building looked so devastated that they'd leave it alone. The coalition airstrikes were increasing in intensity since he'd returned to Mosul and he moved his command post regularly. In the street, a team of men were clearing the rubble left of the apartment building opposite with shovels and a small tractor. It had taken a direct hit during the night from a US Stratofortress B-52 long-range bomber. The whole street had changed appearance each time he came, just in the few days he'd been using this base – transformed by the bombs and shells that fell incessantly on the city.

Another group, including a doctor or nurse, were carrying bodies out of the tangled mess of broken masonry and steel. Further along the road, a huddle of people, men, women, children and an old woman in a wheel chair with a child in her arms, were moving slowly along, building by building. The men walked ahead of the group, stepping cautiously out to test the safety level, then gesturing to the others to follow them to the next staging post. A sniper, shooting from a rooftop along the street hit one of the men, who fell to the ground with a cry.

Karl turned away. He had watched this same scene so many times he'd lost interest in the outcome. There was nothing he could do; he had to reconcile himself to his basic tenet, it was war and in wars people got shot. The sniper might be an Iraqi infiltrator, a jihadist, or just a criminal who enjoyed killing innocent civilians. He didn't know and after his recent meeting with the council he no longer cared. The ISIL leaders and fighters despised the civilians as much as the enemy and wanted them to stay and suffer, not try to escape. Either the group would make it out of the firing zone or not; it didn't depend on him and he had more important matters to attend to.

There were still over a million people in Mosul, moving from place to place, desperately looking for safety, just as he did. Just like the group he'd been watching. Even though the infidels knew the position of every hospital, school and residential area, the bombs hit them just the same. But the north and east sides of the city were even more dangerous, and the Iraqi and Kurdish Peshmerga forces were moving closer to the south of the city. Tomorrow he would move again; he would decide where in the morning.

As he turned from the window, his aquiline features and the livid scar on his cheek showed clearly in the morning light. He said in Arabic, 'This man, Ibrahim; Ali, as you must call him. We know his father and uncle were brave fighters, and we respect him for wanting to follow in their footsteps. But he failed. As his partner, you must ensure he doesn't fail again. You understand?'

'I understand. I will make sure the mission is successful. *Inshallah*.'

'We're probably going to lose Mosul, and other places in Iraq and Syria. It's not important, we'll take other territories, ISIL will continue to spread.' He forced himself to sound convinced and committed, to hide the sense of despair and revulsion that was engulfing him. 'We have to show the non-believers we can take the fight to them. That they can't sit in front of their TVs, eating their Big Macs and drinking Cokes, ignoring what's happening in the world, our world. We must show them they are at risk, wherever they are, whatever they're doing, because we can reach them and hurt them in their own country, in their own home.'

'That's what I want to do and I promise I will do it.'

'Good. Many others like you are going back to their countries with the same instructions. Remember, many small ripples can cause a tidal wave. You can be one of those ripples.'

'I won't let you down.'

'The arrangements have been made for your travel; you should leave tomorrow. Did you get the passport?'

'This morning.'

'And your driver's licence and money?'

'I have it and 1,000 euros they gave me.'

He reached in his tunic and pulled out 1,000 euros in crumpled bills, the cash Aziz had tried to buy his life with. 'Take this, I don't need it.'

'*Shukraan*, thanks, that will help.'

'Read your instructions many times and destroy the paper before you leave. You'll be contacted when everything is ready. *Alhamd lillah rabb alealamin.* Praise be to Allah, Lord of the Worlds.'

'*Alhamd lillah rabb alealamin.*'

The door closed and he sat at his desk and picked up his phone again. 'Come up here now. I want to check on a travel schedule.'

Karl was not the man's real name; he had been born Ali Azim Khan, in Bagram, Afghanistan in 1978, the year before Mohammad Reza Shah Pahlavi was deposed and replaced by the Ayatollah Ruhollah Khomeini, the spiritual leader of the Islamic revolution. Radicalised and indoctrinated by his father, a devout follower of Khomeini's teachings, he was brought up to despise everything that Western culture represented. In September 1996, when the Taliban marched into Kabul, he joined the new regime and took up his adopted name of Abu Karl Ali Azim Afhgani, or just Karl, as he preferred to be called. After the September 2001 attack on the twin towers in New York and the fall of the Taliban government, he transferred his allegiance to al-Qaeda in Afghanistan.

In 2003, after the fall of Saddam Hussein, Jordanian militant Abu Musab al-Zarqawi created al-Qaeda in Iraq to fight against the coalition occupation and in 2004, when al-Zarqawi pledged allegiance to Osama bin Laden, Karl went to Iraq to enlist with them. He stayed with them until bin Laden's death in May 2011, when he joined ISIL as a regional commander in Iraq. ISIL's victories in Syria and Iraq soon validated his decision; thousands of fighters came to enlist with them from almost every country in the world. He knew that three of the caliphate's most crucial ministries, Security, Military and Finance, were run by ex-Saddam regime officers and this had made him feel safe.

Karl was not only a follower of Khomeini's doctrine but also a devout believer of ISIL's dogmas as set out in their propaganda magazine, *Dabiq*. He hated the infidel disbelievers because of their rejection of the 'oneness' of Allah, their crimes against Islam and Muslims, their invasions of Muslim territories and because they encouraged secular, liberal societies which permitted activities prohibited by Allah – atheism, music, women's liberty and sexuality, and same-sex relationships. The list of Western offences against Allah is very long.

After the taking of Mosul in 2014, Karl received a personal accolade and a freshly minted medal at a ceremony in the Great Mosque from Abu Bakr al-Baghdadi, the self-appointed Caliph of the new Islamic State of Iraq and the Levant, spanning Iraq and Syria. Al-Baghdadi had offered him a promotion as attaché to the Military Council, but Karl refused it and other offers that followed. He preferred trying to survive while planning, training and fighting on the ground with his men rather than in a political environment, detached from the reality of the battlefield.

Two triumphs in a lifetime of defeats, he reflected, *and one more defeat to come, when we lose Mosul as soon as the Iraqis and allies get their act together. How blind and stupid we have become, to destroy everything we have fought for.*

Karl turned his mind to the present situation. He

was fully informed of the preparations for the final coordinated assault on the city. Information came from a number of sources; spies in the Iraqi army, ISIL's own secret service, enemy officers and spies who were captured and tortured for information before being executed in ever more barbaric and grotesque public rituals. But the easiest and most reliable source was to watch CNN on TV or his mobile phone, if he could find somewhere where there was a decent signal.

The latest news was that US Secretary of Defence, Ash Carter, had put together a game plan to retake Mosul. Sixty countries with tens of thousands of soldiers were expected to take part in a joint offensive. ISIL had less than ten thousand trained fighters and the same number of local supporters and teenagers who would mostly be sacrificed in the first offensives. They could not fail to be defeated; the pathetically small ISIL force would be hammered into submission like a metal rod on an anvil. It would be the end, not just of the occupation of Mosul, but probably of his life and the other ISIL fighters still trapped in the city.

And trapped they would remain. No one was allowed to leave. Would-be deserters were not given a second chance. To discourage others from attempting to flee the upcoming battle, they were no longer executed by beheading but carbonised by flame throwers, blown apart by bombs, cut into pieces by chainsaws, or torn limb from limb on ropes between trucks. Whatever mad, perverse, sadistic form of punishment came to the minds of the leaders, it became the flavour of the day and no one, including Karl, was exempt from it. It was possible that the ISIL movement could survive the upcoming battle, but Karl knew for certain he could not.

He picked up his phone and chose one the few pictures he had stored. It was of a pretty, young, fair-haired woman with deep brown eyes. He looked at it for a while, then put the phone away in his pocket.

Milan, Italy

After speaking with Karl, Ibrahim started worrying. *What kind of a man will they send to be my partner. He'd better not be like that imbecile Ahmad, in Cologne. At least I tried and almost succeeded, he's been trying for two years without achieving anything at all.*

He laid out the map of Europe on his bed and looked at the journey from Milan to Florence, Rome, Reggio Calabria, then Palermo; it was a long trip. Then he went online and found there was a direct *Frecciarossa* train leaving from Milan Centrale every night at eight o'clock, arriving in Palermo Centrale at four the next afternoon. The ticket was 90 euros. He decided he'd take the train the following night, the 26th, to be sure he was there on time.

He knelt on his prayer mat again and chanted, *Subhanah Alllah, Alhamd lilla*, thanking Allah for this opportunity to make amends for his failure and the chance to finally prove himself as a magnificent martyr. He spent the afternoon wandering around Milan, enjoying the freedom and the bustle of the Italian city, storing up positive energy to prepare him for his journey to Palermo.

TWENTY-FOUR

Istanbul, Republic of Turkey
May 2016

'You were right, Mama. He was the British Ambassador in Ankara for eight years, then he was in Athens and Teheran. That's how he knows these places and languages so well.' Hamid was looking up Sir Patrick Carr's many online entries on their mobile. 'The Queen made him a knight when he retired in 2006. Look, there's a picture of him and Lady Nancy at Buckingham Palace after the ceremony.' He handed the phone to his mother. 'We'll be able to visit the palace when we're in England, it's open to the public, you know.'

'What beautiful clothes they're wearing. It was ten years ago, and Nancy is still as lovely now as she is in this picture. Look Faqir.'

He took the phone. 'I can't understand why such important people are interested in what happens to a bunch of refugees from Iraq. We're penniless nobodies, but they treat us as if we were part of their own family.' He scrolled down the long biography of their newly found friend, 'It's as if ...' he stopped suddenly, staring in disbelief at the mobile phone.

'What is it?'

'Listen to this. It says here that in March 2011, their son John and daughter Patricia, together with their families, were caught in an avalanche in the Italian Alps.

All eight of them, the parents and four children were killed.'

'What?' Hema's face went white, as she and the children crowded around Faqir to try to read the screen.

He continued reading, 'They were skiing on a mountain called Monte Nevoso and there was a huge avalanche. Rescue teams were sent in helicopters and saved two people, but Sir Patrick's family were buried so deeply, by the time they got them out it was too late. The children were the same age as our girls, just starting their lives.' His voice choked, thinking of the risks his own family were taking.

'My God, their children and grandchildren taken from them like that, it's just too cruel.' Hema pulled her children around her, holding them as close as she could, instilling her love into their minds.

They were all quiet for a moment, then Aisha, their eldest daughter, said what they were all thinking, 'Maybe that's why they're interested in what happens to us. They don't have their own family to look after, so they're helping us.'

'We must never speak of this with them,' Hema admonished them. 'It must be hard enough to bear without being reminded of it after all this time.'

When they went to bed, Hema took her husband's hand. 'Kneel down with me and pray.'

'What shall we pray for?'

'That whatever happens to us, our children will grow up to live long and happy lives.'

'*Inshallah*.'

Baaj, west of Mosul, Iraq

The man limped painfully towards Karl, leaning heavily on two crutches. His bodyguards hovered nearby, but he disdained their offer of help. He was a proud man and couldn't admit any frailty, especially in front of a legendary senior commander. The air attack of March 18th in which he had been targeted had almost succeeded in destroying him, but he had somehow survived to tell the tale. Though he was not yet strong enough to fulfil his duties as Caliph of the Islamic State of Iraq and the Levant. It was only a few weeks since Abu Bakr al-Baghdadi had undergone the last bout of spinal surgery and the doctors had not expected him to walk again. His wounds were so serious that the ISIL cabinet had held a meeting to discuss who would replace him if he died. Abu-Ala al-Afri, the caliph's deputy and a former Iraqi physics teacher, was installed as the stand-in leader, but Baghdadi had no intention of letting him become a permanent fixture. He was determined to recover fully.

Like everyone else, Karl had recently heard rumours that his leader had been killed in another U.S. airstrike in Raqqa on June 12th, but the encrypted call he'd received yesterday had dispelled his doubts. He'd been invited to drive one hundred and fifty kilometres to Baaj, near the Syrian border, to pay his respects to the man who had presented him with his most cherished possession, the medal he'd been awarded for his involvement in the capture of Mosul in June 2014. He was happy to get out of the city and rode his motorcycle along the A47 to Sinjar and then 35 km across ISIL controlled territory on a narrow dusty road until he found the property on the outskirts of the small village.

As the once imposing figure approached him, Karl had difficulty in hiding his shock and sorrow. The caliph looked much smaller and was now thin and drawn; he had lost most of his hair and was wearing thick spectacles, looking more like a schoolteacher than the leader of the ISIL jihadists. After solemn greetings and mutual congratulations, they went to sit on a terrace at the side of the house, where they were served tea. Baghdadi had been leader of ISIL since the death of his predecessor, Abu Omar al-Baghdadi, in May 2010 and was almost single-handedly responsible for the growth of the caliphate in followers and in territorial control since that time. *He must be sickened to see how quickly the empire he built is being lost*, Karl thought sadly. *ISIL's leader is a reflection of the state of his caliphate.*

'I heard you turned down another promotion, in Mosul. It's a pity, the man who was chosen isn't of your calibre, he has never achieved anything in his life.'

He demurred, 'I'm still handling a lot of important tasks to prepare the city for the coalition attack.'

They discussed the current situation in Iraq, then the caliph said, 'Do you think it's worth trying to hold Mosul?'

Karl was thunderstruck. *The man is sicker than I thought. Mosul was our greatest triumph and he's talking about abandoning it? Or maybe this is a trap?* He replied, 'Like every decision we have taken since you became caliph, it's a calculation of possibilities and probabilities. If we believe we can prevail against the coalition forces, then we must continue to prepare as we are doing now. If not, then we should save our resources and channel them in another direction, one where we are sure to succeed and boast of a victory, not a defeat.' He waited, hoping his reply wouldn't be interpreted as weakness or treason.

Baghdadi laughed. 'Karl, you are one of the cleverest men I know. Only you could answer that question without actually giving an opinion. Tell me, how many fighters do you estimate we have there? I've asked the council many times, but I never get a straight answer.'

'The problem is not how many men we have, but how many of them are dedicated fighters, prepared to die for the caliphate. When we took the city, we had only about two thousand, but they were worth fifty thousand. Now we have maybe ten to fifteen, but I don't think there are more than ten thousand who can really fight.'

'And the coalition will bring at least one hundred thousand.' Karl said nothing and the caliph continued, 'That's the real answer. It's not a question of holding or losing Mosul, because it's just a matter of time.'

'So your question is really, is it worth sacrificing ten thousand good fighters, men who can be used elsewhere to achieve something worthwhile?'

'And that's your answer. I knew it would be and you'll be surprised to hear I agree with you, but there's nothing you or I can do about it now. I'm still caliph, but in name only. The council leaders may abandon Mosul themselves, but they won't sanction the withdrawal or surrender of thousands of fighters. Even though there are places where those men would make a difference, where we could build a new stronghold and create the caliphate we have dreamed of.' He was quiet for several moments, moving uncomfortably in the chair and holding his wounded legs, a pained expression on his face.

Karl said, 'There are other ways we can hurt the infidels, by attacking them in their own countries. I have sent someone on such a mission, one which will make a great noise and will be noticed and taken as a deadly warning by the infidels, wherever they are. This could be just one of many attacks we could mount. ISIL is not confined to Mosul, or even Iraq and Syria. ISIL must be seen as a global threat that can destabilise governments and populations around the world.'

'I was informed of your initiative, although Abdullah took the credit for it. Is it someone we can trust, someone who will die willingly for our cause?'

'I believe so, in fact I'm sure of it. And If they are successful, we may yet have a noteworthy victory, something which will make the Western powers sit up and realise our threat to them is not limited by geographical presence. Others will follow and ISIL will be like the four winds, blowing from every direction and carrying the same message everywhere. Change your ways, or we will change them for you.'

'If the council leaders leave Mosul, promise me you will go with them and accept a proper post, where you can do something useful, instead of cleaning up after that arsehole, Abdullah. Something where your pragmatism can help them take sensible decisions that can help us to rebuild our caliphate, instead of destroying it.'

Karl saw the man was now exhausted. He stood up

and bowed, 'I'll leave you to rest, Caliph. Thank you for your encouraging words and I promise I will consider them and take the appropriate action. *Alhamd lillah rabb alealamin.* Praise be to Allah, Lord of the Worlds.'

On his ride back to Mosul, Karl's mind was in turmoil. *I can't believe he wants to give up Mosul or change the way ISIL works. Is he setting me up for a fall, or is he just suffering from his injuries and can't think straight?*

Whatever the reasons, he knew he would just have to bide his time to see what actually happened. Baghdadi was no longer in charge and his immediate superior was, as he had described, an arsehole. He put the matter out of his mind and rode back to the grim reality of ISIL's greatest mistake.

Palermo, Sicily

Ibrahim had managed to get several hours of sleep on the night train and reached Palermo Centrale on Friday afternoon, the last leg being the trip across the Messina Strait. On both the train and the ferry boat, he'd travelled without showing any documentation at all, apart from his ticket. Ibrahim had not been on a ferry boat before and stared in disbelief when the train drove onboard on rails that went into the bowels of the vessel. He went out on deck and mingled with the other passengers, chatting with them in English interspersed with a few words from his slowly improving Italian. They told him that a bridge had been planned over the 3 km stretch of water for the last sixty years, but it was still a project. The latest cost estimate was 9 million euros, so it didn't sound as if it would get built any time soon.

From his map, he knew the *Accogliente Ostello* was in the Via Albergheria, in the university area, near the Ballaró Street Market and only half a kilometre from the station. The hostel was a converted old mansion, shabby but clean, mostly used by students. Google Translate told him the name meant 'Friendly Hostel' and he quickly found that was true. The check-in clerk was Tunisian and not interested in his identity papers. He greeted him like an old friend and Ibrahim realised he knew who he was and no questions would be asked. The twin-bedded room was on the first floor and cost 35 euros a night. He filled out a registration card as Ali el Zafar and took his things up to a decent sized room, furnished with a battered wardrobe, a chest of drawers and twin beds covered with multi-coloured quilts. The bathroom was adequate, with a bath and shower, and there was a tiny balcony from which he could see a park through the buildings opposite. He put his clothes away in the drawers then plugged in his laptop to test the hotel Wi-Fi. It worked well, but there was no message from Christian. He would check every day, as instructed.

TWENTY-FIVE

Gelibolu, Gallipoli Peninsular, Republic of Turkey
May 2016

'We have to walk back for about two kilometres, past a Hilton, then another hotel and we follow the main road for one kilometre. We should see a sign for a historic fountain then after another kilometre we come to an empty site in front of the beach. That's where Tony will pick us up.' Faqir handed the map to Hema.

He and his family had just descended from the bus in Gallipoli, or Gelibolu, its Turkish name. The 150 km journey from Istanbul had taken almost five hours and it was now 6:00 pm. Sunset was at about 20:30 and their appointment with the skipper of the Lady Claire was at nine, so they had three hours to eat and find their destination. Tony had texted the details for the bus journey and pick-up point that morning, in time for them to take the metro out to Otogar, where the Esenier bus terminal was located.

Hema studied the map. 'It looks a bit complicated, I think we should walk there while it's still light, make sure we can find it when it gets dark. But we can't trail through the town with all these bags.'

She looked around to get her bearings. They were standing by a busy road with the sea behind them and a residential area on the other side, densely constructed with houses and apartment buildings. 'The ferry boat landing must be a couple of hundred metres along here,' she pointed up the road to the east. 'It's close to the town centre. We'll find a café there and the children can stay with the bags while we look for the beach, then we'll come back for something to eat.'

Near the landing they found a restaurant with a sunny terrace and left Hamid in charge of the family and baggage, with enough lira to buy some soft drinks. It was a typical little seaside town, full of narrow, busy streets and bustling crowds and they followed the skipper's texted instructions, strolling across the town like tourists, easily finding the site, a hundred-metre wide strip of empty land. The white sandy beach in front stretched as far as they could see to the left and on the right was a small rocky outcrop which exactly matched the map. There were still a few sun worshippers lying on the beach, but they expected it would be deserted in the cool of the evening. Satisfied, they went back to the café where the children were enjoying the afternoon sunshine. It was a good spot to spend a couple of hours while waiting for the arrival of the Lady Claire.

Sir Patrick had called Faqir after Tony's text message to explain the reason for the travel schedule. 'Before we leave the marina, the customs and immigration officers always come aboard to inspect. With the drug and people smuggling problems today, they examine every vessel, even those with diplomatic papers, like ours. I don't want you to be on the boat then – they'd check your documents and you could be in serious trouble, they know we're going to Greece and your visas don't allow it. Also, it would be an abuse of my diplomatic immunity and I can't afford to do such a thing. We're going to pick you up on the way to the Dardanelles, then leave you at the appropriate point in the Aegean and continue our voyage down to Mykonos. When the Greeks check the boat there, you'll be gone and I won't know where you are. That way, I don't feel I've abused my position, I'm just giving a needy family a lift for a hundred and fifty kilometres or so. Where you came from or go afterwards is no longer my business, you see what I mean?'

Faqir did see, quite clearly. Paddy Carr hadn't become a successful diplomat without learning how to be flexible and imaginative in finding compromises which suited all parties concerned.

Before he rang off, Sir Patrick said, 'I don't want to appear inquisitive, but are you OK for cash? Tony tells me you'll need twenty to thirty thousand euros for travel expenses, will that be a problem?'

Between Faqir and his family, their fortune was now just over 36,000 euros. *That could leave us with only six thousand for living costs*, he calculated, *but we spend very little and should be in Europe by then. We must be able to make it.* He didn't want to beg from the diplomat; his pride would suffer even more than it already had, but he also suspected he would be refused. If Carr could rationalise his responsibility for their escape as he had, he wouldn't want to sully that argument by helping him financially.

In any event, he realised, as far as their money was concerned, he had no other choice, it was this opportunity or nothing. For some reason, perhaps because of the loss of their own family, Paddy and Nancy were taking a huge risk to help them escape from their plight. If they couldn't get out of Turkey with the help of a British knight and a two-ton luxury yacht, they might as well resign themselves to life, or death, in a refugee camp.

'We can handle that, Sir Patrick,' he answered. 'You're already doing more than we could have dreamed of.'

He thanked the Englishman again, then went shopping with Hema to find everything required for their journey, starting with the items suggested by Tony Miller. He'd advised them to buy thick, warm clothing, plastic rain capes and waterproof hiking boots.

'Don't underestimate this journey,' he'd told him. 'You're going to cross the Balkan mountain range. It's very challenging terrain, it'll be cold and you're sure to get rain at some point. Be prepared for everything and you should make it, but it'll be tougher than anything you've ever done. You should also get another mobile for the kids, in case you get separated. I'll copy everything to both phones, just to be sure.'

After spending most of the day preparing and almost 1,000 euros, Faqir was sure they were ready for the next stage of their flight. But he had no idea what lay ahead of them.

After a polite and respectful inspection by the Turkish officials, the Lady Claire set off from West Istanbul Marina at 3:30 pm, the skipper calculating an average cruising speed of 20 km per hour for the 110 km voyage. At 20:45, Faqir and his family were already waiting with their baggage on the now deserted beach; the sky was cloudy and it was pitch black with a chilly breeze from the sea. No one spoke, each of them praying that nothing had gone wrong and they would be delivered from that place without any further heartbreak. Faqir and Hema were still trying to get to grips with the good fortune that had smiled on them when Sir Patrick and Lady Nancy Carr had entered their lives.

Can it be possible? Hema asked herself. *A tragedy that happened five years ago will cause a miracle to occur today?*

Then, just before nine o'clock, sharp-eyed Malik shouted, 'There, over there. I see the spotlight, look.'

They saw a blinking light and could just make out the shape of a large boat about 200 m from the shore. Faqir flashed the torch he'd brought and a few minutes later a Zodiac dinghy came up in the surf in front of them.

'Come on, you'll have to get your feet wet, I can't come any closer.' Tony Miller helped them into the dinghy, insisting they put on lifebelts. A moment later he opened up the throttle and they headed out towards the Lady Claire.

Hema held her daughters close to her, away from the wind and spray. *I'm not dreaming,* she told herself, *miracles really do happen.*

Palermo, Sicily

Ibrahim had spent Friday and Saturday walking around Palermo, eating in bistros and pizzerias, losing his way in narrow side streets and getting the feel of the town. His memories of Iraq were now foggy and distorted by the American-led war which started two months before his family fled in June 2003. To his surprise, Palermo brought those memories back. The city was a complex hotchpotch of styles and people, a mad mix of European culture and ancient mid-east history. Byzantine mosaics jostled with Arabesque domes and frescoed cupolas. Gothic palaces and baroque churches stood adjacent to souk-like markets, and modern fashionable restaurants and bars were hidden away in the noisy, traffic-polluted streets. He walked past cloisters filled with lemon trees, tiny flower-filled chapels and magnificent old palazzos reached by ancient staircases, to finally arrive at *Teatro Massimo*, Italy's biggest opera house. Ibrahim had liked Milan, but he fell in love with Palermo.

The email message from Christian arrived on Saturday evening from an address in Sri Lanka. '*Your partner Sami will arrive tomorrow, Sunday 29th May, on the Grimaldi Lines ferry boat from Tunis. Carry a bag from H&M and look out for a red jacket. Christian*'. He looked up the ferry company timetable online then went to buy a pair of jeans and some socks from the nearby H&M store. This was not the moment to screw things up.

Dardanelles Strait, Republic of Turkey

'The Strait is about 70 km long from the Sea of Marmora to the Aegean and it's never more than 2 km wide, sometimes less than half that, so it can be a real bottleneck.' It was 10:30 pm and the Lady Claire was navigating the Dardanelles Strait, just off the small town of Burhanli, on the south side of the Gallipoli Peninsular, about 20 km from Gelibolu, their starting point. The Al-Douri family were drinking tea with the Carrs in the comfortable salon and he was showing their route on the navigation map.

'So we might get stuck, like in traffic?'

'It's unlikely, Malik. You probably noticed when we entered the Strait our speed just about halved. We're not allowed to go faster here than ten nautical miles, that's eighteen kilometres an hour and this boat is only forty metres long and we can manoeuvre well, so we should have no problems. But some of the really large vessels, like container ships and tankers, get stuck for hours because they can't pass and at some very narrow points they can hardly turn.'

'I've seen them on TV, the big cruise ships and oil tankers. They must be ten times as big as this one. But I bet they're not half as nice,' he added with an embarrassed smile. 'How far are we going after we leave the Strait?'

'We'll turn north when we get past Sedd el Bahr, that's right at the tip of the peninsular, forty kilometres south-west of here.' He pointed on the map. 'After another fifty we'll be into Greek waters, then fifty more to where you leave us.'

Faqir was calculating, 'So, it's about two and a half hours to Sedd el Bahr and another three to our destination. We should get there around 04:00 in the morning?'

'That's the plan. The sun comes up at 06:30, so you'll have two and a half hours of darkness to go wherever it is you're going.'

Faqir exchanged glances with Hema; they understood that Sir Patrick's vagueness was part of his diplomatic camouflage. Tony Miller had given him several carefully marked maps and sent a lot of information – phone numbers, names, addresses and other details – to his mobile phone. He'd explained in great detail the arrangements for leaving the yacht and what would happen next, but Carr had never mentioned it at all. He was a clever man; if ever he or Nancy were asked, they could deny all knowledge of the family's whereabouts or their destination.

'I think we need to get some sleep, Sir Patrick, if that's possible. Tomorrow is going to be a busy day.'

They said goodnight to Nancy, and Carr took them to the deck above, with its three double state rooms. Within a few minutes, they were all sound asleep. For once, Faqir was not kept awake by worries about refugee camps or money.

TWENTY-SIX

Nestos National Park, East Macedonia/Thrace, Greece
May 2016

The man's name was Tapani and he was over six feet tall with massive shoulders and arms. In the flashlight he looked like a giant, fierce and frightening, wearing a grubby vest and shorts which showed his muscular limbs. The girls stayed close to their mother as Faqir was introduced to him by Tony, who spoke Greek surprisingly well. He had warned them that Tapani didn't speak English, so they would have to communicate by signs and gestures. This was another ruse of Paddy Carr's, to avoid any information being accidently acquired about his own involvement and about the Al-Douri family's destination.

The group were standing on the shore of 45 km2 Lake Vistonida, the largest of the forty-two lakes in the Nestos Delta National Park, an 1,100 km2 expanse of lagoons and marshes on the southern coast of Greece. While the Lady Claire cruised slowly in a circle near the island of Thasos behind them, Tony had come as far into the Delta as possible, bringing the Zodiac on a zigzag route to a point where the EO2, a major road crossing from one side of the Delta to the other, was constructed on a slender strip of land that separated the Aegean waters from the lake. The nearest town, Porto Lagos, was 3 km across the water to the west and at 04:15 in the morning not a soul was stirring.

Their farewell on leaving the Lady Claire had been tearful, the whole family embracing Sir Patrick and Lady Carr. Hema was too emotional to speak; she held them both in her arms for a long moment, this English couple who had lost their own family but had saved them from an almost certain life-sentence of detention and deprivation. Finally, she managed to say, 'If we get to England, God willing, you'll be the first people we'll find, to thank you once again for saving us.'

They piled their bags into Tapani's battered four-metre fishing boat. It was an antique craft, made from aluminium but light and flat-bottomed, suitable for a shallow, rocky river bed and large enough to squeeze them all in. At Tony's whispered suggestion, Faqir handed Tapani 1,000 euros, gesturing that he would receive the rest at the end of the trip.

He shook hands with the Australian and Hema hugged him. 'God bless you and thanks for everything. Please tell Sir Patrick and Nancy once again how much we appreciate what they've done for us. We'll never forget it.'

'Some final words of advice,' he said, 'keep the maps safe, whatever happens on the way, it's vital to know where you are and where you're going, it's a long and difficult journey. And take this to help you if you're ever completely lost.' He opened a small box with a compass inside, explaining the simple system of directional navigation.

'I know the whole family speaks good English. Don't use any other language, even when you're alone, always speak English like a family on holiday, not like refugees.

And get rid of those suitcases and any Arab clothes before you leave. Dress and talk like European tourists, and you'll stand a chance of getting through unnoticed. Never leave your phones unattended and keep them charged up, everything you need is stored in there. If ever you have to get in touch with me, use Hamid's mobile – I've sent a copy of everything to it. Just text one word, the name of the place you're in, nothing else.'

'Good luck and call me when you get to the UK.' Before Faqir could thank him, Tony squeezed his shoulder and ran back across the EO2 then they heard the powerful roar of the Zodiac heading to the Aegean, back to the Lady Claire and civilisation. As if in a dream, they climbed into Tapani's boat and set off to the north across Lake Vistonida.

The 20hp Tohatsu four stroke outboard cruised at a comfortable 20 km/h and in less than thirty minutes they reached the small village of Viotopos Kompsatou on the east side of the lake, where Tapani turned into a narrow inlet, running in a north-easterly direction.

Tapani smiled and nodded his head when he heard Hamid tell his father, 'This river is called the Kompsatos Potamos and we're going north.' He and Malik were now following their progress on Tony's map and compass, with the aid of the torch.

They came across no traffic and were able to maintain a constant speed for about 18 km, then the river bed became rocky and the water shallow, forcing Tapani to navigate slowly by the light of a torch for the last kilometre. Finally, they arrived at a small lake alongside a rocky beach.

'We're at Poliantho,' announced Hamid, as they climbed out and pulled the boat up onto the riverside.

It was now 6:00 am and the first rays of sun were starting to lighten the sky. Their guide signalled to hurry and they grabbed their bags and followed him across the rocks and down a narrow track to an old farmhouse with a garden in front, full of wild flowers and vegetables. He opened the door and Faqir led his family into the first Greek home they'd seen. They walked into a large living room/kitchen furnished with handmade furniture, including a long table and six chairs. The table was set with eight dishes and spoons and a basket of bread. At the end of the room was a metal grill behind which, they discovered later, was a goat pen, fortunately empty, the animals preferring to be outside in the summer months.

By the stove stood a handsome, chubby woman in her twenties, holding a naked baby in one arm, while stirring a large pot with the other. She put down the spoon, gave them a broad smile and pointing at her chest, said, 'Hello, me Kassia,' then at her sleeping baby, 'Makari.'

'You speak English, that's wonderful,' Hema stroked the baby's face. 'How old is he?'

The woman continued smiling and stirring and said nothing more.

'I think that's the only word she knows,' whispered her oldest daughter, Aisha. She put her arms out, offering to hold the baby, and the mother handed him over, still smiling.

The infant must have been about three months old

and smelled of carbolic soap. Aisha put a nappy on him while the woman continued cooking.

Tapani carried their luggage into two small bedrooms, each with bunk beds. Faqir could see no other accommodation in the little property. 'Where will you sleep?' he asked, miming the question.

The Greek man gestured to some blankets stacked in the corner of the living room and said something incomprehensible, giving a thumbs-up sign.

'Thank you,' he said, crossing his heart with his hand.

Makari was now asleep in her cot and Kassia spooned the contents of the pot into the dishes on the table. She beckoned to them to sit and she and her husband pulled up stools with them. The fish stew was delicious and they ate it hungrily, making conversation in sign language as best they could. At 7:30 am, exhausted after the night's events, Faqir and his sons went to sleep in one of the bedrooms and the women in the other. They all slept well, thanking providence for their good fortune and wondering what tomorrow would bring.

TWENTY-SEVEN

Palermo, Sicily
May 2016

A crowd of people were waiting in Palermo port at the pier used by the Tunis ferries. There were only two lines plying the route, the *Grandi Navi Veloci* and the *Grimaldi*, with a total of three voyages per week. According to the website and the ticket seller at the pier, the ferry Ibrahim was waiting for was due in at eleven that morning. It was now one in the afternoon and it still hadn't arrived.

The ferry boat finally docked at two-thirty in the afternoon and he could see the passengers crowding down the gangplank and entering the immigration building. The first couple came through the Schengen exit at two forty-five and the first non-Schengen passenger took ten minutes more. *Sami will be non-Schengen*, he thought. *This is going to take a long time.* He went to sit on a bench near the exit doors, placed the H&M bag prominently in front and took out his Italian phrase book. It was sunny and warm, and he sat reading for over an hour, looking at his watch occasionally and scanning the crowd around him for a man in a red jacket.

'Ali?' He looked up from his book. The speaker was standing in front of him wearing a red anorak and jeans, holding a wheelie bag and carrying a backpack.

Panicked, his English deserted him and he blurted out, '*Aber du bist eine Frau*! But you're a woman!'

'Feckin' brilliant! Well spotted. I'm Samantha McDonnell, everybody calls me Sam, or Sami.'

Ibrahim stood up and she put her arms around him and kissed him on both cheeks. 'We're supposed to be lovers,' she whispered.

Taking her hand, he kissed her on the forehead, as he used to kiss his mother, averting his eyes, trying to recover his composure. He was furious with Karl. He hadn't wanted a partner and now they'd sent him a woman. *Why would he send me a woman? What help could she be?* Trying to justify his reaction, he said, 'I was expecting a man. Sami's a man's name and Karl never told me about you. I was surprised.'

'Don't worry. It happens a lot, me mam should have called me Susan or Margaret, it would have been easier.'

'No,' he stuttered, 'it's a good name. Sami, I like it.'

'You won't mind if we speak English? Me German is really lousy.'

He looked around, there was no one nearby. 'Don't you speak Arabic?' he asked, not realising how patronising it sounded.

'A little bit, but we're not allowed. We've got to speak English all the time. I'll tell you why later.'

Now he was angry again. *They send me a woman and she's already telling me what to do. Women don't give orders to men; according to the ISIL code they are just chattels.* He left her to take her wheelie bag and they walked towards the exit.

'It's a good job you've got that H&M shopping bag,'

she said. 'I wouldn't have recognised you from your photo with the hoodie and sunglasses. And you look much older with that beard.'

Now she's trying to flatter me. 'It's not a clever disguise but I think it's OK.' Then, trying to sound knowledgeable, 'You have to keep your head down all the time.'

'Are we going to the hostel? I can't wait for a shower and a sleep, I must stink. That crossing was feckin' awful and I'm knackered.'

He didn't know the word but interpreted it from her gesture. 'It's very close. A few minutes only.' They walked out of the port entrance and he noticed she was a few centimetres shorter than him. Her hair was fair, brushed back from her face and tied in a ponytail. She turned to speak and he saw she had brown eyes. He was surprised that he found her attractive.

'What's it like, the hostel?'

'It's a very old building. Not very ...' he searched for the word, 'smart, but clean and friendly people.' Then he thought of the problem of sharing a room with a woman, something he'd never experienced. 'The room's not very big. Maybe we can get you a different one, more private. It doesn't cost much.'

'Don't worry. I don't fuss and I don't need much space, just a bed and a shower. Anything with a roof, a bed and running water will be better than living in feckin' bombed out buildings in Mosul.'

'You came from Mosul?'

'Sure and all I did. No sleep for two feckin' days. I came in a car through Syria to Lebanon on the M4 and M5, they're still under ISIL control. That took a whole day, then I flew from Beirut to Tunis and got on that stinking ferry I've just got off, thank you Jesus.'

'How did you get on an aeroplane when you've been with ISIL in Mosul?'

'I can travel anywhere with the Irish passport they gave me. The name on it is Sarah, Sarah Callaghan, so you'll have to call me that from now on. For when we meet anyone and have to give our names. OK?'

Ibrahim nodded, again supressing his irritation at being lectured by a woman, especially one who used such filthy language all the time. He was annoyed and worried. He had never had a girlfriend and knew next to nothing about women. Always an awkward, shy youth, he had spent as much time as possible with his father until he had left for Iraq. His advice was to save himself for Allah or the right woman, and he had followed that advice. He had watched internet porn and masturbated a few times when he was younger but had tried to exercise a strict discipline since his father's death.

His conversion to ISIL and the desire to fight for their cause, thwarted by his mother's illness, had consumed him totally for the last two years. A couple of girls had shown an interest in his soft, gentle manner, but he had either spurned them or never plucked up the courage to encourage them. He had never had sex or seen an unclothed female except on the internet and now he had to share a small room with a young woman. He was shaking with fear and apprehension.

He wondered how old she was, where she came from and why she had gone to Iraq. She spoke English with a strange accent he couldn't identify. He was afraid of being humiliated by his ignorance.

'Are you English?' he asked.

'No, I'm from Belfast.' She saw he didn't understand. 'It's in Northern Ireland, on the coast. It's feckin' cold, not like here. It's lovely here, not as hot as Mosul. I like it fine.'

'How long were you there?'

'Eighteen months. I've been there 'til last week.'

'Were you in the fighting?'

'Sometimes, we all were. But there wasn't much fighting 'cos the feckin' Iraqi army ran away like cowardly shites when ISIL took the town.'

'What does it feel like?'

'The fighting you mean? I was as scared as hell at first. I was like, *what the bejesus is happening*? Pissing me pants all the time. Then you kind of get used to it, the bombs and shells, it's like being in a really loud club. It's not having a place to stay for long that's the worst. You're all the time moving around, outside places, basements and schools and hospitals, anywhere where they might not fire rockets at, and you can hardly ever get a shower or a bath.

'I was in an apartment for a few weeks, but it didn't last, nothing there lasts for long. For women it's worse, having to wear a feckin' *niqab* all day, it's as bad as being blind. In the town the buildings are falling down all around you but most of the time you can't see any soldiers or tanks or anything.' She laughed, 'It's like a really cool video game and you sometimes get a Kalashnikov to fire.'

Ibrahim felt a stab of jealousy at her story. This woman had lived the life he had lusted after, to fight the enemy face to face, on the ground, in the killing fields of history. *She's not just someone to fill a fighter's bed, she was a warrior, that's why Karl sent her.*

He needed to defend his apparent lack of action. 'My father and my uncle were killed in Mosul in 2015,' he said. 'I wanted to go, but my mother was ill and I had a young brother and sister. My real name is Ibrahim bin Omar al-Ahmad.

'They told me,' she said. 'And you built a bomb, but it went wrong.'

'It's not my fault,' he said, defensively. 'It was ready and my mother had another heart attack. Everything went wrong. My family was killed. Hassan, my cousin, was there and he was killed and now I've got his papers.'

'I'm sorry for your family.'

'I want to make it good. I want to show I can make it good for Allah and for ISIL.

'Sure and all,' she said, with a bright smile. 'We'll make it good. That's why I'm here.'

The desk clerk gave Ibrahim a sly wink when Sami entered Sarah Callaghan on the registration card. '*Avere un soggiorno piacevole.* Have an enjoyable stay,' he smiled.

They entered the room and she threw herself on a bed. 'I'm in feckin' heaven!' she said, spreading out across the bedcover.

He placed her luggage by the wardrobe. 'My things are in there,' he said, pointing to the chest of drawers. 'You can have this cupboard.'

Getting up from the bed she took off her anorak and hung it up then looked into the bathroom. 'I don't feckin' believe it, a bath. Thanks, Ali. You'll need to get used to me calling you that. And don't forget to call me Sarah. We mustn't make any mistakes.'

She's telling me what to do again. 'Don't worry, I'll remember.'

She unwound a money belt from her waist. 'Here, there's 2,000 euros, it's for our expenses.'

'Wow, that's cool.' The word made him think of his brother. 'Now we have more than five thousand. If we're careful it should be enough.'

'That's a relief. We don't want to get caught short. Can you run me a bath? Here, put some of this in, please.' She took a bottle from her backpack.

He managed to hold back the angry retort that sprang to his lips and turned on the taps, testing the water with his hand. Satisfied, he poured some of the pink liquid into the water and a sweet, citrus-like aroma wafted up.

'I hope that makes you feel better,' he said, turning back into the room. Sami was in her underwear, about to remove her bra. Her breasts were small and high and a locket and a key on a thin gold chain lay in the cleft between them. Ibrahim thought she looked beautiful. He flushed, averted his gaze and walked to the door. 'It's five-thirty. I'll go and get some food for supper,' he spluttered. 'I won't be long.' Before she could answer, he left the room and hurried down the staircase. He had an erection. *This is becoming complicated*, he said to himself as he walked to the nearest pizza café.

TWENTY-EIGHT

It was 8:30 pm when the Al-Douri family said goodbye to Kassia and Makari. Tapani had been absent when they awoke around noon and they'd stayed on the property all day, away from any prying eyes, looking after the baby and helping his wife with her chores. Kassia never stopped working; she swept and scrubbed every surface in the farmhouse until they could have eaten off the floor, then cleaned and raked her little garden until it was immaculate. There were four goats and six chickens in a field behind the property and she took water and food out for them, coming back with several brown eggs and a bucketful of milk.

Faqir's family were enchanted by the calm routine and simplicity of the day. They'd forgotten what it was like to live a normal life, enjoying the sunshine and fresh air, not having to hide in cellars, being invaded by shelling, bombing, injury or death and the constant fear of being singled out by the security spies. It was a little paradise and they delighted in the few hours of relaxation they passed with Kassia.

At five o'clock she was busy in the kitchen preparing supper when Tapani returned, carrying a bucket of long silvery fish. He greeted them with a smile and kissed his wife and baby, then they sat down to Greek salad and meatballs. She managed to explain to them that the

Greek names were *horiatiki* and *keftedes*. The meatballs were sweet, spicy and chewy, and Hema suspected they might be made from goat's meat but said nothing. The highlight of the meal was a typically sweet dessert, *loukoumades* – fried balls of dough drenched in honey with cinnamon. They were replete when the meal was over, sorry they had to leave on the next stage of their flight.

After the meal, when Tapani was showing the boys how to gut the fish he'd caught, Hema said to her daughters, 'That's what it means to be self-sufficient. They can catch or grow or even make most of what's essential to live and don't need a supermarket or corner shop nearby. Maybe we'll be able to live like that when we get to England.' *If we get there*, she reminded herself.

When darkness fell, it was time to continue their passage in search of freedom and safety. Following Tony Miller's advice, they had reduced their baggage to only backpacks, leaving behind their suitcases, Arab clothing and other items. In Istanbul, Faqir had acquired two larger rucksacks, which would take some of their precious belongings, but Hema and her daughters agonised over what could be taken and what left behind.

Kassia was delighted and grateful for women's clothing, shoes and other items they left, even though she would probably never have the occasion to wear them. They hugged the Greek woman and her baby, thanking her for her kindness. She gave them sandwiches and fruit and they followed Tapani out into the darkness back to the boat.

They would never forget their short stop in Poliantho, nor the simple Greek family who seemed to have nothing and yet had everything. Hema once again thinking of Sir Patrick and Lady Nancy Carr, who seemed to have everything but had lost more than anyone should ever lose.

Monopati, Rhodope Region, Greece

Monopati is 16 km from Polianthos as the crow flies, but the Kompsatos Potamos runs neither straight nor true. It meanders from its source somewhere under the mountains of southern Bulgaria, emerging on the surface in Melivoia, Greece, and running east to merge with a smaller river, then south until it flows gently into Lake Vistonida in the Nestos National Park. It was a bright, starry night and thanks to Tapani's lifetime spent on and around the river, they covered the navigation distance of 30 km in under two hours. They were helped by the dry weather, since during the rainy season the river ran so fast it might be exciting for white water rafters to descend but impossible for any vessel to mount.

They pulled the boat up on the shore and unloaded their baggage for the hike to the Bulgarian border. It was cooler at the higher altitude, a better temperature to cross the 25 km of mountainous terrain, which Tony had described as 'challenging'. Barring accidents and confident in their guide's skilful navigation and knowledge, they should make it before daylight. Hoisting up their backpacks, they strode off behind the Greek giant, who was carrying the two large rucksacks as if they weighed nothing.

Greece-Bulgaria Border

Tapani gestured to them to stay down and be silent. He walked slowly forward, looking around him, not daring to shine a torch. It was almost one in the morning and the moonlight was sufficient to see for a short distance, which was both an advantage and a disadvantage. They were lying on the cold rocky ground in a forested area near Kushla, a Bulgarian village, 5 km from Monopati. If they got past this village, there were no more until Drangova, the largest town in the area, about 6 km away to the north-east.

In front of them was a farmhouse with outbuildings; it was in darkness and the Greek was ensuring it was safe to pass it. If not, they would have to retrace their steps to avoid the dense woods and rocky terrain on either side. There were only cart tracks at this point and no permanent control of the border, but immigration guards rode along the tracks on motor bikes at irregular intervals, to send refugees back to where they came from.

'He's signalling to come forward,' Malik whispered. In the moonlight, they could just make out the figure of their guide waving from the trees on the far side of the property.

They were moving silently towards the corner of the building, when they heard a door opening and a beam of light shone across the gravel path in front of the house. The family froze where they were, just ten metres from the light, shivering with fear and cold.

A woman's voice spoke in Bulgarian, followed by a

man's, then the door shut and they saw him walk from the house along the path towards Tapani's hiding place. The light was extinguished and they could no longer see as far as the trees. A motorbike or scooter engine started up and drove off into the night. Faqir motioned them into the shelter of the building, standing silently against the wall, waiting for their guide to reappear, hardly daring to breathe in case the steam from their breath might be seen in the chilly mountain air.

A moment later, a headlight shone along the path behind them and the motorbike came around the property, driving slowly past their motionless forms, parallel with them, just a few metres away.

'That must have been the border guard, visiting his lady friend.' Faqir broke the unnerving silence, as they watched the lights fade and disappear into the distance.

Then a voice behind them said, 'OK.' It was the first English word Tapani had spoken and probably all he knew; they jumped with fright when they heard it. He signalled to move on and a few minutes later they were heading towards Drangova, two hours away and another 6 km further from the border.

Near Kitna, Kardzhali Province, Southern Bulgaria

'We must stop for a while, Tapani, we're very tired.' Faqir mimed sitting down and resting and the giant Greek nodded and pointed to their right. They had skirted the town of Drangova to the west and at three in the morning, they reached the road to their destination, Benkovski, 10 km away. Walking on the road was faster, but Hema and the girls were exhausted. The Greek led them to a wooded grove where they collapsed onto the grass, stretching and massaging their aching leg muscles.

Their youngest daughter, Lyla, had slipped and twisted her ankle and was helped by her brothers over the last couple of kilometres. Hema carefully removed her boot; the ankle was bruised and swollen. 'Is it hurting badly, darling?'

'It's sore, but I don't think it's sprained.'

'Here, let me help it.' Hema fished in her rucksack for the first aid items she'd packed. She swabbed it with a lotion then rubbed ointment onto the bruise, binding it with bandages taped tightly. She replaced the boot, leaving it unfastened. 'Is that better?'

The thirteen-year-old smiled and nodded bravely, but Faqir looked at his wife worriedly. They had many kilometres to walk in the next few days; the ankle wouldn't have any time to heal and would slow them down.

They rested for an hour and ate some of the food Kassia had given them. Faqir handed Tapani the rest of his fee, 1,000 euros, apologising that it seemed so little, but it was all they had. He needn't have worried, the Greek was overjoyed with the money and kissed each of them in gratitude.

At 5:00 am they reluctantly set off again for Benkovski, reaching the River Varbitza which runs alongside the town an hour later, where they washed the grime and dust off and changed their clothes to look more like casual tourists. At seven they followed Tapani across the bridge to the bus station. With the Bulgarian lev Faqir had purchased in Istanbul, he bought tickets for the six-and-a-half-hour, 300 km bus ride to Sofia, the capital.

They mingled with the crowd of waiting passengers until the bus arrived and Tapani went over to the driver and embraced him, obviously a good friend. He introduced them all, explaining, as far as they could understand, that they were Kurds from Turkey, visiting the country for the first time and asking him to look after them.

The Bulgarian showed them to seats in the front of the bus, indicating that they'd have better views. He went down to stow their bags in the luggage compartment and Tapani came to bid them farewell. It was an emotional moment; all they could do was to embrace the big man and thank God and Sir Patrick Carr that he'd come their way. The driver climbed on board and promptly at 8:00 am, the doors closed and they waved goodbye, wondering how many more miracles they'd need before they arrived safely at their final destination, the UK.

TWENTY-NINE

Ibrahim and Sami were at a café in the Vucciria street market having coffee and sweet pastries for breakfast. It was early, but the sun was already high and warm.

She sat with her face turned up to catch the feel-good rays. 'This is great. We couldn't sit in the sun in Mosul. It was either too hot or there were snipers trying to take your feckin' head off all the time. I think I like Palermo better.'

He didn't respond. Walking back to the hostel with the pizzas the previous evening, he had considered this change in his situation and didn't like it. It was bad enough having a partner criticising his every move or mistake. But a woman, a woman who had gone to Iraq to fight with ISIL in battles that he had only read about or seen on TV; that was much worse. How could he not feel humiliated? Despite what the ISIL code said, she wasn't just a chattel, to be used for a man's pleasure. In Mosul, she had been involved in fighting and survived to be sent here to help him.

She had already accused him of failing to build the bomb properly and that it would be better now she was here. *Such arrogance!* And her behaviour, taking her clothes off in front of him and the disgusting language she used all the time. That wasn't the sign of a serious woman. She had learned bad lessons in Iraq and needed to be reprimanded. What was necessary to accomplish any kind of a mission was *disziplin*. He said the word in German in his mind, then *discipline* in English, *tadib* in Arabic. He would have to instil some into her.

Ibrahim entered the room, fired up and prepared to have an argument. Instead, he found her tucked up in bed and out to the world. In the dim light from the landing, she looked very feminine and vulnerable. Deflated, he went down to the lounge, ate his supper, then sneaked quietly into the other bed without disturbing her. She didn't stir in the night, but he tossed and turned, wondering how to cope with this new challenge.

Now he was still working out how to approach the subject but couldn't pluck up the courage. She seemed to notice his mood and whispered to him, 'Shall I tell you what the Emir has planned for us? He told me I have to talk to you about it. You know, get your opinion and advice.'

He was immediately mollified; she wanted his opinion and advice. But before any discussion he needed to know her better and understand the way she was. 'Let's walk a bit, out of hearing of anyone. We must be very careful.'

They stopped at a stall and he chose some fruit and gave them to the old woman to weigh. 'How old were you to go to Iraq?' he asked.

'Eighteen. I got there in September 2014, three months after ISIL took over Mosul.'

She's the same age as me, he registered. 'But you're not a Muslim. Why did you join ISIL?'

'Me boyfriend was going with two other friends. They're Muslims, but they said I could go with them.

And I wanted to get me own back on the feckin' English for what happened ...' She stopped speaking suddenly, but he didn't notice.

'You had a Muslim boyfriend in England? Are there a lot of Muslims there?'

'In Northern Ireland. There didn't used to be many but over the last few years there's a lot more come, escaping from the wars. His name was Baki, he was me boyfriend, from when I was sixteen. He was older than me, eighteen, feckin' gorgeous. He took me to places, spent money on me. I was like, out of me mind over him, I'd have followed him anywhere. Look, that's him.' She opened up the locket on her necklace and showed him a photo of a young Arab man.

'Yes, he's good looking.' *Too good*, he thought to himself. He saw a wide grin on her face and felt quite envious.

'What about your parents? Were they not worried for you?'

'I haven't got any.' She gave him the same version of events she'd been giving for years. It wasn't true, but it diverted further questions. 'Me old man raped me for years then dropped down dead when I was fifteen, thank you Jesus. Me mam kicked me out to get a job when I left school. She was a junkie, didn't know what the fuck she was doing.'

He pulled a face at her continual foul language but said only, 'A *junkie*?'

'You know, always out of her mind on drugs and booze.'

'Oh, I know what you mean. I'm sorry.'

'It's OK, she died a couple of months later, she was only thirty-nine. That's when I met Baki. He had a good job and a flat. I told you, he looked after me better than anyone else ever did.'

'Where is he now?'

'He was killed by the English and American feckers. In the airstrikes in the February, five months after we got there.'

Ibrahim took a moment to register this. *She had gone to Iraq with her boyfriend and he had been killed five months later, but she had stayed for more than a year afterwards.* 'What happened to him?'

'We went to the north-west part to defend against attacks from the Kurdish Peshmerga. I got out, but they were all killed, Baki and his two friends.'

'I'm sorry, Sami. It must have been very ...' he searched for the word, 'difficult for you.' He looked at her face, but she showed no emotion.

'Your father was killed there as well, and your uncle. I knew them. We lost a lot of good fighters there.'

He stopped dead in the street, thunderstruck by this casual statement. 'You knew my father and uncle?'

'Everybody knew them in Mosul. Very brave men, they showed no fear. Karl told me they were the best fighters he ever had. He knew they'd worked for Hussein, but he didn't care, they fought for ISIL and they fought well.'

Tears came to his eyes and he turned away so she wouldn't notice. His heart was pounding and he thought it would burst with pride at the news. After a moment, he said, 'Was that an important battle, against the Peshmerga?'

'It was very important to keep control of Mosul, you don't know how many fighters we have, a lot less than people think, thank Christ. Karl told me nobody believed they would capture the place in 2014. They had less than two thousand men and the army had about thirty thousand. ISIL has feckin' amazing fighters.'

Again, Ibrahim felt a sense of pride at this praise of his father's reputation. *If she's telling the truth,* he suddenly thought. 'Do you know Karl very well?' he asked, trying not to sound too concerned.

'Jesus, sure and all I do. I was his wife for more than a year after Baki was killed, until last month,' she said casually.

There was a long silence while he assimilated this latest bombshell. They stopped at a bakery and he bought a *bastone,* a loaf of bread. He handed over some change and they continued walking.

'Karl took you as his wife?'

'He never called me that, he was too proud to admit it. I was just the woman he shagged, but I know he liked me.'

'Did you like being his woman?'

'He's a senior ISIL commander in Mosul. Feckin' arrogant but smart as shit. He beat me up a lot, but we got along OK.'

Ibrahim's imagination was invaded by sordid scenes of sex and violence but he just asked, 'Why did Karl send you to meet me when you were his woman?'

'It's looking very bad for them. Karl said they would have lost Mosul already in February if the Iraqis hadn't gone to take back Ramadi first. But now there's tens of thousands of army soldiers and Kurds around the city waiting for the order to attack.'

'How many fighters does ISIL have there?'

'There's about fifteen thousand now, but a lot of them aren't really fighters. Just hangers-on who signed up not to get tortured or killed. They'll be no feckin' use when the real fighting starts.' She spat on the ground, much to his disgust.

'Now the American and Iraqi planes are bombing the shit out of the place, softening it up for the ground troops to move in. Just before I left there was a massive American air strike on the city centre and al-Bajari, the deputy war minister, was killed. Karl's best mate was Hadi, another commander, he died in the same attack. Karl was lucky, he'd just left the building when it was hit, or he'd be dead as well. Feckin' Americans and English coming in and murdering the true believers fighting to take back their own country.'

Ibrahim was fascinated by her intimate knowledge of the war. His loins stirred at the thought of being there and proving his worth. But he knew it was impossible. Their task was decided, they had to execute it; that would be their contribution to the fight. He said, 'Karl's worried that Mosul might be lost?'

'He thinks they'll be feckin' wiped out.'

'And he sent you here to meet me?'

Again, she prevaricated and told him the version of the story she'd rehearsed on her trip from Mosul. 'I told him I wanted to do something better than just screwing him or getting blown the fuck up over there. There's nothing useful I can do in Iraq or Syria, I'm like, just a stupid infidel cow as far as they're concerned. So, I wanted to come back to Europe and do something here, make a real sacrifice. There's lots of Europeans coming back home from ISIL now and there's going to be big trouble. He told me about you and I sort of felt as if I already knew you, with Baki and your father fighting together and everything. It sounded like a good chance to keep the fight going, so he set it all up. End of story.' She bit into an apple and continued walking.

He digested this in silence then, trying to make up for his earlier moody behaviour, said, 'Thanks for telling me all that, I didn't know how my father died until now. I'm glad you told me, but I'm sorry, am I asking too many questions?'

'It's OK, but I'd rather forget about all that and talk about our job. That's what we have to concentrate on now. Getting our job done.'

'You're right. It's what I think as well, we must have proper discipline to get the job done. Come, over here.' He led her to a bench in the park across from the hostel. Swallowing his pride, he said, 'So, tell me Karl's orders.'

'I don't have it written down in case I got stopped on the way here, it's too dangerous. I've memorised everything from Karl and today he said I have to tell you the first part. Is that OK?'

Once again, his initial reaction was to shout, *I'm in charge of this mission. Just tell me what he said.* He forced himself to stay calm, 'I understand. He told me the same thing, to remember everything and not to keep anything in writing. So, just tell me the first part.'

She knew he wasn't happy with the situation, but

there was nothing she could do – Karl's word was law. Leaning up close to him, she spoke into his face, so he could smell the slight scent of her sun cream. 'Tonight, we've got to leave Palermo and go to England.'

Ibrahim reacted immediately. 'England? Karl never said anything about going to England. It was already hard for me to get all the way down here from Stuttgart.' He paused, reluctant to let her know how little he understood about travelling between countries. Finally, he confessed, 'I haven't got the right documents to pass borders and I don't even know how to get from here to England.'

She took his hand, 'We have to go through France, so we take the train from here to Paris at nine o'clock tonight.'

He stared at her in amazement. 'But we don't have time to organise all that by tonight.'

'It's OK, it's all been done. The train tickets are booked and we just pick them up at the station here in Palermo. We get to Paris tomorrow night at the same time, nine o'clock. Italy and France are both in the Schengen zone and the EU. I've got an Irish passport and you've got a German one so there'll be no problems. When we get to Paris, I'll tell you how we do the last part to England, that's the tricky bit and it's why Karl made sure you speak good English. I've got the instructions for the trip to Paris in my memory and I'll tell you all the details when we get back to the hostel.'

'The main thing is, we have to look like we're a couple and pretend we're in love, we'll stand out less than a man by himself. There's a hotel booked for us in Paris.

We have to tell them we've come from England and we're going to Italy to get married. It's what Karl called "a double bluff" – if the police find our trail, they won't know which way we're going.'

Before Ibrahim could assimilate this series of directives, she went on, 'When we get to England, you're going to build another explosive, a much bigger one, and we're going to blow up an important building full of thousands of English feckers. That's what our mission is. That's what we've been chosen for, to give you a second chance and to let me do it with you as your partner.'

THIRTY

Mosul, Iraq
May 2016

Karl had moved his command post again, still on the left bank of the Tigris, but this time to the central-east part of the city. Across the street was the most surreal scene he had ever observed. There was a huge crater in the road in front, created by the previous night's coalition air strikes. An abandoned, burnt-out car that had stood on the street had been blown into the air and was now perched ten metres up on the remains of the terrace of a building opposite him. The terrace was the only part of the facade of the building that remained standing. It looked like a scene from a futuristic movie. It was hard to believe there were almost a million civilians in the remains of the city, still clinging onto what was left of their apartments, living in ruined schools, shops, hospitals, hotels, hiding in basements, or trudging through the streets with a few belongings and what was left of their families, trying to find a way out of this inferno of death and destruction.

A large number of his men were working on that street and others leading towards the bridges that crossed over the river to the historic old town on the west side of Mosul, which he knew would be the scene of the last and bloodiest fighting. They were blasting and digging holes in the tarmac, planting pipe bombs and other primitive explosives that would serve as land mines as the attacking allied forces drove their tanks and armoured cars from east to west across the ravaged city. The fact that there would be virtually nothing left of the ancient capital, some parts of it dating from 400 BC, didn't seem to be of any importance, neither to the ISIL rulers, nor to the infidel coalition forces who were bombing it out of existence. The last phase of destruction would take place across the river, in the magnificent Assyrian centre, and what was left of Mosul would be retaken, two years after he had helped to capture it.

As he watched the destruction of the roads and streets in this last futile attempt to delay the inevitable defeat in that final battle, his mind wandered back over that two-year period and his talk with Baghdadi in Baaj. *How many people, fighters and civilians, have died during that time?* He asked himself. *It must be tens, if not hundreds of thousands. And all for nothing, just to turn back the clock to the day before I led my men to our most momentous victory.*

What was worse, he now feared that he would not even be involved in that last glorious, bloody failure. That morning, a message from Abdullah, still the Mosul supreme commander, confirmed what the caliph had intimated to him. They, along with other senior leaders and some hundreds of fighters, would flee the city before the end of the month for Raqqa, the official headquarters of the caliphate in Syria. This return to Syria was, for Karl, the ultimate loss of face – to run away from the most important battle of their history. To give up the city he had helped to capture, without the chance to lose his life in defending it from the infidels.

Karl was tired and disillusioned. *It used to be a*

dutiful pleasure, important and necessary in the name of Allah, but still a pleasure. Now he wished only that he could stay in Mosul and die fighting alongside his men, though he knew they could not prevail. But even that pleasure was to be taken away from him. He went to meet his command team in the basement of the hotel. Preparations had to continue for the last, vain defence of the city against the upcoming assault, with or without him.

Berkovitsa, Montana Province, North West Bulgaria

After finding a connecting bus in Sofia and enduring another two-and-a-half-hour ride, the Al-Douri family had finally arrived at the small Bulgarian ski resort of Berkovitsa, 12 km from the south-eastern border of Serbia. Following the instructions on his mobile, Faqir led them to the Hotel Shstasti, a simple family hotel near the ski lift, which had three sparsely furnished rooms available on the upstairs floor.

The beds were hard and uncomfortable, but they threw themselves down on them gratefully, happy to rest after their full day of bus travel. Faqir went outside to call the number of Tony's next contact; the Australian had told him the man could just about speak English and he managed to make himself understood. Fifteen minutes later, he was waiting in the empty hotel bar when a tall dark-skinned man with an impressive black drooping moustache came over to him. He looked like a villain in a bad spy movie.

'Faqir?' He nodded and the Bulgarian put out his hand, 'Ivan. Come, we walk a bit.'

On the lawn outside, he lit a cigarette and took a deep drag. 'They start close border now, you know this?'

'Tony told me, but he thought you could still get us through. Can you?'

'Is different now. More patrols, but I know good way where is possible.'

'So, you'll take us?'

'Price is different. Last week was 500 euros, now is 1,500.' He showed the number with his fingers.

'You mean it's nine thousand for my whole family?'

Ivan leaned closer and he could smell cigarette smoke on his breath. 'Tony said you good friend to look after, but now is dangerous time. And house on other side is cost money.'

Faqir was sweating; this was going to cost him three times what he'd expected. They couldn't afford it, he would have to bargain the man down or find another solution.

Ivan saw his expression. 'OK. I take you all family, five thousand. Is not my fault, is fucking Hungarians.' He spat on the ground and took a drag of his cigarette, waiting expectantly.

That leaves us with less than thirty thousand, almost half our money gone already. Once again, he cursed the killers who had robbed Hema of her mother and the family of a quarter of their dwindling fortune. *But we're stuck in this tiny place in the Bulgarian mountains with no other options.* 'OK, if it includes the safe house.'

They shook hands on the deal, agreeing that he would come for them at 8:00 pm the following night, an hour before sunset. That would give them nine hours of darkness to cover the next stage of their journey. Relieved, Faqir went back to the hotel, lay down by his wife on the bed and fell into an exhausted sleep.

THIRTY-ONE

Lieutenant Eric Schuster walked into Max Kellerman's office. 'The Kalk dossier's been reopened.'

Max looked up from the screen, 'Because of the Kunduz-Takhar incident?' He was referring to the kidnapping of over two hundred civilians and the execution of many of them on a highway in Afghanistan that week.

'That might have sparked the decision, but I doubt it, it's everything that's going on in the terrorist department these days.'

'I'm not surprised, the death tally this month is over twelve hundred. They're exporting their terror anywhere they can, especially ISIS. Trying to deflect attention from Mosul and Raqqa, where they're in serious trouble.'

'And it's going to get worse here in Europe, jihadists escaping from Iraq and Syria to take their vengeance on the Western allies they blame for the wars in the first place.'

It was May 31st, a month since the Kalk explosion and two weeks since the last unproductive news announcement and nothing had transpired. Either Ibrahim or Hassan, they didn't know which, was still in circulation and no one knew where he was hiding. The incident chart, still on his office wall, hadn't been updated for days, a testament to the lack of progress in the defunct investigation.

'So they think Al-Ahmad is still a real threat?' Max asked, reminding his boss that his bet was still on Ibrahim.

'Let's say they don't want us to be seen ignoring the possibility of a terrorist at large that we know about but we're doing nothing.'

'What do they want to do?'

'They've agreed to increase the reward to 100,000 euros. I'll try to renew interest with a couple of press conferences and the unbarred photos. I'll do one tomorrow night, want to help me write it? We need a new angle, it's an old story now, so I doubt it'll have any effect, but we have to show willing.'

Max wasn't keen on helping to write an announcement that he wasn't going to give, but he put his feelings aside and bent to the task.

Berkovitsa, Montana Province, North West Bulgaria

It was raining heavily when Ivan led them down the hillside towards the Serbian border, 12 km away to the south west. Faqir and his family had spent the morning picnicking on the meadow near the hotel. Lyla's ankle was still swollen and after Hema changed the dressing, he had carried her on his back. They relaxed in the sunshine for a couple of hours, enjoying the quiet and calm, before returning to pack their bags for the next stage of their journey.

By the afternoon, the weather had changed; the temperature dropped and rain clouds moved in from the east. Faqir had paid only for one night and they prepared to leave the hotel, without knowing where to shelter until evening. The owner, Andrei, a tall skinny man with a shock of red hair, was a suspicious looking fellow, who must have seen a lot of refugees come and go through his establishment. Faqir had said as little as possible to him, worried that he could be a source of problems. As they stood at the door, looking out at the pouring rain, he came up to him. 'I suppose you have an appointment with Ivan later this evening.'

Faqir said nothing, but his heart started pounding. *He must be an informer, paid by the authorities to help them stop illegal border crossings.*

He struggled to answer and the man smiled. 'No need to go out and get soaked. Stay here until he comes. He's a good friend of mine, brings me a lot of business. Come into the bar and have a coffee while you wait.'

When Ivan arrived at eight, it was dark, freezing cold and pouring, and there was no one to be seen. They were wrapped up in warm clothing, wearing their plastic capes. Faqir shook hands with Andrei and they set off with their guide. As usual, he handed him half his fee, ensuring he didn't leave them in the lurch and run off with their precious euros. They followed him down a steep ski path, a 5 km long winding trail towards the valley at the bottom of the slope, surrounded by pine forest on either side. The rocky path was well trodden, but the rain had turned the surface to slippery mud and they made slow progress, helping each other on the treacherous slope, glad of the waterproof boots they'd bought at Tony's suggestion. At 9:30 pm they reached a large meadowland, which Ivan told them was used by the farmers in the villages below, who led their cattle up to pasture in spring until autumn. He stopped in the protection of a huge tree at the edge of the forest and they gathered around him.

'We got 7 km to border,' he said, passing around a water bottle. 'Is danger now for Bulgaria patrols. Serbs doesn't like people come from here if not send to Hungary, is very political.'

They were about to set off across the wide green expanse when he held up his hand to stop them. Putting his finger across his lips he motioned them back amongst the trees, where they waited in silence until they heard the faint sounds his sharp ears had detected. Now they heard mumbled voices and through the rain they could just make out the vague shapes of a large group of people, about thirty metres away, advancing slowly across the dark field. They watched them make their way towards the west until the distant shapes disappeared into the mist.

'Is other group refugees,' he told them. 'On different trail for go direction Senokos. Is bad for us, crossing is easy there, but many people caught by patrol. Is not good follow big group. Other way is hard, but more safe. You can climb up rocky path?'

'Do we have a choice?'

'No, if you want be safe.'

'Are you alright darling?'

'It's hurting a bit Mama, but I'll be OK.' Lyla smiled bravely.

Faqir nodded to the guide and he led them in the opposite direction, along the edge of the forest, stopping after a few hundred metres. 'Go from here,' he pointed to the south, 'is short way cross field, but difficult on other side. Will be slow but maybe no patrol. Wait now.'

They waited for ten minutes; the rain had lessened and a slight breeze rustled the trees in the darkness. Suddenly, the silence was broken by a man's voice, shouting, followed by a gunshot then a woman's scream and the sound of a vehicle, a jeep or motorbike. The flash of torches lit the gloom from the direction taken by the other group.

They looked at each other in shock and fright. What was happening?

'Now go, patrol busy with other group.' Ivan picked up Faqir's rucksack and he carried Lyla in his arms as their guide herded them quickly across the field. 'One kilometre to forest there.'

They hurried across the open pasture land, slipping and sliding on the wet grass, looking fearfully around in the dim light and ducking down instinctively when they heard another gunshot and more shouting. In the protection of the trees on the other side they dropped their rucksacks, catching their breath and waiting for their heartbeats to settle down. Faqir had carried his daughter for almost a kilometre and he knew he couldn't do it much longer. Ivan lit up a cigarette under the cover of his jerkin. The mountain was silent again, only the steady drumming of the rain falling on the trees around them to be heard.

'They must have caught the other group.' Faqir thanked their lucky stars that Ivan had heard them and taken a different route.

'What will happen to those poor people?' Hema was

thinking, *they probably paid a lot of money and they've been taken and it was all in vain.*

'Go camp in Sofia. If come from Turkey, send back. No country want refugees now. Turkey and Bulgaria make fence, is 150 km long for stop refugees.'

'Is it just as bad in Serbia?'

'I get hundred people to Serbia here. Only few sent back. You careful, you OK.' He checked the time on his phone. 'Is ten, time for get moving, six kilometres to border and more ten after. We go, OK?'

He picked up Faqir's bag again and led them up a muddy, rock-strewn path that snaked its way through the forest, one moment climbing uphill and the next down the perilous, ankle-breaking track. The brothers helped Hema and Aisha on the wet, slippery slopes and Faqir was carrying Lyla on his back now, struggling to keep up with the others as she seemed to become heavier with each step. Tony's words, 'challenging terrain', reverberated in his mind as they fought their way across the inhospitable territory of the Balkan mountain chain.

THIRTY-TWO

Paris, France
May 2016

The Hotel Olympia was not far from the *Gare de Lyon* where Sami and Ibrahim had arrived on the TGV from Geneva. It was late and they were too tired to risk getting lost on the *RER*, the Paris underground, so they took the short taxi ride to the hotel. It was in a one-way street and the taxi driver refused to drive around to the other end.

'It's just a minute's walk along on the left,' he told them, taking the 10 euro note and waiting for them to get their bags out before driving off without another word.

They soon understood why. All along the street, there were makeshift campsites of African immigrants living on the sidewalk. Surrounded by trash, junk, mattresses and worse, families were living and sleeping in tents like homeless people. The Mayor, Anne Hidalgo, had announced plans to build a camp for thousands of illegal migrants in central Paris, but it looked like she was simply catering to the existing reality, not planning for it.

Ibrahim was impressed by Sami's reaction when a couple of young kids tried to bar their way on the dark street, asking for cigarettes or money. She pulled a tiny folding penknife from her jeans pocket, waving it in the face of one of them. 'Feck off, you filthy bastards, or I'll give you a cheap facelift,' she screamed.

'Did you learn that in Iraq?' Ibrahim asked as they walked off.

'To be sure I did not. I learned it when I was six in Belfast.'

They had travelled from Palermo to Naples on the overnight train, managing to get a little sleep, then taken high speed trains the next morning to Milan then Lausanne, in Switzerland, arriving in Geneva in time to catch the TGV to Paris. It was after midnight when they arrived at the hotel, exhausted and in need of a shower. The door was locked and the building was in complete darkness.

'Are you sure this is the right place?' Ibrahim asked. 'It looks like it's closed up.'

She laughed and rang the bell. 'Sure and all it is, Karl's friendly agency booked it. He always does what he says.'

While they were waiting, Sami said to him, 'You can keep your hood up, but take your sunglasses off or you'll look daft. Stay back and look at the floor so they can't see you too close up or in case there's a CCTV camera. Give me some money and let me do the talking. Don't forget we're going to Italy to get married. And don't laugh when you hear me talk.'

'Yes boss.' Ibrahim had no idea what was about to happen, but he was beginning to have implicit faith in her.

A light came on and they heard a woman's voice shouting. There was the sound of locks being opened and bolts being drawn then the door swung open and a middle-aged Arab woman in a kaftan appeared in the lighted entrance.

'*Monsieur et Madame el Zafar*,' she cried and ushered them inside, chattering in rapid French they couldn't understand. As she locked and bolted the door again they could see a bar and restaurant in the style of a Greek tavern. In the dim glow from the wall lights the empty rooms looked shabby, worn and tired.

'I'm Sarah and this is Ali.' Sami shook hands with her. 'Do you speak English? Neither of us knows any French.' She had lost her Irish lilt and affected a Kensington accent, sounding like a BBC TV announcer. He stood behind her, looking at the floor and keeping his face in the shadow, wondering how she could change her accent like that.

The woman said she was Algerian, her name was Valérie and she spoke some English. 'We used to get many English tourists. Not anymore.' She looked tired and worried, pushing her hair back nervously.

'Well, it's a shame we've arrived so late but the trip from England was frightful, it took much longer than we expected.'

'*Ca va, ca va*, don't worry, it's better to have customers, even so late. We have a lot of empty rooms, almost all of them.' She told them her family owned the hotel, but business was so bad they'd had to reduce their rates by forty per cent since the terrorist attacks.

'But still we have not many visitors, so we've closed down everything except the ground floor. This country is a catastrophe,' she said wearily. 'Hollande and the unions are crippling the economy. There's always bad things happening and no tourists come here now. Nobody cares about anything anymore, there's so many immigrants around it's just like in a war. My parents are getting old, if things don't change I don't know what we'll do.' She went behind the desk and produced the registration forms. 'Can I see your ID papers? I have to make a copy.'

Ibrahim stood back in disbelief as Sami recounted an incredible story to the woman. 'Valérie, I have to ask you something, we need your help. My name is not el Zafar, because we're not married yet. Ali and I met in London last year when he came there to college and we fell in love.' She took his hand and wrapped her arm around his waist. 'He was supposed to go back to Dubai to marry someone he'd never met, all arranged by his father, but he wants to be with me. So, we're on our way to my cousin's house in Italy to get married there. My mother and father know about it and they're over the moon, but Ali's family doesn't know a thing and we have to make sure they don't find out.'

She took a deep, emotional breath. 'Please can you help us to stay anonymous, otherwise we'll be stopped and he'll be taken back to Dubai.' A tear ran down her face as she looked imploringly at the woman.

Valérie gave a frown but said in a sympathetic tone, 'So you want me to pretend you've never come here? Not to fill out the forms for the Tourist Office?'

'Could you do that for us?' Sami asked, leaning back against Ibrahim, pushing him into the shadow, another tear glistening on her cheek.

'How long will you stay?'

'Just tonight and tomorrow, we'll leave on Thursday. My cousin Keira's expecting us then and the wedding's booked for Saturday. My parents and two brothers are flying down as well, so all my family will be there. Please say you'll help us, we're desperate to get married and don't want to lose each other.'

A calculating look flitted across her face. 'I don't know if I can take the risk. We're supposed to send the registration papers and photos to the police every day. I'd have to charge you a lot more.'

'We can pay a little more, not a lot, but something extra.'

Finally, Valérie agreed to give them a double room for two nights for 300 euros, cash, in advance. 'It's the nicest room we have,' she said, 'We haven't used it for months, but it's clean and ready.'

Sami handed the money over with a sigh of relief, 'Thank you, Valérie, Ali and I will never forget your kindness.'

Ibrahim carried their bags along to room seventeen then went immediately to the bathroom to run the hot water for Sami's bath. 'How did you imagine that story?' he said incredulously. 'Do you really have a cousin called Keira?'

'Don't be daft, it was just rubbish. I was thinking of Keira Knightley, the English actress, she's beautiful. That's called the Irish blarney we're born with. One thing the Irish are good at is telling stories, true ones and rubbish ones.'

'I like that voice you used. It sounded like the Queen of England. Were you an actress?'

'Only in school plays. That's the posh accent the rich folk have, like they're chewing toffee all the time.

Anyway, the main thing is we're here without any record, so the police can't get on our trail. I'm worn out now, thanks for running the bath, I'm going straight in.'

'I haven't prayed for almost two days,' he said, as she started to undress. 'I won't be long and I won't disturb you.' He took his prayer mat along to the empty restaurant and unburdened his soul for fifteen minutes while Sami soaked in the hot soapy water. When he came quietly back to the room she was fast asleep, the same young, vulnerable look on her face he had observed before. He was finding it hard to reconcile the pretty, innocent looking young girl asleep in bed with the tough, foul-mouthed, experienced woman who had fought in Iraq and frightened off two would-be muggers in the street outside the hotel, who gave him his orders like an Emir then lied her head off to Valérie.

She's a clever woman, he thought to himself. He washed and cleaned his teeth without disturbing her then climbed quietly into the other bed. The smell of her freshly scented body lying so close to him gave him an erection, which kept him awake for a while until the rigours of the two days of travel claimed his consciousness.

THIRTY-THREE

Mosul, Iraq
June 2016

Karl was in a massive warehouse in the north-eastern part of the city, where he'd been assigned to another futile task by Abdullah. The area was vulnerable to aircraft attacks and so far, there had been no meaningful build-up of ground troops, but he knew they would soon come and this would announce the final chapter of ISIL's Mosul occupation. Since the loss of the airport at Qayyarah West, he'd been to the storeroom many times, supervising the transfer of the contents from the original installation in the Nineveh ruins close to the Tigris river.

These days he spent a lot of his time underground and he missed the open desert and savage beauty of the Qayyarah region to the south. This was because during their two years' occupation of Mosul, ISIL engineers had created a new circulation network linking most parts of the city with underground tunnels. Kilometres of passageways had been dug with excavating equipment and the hard labour of thousands of civilian conscripts. Working them until they dropped, exhausted or dead, and were shipped off to the many burial pits and sink holes in the surrounding desert. Karl didn't like the tunnels, but it was preferable to being blown to pieces in the streets above them.

It was after midnight, but he didn't mind wasting his nights on senseless projects that would come to nothing.

He'd already had enough of Ekaterina; she was the stereotype of a Russian woman, no conversation and ferocious in bed. After spending a couple of evenings with her he was happy to get away. He missed the clever, funny, mischievous spirit of the Irish girl, but it was too late to do anything about that; he'd taken his decision and now he had to live with it. *Or probably die with it*, he reminded himself.

Surrounding him in the huge open space were dozens of surface-to-surface rockets bearing Russian inscriptions. A tank of mustard gas chemical agent stood at the far end of the space, covered by a tarpaulin to prevent the fumes from escaping. It was late at night, but there were a dozen men working in the gloomy storeroom. The military council was so convinced the project could change the balance of the war, it had been given top priority and a highly respected senior commander, who unfortunately didn't believe for one moment the plan would come to anything. Several of the missiles had been taken apart and two ISIL fighters were dismantling the warhead from another under the orders of a so-called 'chemical weapons specialist'. The plan was to use the rockets to unleash the deadly chemical against coalition troops when they got around to attacking the north-east sector in the forthcoming battle.

Karl had no confidence that they would manage to arm any of the missiles, much less fire them against the enemy. Despite all the hype around the jihadists' capabilities, he was well placed to know how primitive their skills really were. They could construct tunnels under the streets, but chemical weapons experts they were not; they were more likely to blow up the warehouse with him inside than ever to hurt a coalition soldier. He stood by the warehouse door, breathing in the cool, fresh night air and staying as far away from the noxious material as he could.

He had relocated his command post the previous day to a semi-demolished building in the area after news came to him that the Iraqi army was moving troops up from their main encampment in Makhmur, to start using the airfield as a launch-pad to prepare the ground for a push from the south. He reflected on the advice he had given Abdullah to let the infidels take the airport, but he knew the loss had been inevitable and he had once again helped to save many of his fellow fighters. However, he hadn't expected the US army machine to get the place operational again so quickly. It was ironic that the airfield had been previously called Saddam Airbase and was the main base during the war with Iran. *What goes around comes around*, he said to himself.

Near Gornji Krivodol, South-East Serbia

'We stop here for small time.' Ivan lit a cigarette and took a drag.

The route they'd taken from the pasture land to the border wasn't a track; it was a narrow, tortuous, rocky path, often completely blocked by fallen boulders they had to climb over or around. A stream of rain water ran down towards them as they laboured up the mountainside, soaking their boots and legs under their capes. They had ascended to an altitude of 1,000 m then traversed a high barren ridge, crossing the Bulgaria-

Serbia border in a desolate spot about 3 km east of Gornji Krivodol, a Serbian hamlet, with, according to their guide, a population of only seventeen souls. It was now almost 3:00 am – just another three hours of safe darkness left – and they were sprawled on the ground in the forest on a shoulder of the mountain, just above the village and a kilometre inside the border. The rain had finally let up, but they were tired, cold, wet and muddy, shivering in the early morning mist.

The 16 km they had covered from Berkovitsa seemed to have taken a lifetime, with Hema and Aisha needing assistance on the difficult, dangerous climbs up the slippery, muddy trail. Miraculously, so far, there had been no serious injuries, apart from cuts and bruises from the rocks and viciously spiked bushes which seemed to attack them from every side. The boys had taken their father's rucksack in turns while he carried Lyla, but he was dead on his feet and couldn't continue any longer. Ivan had ended up carrying both daughter's rucksacks, but he didn't dare to use his flashlight and every step in the darkness was a potential accident.

Faqir passed around bread, nuts and water, while Hema tended the damage everyone had suffered from the difficult, dangerous passage. Although Lyla's ankle wasn't any worse, she was in no state to walk, or climb on that perilous path and neither was he.

The local map was still clear in his mind. 'It's still another ten kilometres to Slavinja?' he asked, in a whisper.

The Bulgarian hesitated, 'Maybe. Other way is possible.'

'What do you mean?'

He struggled to explain. 'Walking is 10 km, but this part, go down Gornji Krivodol, very difficult. After is easy walk to Slavinja, but ...' He took another drag on his cigarette.

'What's the problem?

'Here is narrow go down for three kilometres, not easy for girls and woman. Is very ...' He held his hand flat, pointing down.

'It's very steep, like a cliff?'

He nodded, 'Is dangerous in dark, now rain makes very bad.'

'You don't think we can make it?'

He took a drag on his cigarette. 'Now is three o'clock. This part two hours in rain, can be more. You carry little girl, you slow and can make accident. After is more ten kilometres for Slavinja, two hours.' He added the hours on his fingers.

'And it gets light at six-thirty.' Malik was listening attentively.

He nodded. 'Walking in day is dangerous.'

Faqir was tired and worried and now he was becoming annoyed. 'You knew from the beginning I had my whole family with me and they've been excellent, haven't complained once. But they can't go any faster, this route is much too tough for them, especially in the rain. It's too tough for all of us, we're not used to climbing in the mountains, not like you. I can't carry my daughter much longer, it's a miracle we didn't have an accident on that last part. And now you're telling me the next part is worse. What the hell are we supposed to do?'

'Wait, wait, don't make noise, you want get caught? Is other way, is longer but more easy.' He took another drag on his cigarette. 'Can cost some money. You want I try?'

The Iraqi was immediately suspicious. He'd heard too many stories about people smugglers who asked for more money before they completed their job. 'What do you mean by "some money"?'

'Wait.' He pressed a number on his phone.

Malik said, 'You won't get a signal here, we're in the middle of nowhere.'

'Mobile here on border best in Serbia and Bulgaria, many new …' He held his hand up high.

'Transmitters, for the patrols?'

He nodded then spoke rapidly in Serbian for a moment, then, 'Thousand euros car take from near place to Slavinja, no need for climb down. Is OK?'

Faqir looked resignedly at Hema, holding her tired daughters. 'Five hundred extra when we get there.'

'OK. Five hundred.' He spoke into the phone again.

'I think I made a bad deal,' Faqir said as they climbed wearily to their feet. 'He looks too happy.'

THIRTY-FOUR

Paris, France
June 2016

It was a bright, sunny morning when Sami and Ibrahim came down for breakfast. A surly looking woman who spoke no English, brought them croissants and coffee, banging the cups and plates onto the table. She walked away without saying a word.

Sami waited until she'd gone. 'No tip for her,' she whispered.

Ibrahim smiled. He was beginning to enjoy her British sense of humour. She could make a joke out of every situation, not that he always understood her meaning, but he knew she was making fun of something. On the long train journeys from Palermo he'd seen a side to her character that surprised him, it wasn't what he expected from someone who had fought as a Jihadist. Her manner was confident, fresh and enjoyable, humorous and sometimes even raucous, but she was thoughtful, in a simplistic, not a complicated, formulated way. She spoke openly and interestingly about everything she saw and heard, and she made him feel happy.

He realised his life in Germany had lacked fun and laughter. His father, Jabbar, was a taciturn, disappointed man who was forced to give up a good life in Iraq by escaping to a country whose language he didn't speak and whose beliefs he didn't share. He had been a member of Saddam Hussein's Imperial Guard, an immediate priority target for the American forces after the downfall of their leader. After several weeks of hiding, he'd managed to arrange new passports for his family to escape to Lebanon and then Europe, ending up in Germany with nothing but the clothes they wore and Iraqi passports in their new names, guaranteeing them asylum then naturalisation in this adoptive country.

During all the years they had lived in Germany, Jabbar had grieved for his birthplace and never given up hope of returning. Then ISIL had given him motivation and opportunity to take a first step towards that hope, in his own country, Iraq. They didn't care where he came from or why he wanted to fight with them and that all he wanted to do was to take revenge on the regime that had destroyed his life. As Abu bin al Khattab, the skills he had learned under Hussein's regime brought him recognition and rapid promotion. A year later he was killed, four thousand kilometres away from his family, just another victim of Western politics and tribal war in a country that was not even his any longer. With her husband dead, Ibrahim's mother withdrew into a lonely, unhappy existence, not going out and constantly berating him for wanting to throw his life away like his father.

After her illness and his move to live alone in the ill-fated apartment, his brother and sister's visits brought him the happiest moments he had known. Then they had all lost that because of his stupidity. Now, when he prayed, any enjoyment he'd experienced brought him a feeling of guilt. *I don't deserve to be happy*, he told himself. *I deserve only to die making it right.* But with

Sami he felt happy and he didn't feel guilty. This made him feel guilty.

Neither of them had previously visited Paris. It was a fine morning and with a map from Valerie they went out to visit the city. First, he bought a Bouygues SIM card for his phone, in case he had to contact Christian or Karl. Then for three hours they wandered around, until their feet hurt. They bought sandwiches and soft drinks and went into the *Jardin des Tuileries*. It was warm and they sat for a while, saying nothing, just enjoying the quiet. Ibrahim brought his mind back to their mission. *Discipline*, he said to himself. *We must stick to discipline*.

He turned to Sami, a strict expression on his face. 'I think you must tell me about going to England and the rest of Karl's instructions. I know you are my partner, but this is my mission and I have to know everything to make sure we execute it properly.'

Sami supressed a smile. She wasn't at all upset by this mild outburst. She sympathised with his discomfort at being answerable to a woman and had been waiting for him to insist on taking control of the project. She was only surprised it had taken so long. Karl was his Emir and she had been his wife, so Ibrahim hadn't dared to make a fuss, until now.

She looked around; there was no one nearby. 'Tomorrow, we have to take a train to a place called Lannion, it's about four hours from here, in northern France. We take the train from Montparnasse station that leaves just after five o'clock. It gets in at quarter past nine, it'll be dark and it's a small town, so there shouldn't be many people around.'

'How much does it cost?'

'Only 40 euros, but then we have a big expense. How much have we got left?'

'After what we gave to Valérie, about four and a half thousand. What's the big expense?'

'When we get to Lannion, someone will meet us at the train station, a Spanish guy called Miguel Novarro. He's seen a photo of me and we have passwords, it's "Redemption", then "Liberation".' Ibrahim was listening closely, trying to memorise everything as she had done. She went on, 'We give him 3,000 euros and he'll drive us to a village called Louannec, on the coast.'

He looked shocked. 'Three thousand? That's most of our money. We can't give so much away, and to someone we've never met. How do you know we can trust him?'

'Karl knows him. He's a Basque separatist from San Sebastian. He was a member of ETA and blew up a train or something in 2001. Anyway, he's still a revolutionary and he supports our movement. Karl told me we can trust him completely.'

Ibrahim looked sceptical, 'What does he do for all that money?'

'He takes us across the Channel to England in a fishing boat, a high speed one. It takes about six hours, so we can set off after dark and get there before light. The immigrant smugglers are charging people three or four thousand each, so it's not a lot.' He was shaking his head. 'What's wrong?'

'It's too much. That leaves one and a half thousand to

buy the materials, but we have to have somewhere to live and that's what costs the most.'

'Wait, that's the best part, there's an empty flat that won't cost anything. We land on the south coast then take a train to a town called Guildford, it's near London. That's where the flat is. I know the address and I've got a key.' She pulled out the chain around her neck and jangled the key. 'We won't have many expenses once we're there.'

He looked at her in astonishment. 'Karl's got everything worked out, hasn't he? What's the address?'

'Flat 1, 18 Watson Avenue, Guildford. It's not far from the station, on the ground floor and quite big. There's plenty of supermarkets and stores around to buy what you need.'

'What happens when we get there?'

'We contact Christian and he'll send us an internet address to get the instructions for the mission. Then we have to work quickly to get it done. Karl wants it to happen before something happens to him in Mosul.'

'Do you already know the target? So we can start planning the attack?'

'No. We won't find out until we get to England in case we get stopped and questioned. He's right about that, I'm not very good at keeping me mouth shut.'

Still delving through her memory, she went on, 'We have to change the euros for English pounds. I've got the address of a foreign exchange office. We should go there now, it's not far from here.' She gave him a wan smile, 'There. That's everything Karl told me. Now we both know the same. Is that better?'

He realised she had understood his discomfort, not feeling in charge of the operation, having to ask her for instructions, feeling foolish, being ordered about by a girl. 'Thanks, Sarah,' he said.

'Sure, that's OK,' she answered. She wondered if he'd noticed that she was trying not to swear so much. Swearing was almost an obligatory part of the Irish vocabulary, but she knew Ibrahim didn't like it. Sami wanted this mission to go well. She owed it to Karl and she was ready to do anything to make it successful, for him.

At the Hotel Olympia, Nina Barras, the waitress-cum-cleaner, finished making the bed in room seventeen. She wiped a cloth quickly over the bathroom sink and bath and folded the end of the toilet roll to make it look like a professional job. There were a few bits and pieces in the rubbish bin and she emptied them into her bucket. A screwed-up paper fell on the floor. Nina was a nosy, suspicious woman and she flattened it out and read it. It was a printed receipt from a railway ticket machine for two single tickets from Geneva to Paris on the TGV. It was damp and smudged and she couldn't read the date. She threw it in her bucket and went out, leaving the room pretty much as she'd found it.

THIRTY-FIVE

Slavinja, South-East Serbia
June 2016

Faqir was counting his money, something he did frequently now. After paying another 3,000 euros to Ivan, his family had almost exactly 28,000 left – 7,000 each. *Just over half of what we started with two weeks ago. Fourteen days on the road and we're only as far as Serbia, not even in Western Europe yet. How are we going to make it?*

After Ivan's phone call, they had hiked along the ridge above Gornji Krivodol to Baljev Dol, an even smaller settlement of just eight residents. The rain had stopped but a cold wind was blowing and they shivered in their damp clothing as their guide led them down an easy slope to the local road for Slavinja. He and Faqir had taken turns to carry Lyla and the boys had done their share. Somehow, they all made it in one piece. Ivan's Serbian brother-in-law, Vlado, an unshaven slovenly looking man, was waiting for them in his battered Transit van and at 5:30 am on Sunday morning, they arrived at his house in Slavinja, 11 km inside the Serbian border.

His wife, Boyka, a tired, disappointed looking woman of about forty gave them a mug of hot tea and had boiled pans of water to fill a tin bath. They washed the mud and dirt from their limbs then dried themselves off and changed out of their damp clothing. She had prepared a thick, spicy soup and they sat around the kitchen table, exhausted but starving, enjoying the hot broth with chunks of homemade bread.

Vlado spoke no English, but Boyka had worked as a maid for an English family in Sofia and spoke it quite well. When Hamid asked if they'd seen many refugees, she exchanged glances with her husband and said nothing more. Since Ivan had spoken of helping one hundred refugees, they assumed their dwelling was a kind of half-way house; it was certainly well placed for that purpose.

Ivan and Vlado went off in the van, promising that Vlado would return to transport them from the house to the bus station the following morning. Then Boyka took them down a narrow staircase to a stone-floored cellar with mattresses and blankets on the floor. Fortunately, it was too dark to reveal the condition of the makeshift beds, but they were too tired to worry about it; at least they were dry, out of sight and safe for the rest of the night.

It was now four in the afternoon and after a few hours of sleep, a wash in freezing cold water and a lunch of home-baked bread and fresh goat's cheese, Faqir was ready to organise the next stage of their seemingly interminable journey. He consulted his map then called the next number stored on his phone. Ivan had been right, the connection was good and a moment later he was through to someone who spoke excellent English, in Novi Pazar, 200 km away in south-west Serbia. Once again, he found himself arranging services to be rendered by foreigners in far off places. Faqir was becoming tired of the stress and worry of putting the safety of his family into the hands of strangers, but he had no choice.

Düsseldorf, Germany

The police TV announcement went out in Germany on Thursday, several times during the day and again in the evening news programme. It was retransmitted there and by a few other national TV stations that night and the following morning. Max Kellerman's boss, Lieutenant Eric Schuster, handled the item, generously not casting blame on Max, but trying desperately to reignite interest in the story, without much hope. The attention span in the modern age being as short as it is, the number of countries where the item was retransmitted was small. The event was old and there was nothing to report except that a suspected terrorist was still on the run, probably somewhere in Europe. He was one of the two shown in the photographs, but it had still not been established which of them he was. The only real change was the increase in the reward from 50,000 to 100,000 euros. Because of the state of emergency still in force in France, the announcement was given greater exposure there and was shown on the hourly news bulletins all that evening and the whole of the next day.

Mosul, Iraq

From his vantage point on top of the university building, Karl could see flames lighting up the night sky far in the distance, to the south. There were half a dozen fires in the area around Qayyarah and Makhmur and several more to the east, near the Kurdish zone, the territory that had been retaken by the Iraqi army with US assistance the previous month. The fires were from burning oil wells, blown up and ignited by ISIL fighters still encircled in the region. During the day the cloud of smoke was more and more visible, gradually expanding on the horizon.

At least we learned something from Saddam, he thought cynically. The scorched earth policy Hussein had employed after his failed invasion of Kuwait when retreating from the allied forces in 1991. Saad, Karl's replacement as ISIL Qayyarah commander, had issued instructions to the trapped militants to burn and destroy everything in sight, to prevent the liberated population recovering from the nightmare occupation they'd suffered, and prolong their misery as much as possible. A secondary advantage was that the black, noxious smoke that billowed out for hundreds of metres around and above the fires literally created a smoke screen which made allied air attacks more difficult. The technique involved was primitive but effective; the jihadists rigged the oil heads with explosives then shot at them from a safe distance until the explosions ignited the oil. To prevent Iraqi firefighter teams from extinguishing the fires, they then planted improvised explosive devices in the desert surrounding the wells.

Once again, Karl despaired at the regime's blind determination to create nothing and destroy everything. The Iraqi people would never forgive the inhuman suffering and destruction their occupation had visited upon them. Any feelings of sympathy for the ISIL cause, once a noble fight against the infidel, had been extinguished by the callous brutality of their rule. Every action of this kind, he knew, was another nail in their coffin; when the coalition forces finally reached the gates of Mosul, the people would open them eagerly and welcome them as saviours, not invaders.

He still missed being in Qayyarah; despite its endless battles for survival, the countless deaths of his fighting brothers and gradual loss of their surrounding territories, the desert was where he belonged and where he couldn't wait to return. With each day that passed he felt more and more frustrated and useless, trapped in Mosul, a city that was being destroyed, its history and future disintegrating until soon, no one would remember what it had been like, or even that it had existed.

He looked at the time; it was nearly midnight and he had a busy day ahead, to be culminated by a meeting of the commanders, called by his boss, Abdullah. *I can hardly wait.* He went back to the Beirut Hotel on his motorbike. He was still sleeping there, but alone – he hadn't felt like company since Sami had left. He knew the reason, but it didn't help to think about it.

THIRTY-SIX

Pirot, South-East Serbia
June 2016

On Thursday morning, the Al-Douris were in a queue for the bus to Niš, the first stop on their nine-hour trip to Novi Pazar, 200 km away to the west, on the other side of Serbia. Apart from a few sniffles, no one seemed to have suffered any serious effects from their perilous passage over the cold, wet, inhospitable, mountain range and they were now resigned to the prospect of another interminable bus ride. Boyka had sent them off in the van with Vlado at 7:00 am for the 20 km drive to Pirot, the largest town in the area. She had prepared sandwiches and fruit for them and changed 200 euros into enough Serbian dinars to cover the cost of their tickets and expenses on the journey. After helping them with the ticket machine, her surly husband drove off without a word and left them to the fifteen-minute wait for the bus. There were already about twenty people queuing and when it arrived, Faqir's family were still at the back of the line, trying to look like casual tourists in the middle of the Serbian town.

As the incoming passengers descended from the bus carrying bags, cartons, crates of chickens, even rabbits and small pigs, Hema grabbed Faqir's arm, 'Look, police, across the square,' she whispered.

The two police officers strolled over to the terminus and started checking the arriving passengers' papers.

The Iraqi smiled confidently and squeezed his wife's arm, saying nothing, while their well-rehearsed children chattered in English. Inside, he was desperately wondering, *how in the Lord's name are we going to get through a Serbian police check with Iraqi passports and invalid Turkish visas?*

The last arrival left the bus and the queue began to move forward, the officers examining each passenger's documents carefully. Faqir delved into his bag and retrieved their passports and the defunct visas, in a vain attempt to look as if they had the necessary documentation. He joined in with his family's English chatter, laughing and smiling as if they were on holiday, but his mouth was dry and his heart beat faster with every step towards the head of the queue. He knew they would never get past this checkpoint.

There were now only two groups ahead of them, a couple with a child and two young men with backpacks, one minute more and it would all be for nothing. Faqir was considering turning around and walking away from the bus stop, even though that would send the same signal as having no documents.

The officers were now handing back the couple's papers. He whispered to Hema, 'Shall we make a run for it?'

Just then, the two men in front of them raced away from the queue and down a narrow street leading to the town centre. The officers pulled out their pistols but couldn't shoot in the crowded square. One of them fired into the air and the other pulled out his walkie-talkie and they both sprinted off to follow the two fugitives.

Faqir's heart was still racing and he was soaked with sweat when the bus pulled away, his family on board and safe, at least for now.

The children settled down, relieved and chattering happily, knowing how close they'd been to disaster. Hema took his hand and kissed him on the cheek, 'Thank God for those other refugees,' she said. 'But that's twice it's happened and I think we're running out of miracles.'

English Channel, France-UK

The boat was called Cabaret and it was a 1992 French-built twelve-metre aluminium *bateau de pêche*. The original Nanni shaft drive had been augmented by two Mercury Optimax 200 HP outboard motors. The vessel was more like a low flying aircraft than a fishing boat, speeding over the water like a hovercraft. Miguel opened it up when they reached international waters, quickly reaching 25 knots, equivalent to 46 km/hour. He pulled back to a steady cruising speed of twenty-two, which would get them to the UK coast in five hours. The water was choppy and it was a dark and rainy night, with poor visibility.

They had left the hotel at twelve-thirty that afternoon to take the *RER* to Montparnasse station, Valérie wishing them '*Bonne chance*', and kissing Sami on both cheeks. She knew where the CCTV camera was in the hall and avoided looking at it, keeping her head down whenever she was in range. Ibrahim looked at the floor and mumbled a quick '*au revoir*' as he hurried out the door with their bags. At the station, he bought two special excursion tickets from a machine on the platform for the

5:08 pm train. It was a three-stage journey; a TGV to Rennes, then two normal SNCF trains to Plouaret then Lannion. At the exchange bureau they had bought 1,200 pounds sterling, which Ibrahim stored in the zipped pocket in Hassan's hooded jerkin, together with the 3,000 euros for Miguel. They had several hours to wait and went to a nearby fried chicken restaurant to spend their few remaining euros on calories before the journey.

It was still sunny and bright when they set off, but the weather became progressively worse as they went further north. By the time they reached Lannion, it was dark outside the carriage window, the rain was pouring down and a heavy mist had rolled in from the sea. On the last leg an inspector passed through checking tickets. Sami spotted him in the next carriage and sent Ibrahim off to the lavatory. She showed both tickets and said in her exaggerated English, 'My fiancé's in the toilet. Awfully sorry.' The man checked the tickets then asked for her ID. 'Certainly,' she smiled, and handed over the ID card given to her in Mosul in the name of Sarah Callaghan.

He gave it a cursory glance. '*Merci, mademoiselle,*' he muttered and moved on.

At nine-fifteen they walked out of Lannion station into a freezing fog and took shelter from the rain under the roof of the station café. Ibrahim was glad Sami had insisted on him buying a waterproof hooded windcheater to put over the sweater, 'You'll need it when we get to England,' she'd told him. 'It's always cold there.' They fastened their jackets up to the neck and waited, shivering in the cold damp and looking nervously around as the other passengers came out. After a few minutes, a small man smoking a cigarette and carrying an umbrella came up to them. He was dressed in dirty yellow oilskins and appeared to be in his mid-fifties, slim and fit-looking.

'*Bonsoir*, Sarah?' he said.

'*Bonsoir*, Miguel. Redemption.'

'*Liberation*,' he replied. He pronounced it in the French way, *leeberaassion*. 'This way.' He held the umbrella over them and they walked to an old blue Renault. By now, the other passengers from the train had dispersed and the street was deserted. He asked them a number of casual questions about their trip as they drove and they realised he was quite fluent in English. Twenty minutes later he parked the car in a yard beside the dark, deserted harbour and they went to a boat tied up alongside. The rain was still falling steadily and the mist had now become a fog.

Sami smiled to herself when Miguel said, 'We're lucky with the weather. It hasn't rained for a week, it's a good sign.'

'Sounds like an Irishman,' she whispered. Ibrahim laughed nervously, without understanding the remark.

A taller man in similar dress said 'hello' and helped them over the side of the vessel. 'This is my brother, Eladio, his English is OK, but not so good,' Miguel told them.

Miguel took them into the wheelhouse. 'You have the money?'

'Here, 3,000 euros.' Ibrahim reluctantly took the bundle of notes from his jacket pocket and the man counted them carefully.

'*Excellent, merci*.' He shoved the money into his pocket

and nodded to his brother who took their bags down a few steps to a cabin below the deck. From the feeble light cast from the wheelhouse they could see there was no other superstructure; the back of the boat comprised a flat aluminium deck with a couple of hatches cut into it. A winch was positioned on the stern, with ropes and folded nets attached to it. The whole boat stunk strongly of fish.

Eladio came back and climbed out onto the quay to untie the boat, while Miguel led them down to the cabin. It was fitted with vertical timber wall cladding and had about one metre seventy of headroom, almost enough for Sami, but Ibrahim had to duck well down. Two bunks were fitted on either side and there was a metre-wide cupboard built into the wall between them.

'Look here,' he said and pulled open the doors of the cupboard. Inside, three shelves ran across the back wall and the whole cupboard was filled with life jackets, ropes, wellingtons, storm oilskins and other gear. 'Help me take these out.'

They pulled the material out of the cupboard until it was empty, then he unscrewed the lower shelf from the two central support brackets and pulled it out. A joint in the wood ran across the planking where the shelf had been. Miguel removed the screws around the section then pulled it away, leaving an aperture the width of the cupboard and forty centimetres high. He shone a torch into the gap; the space inside was at least two metres wide and a metre and a half deep. The floor and walls were covered in stick-on squares of brown carpet. There was a mattress with a folded blanket lying on it.

Sami looked at the aperture with a sinking stomach. She'd always had a fear of being trapped in small spaces, but she just said, 'That's a clever hideaway. You must have used it before?'

The Spaniard didn't answer. 'Put your bags in there and get in to try it,' he instructed them, handing her the torch.

She climbed through the opening and Ibrahim passed the backpacks and wheelie bag to her then managed to squeeze through beside her. The mattress on the floor smelled damp but was clean. She spread the blanket on it and they laid side by side with the wooden ceiling a metre above them. Above, they heard the sound of the ignition turning until the motor fired and settled into a constant hum behind them and they could feel the rocking of the boat as it pulled away from the dockside and started to move slowly out of the harbour.

'You only need to go in here if a customs or immigration officer comes aboard. For a half hour maybe, not more. Is it OK?'

'I think I can manage it, but not for too long.' Sami was supressing the feeling of claustrophobia that invaded her senses. 'Are you alright, Ali?'

'Can we keep the torch on?' he asked, aware that Sami wasn't comfortable.

'No light. It might shine through a crack in the wood.'

'Don't worry, I'll be OK.' She squeezed his hand, grateful for his concern.

'Good, we'll leave it open. We might not have long to prepare it, we have to be ready.' He chose two of the jackets. 'Put these on, you'll be warmer and it might get rough.'

As they climbed back on deck, the boat lurched sideways. Sami gave a scream and grabbed Ibrahim's arm. '*C'est bon, relax.*' Eladio pulled her into the wheelhouse. 'It's because we're leaving the harbour, the sea is good tonight, not like sometimes.' He switched off the interior light and they were surrounded by impenetrable darkness.

The boat headed out into the open sea and Miguel gave them a quick explanation of their course. 'We go north past Guernsey then north-east to Weymouth. There's no more ferries running at this time, so it should be quiet. The route is longer but we can go fast and the immigration checking is not so much. Most traffic is coming from Guernsey or Jersey where they have good immigration control, so there's less in Weymouth.'

Ibrahim asked, 'Where is this place we're going to?'

'It's a small town, near Torquay, that's bigger and has a lot more boats coming in. There's a ferry port in Weymouth where the Border Force operates, but it's closed because there's no ferries. Next to it is a marina for private yachts and it's not busy at night, that's where we're going. It should take six or seven hours so we'll arrive at four or five in the morning when it's still dark and there should be no one around.'

'What about the Border Force on the water?' Sami knew the UK had patrol boats looking out for illegal traffic.

'We'll see them if they're coming our way. We navigate with radar, but we've got AIS equipment with GPS that we switch on and off to see where the other traffic is, but not long enough to be noticed. We haven't filed a sea route with the French Coastguard, but we've done this run many times and I know what to say if we get stopped. We'll have no problems.'

'*Inshallah*,' they both said in unison.

They had now reached their cruising speed and the boat settled into a moderate rhythmic forward pitching movement. 'There's some sandwiches and water in the cabin,' Miguel told them. 'You should eat something then get some sleep, it's another five or six hours until we reach UK waters, so it's a good time to rest.'

Ibrahim and Sami were awakened by Miguel shaking them at four-thirty in the morning. Panicked, Sami asked, 'What's happened? Is something wrong?'

'There's a patrol boat showing on the GPS and he'll see us. We've slowed down and put the sailing lights on to look normal, so you'll have to get in the hiding place in case they come aboard.'

The boat was rocking badly and Sami was starting to feel sickly. 'How long before we arrive?'

'We've only got half hour to run if they don't waste our time. But get inside the cupboard now or we run a risk. You should only be in there for a short time.'

They climbed into the cavity, Sami supressing her nervousness and nausea. A few minutes later, they were lying side by side on the blanket covered mattress and could hear Miguel screwing back the shelf and stacking the material into the cupboard. Then the engine noise became quieter and they realised the boat was slowing down. As it went slower, the sickly motion became more pronounced and Sami felt worse. She squeezed Ibrahim's hand, trying to overcome the feeling.

'Are you OK?'

'I feel shitty, but I'll be fine.'

'Here.' He passed her the bottle of water he'd brought in. 'Drink some and it'll help.'

'Thanks. Sorry to be a wimp.'

A few minutes later, they felt the boat slow down completely until it was rocking and swaying like a cork from the sideways swell. Sami wanted to throw up, but she managed to hold it off, sitting with her head between her legs and breathing deeply. Ibrahim sat up with her and held her hand tightly. 'You're doing great,' he whispered, 'Miguel said it won't be long.'

He's a thoughtful guy, she said to herself. *One of the nicest jihadists I've met.*

Now they could hear men's voices from above deck and after a few minutes the sound of someone coming down the stairwell. Miguel said, 'We're loading English cheeses from Torquay. There's a big demand in France for English cheese.'

A man's voice said, 'Why did you come over in the middle of the night?'

'So we can load early and get back the same day. We do this run from St Malo every week, if the weather's good. That's why we've got the two Mercury's, we're the only boat this size that can do it so fast. It gets picked up by the distributor this afternoon and it's in the shops by tomorrow, still fresh.'

'Who slept here?' They heard him walking around the cabin, picking up things.

'I had a couple of hours, then my brother. It's a long trip.'

'What's in there?' Now the cupboard door opened and they tried not to make a sound, not even to breathe. Sami squeezed Ibrahim's hand so tightly he almost winced, but he kept silent. Sitting close to her in the dark, confined space, he could smell the fear and sweat on her skin, mixed with the scent of the bath essence. He had never known such an erotic sensation. Despite the imminent danger just a few feet away, he felt his penis harden. He kept his knees together and wrapped his arm around them so she wouldn't notice. *It's not a good time for this,* he thought to himself.

Miguel said, 'Just what you see, bad weather and rescue stuff. Should I take it out?'

'Yes. Empty the cupboard.'

He pulled the material out then a knocking sound came from the panel, top sides and bottom and they heard the shelves being tugged and tested. 'Take the shelves out, will you?'

'I'll need a screwdriver. Just a minute.'

A moment later they heard Miguel attacking the screws. Sami bit her fingers to stop her teeth from chattering with fear. It also eased the mounting feeling of sickness that threatened to overcome her. Ibrahim thought of his family, the grief, the planning and patience that had gone into his long journey that might now be brought to an end. The erection went away and he held her other hand tightly, breathing quietly through his mouth, pushing away the black thoughts that tried to enter his mind.

Then Miguel said, 'By the way, where's Roger?'

'Roger?'

'The guy who usually comes aboard, big guy with a limp, speaks a bit of French. Is he OK?'

'Oh, Roj. You know him? His wife's having a baby.'

'*Quelle belle nouvelle.* Tell him *félicitations* from Miguel.'

'You should've said you know him. No need to waste time here. Don't bother with that cupboard. What's under the main deck?'

'Apart from the engine, there's the fridge. Now it's mainly for the foie gras or some of the soft cheeses we carry. We hardly fish anymore now, there's no point.'

'Are you carrying anything now?'

'Foie gras, like we always do. The best in France. Come and I'll show you.'

'I'll need to see the paperwork as well.'

The footsteps went away and up the stairs. After a while they heard the ignition whining and the engine firing then the rocking became a steady rhythm again. The panel came down and Miguel's face appeared. '*Tout va bien,*' he said. 'Those *imbéciles* are gone.'

Sami climbed out and ran up the stairs to puke over the side. 'Jesus,' she said, 'that was worse than Mosul.'

THIRTY-SEVEN

'What a journey, thank the Lord it's over.' Hema stretched her body to get rid of the aches and pains inflicted by their exhausting trip from Pirot. The nine-hour drive had taken more than ten, due to the complications of changing buses three times in a disorganised country where they couldn't speak a word of the language. A third of their marathon 275 km route was to circumvent the border of Albania, which jutted out 50 km into Serbia at that point. At 6:00 pm they had finally arrived in the small town of Novi Pazar, a relic of the Ottoman Empire. The *Sanjak* was situated in a tiny corner of Serbian territory, surrounded on the south by Albania, the west by Montenegro and Bosnia Herzegovina, and the east by the disputed territory of Kosovo.

They were now in the Mika Guesthouse, where they had obtained three rooms for 75 euros including supper and breakfast. Faqir couldn't wait to have a few hours of rest, but first he had to organise the next stage of their marathon. He washed to get rid of the dust and sweat and made sure his family were comfortable. Since they'd done no walking or climbing that day, the bruise on Lyla's ankle was mending. Hema rubbed on some ointment and bound it up again; they had one more hike ahead of them and needed to be in good shape.

'I'm going to call the last number on Tony's list, I

won't be long.' He went outside with his map and phone, praying once again the contact would be honest and efficient. He knew their luck wouldn't last forever, but he had no option but to follow the plan and trust in God.

Guildford, England

Ibrahim and Sami arrived in Guildford on Friday, the day after leaving France. Miguel dropped them at the marina in Weymouth at 5:30 am, then the Cabaret headed for Torquay to pick up a cargo of cheese, just as he'd told the Border Force officer. What he hadn't told them was that he was taking it back to Cherbourg, about 100 km east of Lannion, where he and his brother lived and where the Cabaret was registered. The officer hadn't asked this and it would turn out to be important.

Sami had been right about the weather – it was cold and raining and they were glad of their hooded anoraks as they trudged the ten-minute walk to the station. The first train was at 6:25 am and they arrived at their destination at nine-fifteen, having slept for most of the journey. A town map from the station gave them the bus routes. Watson Avenue was on the west side of town, just three stops away and number eighteen was only fifty metres from the bus stop, an old three-storey building with six flats. Number one was on the ground floor, with a door to the side of the building, away from the entrance hall for the other apartments. Karl had been painstaking in his choice of accommodation.

'That's a relief!' Sami opened the mail box with the

key on her necklace and found the front door Yale key taped on the inside.

The two-bedroomed flat was bright with a small kitchen and a living room, furnished with shabby but comfortable items. Ibrahim was relieved; living and sleeping in the same bedroom as Sami for a week had strained his emotions to breaking point, even though after their conversation in the *Jardin des Tuileries* in Paris, she had tried to become more demure in her behaviour. She realised he was uncomfortable when she used bad language, undressed in front of him or didn't respect his privacy. Sami wasn't used to that, neither in Northern Ireland nor Iraq and she tried her best not to embarrass him and he had noticed. Even so, just sitting next to her in their room, on the trains and buses, or lying close to her in the night and hearing her breathing, smelling her body, either after a bath or when she was sweaty and tired from travelling had become more than he could bear.

He had stopped looking at ISIL propaganda on his laptop; it excited him too much and he was having enough trouble coping with his reactions to Sami's presence. The night before they left Paris for England, lying in the bed next to her, breathing in her perfumed fragrance, he had another erection. After an hour of trying to get to sleep, he was obliged to go into the toilet to masturbate. Afterwards Ibrahim went down on his knees and recited a catechism he'd composed to help him overcome these lapses; *Allah, merciful Allah, help me be stronger. Help me to concentrate on my mission and ignore these feelings of human weakness. I will not fail you this time. Please help me to be stronger, to serve you without weakening again.*

Now they were in England, finally preparing for their assignment, he was determined to be strong. Nothing must get in the way of the mission; nothing else mattered but making a success of this second chance.

Paris, France

Nina Barras finished cleaning room seventeen then went to see Valérie. 'Will you need me any more today?' She'd started at six that morning and wanted to get home to make lunch for her daughter, who was looked after by her mother when she was working.

Valérie consulted the reservations, it didn't take very long. 'I don't think so. We've now got only eight and ten occupied and they're both leaving by lunchtime. The next three bookings are arriving tomorrow and you've already prepared those rooms, so come in early in the morning to finish off the other two and we'll be ready. Why don't you take the rest of the day off and go look after Candice?' Valérie didn't much like the woman, but Nina needed the work, which made her cheap and flexible and that suited their present predicament.

Nina had a small TV set in the kitchen of her flat. She hadn't seen the news for a few days and switched on the midday bulletin to catch up, in time to see a retransmission of Eric Schuster's press conference. She saw the photo of Ibrahim and her heart leapt. Schuster was saying, 'A reward of 100,000 euros will be paid to anyone who provides information leading to the arrest of the suspected terrorist.' Among the several European hotline numbers listed was one in France. Nina scribbled down the number then pressed the keys on her mobile with trembling fingers.

Düsseldorf, Germany

'You've been vindicated, Max. Apologies from everyone concerned, you were right and we were wrong.'

'Why, what's happened?'

'I just received a call from a Superintendent Robert Massinet, at RAID, in Paris.' The French anti-terrorist unit, *Recherche, Assistance, Intervention, Dissuasion* – Search, Assistance, Intervention, Deterrence – was commonly abbreviated as RAID. 'A Parisian woman, Nina Barras, called their hotline number and identified Ibrahim bin Omar al-Ahmad from the TV retransmission. He was staying in the hotel where she works and she saw the news item at lunchtime today. Officers have been to the hotel and confirmed the identity with her and the owner. Ibrahim's grown a beard in the meanwhile, but they said there's no question it was him. He paid cash and there was no record or photo in the register. That's why they didn't get anything from the hotel reporting system.'

'Yes! I knew it.' Max sat back in his chair, relishing the moment; he'd been certain he was right all along.

'But I've got even more interesting news for you.' Eric Schuster's eyes glistened behind the thick lenses of his spectacles.

'I'm listening. Take your time, enjoy yourself. It's not as if it's urgent or anything.'

'There's a woman travelling with him. An English woman!'

'What? Where did he pick her up?' Now Max's pulse was accelerating. 'Do we have a picture of her, a name, fingerprints?'

'There's a CCTV camera in the entrance, but they arrived together very late on Monday night and the owner had switched it off, so there's nothing there. They're on film when they left yesterday lunchtime, but both of them are looking down all the time and you can't see their faces.'

'Shit! So what do we have?'

'The room hadn't been used for a long time, so we might pick some prints. They're working on a photofit likeness with the two women and drawing a beard on his photo. The booking was made online under the name of Mr & Mrs el Zafar and the English woman gave her name as Sarah and his as Ali, that's all.'

'So he's dropped Hassan Al-Balawi and is going under the name of Ali el Zafar. They heard no other names?'

'Nothing at all. Apparently, the woman did all the talking and spun a tale about going to Italy to be married at her cousin's place, but it makes no sense.'

'What part makes no sense?'

'Well, all of it, obviously, but Nina says she cleaned their room yesterday and found a railway receipt for the TGV from Geneva to Paris. Geneva's closer to Italy than Paris, so if they'd just arrived I doubt they'd be going there.'

'Does she still have the ticket?'

'She threw it away, no way we can find it. Forensics are at the hotel, we'll see what they dig up.'

'Where's the hotel?'

'Near the *Gare de Lyon*.'

'So it could be Geneva. Is she certain it was Ibrahim?'

'They're both absolutely sure. The owner is royally pissed off. I suppose she was taken in by the story and tried to do them a good turn. Now she's been arrested for infringing the laws on guest registration and tax evasion. With all the terrorist problems in France, she's going to be in deep shit.'

'And I'm back on the case?'

'I just talked with *BFE+* in Berlin. Since the fugitives have exited German territory, they're stepping out of the picture. They've got very few people and a shitload of ongoing investigations. We want you to take over and coordinate with Massinet to find them in France. Starting with checks on trains, buses etc. out of Paris. They must have left the city yesterday afternoon after they moved out of the hotel. You can organise joint press releases as soon as we get the full report and any other information from forensics.

'Anyway,' continued Schuster, 'I don't have to tell you what to do, you've done better than any of us in working out who we should have been looking for. I'm sorry, Max, sometimes protocol gets in the way. The top brass decided to do it their way last time. This time you can do it your way.'

Max went over to his wall chart and added the latest information. He rearranged a number of pieces of the jigsaw puzzle and drew connecting lines. He could almost see a picture emerging.

THIRTY-EIGHT

Düsseldorf, Germany
June 2016

Max Kellerman was on German TV at seven o'clock on Friday evening – the same time as a French press conference held by Robert Massinet. They had talked that afternoon and agreed to run parallel public appeals. Max was surprised the Frenchman hadn't tried to take full control of the search, which was now concentrated on French territory, but Schuster had obviously spoken convincingly of his understanding of Ibrahim's thinking and likely movements and they agreed to work together until something new came up. Both men boasted proudly of the Europe-wide capabilities of the Atlas Network to locate and neutralise suspected terrorists in the shortest possible time.

The photofit likeness and description showed a slim young woman of about twenty, one metre seventy-five and fair hair tied in a ponytail, they couldn't agree on the colour of the eyes. *Quite pretty*, he thought, *I wonder how they met, why she's with him, what's her job*. The fingerprints lifted from the hotel room were of a man and a woman, but they hadn't matched anything on any database, which probably meant neither had been arrested. He mentioned that the woman had spoken with a high-class English accent, probably from the London area. Ibrahim's photo had been upgraded and enlarged, including the beard. Both policemen emphasised that he was still travelling with Hassan's passport and his photo was shown again with his full name. However, to confuse things even more, they revealed that Ibrahim might now be calling himself Ali el Zafar and the woman appeared to be travelling under the name of Sarah, which was probably not her real name.

Massinet agreed to be deliberately vague about where they were heading or had come from, stating only that they were likely to be travelling from Paris to another destination in Europe. Max was still cautious about the information they'd gleaned from the two women at the hotel. There was no confirmation of any direction they were taking and he was wary of the existence of the ticket receipt; it was just too convenient. They had only the word of the woman, Nina, that it existed and she'd said she couldn't read the date. It could have been lying in the waste bin for days, if it was ever there at all. The proximity of the hotel to the *Gare de Lyon* probably confirmed they arrived on a TGV, but it could have been from a number of places. CCTV footage from all the recent arrivals and departures was being examined, but it would take time to process so much data and once again they were a day late.

After his initial enthusiasm, Kellerman was very unhappy with the confusion around the identities, travel details and the lack of any reliable facts on which they could base a sensible plan of action. He was beginning to regret his eagerness to take the case back; it might end up being a huge embarrassment. *Maybe that's why Massinet agreed to play second fiddle to me,* he said to himself.

The reward also presented a problem; *if we had*

caught them as a result of Nina's information, she would get 100K. But if someone else now identifies them and they're found then they should get it. He decided to leave that conundrum to his superiors and announced the same reward again, 100,000 euros. That might bring a quick arrest and whatever the cost, it was worth it.

Guildford, England

'I need to get another set of instructions to make the TATP.' Ibrahim was typing an email to Christian. *Arrived safely. Need manufacturing instructions. Tx.* 'I think I remember how to do it, but it's better to have the full details again to be sure. We'll check the list for everything we need and where to buy it, so there's no mistakes. Then we have to find out the target and go to visit the place to check it for access, security, and when there's the largest crowds of people. We need to make sure about everything to execute our mission successfully. And it's best to do it first before we start work on the explosives.'

She smiled at the explanation, knowing he wanted to sound important and knowledgeable. *Like most men do,* she thought, *but it doesn't matter, as long as he knows what he's doing and we get the job done.*

It was Friday evening and Sami had returned from the supermarket with groceries, soft drinks and toilet items, hopefully everything they needed for at least a week. It was still raining, and she had invested in an Arriva bus card which would take her all over the town, making sure no one saw her often enough to remember her.

She had also bought a couple of O2 SIMs for their mobiles and while she put the items away, Ibrahim sent off his message to Christian at the Sri Lanka address and swapped the Bouygues French SIMs for the O2 ones. There was an HP printer in the flat and he had downloaded the software onto his laptop, ready to print out everything as it became available. He put on his hoodie and went to a nearby café, bringing back a couple of pizzas. There was a TV in the living room and while she prepared a salad he switched on the BBC evening news, one of the few channels it would receive.

He watched in shock as he saw Max Kellerman walk up to the microphone to give his press conference. After listening to the first few words of the speech, he called, 'Sami, come here, I think we're in trouble.'

'Oh shit!' She came and sat close to him, grabbing his hand, trying to prevent her own from trembling as they watched his announcement. Ibrahim's photo with the improvised beard was quite clear and her photofit likeness was not a bad one. It was followed by a quick extract from a French TV conference, which stated that RAID, the French counter-terrorism unit, was actively involved under the auspices of a European anti-terrorism network called Atlas.

He switched off the TV and looked nervously at her. 'He's the policeman who was at the apartment after the explosion. I've seen him on TV a few times. What do you think?'

It's not the time to panic, she told herself, trying to think about what the police knew and what they were just guessing. *The main problem is those pictures. They're too close for comfort.* 'It's a good job we saw that announcement, it's a good warning. Up to now, there's only one person who can identify us, that woman in Paris. But they don't know we've left France, they've got no idea where we are. So, we've got to make sure we don't get recognised here in England.'

Her confidence reassured him. 'It was just unlucky. She saw me in the hotel when we had breakfast. But they don't have a picture of you because you never looked at that camera on the wall. And the way you spoke, they think you come from London, and you told Valerie we were going to Italy, that was clever. If we're careful, I think we'll be safe.'

'Maybe, but there's things we can both do to make it better.'

'Like what?'

'You trust me?'

'Of course, you're my partner.'

'OK. Come into the bathroom and take your shirt off.'

For the next half-hour Ibrahim had to suffer the humiliation of having his unruly mop of curls cut off then his head shaved by a girl. He was mortified to be handled by her in this way, but he said nothing, annoyed that he hadn't thought of it himself. He also found the sensation of the razor blade rubbing gently over his skin very erotic and had to exercise control.

She rubbed a few drops of her bath oil over his head. 'There, that's better. Look.'

He examined his new shaven image in the mirror. 'You were right, I look completely different.'

She looked him over again. 'I'm wondering about that beard, it's a bloody bushy one. They're showing a photo of you with it, so why don't you cut it off, so you have that stubbly look all the guys have now?'

'OK.' He took the scissors and started to cut it back.

'Wait, I'll do it faster.' She trimmed it down to a short stubble. 'You look really cool like that. I could fancy you meself if you're not careful.'

'I just need some jeans with holes in them and I'll look like a pop star.'

'Or a football player.' Sami laughed. 'We'll have to get you one of those special electric razors, it's easier than scissors. Right. It's my turn now. Go and set the table for supper and don't come in here.'

An hour later, Ibrahim was watching TV to see if there was any more news. He turned as she came out of the bathroom. '*Mein Gott*,' he exclaimed. Sami had been transformed from a pony tailed blonde into a brunette with shoulder length hair framed around her face.

'I was sure this would happen sooner or later. I had everything with me to cut my hair and dye it. What do you think?' She pirouetted in front of him. She had even dyed her eyebrows to enhance the darker appearance.

He thought she looked beautiful but couldn't say so. 'It's great. You look more serious but just as nice. Only in a different way, if you know what I mean,' he said in a slightly embarrassed voice.

'Different from the photofit?'

'Nobody would know it was you.'

'OK, for the next week, you stay in the flat and I'll go out if we need things. When we get the list of stuff from Christian, I'll start buying them and you can prepare the TATP. We'll wait to see if there's any more announcements before you go out. OK?' She went to warm up the pizzas in the oven.

'OK, Sarah.' Ibrahim nodded in agreement. He was getting used to her being in charge. The strange thing was he quite liked it.

THIRTY-NINE

Novi Pazar, South-West Serbia
June 2016

Their latest guide was called Luka, a large, smiling Serbian who insisted on taking Faqir to the local tavern for a glass of Rakija, which he told him was a traditional drink made of fruit juices. What he didn't explain was that the fruits were fermented and the resulting alcohol was strong enough to knock over a horse. He drank both their glasses while the Iraqi nursed a beer and they negotiated his terms of service. The conversation was easier in two respects, firstly because his excellent English came from having lived for some time in London, the second reason was the price.

Luka explained that very few refugees went from Serbia to Montenegro; his main activity had been helping Albanians and Kosovars enter Serbia to travel from there to northern Europe. 'Montenegro's not part of the EU yet, that's why. They're busy negotiating to be members, and to join NATO as well, but you know how complicated the Europeans are, it'll take them years.'

Faqir knew little about the complexities of the Brussels political machinery, but he nodded wisely, determined not to be taken for an ignorant Arab.

'In the meantime,' the Serbian went on, 'it's not a great route, to make money, I mean. Serbia to Hungary was the best, but the Hungarian clampdown has been very bad for business. I've had no customers since then.'

Faqir was astonished that 'people smuggling' could be described as a business, but since the man made his living that way, he couldn't argue. He asked, 'So the price is lower than through other borders?'

The big Serbian roared with laughter. 'Tony told me you would negotiate well, but you don't need to. I know the other Serbs are charging 1,500 euros or more for each passenger, but I'll take your whole family from here to Zaton, for 6,000 euros. That's 24 km inside the Montenegro border, 60 km by car and only 10 km easy walking, plus a house in Zaton for one night. There's a bus to Budva, the resort on the Adriatic coast, every day and it's very cheap. I'll even include the tickets for you.' He took another swallow of the fiery liquid and sat back, smiling at Faqir.

Faqir followed the route on Tony's map; he could see the thin lines of trails in the area. It looked a lot easier than the crossing from Bulgaria. *That's the same price as Ivan, they must have talked together. Difficult to talk him down if he knows that.* He said, 'You guarantee we won't have to do any climbing or impossible tracks and no surprises halfway there?'

'I promise, no surprises. This is a good route, your wife and daughters can do it with no problems and where we cross, it's a long way from any villages or patrols and I always get through easily.'

Faqir held out his hand. 'Five thousand and we have a deal. I'll give you half when we leave tonight and the rest when we get to Zaton.'

Luka laughed and shook his hand. 'Done. One more thing, there aren't many refugees in Montenegro yet, but I expect there'll be a lot more coming, after the Hungarian decision. This is maybe bad for you if they increase their controls. It's a small population, only about 650,000, so you'll have to be careful not to stand out.'

'We speak English all the time now, just like British tourists. In any case, there's nothing we can do about it, just pray we don't get caught.'

'*Inshallah*,' said the Serbian, to Faqir's surprise.

Guildford, UK

On Friday morning, Ibrahim received a message from an email address in Lebanon; it was from Christian. It consisted only of a password and the address of a dating agency, *cupiditi.com*. Once again, he was impressed with their ability to surprise him. If anyone was intercepting their transmissions, they would not expect a dating agency address to be used by an Islamist movement. Two more passwords arrived by separate emails, then a text message arrived on his phone giving brief instructions and the coordinates he'd need.

He opened up the dating site and followed the steps given in the text message. The procedure for entering the Dark Web was more complicated than before and he assumed the situation in Iraq and Syria was causing ISIL to maintain greater secrecy in their communications. In addition, he no longer had the encryption app he'd had on his previous laptop. Several steps later he finally found the PDF he had received in Kalk, entitled '*Instructions Part One*', which, when he entered the third password, provided him with the same drawings, photographs, diagrams and list of materials.

He printed off the first set of instructions and closed the internet connection down. After a few minutes, he went through the same procedure again, receiving and entering additional passwords until he had the second set of instructions and complete list of purchases required to fabricate the *Triacetone Triperoxide*. Now he had twenty pages of instructions, drawings and warnings. He checked them all; everything was as he remembered, he had all the working documents that had been lost in the explosion.

Ibrahim spent the next hour going through everything page by page with Sami. In Cologne, he and Jamil had bought German products and he tried to explain what every item was, so she could find the English equivalent. He was once again impressed at her quick thinking and memory. *She's an excellent partner. I was wrong to worry about having to work with a second person, or a woman.*

He sent off another message to Christian. *Have all documents. Ready to visit. Where?*

Mosul, Iraq

Karl was overseeing a team of 'engineers' in a garage in Mosul old town. They were installing explosives in trucks and cars in readiness for the street fighting that would erupt when the coalition forces swept through the narrow, winding lanes and passageways. Once equipped as motorised bombs, they were driven to random points in the town and left, ready to be started up and driven into the troops as they advanced. He had a list of the vehicles which had been prepared and where they were situated. Over two hundred lethal weapons waiting to be released on the attackers, many to be driven by civilians, forced to carry out suicide missions or see their families massacred before their eyes.

He was fortunate to have escaped an even more gruesome project; rounding up victims to carry out suicide missions when the invasion came. The civilians, young, old, men, women and children, it didn't matter to the ISIL command, would be trapped in buildings when the attacking troops entered, then sent out to detonate themselves, or be detonated by a hail of bullets to blow up the coalition soldiers. There were still almost a million left in the city, those who had been unable to find a means of escape, and now it looked like they never would. The ISIL commanders were stockpiling every type of weapon they could, and that included weaponising the remaining civilians.

Karl was not proud of what had taken place in the city he had captured so bravely two years before, when he had been hailed as a hero of the ISIL Jihad. It was now no more than an evil, sadistic cesspit for the citizens trapped in its fatal embrace and the ISIL fighters who had not yet fled for their lives. He went over to inspect the next batch of vehicles, add them to his list and send them to their designated location. Even if he was forced, against his will, to flee the city with the other commanders in a few days, he still had a job to do. Like it or not, someone had to maintain some form of discipline and plan for the next escalation of this never-ending battle.

His phone pinged and he read the message from Ibrahim. *They're in place and ready to proceed,* he realised. *I knew Sami would get him sorted out. We can still send a message to the world.*

He called the number back on WhatsApp and spoke one phrase in Arabic. Then he said, in French, '*Bon voyage.*'

Guildford, UK

Ibrahim listened to the 30-second call, then changed the SIM in the phone and sat silently for a moment.

Sami went to sit by him on the settee. 'What did he say? Do you know what our target is?'

'He just said, "Fly from Gatwick Airport. *Bon voyage*".'

Düsseldorf, Germany

Max Kellerman was looking at his jigsaw puzzle on the wall and feeling a little more optimistic. The latest press conference had produced something. He'd received a call that afternoon from Massinet. An Englishwoman who resembled the photofit picture had been seen two days ago by a ticket inspector on a train going from Plouaret to Lannion in Northern France, near to several Channel ports. The inspector couldn't recall her name, but he remembered she spoke good English. 'Like the Queen,' he'd said.

They had then found the CCTV footage from the TGV from Paris to Rennes, which showed a couple who could be them. The man was wearing a hood and the woman had blonde hair in a ponytail; they both kept their heads down so it was difficult to be sure of either of them. The CCTV cameras on the two SNCF trains were not working, so they still had no clear photos of what they might look like now.

Massinet was passing the dossier to Pascale Letouffe, the RAID commissioner in Rennes, Brittany. 'I've ordered Letouffe to put his people on alert and carry out an intensive search of the area under the anti-terrorist measures. That means they can enter and search any premises or property without a warrant.'

Looking at the map of the Brittany coastline, Max was sure he knew where they were heading. 'Don't get your hopes up,' he told Massinet. 'I think we're probably too late again.'

'What do you mean?'

'My guess is they've already crossed the Channel to England, from one of those little ports around Lannion, well away from the main traffic, immigrants and border patrols. He's smart, this Ibrahim. We mustn't underestimate him.'

'I'll contact our coastguard people and see if they've spotted anything unusual going on. I'll make another appeal on TV this evening, although I think you could be right. They've maybe flown the coop.' Massinet rang off and Max went to report to Eric Schuster, repeating his conviction that Ibrahim and the woman were on their way to England.

Schuster looked at the map, frowned and shook his head. 'From there it's more likely they'd go to Guernsey, or Jersey or even Ireland. It's the longest possible route to the UK, over two hundred k's. Why would anyone choose that route?'

'For exactly that reason, because nobody would choose

it. Listen, Eric, once you're in a boat, if it's fast enough, the distance doesn't matter. As long as you can get across without being seen, it's the safest choice. They arrived in Lannion at nine-fifteen, when it was dark. I figure they probably left from somewhere like Pont Gouennec or Port l'Épine, one of the small fishing harbours right next to Lannion, here.' He pointed on the map. 'In a fast boat they could be in England before dawn. And I already checked the weather on the Channel that night, it was pissing down with rain and foggy, so they wouldn't be seen. I'm certain they're in England.'

'OK, if that's your intuition speaking I won't argue. You'd better get in touch with the Counter Terrorism Command people in London.'

'I'm also going to ask Letouffe to check out fast boats on the coast around Lannion.' Kellerman strode out of Schuster's office, *we're finally starting to catch up,* he told himself, *still behind, but getting closer.*

FORTY

Guildford, England
June, 2016

'I'll fry eggs for supper. Better not go out so soon after that announcement. And we have to talk about the Gatwick attack, it'll take some planning. I don't suppose you eat bacon? I've got tinned mushrooms and beans, is that OK?'

He was studying the instructions again and nodded absently. Sami went into the kitchen and looked in the cupboard. There was a big, old fashioned iron frying pan and she took it out, made sure it was clean and put it on the stove. It weighed a ton and reminded her of the last time she'd handled a pan like that. She'd told Ibrahim what she told everyone so often that she'd begun to believe it herself, '*Me old man dropped down dead when I was fifteen*'. She tried to push away the memory of that night, but it came back to her as if it was yesterday.

Belfast, Northern Ireland

Sami had just managed to get her mother up the stairs of their terrace house in O'Connor Street and onto her bed. As usual, she'd passed out in front of the television, high on crystal meth and vodka. Nowadays she hardly ate anything and weighed so little Sami could get her upstairs without much trouble. She came back down to the hall as her father came in the front door. She could see by the look of him he'd had a skin-full and went quickly to the kitchen to get away from him.

He limped along the corridor after her, the left leg that had been almost blown off by the English dragging behind. 'Hello me darlin' girl. Come here and give your old man a nice cuddle. Me wife'll be no comfort to us, never bloody is. Come and show me how much you love your dad.' He threw off his jacket and staggered unsteadily towards her, opening up his trousers.

She backed up against the stove. 'I'm havin' me period, go away. Please don't touch me, Dad.'

Now he had his penis out, sticking through his underpants. 'Don't fret yourself for that, girl. I'll do it from behind again, I like it better that way anyhow.'

She looked frantically around as he staggered forward and grabbed the first thing at hand. It was the iron frying pan she'd used to fry the potatoes and bacon for her supper. It was so heavy she held it with both hands. She backed away against the kitchen counter. 'Don't come any nearer or I'll smash this in your face.'

He laughed, 'To be sure, you'd never do such a terrible thing to your own father. Come here and get your knickers down.'

As he lunged forward she swung the pan at his head. He ducked down and she missed, but his injured leg gave way and he fell forward against the edge of the tiled counter. There was a sickening crack and Michael Sean McDonnell fell down on the kitchen floor as if he'd been felled by an axe.

'Sweet Jesus. What have I done?' Sami dropped the pan and knelt down beside her father's body. A red and blue swollen bruise on the temple showed where his head had smacked into the edge of the tile and there was a trace of blood there, on his forehead and a trickle on the floor. She shook him by the shoulders, 'Dad, I'm sorry, Dad. Wake up and give us a kiss, I don't mind, honest I don't. Just wake up.'

He remained immobile, his eyes closed, and she put her face against his mouth, but couldn't feel his breathing. He looked as if he was sleeping, his features calm and relaxed. She thought he looked nicer than he'd looked in a long time. Sami sat on the floor beside the body, adjusted his clothing and fastened up his trousers. *There, that's better, no one will know what you were after doing to me.* She took his hand, trying to understand what it meant to have killed her father. *What'll happen to me? Where'll they send me? They can't let me stay here with me mam. They'll put me in prison or a home where I can't hurt anyone else.* Sami lay alongside him, still holding his hand, trying to sort out her confused mind and after a few minutes, the adrenalin rush faded away and she fell asleep.

It was almost midnight when she awoke and she felt cold. Her father's hand in hers was freezing and she pulled away from his body, the terrifying images coming back to her mind. Sami stood up, looking around the kitchen. There was no sign of a struggle or disturbance of any kind, just the trace of dried blood on the tile and the floor where her father lay quietly and peacefully. She could hear no sound from upstairs and she knew her mother would still be in a deep sleep, a semi-coma in fact, unconscious for at least six hours. She picked up the frying pan and absent-mindedly wiped it clean with a wet cloth, placing it back on the stove top.

I'll have to tell me mam what's happened, she'll bloody murder me when she sobers up. Sami went up to her parent's bedroom. Her mother hadn't budged; she was snoring, lying flat out on the bed in the same position as she'd laid her. She shook her, like she'd shaken her father, trying to wake her up, but the woman just mumbled something and continued snoring. She sat on the side of the bed, thinking about her father, remembering her childhood days when they'd been a normal, happy family. Before his injured leg got so bad it cost him his job and he'd taken to drinking, then her mother followed his example, until that's all they seemed to do.

Finally, she realised, *it's time I called the police, there's nothing else I can do.* Then she thought about having to tell them her father had been abusing her, it had gone on for two years, since her first period. Her mother was out of her mind so often on booze and drugs that she was incapable of pleasing him, so he'd turned to his daughter for satisfaction. *I can't say me dad was fuckin' me, so I killed him. It wasn't his fault. All because those English feckers shot his leg off when he was making a peaceful protest at the border at the wrong time.* Floods of tears came as she struggled to come to terms with the reality of her plight.

Sami went to get her phone and call the emergency service. *Why couldn't he have slipped on something and bashed his head by accident?* Then, thinking out loud, *who's to say he didn't? There's nobody's seen what happened. Me mam can't say anything, she wouldn't hear it if I'd shot him with a pistol.*

Sami thought about it for a while then, making up her mind, she found a jar of dripping, fat her mother saved from the cooking. Kneeling by her father's body, with a piece of kitchen roll she smeared a little on the linoleum floor near his feet and on the sole of one shoe. She put the jar away and threw the paper in the trash, then looked around again. His jacket was lying in the passageway and she picked it up and laid it on a chair in the sitting room, came back and checked everything in the kitchen and hall. There was nothing to incriminate her, no blood except a little by his head and on the tile, nothing to show it hadn't been a tragic accident. With trembling fingers, she took her phone and called 999.

The autopsy showed a very high level of alcohol in the system which explained his lack of attention when coming into the kitchen and that he hadn't tried to prevent the fall – he'd been blind drunk. It took the ambulance an hour to get there after the police called and the estimated time of death couldn't be established to within two hours. Sami's mother didn't seem too concerned to have lost her husband; she still had the army pension he'd been receiving which had paid for the drugs and booze for them both. A verdict of accidental death was recorded and life went on as normal in the McDonnell household.

Six months later, Sami met Baki and moved out to live with him in his flat. Her mother died a few months after that. There were only seven mourners at the funeral at the Newlands Cross Cemetery-Crematorium. Sami had lost her family, but she had Baki.

She switched on the electric ring. 'Supper'll be fifteen minutes,' she called to Ibrahim.

FORTY-ONE

Near Poda, South-West Serbia
June 2016

'We walk 4 km to the border and another four on the far side, then the other van picks us up.'

It was 11:15 pm and the Al-Douris had just climbed down from a Volkswagen van, after a 40 km drive from Novi Pazar. It was a clear, starry night but without lights, on a series of small, narrow roads, the trip had taken over an hour, the last 2 km being no more than a cart track, and they were glad to be out of the vehicle. From his map and the hilly, winding roads, Faqir knew they had come through a mountainous region, but they were now in a flat valley, surrounded by forests. They had passed only two other cars in the last 15 minutes, confirming Luka's statement that there were very few villages in the area, the nearest, Poda, apparently boasting only seventeen inhabitants. He told them that the track they were on continued to the border, but they would walk away from it towards Poda before crossing at a point where there were no roads at all.

Shivering in the cold night air, they hoisted up their backpacks and set off along an easy path that wound gently between the trees, parallel to the invisible frontier. Lyla's ankle was much better and she could walk without pain, while the Serbian carried her rucksack. No one broke the silence as they covered the 4 km in less than an hour, then he motioned to them to wait while he looked around. At five minutes past midnight on Sunday, June 5th, the Al-Douri family followed their guide into Montenegro, the fifth country they'd visited since leaving Iraq a month ago. Hema gathered her children close to her and took Faqir's hand, 'Almost there,' she breathed quietly.

At one o'clock they stopped for a rest, two kilometres inside the border, another two to reach Lazovići, where the second van would be waiting to take them to Zaton. Luka told them it was the only village within 20 km, with a population of two hundred. Since beginning their hike two hours ago, they hadn't seen any sign of man, not a building, road, no cultivated land of any kind, nothing but the vast expanse of forest that surrounded them.

They sat in a clearing under the stars, relishing the majestic, silent beauty of the mountains, so far and so different from the hell that Mosul had become. Hema's mind was filled with admiration for Faqir and happiness for her children. *Somehow, we've made it all this way, surely we can make it to our destination, it might be possible after all.*

'Thanks, Luka,' she said, as he passed around a water bottle and some fruit, when he suddenly held up his hand and put his fingers on her lips. There was no sound and they nervously looked around the shadowy forest that surrounded them. Faqir's heart started pounding again, *dear God, what's gone wrong now, has our luck finally run out? If we're discovered, it's the end of our freedom.*

In the dim light a massive dark shape emerged from the trees; it was a large animal, but bigger than any creature they'd ever seen. It walked low to the ground as it silently made its way on all fours across the clearing. An earthy smell emanated from it and they could see the steam from its breath as it passed in front of them, seemingly unaware of the group of humans who were gazing at it in amazement and fear. The creature stopped near Hamid and Aisha, reaching up with one foreleg to strip some leaves from a bush and stuff them into its mouth. It looked around and they froze like statues, not breathing, making no sound or movement. The 250 kg, 1.2 metre brown bear turned away, continued its path through the trees, and disappeared silently into the darkness as if it had never been there.

On the 30-minute trip from Lazovići to Zaton, the children quizzed Luka about the wild bear. He explained, 'There are a lot of them in Montenegro, because they were never captured and put in circuses and zoos, like they did in my country. The one we saw must have walked from one of the national parks in these mountains, there's two of them in a 50 km radius of here. They're part of the protected area on the borders of Albania, Serbia and Montenegro. In the summertime, the bears travel for hundreds of kilometres through these forests. They don't bother with people unless they're frightened or attacked. I've seen a few of them on this route and they're always quiet and peaceful. It's their forest after all,' he said with a smile.

The house in Zaton was small, clean and tidy, with a wood burning stove and no running hot water. Femija, the owner, was a round, jolly lady in her mid-forties, who spoke no English but welcomed them with a warm smile. From the way she spoke to and looked at Luka, they assumed they were more than just friends, but he said goodnight to them and went off with the driver of the van. It was now 02:30 in the morning and after the last few days of climbing and hiking they were all dead on their feet. Like Boyka, in Slavinja, she had prepared mattresses for them in the cellar and they fell onto them without taking off their clothes or washing and were immediately asleep, the children dreaming of the mysterious creature who had visited them in the forest.

Gatwick Airport, UK

'It's two minutes to the North Terminal, where most of the other flights leave from.' It was Sunday morning and Sami was in the shuttle between the two terminals. speaking to Ibrahim on her mobile. They had decided it was safer for her to go there alone, until they saw a further police announcement. In addition, she had previously flown from Gatwick when she left for Iraq via Istanbul and knew her way around. It was a sunny day and like many of the holidaymakers around her she had on her sunglasses, was wearing a tee-shirt and jeans and pulling her wheelie bag. Ibrahim had bought her a one-way ticket to Paris on a Vueling Airlines flight in the name of Sarah Callaghan in case she was stopped and questioned. It was only forty-nine pounds and he'd paid from the PayPal account.

After Karl's message the previous day, they'd spent a long time looking at the airport website, so Ibrahim could familiarise himself with the layout and floor plan.

He'd never seen one with the terminals joined by a shuttle train and found the idea eminently sensible.

He heard her complain, 'I've never seen such crowds of people. The holiday season's starting. It'll get worse from now on.'

'That's perfect,' he answered. 'If it's like that all the time, it doesn't matter when we go, it'll always be full.'

The direct train from Guildford had taken only forty-five minutes and she'd already walked around the South Terminal which was next to the station, taking note of the positions of the lifts, escalators, shops and the train station entrance, the points where people were congregating in groups. Ibrahim had told her what to look for, the places where maximum damage could be inflicted. The shuttle disembarked, and she followed the procession up the escalator to the North Terminal departure level. Here, she could hardly make her way through the passengers fighting to get to their check-in machines.

'It's the same here.' she said. 'It should be worth doing as long as we don't screw it up. A big noise, well planned.'

'You need to check how we can get close in a car.'

They had discussed this problem at the flat when he looked at the plans. 'We can't take buses and trains and carry the stuff through the station and up escalators or in lifts full of people. We have to go in a car, park near to the entrance and walk in with a case on a trolley. Then we just work out the best place to do it.'

'You can't park anywhere you like there,' she said, 'there's too many cars and buses. The police will stop us and we'll be screwed. I'll look at the car parks.'

Now, she went out of the departure hall to the multi-storey car park just a hundred metres across the street and found an attendant who confirmed it was the short-term car park. 'It's to leave your car for an hour or two if you're meeting someone. It's more expensive, but if you can afford it, it's the closest and most convenient. There's one at both terminals, they're just the same.'

Sami had switched on her English accent again, 'My boyfriend's having an operation and won't be able to walk far. Could we leave the car on the ground floor, opposite the entrance?'

'That's the Premium Service. You leave it on this floor, just behind us. But it costs more and you have to book online in advance.'

'The same at the other terminal?'

'Yes, it's right at the entrance.'

She relayed the information to Ibrahim. 'That's good, Sami, well done. But I've been thinking about something. Can you go back to the other terminal?'

'I have to go back there to get the train. What do you want me to do?'

'You're in the North Terminal, right?' She confirmed it and he said, 'We'll do as if we drove in and parked a car. Go right to the back of that premium part, that's where we would choose.' She walked to the back of the park, where there were still a few spaces available. He looked at his phone. 'It's ten minutes past eleven. So, we park, open the boot, take out the case and we get a trolley.'

'They're right here, you just need a pound coin.'

'OK. So our bags are on the trolley and we go in the terminal to the busiest part of the departure hall.' He was looking at the floor plan on his laptop; it reminded him of his previous target, the *Haus und Heim* department store in Cologne.

A couple of minutes later, she said, 'I'm here, right in the middle. There's lots of people.'

'OK. I want you to take the shuttle to the other terminal, to where you buy the train tickets. Tell me when you get there. See how long it takes from when we parked the car.'

She looked at the time. 'I'll switch off to save the battery.' She pushed the trolley casually away to the walkway leading to the shuttle.

Ibrahim continued working until she rang back. 'Is everything OK?'

'I'm standing beside the entrance to the station in the South Terminal, it's perfect.' Behind her there was a queue at the ticket counters and a constant flow of passengers went past her to the escalators for the station platforms. She shuddered when she imagined the damage an explosion would inflict on the crowds around her.

'That's great, it took exactly fifteen minutes from parking the car, so we know the timing.'

Sami had been in the airport for almost an hour; she was becoming nervous. 'If that's all, I'm coming back home now, there's a security guy walking this way, so I'll have to ring off. See you in while.'

She turned to leave and the trolley bumped into a pushchair with a little girl in a pink dress. The child dropped a raggedy-looking teddy bear and started crying.

Sami picked it up, 'Here you are, no need to cry, everything's fine. That's a very pretty dress.'

The mother smiled at her, 'Thank you. It's chaos in here, isn't it? Everybody rushing off on holidays. We're going to Mallorca, where are you off to?'

'Oh, just a few days in Paris, that's all.'

'That's nice. Well, have a safe flight and enjoy Paris.'

Sami pushed her trolley slowly towards the train departure exit, the woman's words ringing in her mind, 'Have a safe flight and enjoy Paris.'

Two hours later, she was back in the flat in Watson Avenue.

'Thanks, Sami, you did a great job. Did you have any problems, nothing went wrong?'

'Nothing.' She didn't mention her nervousness, nor the woman with the little girl in the pink dress. 'I was just another single woman traveller lost in Gatwick. I even stopped the security guy who came by and asked him the way to the Vueling check-in area. He was bored out of his skull, happy to help me.'

'And there's no special security for the car park?'

'Ibrahim, it's like everything today, they just want to sell you something. As long as you book and pay, they don't care who you are.'

She described her conversation with the attendant and he laughed out loud. 'That's funny. Are you expecting me to break my leg? Is that some more of the Irish *blarney* you tell?'

'To be sure it is. Anyway, it worked, we found out what we wanted. The car parks are the same at both terminals, so it doesn't matter where you leave the car.

The attendant told me they're very busy, but we have a choice of two.'

'Cool.'

'You're wanting to make two explosions, one in each terminal, isn't that right?'

'It would be really important. What they call a "big noise". Karl would be proud of us and we'd be famous ISIL fighters.'

'You really think we can pull it off?'

'I know we can. We park in any terminal, they're the same. We both have a trolley with a suitcase. You stay there and I go to the other one. It's fifteen minutes for both of us to be ready. I call you to check everything is OK then send the message from the other phone and your bomb goes off, then mine. It will be a major attack, one of the best. Maybe even the best.'

She shivered, as she had done at the ticket office. 'I suppose so. No, you're right, it will be the best.'

He didn't notice her reaction. 'But we still have another problem. I had a driving permit, but I lost it in the accident. And anyway, I can't rent a car in my name.'

'Karl thought of that. I've got a licence.' She went to her bag and took the plastic card out. 'Look at the name, Catherine Flanagan, they gave it to me before I left Mosul. It's a real licence, there is such a person and she looks a bit like me.'

He took it from her. 'It's from 2013, that's three years, so you can rent a car. But can you really drive?'

'Sure and all I can. I learned in Belfast. Baki gave me lessons and paid for the test. I can rent a car and drive it.'

'That's really great. I was worried about it.' He

squeezed her hand, then took his away, embarrassed. 'We have to find an agent in Guildford, not a big company, some place where they don't ask for a passport, it's not the same name as the licence.'

'I'll look when I go shopping. What about money? Are you sure we're OK?'

'We've got about a thousand pounds left and 400 euros on the PayPal account. We can pay for the car, the parking and everything we need to finish the work. Nothing will stop us from succeeding this time, I'm sure of it.'

She went to the kitchen door. 'I'll go shopping this afternoon and we'll celebrate with fish and chips tonight. There's a chippie just around the corner. I saw it on the way from the station.'

Ibrahim laughed.

'What's so funny?'

'I like the way your mind goes from one thing to another. From our mission, to the car, to money and shopping, then to what you want for supper.'

'It's a woman thing,' she said.

FORTY-TWO

London, England
June 2016

'And you feel certain they've arrived in England?'

'I've been following al-Ahmad for over a month now, unfortunately always a step behind, but I believe I understand the way he thinks.'

Max Kellerman was speaking on an encrypted line with Detective Chief Inspector Callum Dewar, at Counter Terrorism Command headquarters in the London Metropolitan Police Service. DCI Dewar had been drafted in to CTC in 2012, six years after the unit was formed by the merger of the Anti-Terrorist Branch and the Special Branch. He was now an Assistant Commander in charge of current operations.

'What about the French Coastguard?'

'They have no report of any unusual activity on Thursday night, but I've asked the Rennes RAID unit to check on any boats in the Lannion area that could do the crossing as quickly as that.'

'OK, I'll see if our Border Patrol people have anything and get back to you. I'll also alert the other police and security services of a possible threat. I can't authorise any public warning or statement without some firm proof that they're here, but if you make more TV announcements in Germany and France, it's up to you what you say and it will certainly be retransmitted in the UK.'

'I understand. Thanks, Detective Inspector, I'll arrange

a press conference tonight and I look forward to hearing from you as soon as you have any news.'

Dewar called his assistant in and explained the situation. 'Get the word out and talk to Border Patrol. Ask if they saw anything in the Channel on Thursday night, the second. It would be coming north to our coast from somewhere around Lannion in Brittany. We've only got three boats and apparently the weather was really crappy, so it's a long shot, but worth a try.'

In Düsseldorf, Max Kellerman asked Eric Schuster for authorisation to call another TV press conference. He called Robert Massinet at RAID headquarters to coordinate it with the Frenchman's appeal. He felt he was getting closer to his quarry, he just needed a bit of luck.

Guildford, UK

Sami was writing a shopping list. Ibrahim was dictating the items from his printouts and they were agreeing on the English equivalent of the German material he was familiar with. They had decided she would buy some items every day and he would stay in the house in case his photo was too accurate. There was a shopping centre in Woodbridge, to the north of the town, with DIY and other household stores that would stock everything they needed.

'Don't bother about the nails and screws,' he told her. 'I'll get them when it's safe for me to go out. Just concentrate on the materials I need to make the TATP.'

'How long do think it's going to take?'

'I'll have to do it faster than in Germany.' He thought

for a moment. 'If I make one box a day, that's two to three weeks, I think I can do that.'

'Around the end of June,' she shivered, 'that's when there's more people going on holiday.'

'Great. The airports will be full.' He swapped over the SIMs in their phones and gave hers back with a new PlusNet card in it. 'I've got two more SIMs left, so we'll need some more for the trigger phones.'

Sami consulted the timetable. There was a bus at 15:15 direct to the centre. 'I'll get four to be on the safe side. And I'm fed up calling you Ali, we're not travelling anymore and it's confusing changing names. OK?'

'I don't like the name anyway,' he responded. 'And Sami is better than Sarah.'

'Sure and all it is. I'll see you later.' She took a couple of bags and went out. Now she could do something useful she felt better. It would keep her mind occupied and she might help Karl to finally achieve something before whatever happened in Mosul. *Inshallah,* she said to herself. She tried not to think of the woman with the child in the pushchair, but the image kept coming back.

Near Podgorica, Montenegro

Faqir and his family had caught the 2:20 pm bus for the five-hour trip from Zaton to Budva, a popular beach resort on the Adriatic. The tickets were given to them by their newly found friend, Luka, as part of their deal. The holiday town was about 35 km from the border with Croatia and according to him, not high on the radar for refugee crossings.

Before leaving them, the Serbian took Faqir aside.

'Everybody thinks Montenegro's a beautiful little paradise full of honest people with no crime or corruption. That's not exactly right. There's lots of Albanian, Kosovo and Bosnian drug and sex dealers there, it's a small place, with borders all around and a good harbour and easy coastline and it makes a good base for those crooks. Đukanović, the president, is a tough guy and the police take after him. If you keep your nose clean, you'll be OK, but they really take it out on anybody breaking the law, so watch out.'

Despite Luka's warning, there were no police controls at the terminal and the journey had gone without incident. It was now 6:00 pm and they were approaching the capital, Podgorica, 45 km from Budva. Hema and the children were dozing in the soporific atmosphere of the bus, but Faqir was concerned with the next and most important leg of their trip.

Prior to leaving Zaton that morning, he'd called the last number given to him by Tony Miller; Gavro, a fisherman in Rafailovići, the port next door to Budva. But the number was no longer in service and Faqir had no other way of contacting him. He didn't want to worry Hema while they were preparing to leave and mentioned it only when they were settled on the bus.

Her eyes widened with shock. 'We're on our way there now, what are you going to do when we arrive?'

'I booked a guesthouse in the village online, not expensive. We'll stay the night and see what we can find out in the morning. Someone must know where he is, it's a small place.'

'What if we can't find him? He's our only contact.'

'I'll think of something,' he'd replied confidently.

Now, two hours later, he was feeling less confident. He knew his wife was right, they knew nobody in Montenegro. If they couldn't trace the fisherman, Gavro, he had no plan 'B'. He couldn't call Tony Miller, or the Carrs, they'd already done more than he could possibly have expected. And there was nothing any of them could do from wherever in the world the Lady Claire happened to be at that moment.

There must be a solution, he said to himself. *We haven't managed to come all this way to fail now.* He closed his eyes and tried to get a few minutes rest, but sleep wouldn't come.

Düsseldorf, Germany

Max Kellerman's and Robert Massinet's press conferences were shown on the seven o'clock news in Germany and France and immediately transmitted on all the main European networks. As well as repeating what he'd said on the previous occasions, Max announced that it was believed that the fugitives were now in the UK, probably the south of England. He still had no proof of this other than his own intuition, but he was following DCI Dewar's hint about sowing the seeds of doubt. So far there had been no feedback from Letouffe at Rennes nor the UK Border Force, but it was only a few hours since he'd talked with them and he had to go with what his gut instinct said. The UK TV stations made a lot of noise around this *New Threat to British Security*, and he was grateful for Dewar's suggestion. Although he was disappointed to have no specific information, the pictures had worked before and he hoped he might get lucky again, as he had in Paris.

Just after his appearance, he received a call from Callum Dewar. 'The only vessel stopped by our Border Patrol that night was a fishing boat coming from St Malo. They were about an hour out of Torquay, early on the Friday morning, carrying foie gras and going there to load a cargo of cheese. My officer went aboard at 4:30 am and searched the boat but there was nothing. It was a fast boat and the captain said he did the return run regularly and he even knew one of our men, so I know it doesn't fit with what you're looking for, but I've got nothing else to offer, sorry.'

'Is Torquay a potential target? I mean, anything special about the place?'

'I wouldn't have thought so. Even if they did arrive there I'm pretty sure they'd be going on to London, or Birmingham or Manchester, certainly one of our major cities.'

'Can you ask for a CCTV check on trains and buses coming from Torquay on Thursday morning? We might get lucky.'

Dewar wasn't convinced it was worth the resources, but he agreed, 'Sure, we can get the local people to look, but I think it's a long shot.'

'Thanks a lot.' Max was about to ring off when he had another thought. 'I meant to ask. Did you get the name of the boat?'

'I remember it, Cabaret, like the Liza Minelli movie, you know?'

Kellerman hadn't seen the movie, but he thanked

him then called Letouffe at Rennes, asking him to look for a boat named Cabaret and to extend his alert and search to St Malo. As a little extra insurance, he also asked him to check the CCTV records for trains leaving Lannion on Wednesday night or Thursday morning. He was fairly certain they'd find nothing, but he didn't want Eric Schuster to have any excuse to take him off the case again. He examined his chart on the wall and updated some points, feeling he was missing something but he couldn't put his finger on it. He was sure he knew where the fugitives where, but he needed some proof, something definite to hang his hat on.

Guildford, England

'That's great, I'll start making the TATP tomorrow.' They were in the kitchen and Ibrahim was checking off the purchases Sami had made. There were several items he didn't recognise, but when he examined the detailed description in small print on the back of the bottles and packages, they corresponded with what he'd used in Cologne.

She finished putting away the groceries. 'If you're making two bombs we'll need more stuff, but I didn't want to buy ten bottles of the same hair product, it might look fishy.'

'Fishy? What's that?'

'It might look queer, you know, suspicious.'

'Oh, I get it. Did anyone look at you?'

'Nobody at all. People are so busy looking at their mobiles these days, they hardly even look up to pay in the store. I could be the Queen of England and they wouldn't notice me in me crown.'

He laughed at the image, then checked the time. 'It's almost seven o'clock. I'll look at the news on my laptop, there might be something about us.'

They found the news items with the retransmission of the German and French press conference.

'What do you think about that?' Ibrahim was feeling more confident.

'It sounds like that German feller, Kellerman, hasn't got a clue who we are or where we are. There wasn't any real information about our travelling, he's just guessing. And they're still showing you with that bloody great beard, so I think we've done a good job of fooling them.'

'I think you're right. We should be safe for now if we don't get careless. But I still want to work faster than in Cologne.' Ibrahim put on his hoodie. 'I'm going for the fish and chips.'

Rafailovići, Adriatic Coast of Montenegro

A local bus service connected the string of beach resorts along the coast, known as the Budva Riviera, and the Al-Douris passed a number of glitzy, upmarket beachfront hotels before arriving at their modest lodgings, the Kod Baltazar Guesthouse, at 8:30 pm. When Faqir introduced himself in English to the woman at reception and showed her the online booking confirmation on his phone, no questions were asked. She and her husband were the owners and they welcomed the family, showing them three small, clean bedrooms, against a cash deposit of 100 euros. After their first shower in three days and a change of clothes they strolled along the promenade in search of a local café for a meal, Faqir's ulterior motive being to enquire after the man he was supposed to meet.

The owner of Mirko's Café, not surprisingly, was Mirko, a skinny little man of about fifty, with a sad, drooping moustache that belied his sunny, happy nature. The beach terrace was packed with holidaymakers and Faqir asked for a table inside the café where it was quiet. Like most people in the restaurant trade, he spoke English and when he brought their fresh grilled fish, Faqir asked, 'A friend of mine told me there's a boat owner called Gavro who might take us out for a day's fishing. Do you know how we can find him?'

The man looked nervously around the empty room. 'I know him, he used to fish for us, but he hasn't been here for a while.'

Faqir let the matter drop until they'd finished their meal, then he sent Hema and the children outside for a walk along the beach. He asked Mirko for the bill and offered him a cognac and they sat and chatted for a while.

After some gentle probing, the owner leaned close to him and said, 'They say Gavro was arrested for smuggling people from Albania and Bosnia into Croatia. It's impossible now for people to get into Europe through Hungary and Bulgaria and it's less than 40 km from here, so it's becoming a popular route.' He looked slyly at him and sipped his brandy.

Faqir's heart sank. He knew exactly how close the Croatian border was, just a two-hour sea trip along the coast. The country was a member of the European Union and crucially, had applied to be a part of the Schengen Zone. From everything he'd been told, it was the easiest part of their itinerary and was just a step away from Italy and Slovenia, both Schengen countries. Now, he realised that since the Hungarian border was in the process of being closed, the people traffickers' attention had turned to alternative routes and Croatia was an obvious candidate. They had arrived just a few days too late.

What's worse, he told himself, *Tony's contact is in prison and I don't know a single person here.'*

He finished his drink and tried not to look worried. 'That's too bad. The children were looking forward to a fishing trip.' Putting the cash on the table, he stood up. 'That was really good, thanks a lot.'

The café was now empty and Mirko walked to the exit with him. 'Call by in the morning. I know another fisherman who might be able to take you out.' He patted him on the shoulder and closed the door.

Faqir went to find his family. *We just have to pray for another miracle, Inshallah.*

FORTY-THREE

Karl had been called to a meeting in Mosul with eight other senior commanders. They were listening to Abdullah, still supreme commander of the city, confirming the details of the plan of retreat for them and fifteen hundred fighters to the caliphate capital in Raqqa, Syria. Since the continuing attacks on Qayyarah and the growing evidence of US support, it was now just a matter of time before the Iraqis succeeded in crossing the Tigris and Mosul would be facing a three-sided attack from the south, west and north. It was too late to move the Qayyarah HQ to Hamam Alil and when the town fell it wouldn't be long before the final battle for Mosul followed. And now he was listening to the supreme commander explaining how they would run away from that final battle.

The defence of the caliphate city was becoming more impossible with every day that passed. After months of losses from murderous defeats, executions and desertions, he estimated the number of fighters still in Mosul at about twelve thousand. But half of them were of no practical use except as suicide bombers. Realistically, he knew it didn't really matter anymore what they did or didn't do, but what was still important to him and a few thousand like him, was how they died. With honour on the battlefield or like cowards, running away with their tails between their legs.

It's interesting, Karl reflected. *When any of my fellow commanders made a strategic retreat to save lives, they were cruelly humiliated and executed. Now we're going to guarantee the fall of the city by taking fifteen hundred fighters to escort the senior commanders to safety in Raqqa. This is not just hypocritical cowardice, it's madness. The ISIL command has become insane.*

A picture of Sami flashed though his mind. He was surprised to realise that he missed her. Her quick wit and straightforward, independent manner and her body beneath his. He'd had no news of her or Ibrahim since he'd called with the Gatwick instruction the previous Saturday, but he'd seen the various German and French press announcements about them on the Al Jazeera news channel. He was neither surprised nor disappointed to learn that his jihadist partnership had been partly identified; like Sami he'd known it was likely. In fact, he was more encouraged by the media interest, knowing they'd made it to the UK, and by Kellerman's vagueness about their travel details. Sami was smart and dedicated; he knew that with some luck and careful camouflage they could still achieve their objective. After the carnage in France, there might be even more in England.

'Does everyone understand?' The supreme commander's voice interrupted his reverie. He joined a chorus of voices shouting out, 'Yes commander, Move out on 5th July. *Alhamd lillah rabb alealamin.* Praise be to Allah.'

Inshallah, Karl whispered to himself. *If the city doesn't fall before that.*

Rafailovići, Adriatic Coast of Montenegro

At ten in the morning, Faqir walked along to the beach café, his hopes high. He'd told Hema the previous night the reason for Gavro's disappearance, cushioning the blow by repeating Mirko's last words.

'He knows someone else?' She asked, then, 'If he's been caught and put in prison, it must be more dangerous than we expected.'

'Maybe he was just careless. Or it might not even be true, just a story. You know how people like to gossip, he might have gone away for some other reason. Anyway, my love, we can't stay here, we need to find a replacement and if we're lucky, it could be through Mirko.'

That morning, he'd paid for another two nights at the guesthouse to ensure they wouldn't lose their rooms and his family had gone off to enjoy a day on the beach, the first day of real relaxation they'd had for over two weeks.

There were a few customers on the terrace and Mirko took him into the café, where a man was sitting with a glass of white wine. He stood up and held out his hand, 'Hi, I'm Alexi.'

He was of average height, about thirty, with dyed blonde hair and a stubble beard, wearing jeans and a tee-shirt, with the logo, 'Feed the World'.

Faqir noticed his hand was soft and clean, not the

hand he'd expect a fisherman to have. 'I'm Faqir, Mirko told me you take people out fishing?'

In fluent English, he said, 'People hire me for all sorts of trips, I'm very flexible.' He gave a broad smile showing an immaculate set of teeth, as if he'd just had them whitened and polished. Faqir noticed the smell of after shave and felt suddenly grubby and sweaty in his worn, stained clothes.

'Good. Why don't we walk along the beach and plan a fishing trip then?'

He smiled again. 'Sure, no need to take up Mirko's time. See you man,' he said, punching Mirko on the shoulder and leading the Iraqi outside.

They walked along the hardened sand near the water. Alexi lit a cigarette and took a drag. Faqir was astonished that the Eastern Europeans seemed to smoke more than the Arabs. He had been a twenty-a-day man until ISIL had stopped paying him and he couldn't afford to keep it up. *That's one beneficial thing they did for me*, he reflected.

'Have you ever been across into Croatian waters? I hear the fishing's very good there.'

'I'm a Croat, from along the coast. I go there all the time,' he replied.

'Do you take customers there with you, for the fishing, I mean.'

'It depends on how much they pay.'

'What's the going rate for a family of six?'

Alexi stopped and looked him up and down, as if he was calculating the Iraqi's value. Faqir was glad he didn't look smart and rich. He sucked on his cigarette again and said, 'The going rate is two thousand a head.' He turned and walked on.

Faqir had checked their money again that morning, as he always did. After the last crossing and the other minimum local expenses, they had 22,500 euros between them. *That would leave us with only ten thousand. We can't manage with so little, it's just not possible.* He said, 'Gavro was going to take us on a trip for only five thousand.'

'I hear he ended up in prison and his customers are being held to be sent back to Albania. It's not worth taking a risk like that for 5K, not for me and not for you.'

By the time they'd walked to the end of the beach, Faqir had negotiated the price down to eight thousand and he knew he wouldn't get it any lower. 'OK,' he said. 'Provided it's a good boat. Where is it?' Alexi led him over an outcrop of rocks to a small cove where a boat was drawn up on the edge of the sea, the outboard pulled up out of the water.

He was relieved to see it looked like a solid vessel, not an inflatable dinghy. He'd heard enough stories about them being used to leave abandoned refugees floating helplessly in the sea waiting for rescue by the coastguards. 'What kind is it?'

'A Dory, it was built by a friend of mine along the coast. It's a V-bottom, really good in a heavy sea.'

Faqir looked it over. It was white with the name 'ORCA' painted in the middle of a red stripe running along the side. He knocked it with his knuckles and it sounded solid, made of some kind of plasticised wood.

There were two benches running along the sides from a small wheelhouse at the stern in front of the Suzuki motor. 'What's the engine size?' he asked, trying to sound less ignorant than he was.

'Fifty horsepower. It's a six-metre boat, but light, so it's got plenty of punch. In good weather, low seas like now, with me and six passengers we can cruise comfortably at 15 knots, that's about 28 km per hour, no problem, just ninety minutes to the border. There's very good fishing off the coast at Čibača, so that would make a two and a half-hour trip.'

The Iraqi had studied his map and knew exactly the spot Alexi was proposing, a small village on the Croatian coast, just 4 km from Dubrovnik, the largest town in the area. Tony had told him it was a very popular holiday destination and they could easily lose themselves in the crowds of tourists, out of sight of official eyes. 'What's the best time to go fishing?' He kept up the pretence, even though it was becoming farcical.

'Any night after dark's a good time. Not many other boats around to interfere with your sport.'

'How about tomorrow night?'

They walked back along the beach, agreeing the details of the trip. Faqir felt as if an immense weight had been lifted off his shoulders, he couldn't wait to get back to give his family the news – he'd found a boat and driver to get into Croatia and it would cost only 8,000 euros.

Guildford, England

'How's it going?'

Sami had just returned from another shopping trip;

this time she'd brought back six polythene boxes. They were larger than those Jamil had bought in Kalk, 30 x 20 x 10, with red lids. He went to place them with the other material in a cupboard, trying not to think of his brother and sister all that time ago.

'No problems. The first batch is ready.' Working that morning, he'd produced the first quantity of TATP, enough for one box. He'd pushed the kitchen table into the corner of the room, to use as his workshop, leaving space at the sink and cooker for Sami to prepare meals. 'I'll make sixteen boxes to fit in two containers. I'm sure I can make it in three weeks.' He knew from his previous experience the material was not as unstable as the ISIL warnings indicated, but he worked with as much care as before to avoid another accident. 'I'll put everything in this cupboard, behind the table. Don't touch anything here or you might cause an accident.'

'There was a woman looking at me a bit funny in the supermarket,' Sami said.

He spun around, the boxes still in his hands. 'What happened, did she recognise you?'

'Kind of. She was in the queue at the cashier's and she asked me if I come from Belfast. Then I remembered her, she used to work in the pub near me mam's flat.'

'What did she say?'

'She asked me if I'm living in Guildford, so I said I was just visiting me auntie for two days then going back to O'Connor Street. That's where we used to live.'

'Does she live here?'

'Up beside the supermarket, so I'd better not go there again.'

'She's known you all your life, that's why she recognised you even after the changes you made.'

'As long as she doesn't see me picture on the news and put two and two together.'

He thought for a moment. 'Do you think I look much like my photo now?'

'Not to somebody who doesn't know you. But I still don't think you should chance going out if you don't have to.'

'OK, you'll have to buy the material and I'll work faster to be ready sooner, to be safe.'

Ibrahim tried to sound unworried, but he was becoming nervous. Their luck had held for a long time, but it wouldn't last forever.

Rafailovići, Adriatic Coast of Montenegro

'You're sure you can trust him, this Alexi? Until now, we've been lucky that Tony's contacts were honest, decent people, but we know nothing about this man.'

Faqir and his family were taking the day off. Earlier that morning, he had visited a small foreign exchange agency in a back street behind the hotel-lined promenade. He figured he'd get a better rate than in a hotel to buy kuna, the Croatian currency. Croatia was one of the few EU countries not to accept the euro and he didn't want to find himself unable to pay local expenses. He'd bought 200 euros' worth, not knowing how long they'd be in the country. After paying Alexei, their stash of euros would be reduced to fourteen thousand. He tried not to think of how little that was.

Hema and the girls had purchased food and drinks

from the market stalls and they were camped on the beach, with towels from the guest house. The children were enjoying the deep blue, calm, warm waters of the Adriatic, the first real ocean they'd ever dipped a toe into. They could all swim, courtesy of their local public swimming pool in Mosul, before it was closed by the ISIL invaders to prevent anyone from enjoying themselves, and they were revelling in it.

Faqir had been expecting this response from his wife; she was more suspicious, less naive and, he knew, smarter than him. 'The only reference we've got is from the café owner. After he'd left, I asked Mirko what he knew about him, how long he'd known him, that kind of thing.'

'And?'

'He's a Croat from Dubrovnik and married a girl here in Rafailovići five years ago and has lived here since then. I got the impression the girl's related to Mirko, maybe his niece, but I didn't like to ask. He was working as a fisherman, but from what was said, I think he's been doing some people trafficking. He drove off in a smart car, the kind you can't buy on a fisherman's wages. But he said he's got a good reputation in town, never been in trouble and he thinks he's honest and can be trusted.'

'And we can't exactly walk around the town looking for someone to help us get across into Croatia. We don't have much choice, do we?'

'I think we were lucky to get to know Mirko. Without his contact, we'd be stranded, stuck in this place until our money runs out, then probably shipped back to Turkey. Alexi's probably our only option.'

'The children would be happy to be stuck here for a while.' She was watching them swimming out and diving into the rolling waves to surf them back to the beach. 'I can't remember them ever being so happy and carefree. After the last couple of years of pain and misery, it's a wonderful sight.'

'So, what's your decision?'

'You're right, we've got to keep moving while we still have some money left. It's always the same, we'll just have to trust this man and hope he's honest.'

Faqir helped his wife up from the sand, putting his arm around her shoulders as they walked across the beach to join their family in the warm, shallow sea. *Tomorrow night we'll take another step towards freedom and a new life for all of us. Please God, don't let anything go wrong.*

FORTY-FOUR

Mosul, Iraq
June 2016

'Qayyarah's under a massive attack and Saad's been killed.'

It was 4:00 am on Wednesday and Karl had been woken by his phone in the Beirut hotel after another frustrating day, supervising pointless, unproductive defence preparations in the old town. There were now so many booby traps, containing IEDs – improvised explosive devices – in and under the streets, buildings, vehicles and even the bridges over the Tigris. It was becoming too dangerous to walk above ground, even though he hated scurrying around in the tunnels like a rat.

He said nothing; he knew what was coming. Abdullah was so predictable he could have written his next instruction down before it came over the phone.

'Get down there and take over. We can't afford to lose Qayyarah, it'll mean the end for Mosul.'

'So, I'm back to being south-west field commander again?'

'Don't waste my fucking time asking stupid questions. Get down there now!'

Karl thought back to Abdullah's message outlining the plan of retreat from Mosul to Raqqa. *Last week he's telling me I have to leave my men and flee like a cowardly chicken and today he wants me to go to try to save Qayyarah, which will probably fall because of his and Saad's incompetence and he forgets to mention I'll probably be killed in the process.* His patience finally snapped. 'You're forgetting all the vitally important work I'm doing for you here in Mosul, Abdullah. Besides it's four in the morning and I'm still tired. I'll go down there when I've got time.' He closed the phone, wondering if he'd gone too far this time.

Knowing what was likely to happen, he got dressed and was packing his travel bag when the phone rang again. This time it was Major General Abu Omar al-Hashiri, a member of the ISIL Military Council, in Raqqa, Syria. 'Good morning Karl, I have important news for you. The council wants you to take over again as south-west field commander in Qayyarah. It was a mistake to move you out and it's rectified with immediate effect. We're counting on you to get down there immediately.'

'Very well, sir, I'm on my way.' *Small victories are sometimes the most enjoyable*, he thought to himself as he ran to get his motorcycle. Although he knew Abdullah would never forgive him for this snub to his authority and would make him pay for it in spades, he felt better than he had in a long time.

As he rode down Highway One, the night sky was lit up across the horizon. In addition to the dozens of oil well fires that were burning to the east, he could see the lights and rocket flashes from the aircraft above and flames and explosions around Qayyarah. *This is a coordinated air and ground attack, shit! Those idiots Abdullah and Saad should have moved the HQ to Hamam Alil, like I told al-Jbouri in April. It's too late now, we're going to lose our Qayyarah installations along with our best fighters. And maybe it's my turn as well.*

Qadir, who had been his last aide, was still there. He had lost an eye in a previous attack but took up his post again when he came back from the clinic. 'Karl, great to have you back. It's been a fucking nightmare since Saad took over.'

'What happened to him?' Both men had to shout over the sound of the constant explosions.

'Rocket attack from Qayyarah West. They've got it operational again and we've got air attacks from there and from the coalition aircraft hitting us from both sides. And there's thousands of Iraqi and Peshmerga troops converging from the airfield and from Makhmur. Looks like it's the end game.'

'How far have they advanced?'

'They're in control of the road from Makhmur to the river, they've got tanks parked there now. We're holding them at the east side of the bridge.'

'They've retaken Kabaruk?' Qadir just nodded. 'Fuck! So they're 5 km away.' The village, at the east side of the Makhmur Road bridge, was one of the pivotal points of the Qayyarah battlefield. It had been taken by the Iraqis and retaken by ISIL a dozen times in the last few months. Karl envisaged the scene, Iraqi tanks parked at the blockade on the east side of the bridge across the Tigris and ISIL fighters holding the west side. If the Iraqis got across, they had an open road from the south to Qayyarah and the west side was already under threat from the Qayyarah West airfield. 'How did we lose the road?'

'Last night, there was an attack on Tall 'Azbah on the other side of the river by US and Iraqi forces from the airfield. Saad sent men from Kabaruk to defend Tall 'Azbah. While we were fighting there, the Iraqi tanks came rolling along from Makhmur with a couple thousand troops. By this morning they'd taken the town and the road up to the bridge. We lost over fifty good fighters.'

'Saad's greatest crime was he didn't get killed soon enough.'

'He checked with Abdullah before he gave the order.' Qadir tried unsuccessfully to hide his smile.

He forgot to mention that when he called. Karl couldn't believe the stupidity of both men to fall for such an obvious ruse. The Makhmur Road bridge was the only way across the Tigris between Tikrit, 150 km to the south and Mosul, 60 km to the north. Holding the bridge and the two villages on either side, Kabaruk and Tall 'Azbah, had been the key to keeping Qayyarah in ISIL hands. Now, two over-promoted imbeciles had given away the east side and it was just a matter of time before the tanks destroyed the blockade on the west side.

He said, 'The Iraqis have learned a lot from the Americans and those fucking imbeciles, Abdulla and Saad, have learned nothing in their entire existences. What happened in Tall 'Azbah?'

'As soon as they'd taken Kabaruk and got to the bridge, they pulled their forces out and left it to us.'

'For the time being, you mean.' He drank the hot bitter coffee that Qadir handed him, cursing the incompetence he was witnessing. 'What's our strength?'

'Two hundred men in Tall 'Azbah and five hundred here, more or less.'

'Arms and equipment?'

'When Tall 'Azbah was attacked, Saad got a hundred men sent down from Hamam Alil, with trucks and a shitload of armaments.'

Karl laughed, 'Very precise measurements, Qadir. So, Saad did something right, in the end. Have you had a drone up there?'

He studied the file of photographs from the drone and compared it to the map Qadir had prepared with numbers and notes of the opposing forces and equipment. 'I see ten tanks there on the road near the bridge, right? Have they had time to protect them?'

'Those pictures were taken two hours ago. It doesn't look like it, and it's not easy to protect them on the road like that. They're expecting to use them again quickly, maybe tonight, to push across the bridge and open up the west side of the river.'

He thought about this for a moment. 'Those barges we used to get oil workers and equipment across before the Iraqis took back the oilfields. They were tied up beside the refinery dock. Are they still there and working?' Karl was referring to the motorised barges used to ship oil upriver to Mosul from the oilfields and the refinery, before it had been abandoned.

'There's still a couple operating, and we've sent a few sorties over in them. What's all this about?'

'Hang on. How many booby-trapped vehicles have we got here?'

'Thirty or forty. You remember we brought a lot

back from Al-Nasr a few months ago, they're in that oil storage facility behind the mosque.'

'Including light jeeps and cars? Let's take a look.'

They ignored the shells and rockets exploding around them as they ran to the warehouse, where thirty-some vehicles planted with explosives were stored. Karl looked them over, 'OK, he said, there's plenty of suitable vehicles. Take me out to the dock.'

The riverside was only 4 km away and there were two 70 metre barges tied up alongside the dock, with a fighter standing guard. Under Karl's instructions, he started the engines and they sounded OK.

'Can you load vehicles on one of them and get them off on the other side?'

'No problem. It's about time we used them for something.'

'Get one ready to be loaded tonight.'

Qadir drove them back to the storage warehouse, where Karl selected twelve vehicles and explained what he wanted. Within an hour, a dozen 'experts' were adding explosives to the vehicles he'd chosen.

Düsseldorf, Germany

Max Kellerman was on the phone with DCI Callum Dewar; he had some news to share. Thanks to the anti-terrorist measures introduced by the government after the atrocities of recent years, the French police had been unusually assiduous. As well as looking for Cabaret in Lannion and St Malo, they had searched all the local registers of ships between Le Havre in Normandy to Brest, in Brittany. The only vessel they'd found named

Cabaret was a twelve-metre aluminium fishing boat, registered in Cherbourg to a company called *Pecheurs de l'Espagne*. The owners were two brothers, Miguel and Eladio Navarro, from San Sebastian in the Basque country on the northern Spanish coast. 'And you know what that might mean,' he added. The police were sending a team to check the boat and interview the owners. He'd pass on any further information as soon as it became available, but he was certain they were on the right track.

Dewar had nothing to report on the CCTV checks they'd done on Torquay trains and was obviously still unconvinced that the terrorists were in the UK. He wished him luck, hoping Kellerman's judgement was wrong. He'd received that morning the updated statistics on the terrorist threat from the Home Office and it didn't make good reading. More than twenty thousand potential jihadists were on the MI5 surveillance list, with active monitoring and investigation being carried out on a further three thousand representing a hard and immediate threat to security. The government's 'Prevent' strategy seemed to be creating more criticism than praise from the population that it was designed to protect, despite the 29,000 deaths from global terrorism in 2015. Sixty-four of these terrorist attacks were ISIL related. Only the dedicated and professional vigilance of international security services, like his, had prevented much more loss of life from aborted murderous missions.

Dewar returned to one of the sixty-five other cases his department was involved with at the moment. He didn't need any more work, and especially not looking for two needles in a haystack who had successfully avoided capture in Germany and France for over a month and were probably not in the UK. *At least, I hope to God they're not,* he prayed silently.

Qayyarah, Iraq

'OK, you all know your targets?'

It was midnight and after a day of intermittent air strikes and constant missile and rocket fire from both sides, there had been a couple of hours pause in the fighting. The stand-off hadn't changed; the bridge was still a no man's land, the Iraqi tanks holding the east side and the ISIL forces, with additional fighters sent from Hamam Alil at Karl's command, defending the west. Under cover of darkness and the heavy smoke clouds from the burning oil wells, the twelve modified booby-trapped vehicles and the same number of pick-up trucks had been transported by barge across the 200-metre width of the Tigris to the east side of the river.

He had just finished briefing his attack team, the twelve suiciders who had volunteered to drive down the hardpacked sand track to the Makhmur Road bridge and the twelve pick-up drivers who would escort them. His plan was a variation on the original charge against Mosul, two years ago. The open trucks were mounted with light machine guns and spotlights, each with just two fighters carrying assault rifles and handheld rocket launchers. There was a delicate balance between weight and force to be respected in the desert and weight always won out, otherwise they'd be stuck in the sand, sitting ducks. He would lead the charge in one of the open trucks; although he would have happily given up his life in a suicide vehicle, he knew he could contribute more by staying alive.

He gave the signal and the heavy rocket launchers and mortars in Qayyarah started their covering bombardment, firing at the Iraqi encampment on the east side of the bridge, while his vehicles sped off south, down to the Makhmur Road.

In a few minutes, the convoy reached the road at the entrance to the bridge, blocked by the Iraqi tanks parked in lines, about 3 metres apart. The fighting trucks bore down on the temporary encampment, where the coalition troops, buoyed by their success that morning, were still digging in and building their defence barricades. Taken totally by surprise when they saw the jihadists coming down on the east side of the bridge, they panicked and struggled to organise themselves. Under the cover of the continuous barrage of rocket and mortar shelling from Qayyarah, the ISIL fighters carved a swathe of death and destruction through the camp.

In the midst of this mayhem, the suicide volunteers inserted their vehicles into the line of tanks, stopping in between them on each side and back and front, before detonating their explosives. The modifications ordered by Karl that morning consisted of additional massive bombs attached to the front and back bumpers of the suicide trucks, at the height of the tanks' caterpillar tracks. His plan was almost completely successful, most of the tracks being either destroyed or damaged, rendering the tanks immovable. They were now stuck on the road, blocking the bridge and preventing the coalition forces from advancing across the Tigris. Karl had reversed what had been a position of attack for the Iraqis into a position of defence for ISIL.

Now the jihadists took advantage of the panic and disorder in the Iraqi ranks; more ISIL fighters stormed across the bridge and the camp was invaded by one hundred fighters, determined to push the infidels back and retake the east side of the Makhmur Road. The Iraqi troops had no stomach for this kind of close combat and began to retreat back towards Kabaruk. The battle raged for the rest of the night, dozens of men on each side giving up their lives for their cause. By daybreak, Karl's fighters had won ten hard-earned kilometres of extra security, between the east side of the bridge and Kabaruk, and the bridge was now blocked by the disabled tanks. His bet had paid off and so had that of the military council. Six of his pick-up trucks had made it back across the river to Qayyarah, including his, and he'd bought some time at a cost of twenty-five men, but he knew it wouldn't change anything in the end, and the end was approaching very quickly now.

His phone rang as he was driving back to Qayyarah; it was Abdullah. 'So, you're a hero again, Karl, and back in charge of the south-western region. You must be happy being the council's favourite commander. Long may it last.'

Sounds like it won't last long if he has anything to do with it, he said to himself. Aloud, he answered, 'Thanks, Abdullah. Looks like you're going to have to find another second in command for Mosul. Good luck.'

FORTY-FIVE

'Major Kellerman is calling on line one.'

The DCI reluctantly marked his place in the briefing document he was studying and picked up the phone. 'Dewar here.'

Max wasted no time on formalities. 'We've got a report back about the Cabaret. The boat was harboured in St Malo on Thursday night. It's in the port register, so we know they definitely sailed from there to Torquay.'

'Right, that corresponds with the Border Patrol report.'

'The RAID people have been to inspect it and it's a high-speed boat with two Mercury engines. They reckon it could make up to 20 knots at a push.'

'Good, also what my officer told us.'

'Wait. Below decks there's a cabin with a large cavity between two bunks that goes all the way to the bulkhead, hidden by a cupboard with shelving, full of wet weather clothing, rescue material and stuff like that. The cavity's lined with carpet tiles and it's large enough to hide a couple of people.'

'I understand.'

'The owners said they sometimes use that space for their children to sleep when they take their families on sea trips.'

'Sounds reasonable. Go on.'

'The RAID officers searched the cavity and found something on the floor.'

The Assistant Commander didn't appreciate dramatic pauses. 'What did they find?'

'A small printed manufacturer's card. One of those cards they supply with certificate of origin, materials, quality check and all that, to comply with EU regulations.'

'Do they know what it came from?'

'They think it's from the pocket of a backpack, that's where they often put them. They scanned the card to me and it's a Vietnamese manufacturer, but there's a name stamped on the back.'

Another pause, then, 'It's the name of a German distributor in Munich. I've already got someone checking with them that it's a backpack.'

'And your theory is that your Cologne bomber, al-Ahmad, was carrying that backpack and hiding in the cavity when my people boarded the boat?'

'I feel certain of it.'

Dewar didn't like the inference that his Border Patrol officers couldn't find a fugitive terrorist in a cupboard. 'Hang on a minute. You told me there was various kinds of material in the cupboard and I suppose this cavity was also a storage place. So it's highly likely that there's been all kinds of luggage and bags in there as well.'

'I suppose that's possible, but why was it hidden?'

'Was it hidden? You said it was behind a shelved cupboard. I know boats, and that's very common. If you want shelves for the cabin you have to actually build a cupboard across the bulkhead.'

'But we know the Cabaret was en route from St Malo

to Torquay on Thursday night just after the two fugitives arrived in Lannion and now we've found proof that a German bag or something like that was in this hiding place. To me it's obvious they were on that boat and now they're in England.'

'I'm sorry, Major Kellerman, but this is all conjecture. Lannion is miles away from St Malo and that card could have fallen out of a piece of luggage, if that's what it was, at any time. I've already got all our services on alert, but I can't start a nationwide manhunt on such flimsy evidence.'

Kellerman thought for a moment. 'OK, I'm going to get Rennes to fingerprint the cabin and cavity area. We've got their prints from the hotel and we might be lucky. Can you please interview the officer who went aboard and ask him specifically if he looked in that cupboard and the cavity behind? And can you get confirmation that the boat arrived in Torquay?'

DCI Dewar made yet another note on his 'to-do' list. 'I'll get to it as soon as I can, but I wouldn't read too much into it.'

Max Kellerman cursed and slammed the phone down with a bang. He looked over at his incident chart on the wall. He was sure it pointed exactly in the direction he wanted Dewar to go. The problem was, he still had no definite proof. 'Why the hell can't people see what's right in front of their noses,' he shouted out loud. 'I bloody well know I'm right!'

He gave no news conference that night nor the following but showed only a photograph of Ibrahim and the woman, with a text on the screen that read, 'If you have seen this man or woman, please call the following number immediately. Do not approach them, they may be dangerous.' He knew the item wouldn't be retransmitted to other countries – it just wasn't exciting enough.

Guildford, England

'I was just thinking about something.' Ibrahim was filling the third polythene box with TATP.

'And what might that be?'

'How many people do you think were around the places in Gatwick where you said we should explode the bombs?'

'That's a bloody difficult question. What distance do you mean?'

'In a twenty-metre circle.'

Sami tried to recall the crowds around her at the airport. 'If there was twenty-five around me at 5 metres, then the same for each 5 metres more, that would make ...'

'One hundred,' he interrupted. 'In two places, it might be two hundred people. That's a good number.'

'A good number for what?'

'Listen Sami. The Paris massacre was the biggest one so far and that was only about one hundred and thirty people. If we kill more than that, we'll be the most famous jihadists in history. Karl and all of ISIL will be proud of us and we'll make a great noise.'

Sami suddenly felt sick. The words of the woman with the little girl came back to her, '*Have a safe flight*'. She thought of the crowds of holidaymakers in the airport, happy and excited at the prospect of flying off to a sunny, foreign place to enjoy their fortnight away from some boring and underpaid job. In different circumstances, she could have been one of those people. Somehow, fighting in a bombed-out city against anonymous missiles and shells wasn't the same as blowing up a crowd of real people. Women, children, people who weren't guilty of anything except being in the wrong place at the wrong time. *Like me poor old Dad*, she realised.

When she didn't answer, Ibrahim said, 'The Imam Mohammad told me, "All these steps will become a stampede that will make the infidels flee from the power of Allah".'

'Write down the things you need and I'll go to the store before it gets too busy,' she replied. 'I'm going to get ready now.'

She went out wearing the thick-framed sunglasses she'd bought at the supermarket after her encounter with the ex-barmaid from Belfast. She didn't look out of place in the warm sunshine and was much less recognisable.

Near Popovići, Adriatic Coast of Croatia

The Adriatic no longer resembled the deep blue, calm, warm ocean whose soft waves had lapped onto the golden sands of Rafailovići for the last two days. It was a cloudless night and Alexi had taken the Orca out about 2 km from the shore to avoid detection. A cool Bora wind from the north-west had come up after they'd left the protection of Sveti Nikola, a small islet in the Bay of

Bečići, and out on the open sea the water beneath them was black and choppy.

Faqir had asked if there were any lifejackets, but the Croat just laughed, 'Of course, but this is no problem. There might be a bit of rain but nothing this boat can't handle. You'll be fine if you just sit still and hold on.'

As they sailed north, the wind caused the 20-centimetre waves to push against the side of the boat, rocking it sideways. The whole family were feeling the effects of the swell, Faqir and Hema more than the children, since they were sitting in the bow of the vessel. Malik and Hamid were aft, next to the wheelhouse, keenly observing the navigation and operation of the boat. Alexi dropped his cruising speed to just over 20 km per hour, meaning a longer time on the water, but with less movement.

Just before one in the morning, they had passed the Montenegro-Croatian border at Njivice, about 37 km from Rafailovići, their starting point. It was now 2:15 am and they were in Croatian waters, about a half hour from their destination, Čibača. At that moment, the sound of the engine died down to a murmur and the boat slowed to a standstill, bobbing about even more, and accentuating the swell. Hema hung on to the gunwale, fighting to supress the nauseous sensation.

'What's wrong? Why are we stopping?' Faqir looked around anxiously. Was there another vessel in sight? In the moonlight, there was nothing as far as the eye could see, except the occasional faint blink of lights from the shore.

Alexi came out from the wheelhouse to stand between the benches in front of them, holding onto the partition and lighting a cigarette. 'It's OK, guys, don't worry. I just figured it's a good place to stop for a talk.'

The Iraqi suddenly had a bad feeling. 'It's not a good place, the boat's moving all over and my family are feeling sick. We can talk when we get to the shore at Čibača.'

'Sorry, Faqir, but that's not the agreement. When we made our deal, it was to go fishing off the coast at Čibača, not to take you ashore. You know as well as I do, that would be illegal without going through the immigration controls. Of course, you could all get out and swim ashore, it's just 2 km and the sea's only 50 metres deep here.' He flashed his perfect teeth and took another drag on his cigarette.

The Iraqi cursed the language he'd used when they'd spoken on the beach. He'd kept up the pretence of a fishing trip and now Alexi could insist he'd misunderstood. He knew he hadn't, but it made no difference. No wonder he'd beaten him down on price so easily, he'd never intended to take them ashore for 8,000 euros – this was going to cost a lot of money. Money he didn't have or couldn't afford to give up. He felt furious with himself and anxious for his family.

'So, what exactly are you saying, Alexi?'

Hema had said nothing up to now, but her worst fears had been realised; the man was a crook. Her suspicions had increased when he'd insisted on the full payment of 8,000 euros before they left Rafailovići. She squeezed Faqir's hand, whispering, 'Don't provoke him.'

'I told you the going rate for the trip was two thousand a head,' he said. 'I was wrong. Since the Hungarians started their shutdown, it's gone up to three. For that, I might risk the immigration problem.'

'That's 18,000 euros!' Faqir stood up and took a step forward, his fists bunched. 'I don't have that much money and even if I did, you know that wasn't the deal. You've brought us out here to blackmail us into paying more, because you think we've got no other option.'

'Shut the fuck up and sit down.' Alexi pulled out a gun from his jerkin and pointed it at him.

Malik and Hamid sitting in the stern, closest to the Croat, looked at each other, bracing themselves for action as Hema gasped when she saw the dull flash of metal in the moonlight. 'Stop, Faqir, sit down, there must be a way to solve this. Alexi, he's right, we don't have that money, you have to settle for less.'

'That's more like it. You're smarter than this fucking idiot you're married to. If you haven't got the cash, I'll have to take something else.'

Faqir was still standing unsteadily near the bow of the boat, 'What do you mean? We've got nothing else of value. Everything we've got is in our backpacks and it's worth nothing at all.'

'You've got two daughters, good looking, probably virgins. They're worth a few thousand in Albania or Bosnia.' He took a last drag and threw the butt overboard.

'You fucking bastard, I'll murder you for that.' He was about to throw himself at the Croat when he pointed the pistol at Hamid's head. Hema screamed out and Faqir stopped, 'Don't do anything stupid, Alexi. We've still got some money, you can have it, just don't threaten my family.'

'Don't tell me what to do, you fucking Arab refugee.' He raised the gun again, pointing it at the Iraqi.

'Now!' Malik reached up to grab the pistol, while Hamid threw himself at the Croat, knocking him off balance. He fell sideways and the weapon exploded before Malik could tear it from his hand. Hamid grabbed Alexi's ankle, twisting and pulling his foot off the deck and pushing him onto the gunwale. Together, they wrestled him off his feet and manhandled him over the side of the vessel, where he hung by one hand, trying to aim the gun at them. A shot rang out again, but neither was touched.

'Throttle up,' Hamid shouted and Malik stepped into the wheelhouse, pushing the hand throttle up as far as it would go. The engine roared as the Orca jumped forward and Hamid stamped on the Croat's hand until he let go. He screamed as the waves dragged him away and the boat raced off, the brothers looking back at him until he was no longer visible on the ocean surface.

'Throttle down,' Malik pulled the lever back to the bottom and the boat slowed to a crawl, the screaming engine now silent.

'Good job, bro.' The brothers turned to their family in the front of the boat. 'Oh no, what the fuck, what happened?' Hamid switched on his torch to reveal the devastating scene.

Faqir was lying on the deck between the benches, his head in Hema's lap, their daughters kneeling by his body, wailing and crying, desperately pressing a handkerchief to his stomach, a handkerchief they could now see was soaked in blood. His eyes were wide open as he looked at them all in turn, trying vainly to speak, but the blood was bubbling from his mouth and the decking was soaked beneath his back. They saw immediately that the bullet must have pierced a main vessel or an organ for there to be so much blood. Hema seemed paralysed with shock; she looked imploringly at Hamid and he struggled forward to kneel by his father's side in the narrow space, but he knew nothing could be done; they had no medical supplies, equipment or the knowledge to stop the bleeding. He could do nothing except to watch his father dying in front of them.

The boat was now rocking dangerously as the wind pushed the waves against the side and Hema shouted out with fear. Malik rushed back to the wheelhouse, peering through his tears at the compass as he brought the Orca back onto a north-westerly route, parallel with the coast. He tried vainly to block out the scene in front of him, wondering what they would do now, how could they manage without their father who had somehow brought them safely out of Iraq, across five countries, to the brink of making it into the EU, only to be murdered by a filthy, blackmailing Croatian people smuggler who wasn't fit to walk in his shadow. *What's worse*, he said to himself, *it was me who caused his death. I grabbed the gun and it went off and killed my father.* 'I'm sorry, Papa,' he screamed into the wind. 'I didn't know what would happen. Please forgive me.' He wiped his eyes then tied the wheel in position, set the throttle at 5 km/h and came forward to join his grieving family.

It was 2:00 am and the Orca was now moving in a circle

at 5 km/h off the Croatian coast opposite Čibača, their original landing destination. Faqir had died without speaking, a few minutes after the shooting, his body unable to halt the bleeding and his family incapable of doing anything to prevent his death.

After a long, anguished period of crying and praying, Hema and the girls cleaned Faqir's body with seawater and changed him into a clean white shirt and trousers. They washed the blood away from the deck and laid him on a sleeping bag in the dark passageway. After praying again, finishing with the Lord's Prayer, they sat quietly, holding hands, each of them with their own thoughts.

Finally, Hema said, 'We have to decide what to do. Your father can't look after us any more, we have to fend for ourselves, to finish this journey we started together. His death mustn't be in vain, we owe it to him to get through as he wanted, to find a new life in Europe, away from the death and destruction we've suffered all these years. It's time to talk together as a family. We can't change this terrible tragedy, we must accept it and somehow agree on how to survive and move on.'

'First, I have to beg your forgiveness, Mama, Hamid, sisters.' Malik kneeled and put his hand on his heart. 'It was me who tried to get the gun from Alexi and it went off. That's what killed Papa, it was my stupidity. Please forgive me.' He leaned forward and pressed his forehead to the deck.

Hamid pulled him back up. 'It wasn't your fault, we both attacked him. If we hadn't, he would probably have killed Papa anyway, taken our money then shot all of us and thrown us over the side. That Croat was a piece of filth, a murderous, blackmailing crook.' He spat over the side. 'It's no good saying this was your fault, or my fault, or anybody's fault except the bastard who pulled the trigger. He was ready to shoot and we had to stop him. Now we have to decide what we should do next.'

'Malik's right, there's no blaming anyone except that treacherous monster. We have to talk about the immediate problems.' Hema steeled herself. 'The first one is how to bury your father's body. We can't take him back to Montenegro and we can't take him ashore in Croatia. We'll be arrested immediately and shipped off somewhere to a refugee camp.' The tears poured from her eyes as she implored her children, 'What shall we do?'

FORTY-SIX

Düsseldorf, Germany
June 2016

'I've obtained a full report from the Border Patrol officer who boarded the Cabaret.' DCI Dewar was on the phone with Max Kellerman again. This time it was he who had initiated the call.

'What did he say?' Kellerman was immediately interested. At the moment he was at an impasse; the RAID officers had fingerprinted the whole boat, inside and out, but had found no prints to speak of and none to match those found in the Paris hotel. He was wondering why the boat would show hardly any fingerprints, unless it had been scrupulously cleaned.

'Apparently, he was going to open up the cupboard to inspect the cavity, but when he found out that the captain knew one of our officers and made the trip regularly, he decided it wasn't necessary. He checked the rest of the boat and the cargo and let them continue to Torquay.'

'And is that where they actually went?'

'Yes. I just received confirmation that the boat arrived there on Thursday morning early and they loaded a batch of cheeses and left before 9:00 am.'

Max explained that they had found very few fingerprints on the boat. 'I think that's a suspicious sign. It's quite possible the fugitives were hidden behind the cupboard and they cleaned the whole place afterwards to get rid of any fingerprints.'

'Maybe, but fishermen usually wear gloves, because of their rough work in wet, cold conditions, so we have no proof or otherwise of that. But I was thinking of something else.'

Max didn't agree, but said nothing and Dewar went on, 'We know they were going from St Malo to Torquay on the Wednesday, because we have proof of their departure and arrival. But you told me the boat is registered in Cherbourg which is about a hundred and twenty k's away. I'm wondering why they were in St Malo and not Cherbourg the night before they were going to make a Channel crossing. It's a detour of 240 km. And, of course, Lannion's about the same distance from Cherbourg as St Malo, so the whole thing doesn't chime quite true to me.'

Kellerman could see where he was going with this. 'You said they were carrying foie gras, right?'

'That's what the officer saw in the cargo hold.'

'Did he get a copy of the paperwork from them? Do we know where and when they loaded it?'

'I'll get back to him and if we've got it I'll scan it to you ASAP.'

Kellerman put the phone down and went straight to his wall chart. This time he used a red marker and underlined the word, 'Invoice'.

Dubrovnik, Dalmatian Coast, Croatia

Hema and her children were sitting on the terrace of a café in the *Stradun*, a large limestone paved square surrounded by shops and restaurants in the walled town of Dubrovnik. It was a warm, sunny morning and every establishment in the square seemed to be full of tourists. They toyed with their breakfast, attempting to look happy and relaxed but full of anger and sorrow after the awful events they'd just lived through.

The decision of how to dispose of Faqir's corpse had been traumatic for all of them. Hema was right, they couldn't take a dead body ashore, anywhere, for fear of the consequences, but the alternative was abhorrent to their Christian upbringing. Finally, after a long and painful discussion, they agreed there was only one possible resting place for him, the bottom of the sea. Once they made this decision, the others became easier, and they formulated a plan of action. They set about examining the Orca.

'See this, Mama. That Croatian never had any intention of helping us.' In a tool cupboard in the wheelhouse hung a single life jacket, there were no others on the boat. 'If we'd had a storm and the boat capsized, there'd be only one survivor.' Malik spat over the side of the boat. 'He didn't deserve to die by drowning, it was too easy.'

'Shush, Malik. Let the dead rest in peace. Look at this, it's just right.' She unfolded a large, yellow, heavy plastic coat. 'It's large enough to wrap around your father's body.' Her voice choked at the words, but she went on, 'We have to find something to weigh it down.'

He opened a trapdoor in the deck planks revealing a dank, dark space underneath and shone his torch into the opening, 'Here, Mama. Everything we need.' There was a coil of sturdy rope and pieces of scrap metal and broken equipment, ballast to steady the keel of the boat.

Unknowingly, Alexi had provided everything needed to bury the body of the man he'd murdered so callously.

'Now. Very carefully, my darlings.' Kneeling by the body, they lifted Faqir gently onto the bench seat. Under the moonlight, his face looked rested and relaxed, the creases from the stress of the last few weeks gone from his forehead; he seemed to be at peace.

They began the dreadful task of dressing the corpse. Wrapping the waterproof coat around him, they weighed it down with pieces of metal inside and in the pockets, then fastened it up and lashed it tightly around his body and legs with rope to prevent it from opening. Only Faqir's face could now be seen, still and serene inside the bulky wrapping.

'Please take the boat out, Malik.' He opened the throttle and headed due west, for five kilometres, where the seabed was over 150 m below them.

After saying more prayers, Hema leaned over her husband's body and gently kissed his cold lips. Her tears poured down onto his face as she whispered, 'Goodbye, my dearest husband. Thank you for bringing us out of that dreadful place and so near to safety. May the good Lord look after you and keep you safe until I join you again.'

After each of the children did the same, they fastened the flap of the oilskin over his face and firmly around his head. Then, together they lifted the body and gently rolled it over the side of the Orca. Faqir Al-Douri's lifeless corpse disappeared into the depths of the Adriatic, never again to be seen by them, and hopefully no one else.

They kept vigil for as long as they dared in the

choppy swell, finally heading back just before four in the morning. Sunrise would be at 05:30 and they had no time to waste. Malik brought them into the shore just off Čibača; as originally planned and Hema and her daughters disembarked onto the beach with their belongings. With their mother's admonishments in their ears, the two brothers took the boat out west for half a kilometre, where the ocean depth was over 20 m. Malik killed the engine and pulled the outboard up out of the water. His brother took a screwdriver from the toolkit, put on the lifebelt and dropped into the sea at the rear of the craft. Hamid pushed the blade again and again through the wooden stern below water level, while Malik did the same from the inside and in a few minutes, they created a ragged hole in the hull. He climbed back on board and together they smashed through the planking with chunks of metal, until the sea started to leak in.

The heavy outboard motor weighed down on the stern and water poured into the hull of the boat. It was going down fast. The brothers jumped into the warm ocean and sharing the lifebelt, swam away from the sinking vessel, treading water until they saw the bow slide beneath the waves. The Orca submerged into the inky depths of the Adriatic Sea; now there was nothing to prove they'd ever been here, nothing at all. The wind was still pushing the waves towards the shore and they quickly swam the 500 m back to join their family on the beach. It was time for their hike to Dubrovnik.

'It's got two bedrooms which can take five people, a hundred euros a night cash, no questions asked. Shall I confirm?' Hema nodded and he said, 'That's cool, we'll be there in an hour for the keys. See you later, Peter.'

Hamid had found a private advertiser online offering cheap B&B accommodation, a holiday villa which was empty until the end of the month. He'd also ensured that there was a Wi-Fi connection. The neighbours had the keys and would take the payment. Another problem solved.

'It's incredible what you can find on the internet, and how trusting people are.' Hema shook her head. 'What if we were crooks or murderers like that awful Croatian, we could kill them in their beds and steal everything.'

'We're just not used to it, Mama. Everybody uses it like the corner shop we had in Mosul, only it's a lot more useful to us here than it was there.'

The house was clean and tidy. They threw off their dirty clothing, showered, then lay down on the beds and couches available. Sleep didn't come easily for any of them, but the exertions and stress of the night finally caught up and they slept until late afternoon. In the evening, they joined the crowds walking around the town, along the top of the famous stone walls that surround it and through the central square, trying to look like innocent holidaymakers. Tony Miller had been right; it was the perfect place to hide in plain sight.

Guildford, England

'It's taking longer than I expected.'

'And why do think that is?' Sami put down the shopping bag with her latest purchases. 'Are you doing something different?'

'I was thinking how slow the process is, the way they tell you to do it in Christian's instructions.'

'Probably because that's the safe way and any other way would be dangerous.'

'I suppose so, but maybe they never tried a different way.'

'And so you did?'

'Yes, I was trying to make it faster, so we could plan the attack sooner.'

She had another vision of the airport full of holidaymakers. 'What did you do?'

'I put two times the amounts of everything to make two batches of TATP each day instead of one.'

'And you didn't blow the place up, that's good.'

He laughed, as he always did now that he understood her sense of humour. He was sure she'd make a joke even if she was lying on her death bed. 'No, but it didn't work. It didn't mix the way it should. The way it does with Christian's instructions.'

He showed her another box of the explosive material on the table. 'Look. That's only the fourth box I've done now, after four days, and I can't do it faster. If it takes the same time for the rest, that makes two weeks more.'

'Is that when you'll have everything ready?'

'No, that's just the TATP, then I have to build the bombs with the detonator and shrapnel and everything, but it won't take more than a day.'

'We'll still be ready by the end of the month. That's what we planned, the last week in June, when the holiday season gets going.'

He looked embarrassed. 'It was a stupid idea. I've

wasted a lot of stuff, you'll have to buy even more now. I'm sorry.'

She quaked at the thought of more shopping trips, but said, 'That's OK, just make another list and I'll get it done.'

'There's one thing that isn't on the list. We have to think of the best containers for them, in Cologne I used a box made from hard cardboard.'

She thought for a moment. 'For the airport we'll need to have suitcases or it'll look funny. Soft ones, not new, a bit battered. I'll look for some in a charity shop.'

'Great idea. I'll write the measurements down for you. The boxes have to fit well but with enough space for the material around and the trigger phone and everything.'

'I'm looking for a cheap car rental place as well, like you said, where they don't ask too many questions. There's a couple listed online, I'll have a look at them.' She started emptying the shopping bag. 'I got fish fingers for supper, I can do some beans and chips with them, is that alright?'

Düsseldorf, Germany

Max Kellerman had just received confirmation from the Munich distributor. The card found in the cavity on the Cabaret was from a backpack included in a batch imported in December 2015, ready to distribute to stores for the 2016 spring season.

That means the backpacks wouldn't be available in the stores until February or March, he reasoned. *Ibrahim must have bought it after he fled from Cologne in May and it fell out of the bag on June 3rd. The timing's perfect.*

Max was starting to feel more optimistic again and began to write a report to Eric Schuster to seek approval for a formal approach to the Counter Terrorism Command at London Met. He wanted a full TV and newspaper campaign in the UK with confirmation of the terrorist's presence in England and a new reward offered in sterling.

An email flashed across the screen and he opened it up. It was the scanned copy of an invoice from DCI Dewar's office for 50 kilos of foie gras, addressed to *Pecheurs de l'Espagne,* from *De la Ferme Bretonne* in Cherbourg. The delivery date was Wednesday, 1st June and the delivery address was *Quai des Flamands, Cherbourg-Octeville.*

He whooped with excitement. This meant the Cabaret had taken on the cargo in Cherbourg on the Wednesday and then sailed down to spend the night in St. Malo. Why? Why had they sailed for 120 km in the wrong direction, only to sail back the next night to cross the Channel to Torquay? He knew the answer to the rhetorical question. *So they could sail along to Lannion to pick up two terrorists and transport them to England.*

He immediately called back his contact at Rennes to ask him to question the two brothers. Why had they spent Wednesday night in St Malo when they were sailing across the Channel to Torquay the next evening? *Let's hear what they've got to answer to that.*

Max updated his chart then finished his report and took it along to Eric Schuster. Now he might get some action out of DCI Dewar.

Guildford, England

Ibrahim and Sami watched the retransmission of Max

Kellerman's press conference on BBC News that evening. Once again, he'd failed to convince DCI Dewar to go public until they had something definite. Included in his statement was a piece from Superintendent Massinet's previous appeal, but he knew the French had lost interest; they were as convinced as he was that the fugitives were now in the UK.

'Still no change.' Sami switched the laptop off. 'If they'd been sure we were here there would have been an English cop talking, so they still don't know where we are.'

'Or what we look like. You look really different from that drawing and with my shaved head and stubbly beard we don't look anything like the people they're looking for.'

'You're right. No need to worry.' Sami had been worrying since her visit to Gatwick and her meeting with the barmaid, but it wouldn't help to say so.

FORTY-SEVEN

Max Kellerman was in his office at the SIB at eight on Saturday morning. Monika had accused him of becoming obsessed with the al-Ahmad case and he knew it was true. Now, he wished he'd spent the day at home with her – the latest news wasn't good.

Yesterday, DCI Dewar had still stubbornly refused to instigate 'a panic epidemic' in the UK by broadcasting the presence of two dangerous terrorists without reasonable proof that they had been on the Cabaret on Thursday night. Max had hoped the boat's overnight stay in St Malo would provide such reasonable proof, but it hadn't.

A long email from Commissioner Letouffe in Rennes had arrived last night, informing him that Miguel Navarro's ex-wife lived in St Malo with their handicapped daughter. She told the local officer who called at the house that they had spent Wednesday night and Thursday there then left to sail to England at about nine in the evening, as they usually did when they came down before crossing the Channel. The policeman knew the family and believed the woman was telling the truth.

Kellerman reckoned it would have taken the Cabaret about three hours to cover the 100 km trip along the coast to Lannion. He added another hour for entering and leaving the harbour and picking up the two fugitives, therefore setting off for Torquay at 1:00 am at the earliest. The boat was one hour out of Torquay when the Border Control office boarded at four-thirty on Friday morning. They would have had to cross in three and a half hours to meet the time frame.

Kellerman was dejected. He knew that no boat, however fast, could have made the crossing in such a time, but he was certain that the fugitives had crossed the Channel on Thursday night in the Cabaret. *Someone's lying and it can only be the ex-wife. They spent the Wednesday night in St Malo but they must have left the next morning or afternoon for Lannion. It's the only explanation that makes sense.*

He followed that line of thought. *If the* Cabaret *was still in St Malo on Thursday afternoon, someone might have seen it there or, if not, somewhere along the coast towards Lannion.* He emailed Superintendent Letouffe in Rennes and begged him to look for any witnesses to the Cabaret's whereabouts. Then he sent a message to Callum Dewar to explain his conundrum. It was unlikely that the DCI would change his position, but he had to keep up the contact. Sooner or later Ibrahim and the English woman were going to turn up in the UK and they needed to be ready. There was still nothing to warrant a new TV announcement; he needed something to reinvigorate the investigation, but he had nothing. On his way home, he bought a bouquet of flowers for Monika. It was the weekend after all.

Dubrovnik, Dalmatian Coast, Croatia

Hema and her family had been in the villa since the previous afternoon, talking together for hours, reminiscing about their life in Iraq, both good times and bad. Remembering how Faqir had always found solutions to their problems, protecting them from the worst excesses of the ISIL regime and managing to get them safely to this place. At last, exhausted and drained by the recent events, they said their prayers then tumbled into bed, sleeping well into the morning.

This morning, they were feeling rested, slowly coming to terms with the tragic loss they'd suffered. As Faqir would have wished, they were now discussing their next steps, though he was no longer there to lead them. Tony's texts, still saved in Hamid's phone, ended at this point. They knew they would never have got this far without the Australian's help, but his contacts apparently extended no further. The last map was of Croatia and its borders with Hungary, Serbia and Slovenia and the only remaining clue in his instructions was, *SLOVENIA?*

'Listen to this.' Hamid was researching online reports about Slovenia's refugee laws. 'It says here if you ask for asylum at the border, they let you in if you haven't previously registered in any other EU country.' He read from the article, '*Only migrants requesting asylum or entering on humanitarian grounds will be allowed into Slovenia*'. That should apply to us, we're not registered anywhere, except Turkey, but that was just to get our visas, so it's probably not the same thing.'

'I don't see how that helps.' Aisha took the mobile and read the summary he'd found. 'We don't want to stay in Slovenia, it's a tiny place with lots of refugees already. We'd be no better off than anywhere else we've been.

We've got to get to England, that was Papa's plan and that's what we have to do.'

Hamid interrupted, 'That's not what I mean, listen. We're all under 18 years old. Now our father's gone, Mama's got four minors to look after. Minors have a special status in the EU laws and so do mothers with children, that's what *"humanitarian grounds"* means. Our passports prove we're from Iraq and they don't send people back there. I'm sure we'd get asylum papers, then we can cross to another EU country without anyone even knowing.'

Hema was interested now. 'Hamid, show me a map of the EU.' He found a map with the EU countries shown in blue and gave her the phone. 'I see what you mean, it's right next to Italy and Austria. You think we could just go across those borders without any problem?'

'It's the Schengen zone, Mama, they don't check passports or anything. If we get on a train in Slovenia we can get off in any EU country, then we can get to England.'

'He's right, Mama, we can't go anywhere else except north.' Malik counted on his fingers. 'We don't want to go backwards to Serbia or Montenegro, Bosnia's not even a choice and we'll never get into Hungary. Tony's last message says Slovenia and there's no other option. If we get there, maybe we can reach either Austria or Italy. So, what we need to decide right now is, how do we get to Slovenia?'

'Ok, let's look at the crossing points.' Hamid brought up the border map on the screen. 'Coming from the coast, it looks like the best crossing is at Rupa, see? It's on the E61 highway that comes down from the capital, Ljubljana. We'd have to go all the way north along the coast to this town, Matulji, it's about ten kilometres from Rupa.'

Aisha frowned, 'There'll be a lot of refugees trying to get through there. It looks like the only crossing in that area.'

'Maybe.' He checked some other sites. 'No, there are a few around there but Rupa's the biggest. Wait.' He read through another report. 'This one says most of the refugees from Croatia come by land through Serbia across the north of the country, on the E70 highway that goes past Zagreb. The way we'll be going, by the coast, doesn't seem to be very common.'

'That's why Tony Miller sent us this way.'

'Right. So, if the crossings are less busy near the coast it makes more sense for us to go further west, away from Rupa.'

'Guys. Whichever crossing we choose, we've still got to get from here to the border. That's what we need to agree on now, how do we get there?'

Hema listened to the discussion amongst her family with growing confidence and admiration. Faqir might be lost to her, but their children had inherited his gift for logical planning and foresight. 'We can't take the risk of flying again,' she intervened. 'There are too many controls at the airports. Look up the alternatives, ferries, buses and trains. How far is it, Hamid?'

He checked the map. 'It's a long way, about 600 km by road.'

Five minutes later, they'd established that the fastest

and most efficient transport was, once again, by bus. The train was impossible; there was no station in Dubrovnik. The nearest was in Split, four hours away, whereas there was a direct bus service to Rijeka, a large port, 20 km from the Slovenian border.

'Look Mama, there's an Arriva bus tomorrow morning at eight in the morning, getting to Rijeka at 8:30 pm. We can be right next to the Slovenian border by tomorrow night.'

'Twelve and a half hours in another bus, my God, I don't think I can manage it. How much does it cost?'

'It's 2400 kuna for all of us.'

'I don't have enough kuna, do they accept euros?'

'Both prices are here, wait.' He calculated, 'It's 180 euros.'

Hema had now adopted Faqir's obsession with money. Alexi had taken his blood money with him to his watery grave, but the dwindling balance of their fortune was held between her and the boys. With some luck, she figured they could reach the Slovenian border with a bit less than 14,000 euros.

'What does everyone think?' There was a unanimous show of hands. She sighed resignedly, 'Alright, find the directions to the bus terminal, Hamid. We'll spend the rest of today on the beach to get ready for yet another journey, then have an early night and get the bus in the morning.'

Guildford, England

'I think that's the lot.' Sami laid her shopping on the table, checking the items off against Ibrahim's printout.

'Was everything all right, no problems?'

It was a week since her visit to Gatwick and she had been out every day, sometimes more than once, to buy products from many different stores, slowly and unobtrusively, just as he and Jamil had done in Kalk. He still tried to avoid thinking about his family; it was counter-productive. Sami helped in that, keeping his mind on their assignment, planning the details together.

'Don't worry, no one noticed me.' She tried to shake off the feeling of nervousness that overcame her every time she left the flat.

'Everything's there. One more shopping trip and we'll have enough to complete the job. And I found those electric toasters online I told you about, the ones I used in Cologne. I bought two of them with PayPal, but they have to be picked up tomorrow from a delivery place in town.'

'Give me the address and I'll get them, in case they want an identity or something.'

'Cool. When I'm ready, I'll buy the stuff for the shrapnel. Women don't usually buy things like that and it might look funny. There's no risk, nobody's going to recognise me here.'

She noticed how he was picking up speech habits from her, *he would never have said 'funny' like that when we first met*. 'Sure, and that's fine with me. When do you think we'll be ready?'

'At this rate, one box a day, I need another ten days.' There were now five polythene boxes of the TATP in the kitchen cupboard; by Tuesday he should have enough for the first suitcase. Sami had found two in the Oxfam shop near the station for twenty pounds, both made from cheap canvas, one in tartan and the other in a floral pattern. They were the right size to take eight boxes in two layers of four with enough space around them for the shrapnel and packing.

After his mistake in trying to accelerate the process, Ibrahim was working as quickly as he could without tiring himself; if he got tired he was likely to make a mistake and ruin the weeks of planning and preparation. And he didn't want Sami to be involved in the manufacture; if anything went wrong he wanted it to be his fault. It wouldn't be fair to her, she was doing enough by shopping for the materials and assisting and supporting him. He knew he was pushing himself hard to make enough material for two explosions in such a short time, but he was determined to outdo Paris and Brussels – to make the biggest demonstration of ISIL force there had ever been in Europe. Karl and all their jihadist brothers would be proud of them; their names would go down in history and never be forgotten.

'Sure, and that's just perfect, 'cos I found a rental car company as well. It's a little place near the station. Second hand cars, fine for us and they won't pay as much attention as the big companies. I didn't go in, but I called them, and they said they've got a couple of five door hatchbacks for twenty quid a day. They told me it's a quiet time for them here in June and they're pretty sure to have one if I give them a couple of days' notice. So, I think that's sorted.'

'You're doing great, Sami. I'd never have got this far without you helping me like this. We make a good team.'

'Sure and all we do, I'll put the kettle on.' Her mouth was dry as she went to the sink. Time was getting short.

FORTY-EIGHT

Near Split, Dalmatian Coast, Croatia
June 2016

Once again, there had been no control at the bus terminal, but there was a large crowd of waiting passengers. As last-minute travellers, the Al-Douris were unable to get seats together and were split up into three lots. Hamid was sitting on his own, which suited him, since the bus had Wi-Fi and he could explore the various crossing options available at the border to discuss later with his family. It was a clear, bright day and the early part of the trip had taken them along the coast road, providing magnificent views of the shoreline and the deep blue ocean they'd sailed on just three days before.

Hema couldn't stop her mind going over her last moments with Faqir, the man she'd loved and cherished since she was sixteen years old and who had been taken from her so suddenly and cruelly. After a while, she fell into a doze, dreaming of happier times in Iraq, before the US invasion, before ISIL, when their world seemed to be a better place, a place where even a brutal dictator like Saddam Hussein hadn't spoiled their life together.

They were now about 160 km into their 600 km journey and a number of passengers had disembarked at Split, so the family could sit together on the back seats; it was a little cramped, but they felt more secure. Hema handed out snacks and drinks to them all and they picnicked happily as the bus took them further north, nearer to the Slovenian border. They discussed the options Hamid had discovered from his research and little by little, they formulated their plan for the next phase of this seemingly interminable journey into the unknown, only five remaining of the seven who had set out from Mosul just a month before.

How many of us will make it all the way? Hema asked herself, now reconciled to the reality of their new status as vulnerable refugees with no means of protection and soon, it was likely, no remaining financial resources. She realised Hamid was telling a funny anecdote he'd read on the internet about refugees. Putting aside her fears she laughed aloud with her family. It was the here and now and she had to make the most of it.

Guildford, England

'What's the balance on the PayPal account?'

'There's three hundred euros left.'

'Good, I've just found two Sony Ericsson W995 phones for twenty-four pounds each, that's about 60 euros all together. They've got a vibrate function, so they'll work fine. I'm going to order them now.'

That morning Sami had picked up the electric toasters he'd ordered from a collection locker in town. He was now buying second hand phones on a specialist site. He needed a trigger phone for each device and would use his own mobile to call them.

'Where will you get them delivered?'

'I'll have to give this address; small companies don't have a collection system. We'll have to use Klaus

Ritterman's name for the order and put a label on the post box in the entrance.'

'There's some in the drawer. I'll do it on my way out to the shops.'

'Thanks, Sami, I'll see you later.' Ibrahim was still amazed that people in the UK went shopping on a Sunday; in Germany, nothing was open, but it was useful to them to be able to shop for small quantities every day.

The post boxes were in the entrance hall of the building and as Sami was sticking the label on theirs, a teenage boy came down the stairs. 'Hiya,' he said. 'You must be the new lady in number one. I'm Craig Hill, we live on the second floor in Flat 4. What's your name?'

Flustered, she went to get past him. 'I'm Sarah,' she said. 'Nice to meet you.' She hurried away from the flat, cursing herself for using the name Sarah. Because the door to their flat was away from the others, until now she'd been able to time her comings and goings to avoid meeting anyone. Now, someone knew who was living there. Sami was becoming very afraid of being recognised.

Rijeka, North-Western Croatia

Hamid had been busy on the bus Wi-Fi. He'd found an empty apartment near the port in Rijeka for 100 euros per night. If everything went as planned, they'd only need it for one night. His mother agreed, and he confirmed they'd be arriving in a few hours. Although the death of his father had affected him more than he could possibly show, in a peculiar way he was enjoying being the new source of information in the family. His brother, Malik, was a stronger and more impetuous character; he'd never back away from a fight, even in the face of certain defeat. In Mosul, Hamid had always lived in his shadow and suddenly, he was advising the family on the important and vital decisions they were faced with. It was a good feeling.

They walked to the apartment, following the route online. It was ten minutes from the bus terminal and he was proud when they found the building immediately. The Dutch owners, a young couple named Jan and Sophie, lived in the adjacent apartment and showed them around the flat. It was tiny – a living room, kitchenette and one bedroom – but a lot better than some of the accommodation they'd had to put up with in Bulgaria and Serbia.

A half hour later, they were sitting in the living room, enjoying pizzas and discussing the pros and cons of the border crossings they could use. Hamid showed them the routes to the forty control posts they had available. They ruled out Rupa, the largest in the area; it was close to Rijeka and accessed by two major roads, the E61 and the D8, so it would be too busy. Up in the north-west corner of Croatia were two smaller posts, but they were also on the route of two main roads.

'Look,' Hamid showed them the sketch he'd made of his preferred route. 'Between those busy crossings you've got this tiny one called Požane, there's nothing there except a border control with a single lane. It's a few kilometres from a place called Buzet and there's a bus from here to Buzet that takes an hour. We can walk from there to the border post in another hour and it will probably be quiet because it's on a minor road and not easy to get to if you're not driving.' He put his sketch aside. 'That's where we should go.'

'Have you checked the Slovenian side?'

'Yes. It's a kilometre walk from Požane at a place called Sočerga. It's a bigger post but there's no town there either.' He showed them the photos of the isolated guardhouse and manual crossing at Požane and the triple-lane automated post at Sočerga. 'That's where we'll ask for asylum, if we can talk our way through at Požane.'

'How much does the bus cost and how often does it run?' Hema asked, pragmatic as always.

'Once a day at a quarter to one and it's 60 kuna each. With an hour's walk, we'll be there by three o'clock.'

'Good, that will get rid of our remaining kuna. OK, everyone, let's vote on Hamid's proposal. Who thinks we should take the bus to Buzet tomorrow and try the crossing at, what's it called?'

'Požane.'

'Hands up who agrees.' They all raised their hands. 'A good debate and a unanimous agreement. Well done Hamid and all of you, I'm impressed, and your father would have been too. We'll leave at midday tomorrow to get the tickets and make sure there's no last-minute problems.'

Guildford, England

It was six o'clock when Sami came back with the next

batch of items on her list. They checked everything as usual then she sat on the settee.

'I finished another box today. That's six, almost enough for the first case.' He went over to her when she didn't reply. *She looks tired, maybe a bit nervous?* 'How was the shopping?'

'I'm knackered. It must be all the worry about being stopped in the shops. I was like, *I know everybody's looking at me*, all the time.' She didn't mention Craig Hill, the neighbour's boy she'd met in the hall. It wouldn't help and might unnerve him.

He was surprised at her reaction. *She's been bombed and shelled and now she's worried about being caught shopping.* 'You sit there and rest,' he said. 'I'll run your bath then go for something for supper.'

She was wrapped in her dressing gown when he came back with fish and chips, steaming hot and wrapped in reams of paper. It was Sami's favourite meal and they'd had it twice since arriving in England. She heated up a pan of frozen peas and set two places on the coffee table in the living room. The smell of the bath essence on her skin excited him, but he ignored the feeling and chatted quietly with her over supper, asking about her life in Belfast, laughing at her witty remarks. Afterwards, he washed up then they sat and watched the news, to see if there were any new announcements about the terrorist bomber and the English woman.

The announcement that caught their attention had nothing to do with them. Sami laughed when she saw a referendum had been called for the UK to leave the EU. 'I didn't even know about it, we had other things to worry about in Mosul. Just wait 'til we carry out our attack, they might change their minds and ask for French protection.'

Ibrahim smiled at her pantomime; he knew nothing about politics and cared less, but he was pleased to see her more relaxed and laughing again. Since the night of his weakness in Paris, he had managed to stay strong. Being in a separate bedroom helped and he avoided going into the bathroom unless he was sure she was elsewhere. He ran her bath every day; it had become a ritual. Usually, after their supper, he went into the bathroom and ran the hot water, pouring in a little of the perfumed liquid. The bath essence and a few cosmetic items were Sami's only luxuries; they lived a very frugal life to ensure their money would last and like Ibrahim, she bought only basic necessities.

She doesn't need make-up anyway, he thought, as she sat next to him on the worn settee, looking at photos on her mobile phone. The reflected light shone on her unlined face, highlighting her deep-set eyes.

She noticed his sideways glance and smiled. 'What's on your mind?'

'Nothing,' he stammered. 'I was just wondering what photos you're looking at.'

'Here, look. That's Karl. You've never seen him before.'

The man in the photo was very dark-skinned. He had a livid scar down his cheek which showed up white on the screen. His features were sharp and cruel, and his smile only skin-deep. He looked as if he didn't like being photographed.

'He looks very ... fierce. A true fighter and leader.'

'He's the strongest man I ever met. I took this picture just before I left. They don't like to be photographed unless it's for propaganda. Except the idiots who cut people's heads off and pose for show. They make themselves the targets, not the clever planners and fighters like Karl.'

'Did he convert you to the ISIL cause?'

She laughed again, a lovely feminine sound. 'No bugger converted me to any cause. I'm a catholic and I'll always be a catholic. I don't believe in causes, I believe in revenge. I thought it would be a way to get me own back on the English for what happened to me father. Me life's been fucked up, sorry, I mean messed up, since I was a kid because of what they did to him. The only people who were good to me after that were Baki and Karl. I might as well fight for what they were fighting for, that's all. The rest is all political crap.'

'So it was because of your father, the same as me?' She just nodded and he felt a deep pang of jealousy. *She went out to the war with real fighters and I stayed at home and killed my family. I'll prove to her I can be just as strong as them. I just need to get the chance again.*

They watched an old Clint Eastwood movie, a spaghetti western. She fell asleep halfway through it, but he watched it right through to the bloody end, 'To improve my English,' he always told her.

At the end of the movie, he switched off the TV and gently shook her awake. 'Time for bed, Sami. Thanks, you did a lot today, tomorrow I want to fill another box.'

FORTY-NINE

At 6:00 am Ibrahim made a mug of tea and found the BBC news on his laptop. What he saw caused him to step back in incredulity. He switched on the TV and rushed into Sami's bedroom. 'Come and look at this. See what happened last night.'

Images were being shown of the massacre at Pulse, a gay nightclub in Orlando, Florida. A 29-year-old security guard, Omar Mateen, had shot and killed forty-nine people, wounding fifty-three others. As the camera moved around the floor of the club, they saw bodies lying everywhere, men and women, mostly Hispanic people. The newsreader said that Pulse had been hosting a "Latin Night" and most of the victims were young Latinos.

The camera focussed on a body lying alone, covered in a police issue blanket. 'This is the terrorist, Mateen, who was killed by officers of the Orlando Police Department after a 3-hour stand-off. In a 911 call shortly after the shooting began, he swore allegiance to Abu Bakr al-Baghdadi, the ISIL leader, and said the US killing of Abu Waheeb in Iraq the previous month, "triggered" the shooting. He later told a negotiator he was "out here right now" because of the American-led interventions in Iraq and Syria and the US must stop their air attacks.'

They watched the programme in silence. After a

few minutes Sami suddenly felt sick. She went to the bathroom and threw up, then sat there for a while, reliving the images in her mind. Her thoughts strayed to the holiday makers in Gatwick Airport, happy and excited to be going off for their annual vacation, the child in the pink dress and her mother's words, '*Have a safe flight and enjoy Paris.*' She opened the locket at her neck and looked at the photo of Baki. Then Karl's instructions came back to her and reverberated in her mind, '*But he failed. As his partner, you must ensure he doesn't fail again*'. She drank a glass of water and went back to sit beside Ibrahim.

The announcer was saying, 'This is the deadliest incident of violence against LGBT people in US history and the deadliest terrorist attack in the US since the Twin Towers disaster on September 11th 2001.' She forced herself to watch until the inevitable debate started between two announcers and various 'terrorist experts' and he switched the set off.

Just as he had felt after the Belgian attacks, Ibrahim's first emotion was a feeling of dejection. Here he was, travelling around Europe with an Irish girl he hardly knew, to build a complicated and dangerous 'engine of destruction'. Trying for a second time to achieve a tiny triumph, to make his own sacrifice, insignificant perhaps, but for him a necessary catharsis after the death of his family. And suddenly, without fanfare or warning, just like that, one American maniac goes into a night club with an assault rifle and pistol and kills or wounds a hundred people. *Where's the justice in that?* He asked himself.

Finally, he said, 'What did you think of that?'

She shook her head, trying to get rid of the images. 'I'm glad it happened in the States, that's my first reaction. Those bastards are worse than the English.'

'But I mean, the attack. It was so simple, so easy. No real planning or building bombs or anything like we're doing. He just walked into a night club and killed fifty infidels. We'd be lucky to kill so many with our two bombs. Maybe we're just wasting our time.'

Sami swallowed hard and thought again about Baki, Karl, their mission. 'You know, Ibrahim, you're sometimes a very naïve guy. Not all jihadists are clever and plan things carefully. They don't all have your patience and dedication. That guy got lucky, he made a big noise almost by accident. We've got to do it professionally, show them they'd better watch out, 'cos while there are people like us around, nobody's safe, and that's what they should be worried about. We've got a job to do and we've got to get on with it.'

She got up. 'I'll do some toast and eggs. Get ready, you've got another box to fill.'

Düsseldorf, Germany

Max Kellerman was dejected. The RAID team in Rennes had come up with nothing to support his theory that the Cabaret had left St Malo on the Thursday morning and not the evening. The weather had been so lousy there was no one outside and if there had been, they would have seen virtually nothing. Without something concrete linking the boat to Lannion or to the terrorists, he was stymied. DCI Dewar had made it abundantly clear he needed more than circumstantial evidence.

He thought back over the history of the affair, event by event, place by place, re-examining each piece of evidence, each witness statement, each report, everything in the dossiers of documents and notes he'd amassed over the past month. He double checked everything with his jigsaw puzzle chart that now took up most of his office wall. *There must be something I've missed. Some action I could have taken and didn't. The answer must be on the Cabaret, but I've failed to find it. What more could I have done to find some trace that they were on that boat?*

The word 'trace' rang a bell in his mind. There was one final check they could make that he'd overlooked; an examination of the carpet in the cavity where he was convinced they'd hidden. If there was something caught on the fibres of the carpet that carried Ibrahim's DNA, the tests they'd done after the explosion would provide enough common strands from his family to make a ninety-nine per cent identification. *Then DCI Dewar will be obliged to take action.*

Kellerman called Commissioner Letouffe in Rennes and asked him for one final, urgent favour, to organise another search of the Cabaret. This time, a forensic search, looking for skin or hair, or anything that might lead him to Ibrahim bin Omar al-Ahmad and the mysterious English woman who spoke like the Queen.

Rijeka, North-Western Croatia

It was 11:30 am and Hema was packing for their latest move. Apart from a few precious items she couldn't bear to part with, Faqir's belongings had already been consigned to a church charity stall in Dubrovnik. Now, she was encouraging her children to discard anything they hadn't used and were unlikely to need on the rest of their trip. They had six heavy rucksacks between them and more walking to do; between Buzet and the border would take at least an hour and they had no idea what awaited them afterwards.

Her sons had the minimum of items with them; they were less attached to personal belongings, but Aisha and Lyla couldn't decide what to leave behind.

'We've got to reduce by one bag, so be ruthless and get rid of as much as you can, especially anything non-European.'

They finally agreed on what they could live without and packed the discarded clothing in Faqir's rucksack, to take to the nearest market stall or second-hand shop. As they finished packing there was a tap on the door. Hema looked around to ensure there was nothing incriminating then went to open it.

It was Sophie, the owner and neighbour. 'We wondered if you'd like to join us for lunch today. Jan is doing a barbecue on the terrace and he always cooks enough for ten. It's lovely out there, so, if you've nothing better to do …'

Hema thought quickly. 'That's very kind, but I'm sorry, we can't come. We're getting ready to hike to the castle above the town. It's supposed to have wonderful views over the whole coast.'

'That's OK, don't worry. It's a beautiful walk and you should do it if you've got the time.' She looked around at the rucksacks. 'Are you leaving? I forgot to ask yesterday.'

'No,' Hema answered quickly. 'We were just reorganising the luggage. I was about to come and ask if we can stay again tonight. Will it be alright?'

'Of course, the flat's empty until Saturday.'

Remembering Faqir's ploy in Bulgaria, Hema fetched her purse. 'Here, I'll pay you now, in case we're late getting back.' It almost broke her heart to hand over another precious 100 euros, but she figured it might be good insurance.

'Thanks, if you're back early, knock on our door and we can have a nightcap. Have a great hike.'

Sophie left them and Hamid said, 'Do you think she's suspicious?'

'What do you mean, why?'

'All the rucksacks packed and ready to go, it looks a bit strange if we're staying tonight.'

'I've paid her, so I don't see why she'd be suspicious. Anyway, there's nothing we can do about it, so let's get finished and on our way. Then it doesn't matter what she thinks, we'll be gone.'

They packed the last items, hoisted up their bags and went out into the hot street. Faqir's packed rucksack was left at the nearest clothing stall in the market then Hamid led them to the bus terminal, where they obtained tickets to Buzet. After waiting for a half hour, they climbed onto the bus with a dozen other passengers.

Hema looked around the bus; as far as she could see, there was nothing untoward. *So far, so good.* She settled back and joined in her children's conversation.

Guildford, England

'Hiya Sarah.' It was early afternoon and Sami was walking away from the apartment building in Watson Avenue to catch the bus for the supermarket.

'Oh, hi, Craig.' He had come out of the main entrance just behind her and ran to catch her up. She walked faster to get away from him, keeping her face averted, but he ran alongside, chattering away.

'Will you be staying here for long? There was a man staying in that flat last year but not for long. Most of the time it's empty. I'm glad you're staying there, everyone else in the building is really old. We've lived here for five years, it's near the school. That's where I'm going but we break up for the holidays on Thursday for six weeks, that's pretty cool eh? Have you got any kids?'

'No, I haven't. I'm only staying a few weeks, it's not my flat, a friend let me stay here until I find one.'

'Are you married? I haven't seen you with a guy, only by yourself. I'm surprised 'cos I think you're really pretty.'

She looked desperately around; she wasn't as invisible as she'd imagined. How had he seen her? *His room must face the entrance*, she realised. *He must spend his time looking out the window.* A bus approached the stop nearby. 'That's mine. See you.' She ran to jump on, not even noticing what number it was.

Sami stood on the platform and watched him walk

away, her heart in her mouth. The bus turned a corner and she realised it was going in the wrong direction. She got off at the next stop and walked back along the street. It had started raining and she didn't have an umbrella with her.

Rijeka, North-Western Croatia

'So, they're staying another night? That's good, we can do with the money, every little helps.'

Jan and Sophie were having their lunch on the terrace of their apartment, overlooking the River Rjecina, where they had a small sailing dinghy moored. Jan worked for the Dutch Foreign Office and had taken this well-paid, two-year posting at the consulate to save enough money to get married when they returned to Rotterdam. They had quickly adopted the local customs and today he'd worked until lunchtime then taken the afternoon off to have a late leisurely lunch with his fiancée. It was 3:00 pm and they were finishing off a bottle of Plavac Mali, a red wine from the south coast, both feeling replete and relaxed.

'All their rucksacks were piled in the living room. It looked like they were leaving right then, but the mother paid for tonight, so they can't be.'

Jan was a typical Dutch government employee, an EU man through and through, with all the narrow-minded, petty fixations of their functionaries. The comment nagged him and after washing up the dishes, he said, 'What did they say they were doing this afternoon?'

'Hiking up to the castle.'

'Let's just take a look. They won't be back for a while and in any case, it's our flat, we've got every right to check on our tenants.'

The apartment was completely empty; not a personal possession to be seen, no toilet items, not even a toothbrush, no clothes and no rucksacks.

Sophie looked around at the unoccupied space. 'They've gone, everything's gone, they can't be coming back.'

'That's what it looks like, so why did they pay for an extra night if they were leaving? Hmm, it seems very peculiar. Have a good look around.'

It didn't take long to search the tiny apartment, but there was nothing to be found, nothing to show the Al-Douri family had ever been there. Disappointed and now suspicious, as they went to the door, Sophie took one last look around and saw the cushions on the well-worn couch were strewn across the seat. Obsessed with tidiness, she went to put them back in place. Hidden under one of them was a sheet of paper. She unfolded it and looked at the sketch and notes drawn on it in pencil.

'What do you think this is?'

'It's a map of the border with Slovenia.' He snapped his fingers. 'Those people must be refugees, they're trying to get into the Schengen zone. It even shows which control post they're going through and how they'll get there. Look, the bus departure time, the road numbers and everything are all marked here. Some of these scribbles are in Arabic, they must be from Syria or Iraq, illegal immigrants trying to use Schengen to get into one of our western EU countries.'

She looked at her watch. 'It's three o'clock. They were leaving when I saw them at midday, so they must be arriving at the border soon. I hope they manage to get through.'

'I bet they're not going through the control post, if they haven't got proper papers they'll be looking for a place to get around it. They've probably got a smuggler waiting there to guide them across.'

By now he was red in the face. 'Calm down, Jan, they're a very nice, polite family. It's not our business where they're going.'

'That's just what's wrong with the world today!' He shouted at her. 'Nobody cares about people breaking the rules and it's causing chaos. We can't let these bloody displaced persons just cross the EU without proper controls. I'm calling our head of security, he'll know what to do.' He pulled out his phone and pressed the number.

FIFTY

North-Western Croatia, near the border with Slovenia
June 2016

Police Inspector Horvat Puškarić of the Croatia Border Police Directorate was furious. As if he didn't have enough to do preventing illegal immigrants from entering his country, now some interfering EU jobs-worthy was making a fuss about a family purportedly trying to leave for Slovenia. In his opinion, he should be helping them to leave and not preventing them, but since his country had become the 28th member of the mighty European Union in 2013, he spent half his time cow-towing to their frequent panic attacks. Once again, some political do-gooder had got their knickers in a twist for no good reason and he was just collateral damage in the farrago. He was driving a jeep along the razor wire border fence erected by Slovenia the previous year, looking for a needle in a haystack – a family trying to get through the border at one of the many areas where the fence was non-existent.

Puškarić was wondering why a refugee family would try to penetrate the fence during the day. There were plenty of people smugglers who knew exactly where the unfenced gaps were and who would guide them through for a relatively small sum. *Why not wait until dark, like any sensible fugitive?* He asked himself. He was now nearing the D201, the road that went through the Požane control post and decided he'd call in to see if there'd been any unusual activity. He turned onto the road and drove back up from the border to the guardhouse.

The walk from Buzet to the Požane control post took the Al-Douris less than an hour; they were so much fitter now than when they'd left Iraq a month ago. Hema was proud of how her children had adjusted to the death of their father and were now a well organised team of survivors, determined to fulfil his dream of finding a new life in a safe and peaceful place.

'That's the guardhouse, just ahead. It's got a barrier across the road. I can see a couple of cars coming from the other side but nobody on this side. Are you OK, Mama, you know what to say?'

'I hope so. It depends on what questions they ask – your Papa was much better than me at convincing people to do things.'

As they walked up to the control post, which was no more than a small cottage, surrounded by open countryside, the leading car stopped on the other side of the barrier. A man in uniform examined the driver's documents then the barrier lifted up and the car came through and drove past them.

Hema summoned her courage and walked up to the officer. 'Do you speak English, please?'

He looked at the family in surprise, peering up the road behind them to see if there was a car that had brought them here. 'I speak a bit.'

She took out their Iraqi passports and birth certificates and handed them to the man. 'I'm Hema Al-Douri and these are my four children, all under eighteen. We're refugees from Mosul and we wish to enter Slovenia to seek asylum.'

'You mean Mosul in Iraq? How did you get here to Croatia?'

'It was a very long and dangerous journey, but we don't want to stay here, we want to seek asylum in Slovenia. You know we can't go back to Iraq, or we'll be killed and we have the right to seek asylum according to the EU laws.'

The man looked nonplussed. 'I've never had a family ask for asylum in Slovenia, only here in Croatia.'

The second car they'd seen had pulled in beside them and another man in uniform came over to them. 'I'm Inspector Puškarić. What's going on here?'

The border guard explained the situation in rapid Croatian and he turned to Hema. 'You're the family that's trying to get into Slovenia illegally?'

She was taken aback by this accusation. 'I don't know what you're talking about, there's nothing illegal about what we're doing. We're here at the control post making an official, formal request to enter Slovenia to seek asylum.'

Malik, aggressive as always, asked, 'Who told you we're trying to get into Slovenia illegally?'

The inspector looked momentarily embarrassed. 'We had a report about an illegal attempt by a family of five, I assumed it was you.'

Hamid thought quickly, 'The only people who know we're here are the Dutch couple whose apartment we rented last night. Did they make the report?'

Puškarić looked even more embarrassed as another

car pulled up on the Slovenian side of the barrier and the border official went to attend to the driver. He said, 'Why don't we go into the office and you can tell me how you got here and what you want?'

He led them into the converted living room and they stood by the counter. He looked at the documents Hema handed over. 'I've got seven passports and birth certificates here and there's only five of you. Where are the others?'

'Both my mother and my husband were murdered by bandits on the way.' Tears came to her eyes and Aisha put her arm around her shoulders.

'Now there's just you and your four children? I'm sorry to hear that.' He looked at their birth certificates, 'I see they're all under 18 years of age.' He returned the documents. 'How did you get from Iraq to the Slovenian border?'

'We came through Turkey, Greece, Bulgaria, Serbia, Montenegro and ended up here. We've been travelling for a month, mostly on foot.'

Puškarić raised his eyebrows, obviously impressed, but he didn't ask how they'd crossed so many borders. 'Have you been officially registered in any of those countries?'

Hema shook her head. 'We don't want to be registered in any country until we get to Slovenia, that's why we're asking to leave Croatia.'

'You know it's almost impossible to go through Slovenia into other EU countries? The so-called Balkan Route is being closed everywhere.'

'Yes, we know. That's why we want to apply for

asylum, so we can wait there until we get permission to move freely.'

He was impressed with her honesty. 'That can take years, you know that?'

'We'll just have to take that chance. If we could survive Mosul, we should be able to survive that.'

Hamid interjected, 'Inspector, you can't send us back to Mosul, because we're Christians and we'd be murdered, so you'd either have to grant us asylum here in Croatia or let us apply in Slovenia. If you help us to get through, it's one less family for you to worry about in your country.'

'You're a Christian family? How did you manage to stay alive so long in Mosul?'

'Our father was a clever man, we kept out of trouble and they left us alone. None of us have ever done anything wrong until we fled a month ago to get to safety. Now, we're just one kilometre from finishing our journey.'

The inspector supressed a smile. *This is not your normal family of refugees,* he realised. *They've thought this through very well. The boy's right and what's more, I agree with him.* He looked at the passports again. 'Do you mind telling me what happened to your mother and husband?'

Hema steeled herself. 'We had visas to cross Turkey and were heading for Istanbul, but we were attacked on the road at night by a gang of robbers. They shot my mother dead and took our money.'

Malik took over, knowing she couldn't continue. 'My father was murdered by a Croatian crook near Dubrovnik and he stole most of what we had left. We're so tired of travelling and being attacked and robbed and having our money stolen from us until we've got almost nothing left. We're desperate to get somewhere where we can ask for asylum and wait until we can travel legally to settle in a safe and peaceful country.'

The inspector was thoughtful for a while, saying nothing, then, 'Just wait here for a moment.' He went outside and spoke to the border guard.

Hema smiled through her tears at her children. 'Thank you, boys, you did better than I did. Now we just have to hope this policeman is a decent person with a heart.'

After a few minutes he came back. 'You're sure you want to apply for asylum in Slovenia, even though it could take a long time before you can move on?'

They all nodded assent.

'Right. Come with me, the guard will let you through as long as I'm with you.'

A car had just arrived on the Croatian side of the barrier and he went to speak to the driver. The man looked surprised but nodded his head and got out to open the boot of his vehicle.

'Ladies, put your bags in here and get in the car with this gentleman. He'll follow me and the boys to the Slovenian control post.'

As if in a dream, Hema and her daughters dumped their rucksacks in the boot and climbed into the back seat of the car. Hamid and Malik did likewise in the jeep and the border guard raised the barrier. The two vehicles drove in convoy for a kilometre across the border to the Slovenian control post at Sočerga. They retrieved their luggage and thanked the driver, who drove off on the D208 towards the capital, Ljubljana.

Puškarić led them over to the Slovenian control office, where a bespectacled man was working at a computer terminal. He looked up and smiled when he saw the Croat. 'Horvat, what are you doing in my country?'

'This is Police Officer first class Mlakar, he's a good friend of mine, speaks English and is an honest man. Ivan, this is the Al-Douri family, from Mosul, Iraq. Mrs Al-Douri, please tell Officer Mlakar why you are here.'

Hema took out her family documents again and laid them on the desk in front of the policeman. 'Officer Mlakar. I am a widow and these are my four children, all under eighteen. We are refugees seeking asylum in your country.'

Inspector Puškarić shook hands with all of them. 'The rest doesn't concern me, unless you come back across the border into Croatia. I'll leave you in the good hands of my friend Ivan. God bless you all and help you find peace and safety. You deserve it.'

FIFTY-ONE

Düsseldorf, Germany
June 2016

Several strands of black hair. Almost definitely from a person of African or North African origin. Also, some blonde hairs from a woman. Please send DNA for comparison to RAID forensics in Paris.

'YES!' Max Kellerman shouted out with delight. After so many anti-climaxes, he'd finally struck gold. The email had just arrived from Pascale Letouffe in Rennes, asking him to transmit the Kalk file from the SIB, Düsseldorf to Paris. He instructed the head of forensics to send the dossier then he called Letouffe.

'What do you think?'

'It seems obvious they were on that boat and now they're in England. There's no other reasonable explanation.'

'I'm sure you're right. Thanks for your help on this, you did a great job.'

'You're welcome, if we've helped you and the UK to avoid another atrocity, it was worth the effort. Now I'll get back to worrying about the threats we've got in my own country, there's plenty to do. Call me if you need anything more.'

Kellerman rang off and went through to Lieutenant Schuster's office with the printout of the message.

'See this? This week we'll find out I was right all along. Ibrahim bin Omar al-Ahmad and a blonde English woman who speaks like the Queen are in England and have been since last Thursday. Letouffe agrees with my conclusion and if Dewar had taken notice of me they'd probably have found them already. I'm calling right away to get him moving before it's too late.'

'Calm down, Max. That's great news, well done. But if French forensics are like ours, they're inundated with work, so you might not get confirmation for some time, especially if Letouffe thinks you're right. It's no longer a French problem, so it'll have a low priority. You still can't expect Dewar to announce a state of emergency on the basis of your intuition. We've got to wait until we get confirmation of these tests, then he'll be convinced and pull out all the stops. MI5 and the other UK security and anti-terrorism units are the best intelligence services in the world and they'll have procedures to put in place at the drop of a hat. Just be patient until we get the result in conclusive form and we'll go straight to the top brass here and make sure Dewar takes us seriously.

Kellerman went back to his office and updated his chart on the wall. Despite Schuster's advice, he planned to call DCI Dewar to put him on notice. He was certain they'd have to start a manhunt in the UK very soon; Ibrahim and the woman were there, it was beyond doubt.

Vrhnika Asylum Centre, Western Slovenia
The refugee centre was tiny, an encampment of about one hundred tents in all. A small part of the property was sectioned off as the Asylum Centre, for those refugees who had applied for international protection, including the Al-Douris. Some of the tents in their area

were empty and the surroundings were clean and tidy, compared to the refugee holding zone, which looked overcrowded and badly kept. Unlike the enormous Domiz II camp in Duhok, the whole camp seemed quiet and well-organised, with hands-on management by the IOM, the International Organization for Migration, and the local authorities.

Alice Newman, an English representative of the IOM explained that the occupants of the holding zone were refugees without identity documents. They were waiting to be returned to the country from which they'd arrived, usually Bosnia, Albania or Croatia, within two or three days. However, the system was so overburdened it often took weeks or months before they were moved out of the camp and more were arriving every day. 'It's better if you don't cross over into that zone,' she told them, 'it can be rough sometimes.' The Al-Douris needed no persuasion to follow her advice.

After Inspector Puškarić had left them at the Slovenian control post, Officer Mlakar had examined their papers and questioned Hema as the Croatian officer had done. By now, she and her family were accustomed to responding to officials and he completed his questionnaire rapidly. At six that evening, a minibus arrived to transport them 60 km to the nearest Centre for Foreigners at Vrhnika, about 21 km from Ljubljana. They reached the camp at 8:00 pm, where they were registered and allocated a tent large enough to sleep all five of them. There was an onsite store where they could buy food and by 10:00 pm they were all asleep, as usual, exhausted by the travel and stress they'd endured that day.

At eight the next morning, they were taken to the medical centre where a nurse carried out a rudimentary examination, declaring them all to be fit and healthy. From there Alice accompanied them to the administration centre for processing. She helped them to complete an International Protection Application and explained the Dublin procedure, which ensured they hadn't previously sought asylum in another country. Their fingerprints were taken and sent off to be compared in the EU's central fingerprint database, to confirm their claim.

'If the application is clean, you'll stay in the Asylum Centre until we obtain approval for your asylum status,' she told them.

'What happens then?' Hema asked.

'Your dossier will go to the Immigration Service in Ljubljana for consideration of temporary residence permits.'

'How long does that take?'

'We've had cases approved within a couple of months, but it can sometimes take years to sort out. There's so many refugees in Slovenia now, it's impossible to process the applications in a short time. But your dossier is different – a widow with four children will get a high priority. I'm going to push as hard as I can for a fast decision because of your circumstances. We're concerned about the fate of young people in these atrocious situations and that'll make a big difference. Please be patient and let me do the best I can.'

Hamid asked, 'What happens after we get the temporary residence permits? I mean, if we get them.'

'You'll be free to leave the camp and live normally in Slovenia.'

'Then we can go to another EU country?'

'You can, but you'll have to obtain temporary residence permits there, just like here, otherwise, you could be sent back.' Alice took Hema's hand. 'I know it all seems very complicated and will take time, but the worst part is over for you. You've survived an amazing journey and now I'm going to help you get the permits you need to get back to a normal life.'

They thanked the IOM delegate and went back to their tent to prepare something for lunch. Hamid looked around at the razor wire fence that surrounded the entire camp and the police control post at the entrance – no way to get out without proper documentation. Their plan of simply getting on a bus or train to Italy or Austria was on hold until they could leave the camp legally. The problem was they had no idea how long that would take.

London, England

'When do you expect to get the results?'

Max Kellerman had just informed DCI Callum Dewar of the discovery of the black and blonde hairs on Cabaret. He'd tried not to sound too pleased with himself; that would come later, when they got definite proof that he had been right all along. 'I sent the DNA file from Cologne to RAID forensics in Paris immediately. Superintendent Letouffe expects them to have them sometime this week, depending on their workload.'

'But you already know what to expect, right?'

'There's no doubt in my mind, but I'm happy to wait for the definite proof if you are.'

'Hmm. I'm beginning to think your intuition can be trusted, so far you've guessed right. Are you making a press announcement tonight?'

'There's no point. The last one didn't even get retransmitted in the UK. There was nothing new in it and the TV stations have no interest in old news. Why did you ask?'

'I think it may be time we started some initiatives over here. If they've been in the UK for over a week, as you believe, they must be getting ready to do something and I don't want to be the last to know. I can't risk an atrocity here in my country, we've got enough problems worrying about the effect Brexit will have on our security, if the vote goes the wrong way next week.'

'I don't envy you. Brexit would be a challenge for all of us, especially you guys in the firing line.' He decided not to get into a discussion with the Englishman about the 'for and against' arguments. 'What were you thinking about our case?' He emphasised, 'our', hoping Dewar would take the hint.

'Would you be willing to fly over for a joint meeting of our counter terrorism units, the CTSFO and S015? I've already briefed them on our previous discussions, but if you're right, we'll be going into a COBRA situation and I'd like my people to be on top of things when that happens.' Dewar had already had a meeting that morning with the Minister of Defence, fresh out of another Cobra meeting, who had briefed him on the status of recent Russian fleet movements in the North Sea, *more problems to worry about.* 'What do you think the timing will be, assuming your theory's correct?'

'They won't have access to ready-made explosives over there, your people would know if someone had been stockpiling TATP or anything of the kind. They'll have to manufacture it, like he did in Kalk. He'll want to build a big device, because he failed the first time and he'll be desperate to make a name for himself. That's what they're doing right now, and it'll take them a while; it's a dangerous job and can't be done quickly. I think we still have some time before they'll be ready. In any case, my boss wouldn't let me leave without having the DNA proof.'

'Why don't we talk again when you get it, if it's conclusive?

'OK. In the meantime, I can write up a report to give you a clear picture of Ibrahim bin Omar al-Ahmad and how he's behaved from the start. I know less about the woman, but we can create a working hypothesis. You might want to share it with your teams, then when we get the confirmation from RAID, you'll be ready to move very quickly. If you're fine with that I'll get the OK from my boss and confirm back.'

Dewar put the phone down with a worried frown. If the DNA result was positive, the matter would suddenly spiral into a very dangerous threat to the British people. Although he hoped and prayed it wouldn't come to that, he had a presentiment that Keller's instincts were well honed. The German's report would help him to prepare his officers. If something was going to happen out there, he had to find it and neutralise it; he couldn't take the risk of not following up every potential threat. He sighed and turned back to his work pile.

Vrhnika Asylum Centre, Western Slovenia

'I've got some good news for you, I wanted you to hear it as soon as possible.' It was nine in the evening and Alice Newman, the IOM representative, had run along to the Al-Douri's tent to share the information she'd just received.

They waited in a hopeful silence while the delegate got her breath back. 'Because of your special humanitarian status of widow and young children, they rushed through the Dublin procedure today. I've just learned the result.'

'And it was clean?' Hema was praying there had been no record kept by any of the immigration officials Faqir had met during their journey.

'Absolutely clean. No previous registrations of any kind, anywhere. I can start to process the International Protection Application. In the meantime, you'll stay here in the Asylum Centre, no need to transfer to the refugee part of the camp.' Alice smiled with pleasure at overcoming this first hurdle.

Hema thanked God for her husband's preparations for their escape and his quick-witted handling of the official barriers they'd encountered and overcome. 'That's wonderful, thank you so much for helping to get it done so quickly.'

Her children each came to shake Alice's hand and thank her until she was embarrassed at the attention. 'Let's hope we can keep up the progress. I'll follow up on the application in the morning, but it will definitely be granted. That means I can get onto Ljubljana to start the procedure for your temporary residency permits.'

She left them and Hema said, 'Maybe we won't have to kill the guards or jump over the fence. What do you think Hamid?'

He took the sarcastic remark in good grace, 'Don't worry, Mama. I've got lots more plans in case the application fails.'

Later that night, Hamid sneaked out of the tent with a torch and his mobile phone. He looked up a number then composed a text, rereading and correcting it several times until he was happy with the message. He hesitated for a moment, then pressed *Send*. No one noticed as he crept back to his bed.

FIFTY-TWO

Guildford, England
Saturday, June 18th 2016

'I made a toasted cheese sandwich for you. Stop working and come and sit quiet for a while, you've been at it since eight o' clock.'

He came and sat beside her. The sun was streaming in through the window and the shabby living room was friendly and welcoming. He said, 'One more box done, that's twelve, only four more and we're ready. But I'm a bit tired, I don't think I'll work this afternoon, in case I make a mistake.'

Sami handed him a sandwich, 'You OK?'

'I'm cool, just tired. I didn't sleep very well last night.'

Once again, he surprised her with his improving vocabulary. 'I'm not surprised, you've never stopped working for two weeks. Take it easy today and sure you'll be fine.'

'Thanks, this is good.'

'That's your coffee in the blue mug.'

They sat quietly for a while, then Ibrahim asked, 'What do you think of my stubbly beard now?'

'I like it fine, but you need to let the sideburns grow a bit. And you've got some ginger hairs that I couldn't see when it was all bushy, it must be from your Irish ancestors.' He smiled at the joke, enjoying the sense of intimacy. 'Nobody's going to spot you now. Even without the hoodie, your shaved head changes you a lot.'

'Good. On Monday morning I'm going for the nuts and bolts. I'll show you how to do the first case in the afternoon. How to pack it tight and make sure it doesn't move about when you carry it or push it on the trolley.'

'You think we'll be ready by then?'

'Wednesday I'll be finished, even if I take this afternoon off.'

'We'd better fix the date for Gatwick, so I can book the car and the parking.' She looked at the calendar on her phone. 'Next Saturday's the 25th, lots of people will start going on holidays. The airport will be crammed.' As she said it a cold spasm ran up her spine.

'That gives us a week to be completely prepared. You're right, Saturday is a good day for people leaving on holiday. We can book everything today. We need to buy two cheap tickets as well, in case we're stopped.'

They spent some of the PayPal balance on a Premium Service space at the North Terminal short-term parking for midday on Saturday, June 25th and two economy one-way tickets to Belfast. Ibrahim sent a text to the number of Karl's last call, saying simply, 'Saturday 25'. A few minutes later, he received a reply, '*hza tayibana wafaqak allah,* may Allah bring you luck'. He changed the SIM for what he hoped would be the last time.

Later, Sami went out to the car rental shop to book a four-door vehicle in the name of Catherine Flanagan. He admired her through the window as she walked away from the flat in the sunshine. *In a week we'll be the most famous jihadists in history. An Iraqi man and an Irish woman.*

Qayyarah, Iraq

'They're putting in anchors for a pontoon bridge and building a concrete pier on the east side. The Makhmur side,' he added, in case Abdullah didn't understand his compass references. 'And there's a dozen boats bringing materials across to the west side to start work here.'

Karl was reporting to the supreme commander, from a viewpoint near Tall 'Azbah on the western side of the Tigris river, a couple of kilometres south of the Makhmur Road bridge. Through his binoculars he could see the partly constructed pier surrounded by trucks with hydraulic cranes being operated by Iraqi soldiers. They were unloading steel Treadway units to be assembled on the site. Other trucks with twin boom arms were unrolling the 10-metre inflatable rubber pontoons on which the bridge would be laid. He estimated the span of the river at that point at about two hundred metres, twenty lengths of Treadways. The vehicles also had extra-large air-brake tanks that would serve to inflate the pontoons before they were placed in the water. He'd seen this type of US designed 'Assault Float Bridge' in Iraq in 2004 after the US invasion. Once the second pier was built on the north side, the bridge could be quickly rolled out on the pontoons. Then the tanks and heavy armaments which were still stuck around Kabaruk would be free to cross the river onto the Qayyarah side.

'That's because you stopped them from crossing the Makhmur bridge,' Abdullah answered grudgingly. 'As long as we keep them cooped up on the other side of the river, Qayyarah remains a blockade for their advance on Mosul.'

He's learning fast, quite amazing. Aloud, Karl said, 'They're too far away for us to attack them from Qayyarah and I don't have the manpower and equipment to start another front. I've got my hands full holding the bridge and preparing for whatever they're going to do with the troops and armaments they've been flying into Qayyarah West.'

'You know I was never in favour of abandoning the airfield. Remember, I told you so at the time.'

Karl smiled when he heard this retraction, three weeks after the event. He'd gotten used to being blamed by his boss for everything that went wrong and getting no credit for what he achieved, but it made no difference, he knew he was much too valuable to be dispensed with at the moment. His reputation had carried him through all these years and would continue to do so, until the last battle took him out of the fight. *Inshallah.*

The number of ISIL fighters continued to diminish through killings, desertions and executions and now there was a new insidious threat to their fighting force. The previous day, a French special forces officer had been caught masquerading as an ISIL soldier. Under torture, he'd confessed to being part of a group of forty special agents sent in by the French government to assassinate fighters from their country who might return to commit further atrocities like the Paris massacre.

Clever tactics, had been his reaction to the news. The French authorities couldn't carry out 'search and kill' assignments on their own territory, so they were exporting them to his battlefield. There were hundreds of French fighters in ISIL and they were loyal and ferocious; they were needed. Karl didn't usually approve of the torture techniques used by the security officers, but on this occasion the information could be of real value in tracking down the other undercover officers and helping to protect further losses to their dwindling human resources.

He decided to ignore Abdullah's remark. 'The point is, we can't do anything to stop them and it won't take them more than a week at most to get the crossing in place. Then we'll see some heavy stuff coming from the south to meet up with the airfield forces.'

The supreme commander was silent for a moment, then he said, 'If we can't attack them from Qayyarah, how can we get rid of that bridge?'

That's a more proactive approach, Karl thought. 'Let me think about it and try to work up a plan.'

'Time is short. I'll expect it quickly. *Alhamd lillah rabb alealamin.*' The line went dead.

Vrhnika Asylum Centre, Western Slovenia

'Is there any news for us, Alice?'

At 8:00 pm, the IOM office was quiet, in fact the whole camp was usually quiet, day and night. The greater discipline and organisation of the Slovenian authorities and the smaller number of occupants meant Hema and her children felt a lot safer, but memories of the violence at the Domiz camp ensured she never left them out of her sight.

It was five days since the Al-Douri family had arrived and they'd heard nothing from Alice since her announcement of their clean Dublin report. They had no idea how long they'd have to wait for approval of their right to live freely in Slovenia and hopefully, move on to another EU country in due course.

'I sent the signed application to the IOM central office on Wednesday. All I've heard is they've received it and it's been given a priority rating. I'm afraid it's out of my hands now. We've got thousands of applications to process and a lot of them are high priority, families with children like you. I'll follow it up on a weekly basis, to try to push it through. It won't be as quick as we'd like, but I'll try to make sure it's faster than the average.'

On a weekly basis. Hema's heart sank when she heard those words. *We could be here for months before we get to the head of the queue.*

'Does anyone except the authorities know you're here? Any friends or family in Mosul or anyone in Europe?'

Hamid replied, 'There's nobody we can contact. Contacting anyone in Mosul is too dangerous for them and we don't have any family outside Iraq. My grandfather was in the UK for a while, but he went back a long time ago.'

'All of our grandparents are dead now,' added Aisha, 'there's only us left of the family.'

Hema listened to her children with a poignant mixture of sadness and pleasure. After all they'd been through, they'd earned the right to speak for themselves and she was proud to hear them do so.

Alice placed the dossier one top of the pile. 'I'll call head office first thing in the morning and let you know if there's any news.'

They said goodnight and walked back to their tent, wondering how much longer their journey to freedom would take.

FIFTY-THREE

'How big is the boat?' Abdullah's voice was thick, as if he'd been drinking all night.

'It'll take two tons of explosives, enough to destroy the pontoons and one pier, if we get it in the right position.' Karl was standing on the dockside near the Iron Bridge, in the centre of the old city, looking at the *Saladin*, a steel-hulled ferry boat that had taken up to 175 citizens and tourists alike back and forwards across the Tigris in the years before ISIL had taken over and stopped it from operating. It had been a popular attraction, painted in bright colours, with wooden benches on the top deck where passengers could sit and view the historic buildings on each side of the river as they enjoyed the short crossing. Now, like every forbidden form of pleasure in Mosul, it lay unused, paintwork filthy and peeling, metal rusting, woodwork rotting, the broken windows like a series of black holes along its 35 m superstructure. The Saladin looked like a ferry boat on the River Styx, ready to carry the dead to the underworld of Hades.

'It's about eighty k's to Al Qayyarah on the river. What speed can it do?'

'With that load, about 5 knots, that's about eight hours sailing. We can't let the Iraqis see it on the river, so we'll do the trip in darkness. That means setting off around eight at night to get there by four the next morning.'

He silently cursed the fact that the barges he'd used for the attack on the Iraqi tanks at the Makhmur Road bridge had been lost, destroyed by two 724 Hellfire missiles from an RAF Reaper drone on the day after they ferried his vehicles across the Tigris, a week ago. Now they were on the bottom of the river and there was not another operative vessel between Mosul and Qayyarah large enough for the job. *I wish we were as quick and accurate at retaliation as the infidels,* he said to himself. *If they hadn't sunk those barges I could have been at that pontoon with one hour of sailing, a piece of cake. Now, I might as well send a messenger ahead to advertise our arrival.*

Abdullah interrupted his thoughts. 'How long will it take to load?'

Karl had already discussed this with Wadi, the engineer he'd commandeered from his old unit in Mosul. 'We'll have to get it moved along the river to a dock where we can get a loading crane alongside. We think we can get the engine running again, probably by tomorrow. Then we should be able to get it loaded and equipped in two days.'

'So, it could be ready to leave on Wednesday night. How many men do you need?'

'We need to get an anti-aircraft cannon fitted on the top deck, you'll want a gunner and two ammunition loaders for that. Then, apart from the pilot and mechanic, half a dozen guards with machine guns and assault rifles.'

There was silence for a few moments, then, 'It's approved. You lead the expedition personally.' The phone went dead.

He said to the engineer, 'Get a mechanic started on checking the engine. Find the nearest point where we can load the munitions and equipment. I'll get in touch with the supply officer. I want a ZU-23 cannon with a thousand high explosive shells and two tons of munitions on that wreck by Wednesday night.'

Karl climbed onto his motor cycle to ride back to Qayyarah, the place he'd always felt most at home. He was more pensive than usual, reflecting on Abdullah's last instruction, an order he couldn't refuse to take, since it would label him as a coward, a label he had never worn and never would accept or deserve. It looked like his living legend period was not going to last much longer.

So that's how it's going to end. This time Abdullah is signing my death warrant, as whoever's on that boat when it explodes will be vaporised. Fine, he decided, it's a lot better than running away like a craven coward from the last battle for Mosul. Let's hope it makes some difference, otherwise it's a criminal waste of two tons of explosives.

Guildford, England

Ibrahim had finished the thirteenth box of TATP that afternoon. He'd told Sami that thirteen was his lucky number and they'd celebrated with her favourite supper, fish and chips. Now he was soaking in the bath he had run for her. He'd been doing this regularly for some time. He loved to fill and empty her bath and lately, when she had gone to her bedroom, he would strip off and bathe in the still warm water, enjoying the delicate smell of her perfumed bath oil. He shaved his head, the soft oily water making the blade run easily over his skin. In Germany his family never had a bath; the municipality water price was too expensive and his mother had been miserly in managing their consumption. Each member of the family was allowed only a minute under the shower and to run a bath wasn't even an option. He didn't know who paid the bills for this flat, but it wasn't him or Sami, *so why not enjoy it*, he'd decided.

As often happened, the warm perfumed water brought him an erection. He climbed out of the bath and towelled himself off, then splashed cold water on his face, determined not to give in to the sexual arousal. He had been strong since their arrival in England and he was proud of the surprising discipline he was capable of. He stood at the wash basin, silently praying to Allah and waiting for the feeling to die away. The bathroom door opened and he spun round in surprise, holding his penis, trying to hide it under his hands. Sami was standing there. She was naked. Her creamy skin seemed to shine in the gloomy hall light. Her breasts were small and high, the nipples sticking out proudly, and a tuft of dark hair showed below her flat stomach. He had never seen anything so erotic in his life.

She said, 'You can fuck me if you like.' Seeing the embarrassment and trepidation on his face as he tried to hide his arousal from her, she said, 'It's alright, Karl wouldn't mind and I want you to.'

Taking him by the hand, she led him to her bedroom, lay down on the sheet and pulled him down beside her. She placed his hand between her open legs, stroking his fingers gently between her legs. Wrapping the fingers of her other hand around his throbbing penis, she squeezed the organ a few times. He suddenly cried out and ejaculated over the sheet. '*Oh mein Gott*. I'm sorry, Sami, I'm sorry. I've spoiled it for you.'

'It's alright. Don't worry, it happens a lot. Just leave it to me, I'll bring it back for you.' His fingers were still moving between her legs and she pulled his head down to her breast, gently massaging his penis until his erection returned, then guided him expertly inside her, wrapping her legs around his back to keep him close. Sami didn't kiss him. She had kissed no one since Baki's death, not even Karl.

He thrust himself into her again and again, faster then slower, until she cried out, 'Now. Push now, harder, faster, harder.' As Ibrahim gave one last frenzied thrust he was smitten by the most wonderful feeling he had ever experienced. It was as if his mind had exploded with the exquisite pleasure of the moment.

'*Shukraan ealaa allah,* thanks be to Allah,' he shouted out loud and fell by her side, satiated and happy. He didn't feel guilty. And that didn't make him feel guilty.

FIFTY-FOUR

London, England
Monday, 20th June 2016

'What's the latest situation?'

'No change, I'm afraid. I spoke to Letouffe again, but he's received nothing back from Paris. I get the impression that since he's sure they've left France, it's not one of their top priorities.'

DCI Callum Dewar was quiet for a moment. 'He's as convinced as you are then?'

'His exact words were, "They're in England. There's no other reasonable explanation".'

'I see.' Another pause. Dewar had just come out of a meeting with the Minister of Defence, where he'd reported his concerns about Kellerman's theory. The minister had replied, 'Don't leave it too late, or the press will have a field day, "*Another terrorist plot our security forces ignored*".'

'Can you come over on Wednesday to brief my people?'

Max asked, 'Even without the final DNA proof?'

'You're bound to get it within a couple of days and you'd be more useful here when you do. Can you come?'

Düsseldorf, Germany

'I've agreed to go to London to address a meeting of all the UK security departments. DCI Dewar invited me,' Kellerman added quickly.

'So, he's finally taking you seriously? What happened, I haven't seen the DNA results from Paris?'

'No such luck. You were right, they've got more work than they can handle. It'll be a few more days, but Dewar's pretty convinced I'm right about Ibrahim. It might just be a "CYA" precaution, because the Brexit vote this week could put a lot of pressure on him, but I don't think so. He seems to have a good nose and he agrees with me it's a serious risk. He's already talked to his people and he wants me to brief them with a full history of the background and my theory of what's happened over the past few months.'

'You've got a pretty full schedule. When does he want you to go?'

'Wednesday morning. I'm hoping we'll have confirmation by then, but he agrees it's better if I'm there, if and when the shit hits the fan. Letouffe and I are certain they've been in the UK for a couple of weeks and they'll be making a move any time now.'

Schuster deliberated the options for a moment. *If he doesn't go and there's an attack and we miss it, we'll look bad. On the other hand …* 'OK, I approve it, but I want you back by the weekend if nothing transpires. Once you've briefed them, I don't see what more you can do. There's no point sitting there twiddling your thumbs when we've got shitloads of work here.'

'Understood. I'll be back in the office next Monday. Unless I can get serious kudos for SIB by staying over there and finding Ibrahim and his girlfriend,' he added slyly.

Max sent a quick note to Callum Dewar to confirm his

arrival on Wednesday. *This time I'm sure we're ahead of them*, he said to himself.

Guildford, England

Ibrahim was very quiet in the morning. He was up first and busied himself washing the dishes from last night's supper and setting the kitchen table, saying only, 'Good morning Sami,' when she came out of her room.

After their sexual encounter, he'd lain alongside her, his mood gradually turning from one of happiness and fulfilment to self-deprecation and guilt. When she was sound asleep, he sneaked quietly away and into his own bed. His mind was in turmoil and he couldn't sleep. Through some twisted kind of logic, he now felt a sense of failure at what had happened. He'd failed to fulfil his pledge to Allah and this time not just by self-abuse to relieve his tension.

This time, I've had sex with a woman. And not just any woman. He didn't even want to think about it. Sami was his partner, an experienced and respected jihadist who had come from Iraq to help him plan and execute this attack in England. How could she take him seriously after what had just happened? How could he command her respect as leader of the mission and expect her to listen and obey?

She will see me as weak and easily influenced, an inexperienced youth who doesn't know how to control his sinful urges. She said Karl wouldn't mind, but I don't believe her. He would be outraged at this display of weakness six days before the most important moment of our lives.

He knelt by the bed and recited his catechism, seeking forgiveness and strength from almighty Allah. Finally, he managed to sleep for a few hours then showered and dressed, dreading her appearance, afraid to face her and be forced to cope with this changed relationship.

Immediately aware of his apprehension, she simply said, 'Sit down and I'll make the breakfast.' She fussed quietly for a while then put a plate of poached eggs on toast in front of him. 'I'm not hungry,' she said. 'I'll go to the corner shop and get a few groceries. What do you feel like for supper?'

He ate his meal slowly in the quiet flat, wondering how she could read his mind that way. How she could bring him the greatest moment of pleasure he'd ever experienced then act as if nothing had happened, just go off to the shops and leave him to dwell on his own feelings, give him time to get his head sorted out. *She's clever*, he thought, once again.

Mosul, Iraq

Karl had returned to the city from Qayyarah early that morning to supervise the moving of the Saladin a kilometre along the river to one of the few loading bays that was still in functioning order. The whole day was spent by Wadi and a couple of mechanics in cleaning and tuning up the two four-stroke diesel engines, which were about thirty years old and caked in rust and filth. The propeller shaft and screw were in decent condition and required nothing more than a thorough cleaning and greasing. Fortunately, the engineer was a patient and thorough man and at 10:00 pm, the crankshaft started rotating, the pistons pumping and the screw churning the filthy water to push the massive vessel from its moorings to its new temporary berth.

By nightfall, the Saladin was tied up and ready to install the cannon and load the shells and explosives Karl had ordered from the munitions officer. The only problem was that nothing had been delivered – the bay was empty.

Guildford, England

'This is what I use for the shrapnel.' Ibrahim spilled some of the nuts, bolts and nails he'd bought at the DIY shop onto the kitchen counter. 'It doesn't matter what it is as long as it's small and made of metal, but it's easier to buy this kind of things for the house or the car, everybody does.'

Sami knew about shrapnel. She'd seen the results of suicide bombs in Mosul and it wasn't pretty. She said, 'Is that enough for both cases?'

'I have to buy some more tomorrow. I don't mind going out now, nobody's going to recognise me.' His sideburns framed his face with the stubble beard that looked quite different from the riot of curly black hair that he'd previously worn. Together with his shaven pate, he no longer resembled Ibrahim bin Omar al-Ahmad.

'The phones arrived while you were out. I had to answer the door to collect them, but I hardly opened it and didn't put the light on, so the delivery guy didn't really see me. I took the label off the post box after he left, just in case.' Again, she didn't mention the boy upstairs, that was last week, and she hadn't seen him again.

'Let me have a look.' He checked the Sony Ericsson mobiles. 'The batteries are OK, that's good.' He put a BT SIM in each one, then called his own phone. 'Perfect. Things are going great. I got another box finished this morning, that makes fourteen. If I go out again tomorrow, the last one will be ready by Wednesday, so we're OK for Saturday, no problem. Do you want to show me how to prepare the cases?'

He placed one of them on the coffee table in the living room and laid sheets of tissue paper on the bottom. 'Here you lie the bed of metal, then the first four boxes of TATP on top, then some more shrapnel and the other four boxes on top of that. The cases will weigh about fifteen kilos, so they're easy to lift into the car and onto a trolley. You put the toaster and a Sony Ericsson detonator phone in the box last of all, then surround them all with the shrapnel all around and on top, then some more sheets of tissue paper. That's the most difficult part, connecting them up and testing them. I'll do it on Friday, so we don't risk anything going wrong before we're ready.'

She knew he meant an accidental explosion like the one that had killed his family in Cologne, but just asked, 'How does the detonator work?'

'The phone signal switches the toaster on and it heats up the TATP. It takes just a few seconds and the explosion burns through the paper and canvas and blasts the metal all over the place. The Sony Ericssons have to be programmed to only work when they're called from the trigger phone, so there's no mistakes. I'll use my mobile for that, I won't need it anymore afterwards and it'll be destroyed in the explosion.' He laughed, 'Like everything around us.'

Sami turned away. 'I forgot to get milk this morning, there's none in the fridge.' She checked the time. 'I'll go to the corner shop, they're still open. What do you fancy for supper?'

'Are you feeling ok? You're very quiet.'

'I'm just fine thanks.'

'Are you upset about last night?'

She laughed. 'Don't be bloody silly, I enjoyed it. I haven't had sex for a while, it was just what I needed. I'll get some salad and you can go for a couple of pizzas later, OK?'

Ibrahim watched her walk past the window on her way to the shops. The weather was sunny and warm; she was wearing a sleeveless top and shorts and he thought she looked lovely. *That's all it was,* he said to himself. *She hasn't had sex with anyone since she left Karl. I just happened to be around at the time.* He knelt down and repeated his catechism out loud; he wouldn't weaken again.

FIFTY-FIVE

Mosul, Iraq
Tuesday, June 21st 2016

'I want it near the stern of the boat in the centre of the deck. You'll need to cushion the vibration with rubber mounts.'

The installation of the cannon on the ferry boat was finally under way. It had arrived on the back of a pick-up truck with a crane and been lifted onto the deck with several pallets of shells. It was midday and Karl was still waiting for the remainder of the explosives to arrive. He knew now the time estimate he'd given to Abdullah had been wildly optimistic and he would read him the riot act for being late. If the munitions were there by the next morning, with the dock crane working day and night, he figured they could have the ferry boat ready by Thursday night at the earliest. Then they had to get out of the city in the dark, hoping the enormous floating suicide bomb wouldn't be hit by a stray missile.

In any case, he thought to himself, *it really doesn't matter where or when the explosion occurs, here or in Qayyarah, today, the next day, next year. It will make no difference at all and I won't be around to worry about it anymore.*

Guildford, England
'I've just had an idea.' Ibrahim had finished the fifteenth

box of TATP and placed it carefully in the cupboard with the others.

'And I've just made some tea. Come and have it and tell me your idea.'

He sat on the settee and she carried the mugs over. 'What is it?'

'We should drive to Gatwick and do what they call a dummy run. You know, check the route to get there, the parking, the departure areas and all that. Make sure there's no surprises on Saturday. What do you think?'

'You mean rent the car a day early, on Friday?'

'Will that be a problem?'

She looked at the time. 'I'd better go there now, to make sure. They don't have that many cars and they might have to change if we want it for two days.' She gulped the last of her tea. 'It'll cost another fifty quid, is that OK?'

'We've got plenty of money left. After Saturday we won't need it, will we?'

It was raining and she picked up her folding umbrella at the door. 'What time do you want the car on Friday?'

'After we get the two cases finished, in the afternoon about two o'clock?'

'I won't be long. I'll get some eggs for supper tonight.'

As she reached the street, she turned and glanced back at the building. Craig Hill was looking out of his window.

Vrhnika Asylum Centre, Western Slovenia

'Hello Alice, you asked us to come over. What is it, has something happened?' Hema and her children had been preparing something to eat when a young boy had arrived at their tent and asked them to come to the IOM office.

Two men in suits were sitting next to Alice's desk, which was covered in paperwork, more than when they'd last seen her, three days before. She looked flustered and quickly got to her feet as did both men.

'Good morning Hema. This is Oswald Bissel, head of the IOM regional office in Ljubljana.' The younger man shook Hema's hand. 'And this is Mr Ronald Lambert, the deputy British Consul in Slovenia.' After shaking hands, he ushered the family into a salon with seats for them all. Alice served coffee and water and they sat expectantly.

Hema's heart was in her mouth. *What's happened now? There must be a problem to bring these important people here.* She said, 'Has our application been turned down?'

Lambert smiled, 'That's not why we're here, Ms Al-Douri. On the contrary, we have good news for you. Unusually good news, something I've never encountered before. That's why we've come here to meet you and your children. Let me explain what has happened.'

Guildford, England

It was half past four and Sami was walking home from the bus stop; it had stopped raining. She'd gone out twice to arrange the rental car and buy items for the last batch of TATP and the groceries they'd need up to Saturday. She didn't think she'd need to go shopping again. The feeling was good; she could relax in the flat and not be afraid of being recognised outside. The separate entrance to number one meant up to now she'd managed to avoid meeting anyone except Craig Hill, but the worry of being identified and stopped had increased each time she went out until she was in a perpetual state of nervousness, almost paranoia.

As she turned into the entrance drive she looked up at the second floor. Her heart raced, and she looked down again. He was sitting at the window of what must have been his bedroom, looking out at her. She could see the top of a computer screen in front of him. *He probably sits there doing his homework and playing computer games*, she thought. *I wonder if his parents are there?* She went to the door of number one and stopped for a moment to calm her nerves.

Ibrahim heard the key in the lock and called out, 'Hi, Sami. I've just put the kettle on.'

'Great. I could murder a cup of tea, I've had it for today.' She went into the kitchen to put away the groceries.

'Any problems?' He came over to her, a worried look on his face.

'No, it's just we're so close to the date, I'm nervous all the time I'm out and it's killing me.'

'No need to worry anymore. I just came back with the rest of the shrapnel stuff, so if you have everything you need we don't have to go out again.'

'When did you come in?'

'A few minutes before you. Why?'

She saw Craig Hill's face at the window again. 'Did anyone see you?' she asked casually.

'Nobody, and the guy at the till in the shop never

looked at me. No problems, I'm the invisible man,' he laughed.

'That's all right then. I'll make the tea then we can plan Friday's dummy run.' She tried to shrug aside her fears. 'How many boxes have you done?'

'We've got fifteen. One more tomorrow and we'll be ready to pack the cases on Friday morning.' He laughed again. '*Pack the cases*, it sounds like we're going on a holiday.'

'I suppose we are, kind of. Except we won't be coming back.' She took two mugs and poured scalding water over the tea bags. 'Tea's ready.'

Vrhnika Asylum Centre, Western Slovenia

'I still can't believe it. It's like a dream, a beautiful dream.'

'It's real Mama, this nightmare's almost over. We're going to England. Hurrah!' The other children joined in Hamid's cheer, almost splitting her eardrums.

'But I don't understand how it happened, how they knew we're here and about your father and everything we've been through. How could they know all that?'

After announcing he had good news for them, Assistant Consul Ronald Lambert had recounted an amazing story. The British Consul in Slovenia had been requested by the Home Office in London to approach the Geneva HQ of the International Organisation for Migration on behalf of a family from Iraq, the Al-Douris, who were presently in the Vrhnika Asylum Centre. An application had been made to sponsor the family for asylum in the UK and subsequently, application for British citizenship. The applicant and sponsor was Sir Patrick Carr, an ex- diplomat, credited with the successful resolution of many problems and disputes at an international level in the Middle East during a long and distinguished career.

Sir Patrick's reputation and circle of friends were such that the British Home Secretary made a personal request to the IOM, which quickly became an order to grant asylum to the family in Slovenia and to offer reciprocity in the UK. The paperwork had been accomplished in record time and the two men had been instructed to visit the camp personally to impart the news to the family and arrange for their departure to London.

Hema had sat silent, thunderstruck by this news. While her children were high-fiving each other and the officials and thanking them for this heart-lifting news, tears ran down her face. *Why isn't Faqir here with us? Sir Patrick is doing a wonderful thing, but it wouldn't be possible if my husband hadn't performed miracle after miracle to get us out of that death trap in Mosul. Why did he have to go before we finished our journey?*

Alice came over and put her arm around her shoulder. 'I know what you're thinking, Hema. Faqir can't join us in celebrating this wonderful news. But he gave his life to save you and your children and that's what you must remember. This chance to make a new life is because of his sacrifice and you have to accept it and make the most of it. That's what he would want, you know it is.'

Before they said goodbye, Mr Lambert asked, 'I don't want to be rude or indiscreet, Ms Al-Douri, but could you tell us how you got to know Sir Patrick and Lady Carr? If you don't mind my saying so, it's an unusual friendship.'

Hema replied carefully, 'We met them in Istanbul and spent some time together. But I never expected such kindness. They're doing so much for us, we're all overwhelmed.'

She glanced nervously at Hamid, when he said, 'They even invited us onto their yacht. It's fabulous.' Then he added, 'I would love to sail on it one day.'

Now, after praying with her family and thanking God and her husband for their deliverance, Hema had finally accepted Alice's advice and was addressing their new situation. 'How could they know all that?' she repeated.

'I have a confession to make, Mama.' Hamid handed her his phone. There was a text message on the screen.

She looked at it then kissed his forehead, seeing clearly what had occurred. 'Read it out for us.'

'Dear Sir Patrick, Lady Nancy and Tony. On behalf of my family, I want to thank you for your kindness to us all. We followed Tony's instructions and are safely in the refugee camp in Slovenia. There was a bad problem with a Croatian crook and our dear father was lost to us which broke our hearts. Our mother and the rest of us are well and we have applied for asylum and hope to come to England and see you there some time. Thank you once more and God bless you for your kindness to our family. Hamid Al-Douri.'

FIFTY-SIX

'I just got a call from Letouffe. He thinks we'll have the results by tomorrow. They're getting through their backlog.' Max Kellerman was speaking to Callum Dewar in London. He was embarrassed at the lack of progress; for a week he'd been promising proof of the fugitives' flight to the UK and he still couldn't show any. He was surprised Dewar seemed to be taking him seriously at all.

'I'd still like you to come over today if you can manage it. Everything's set up and my people are looking forward to hearing from you.'

'I agree, I'll feel better if I can share personally what I know with them. And when we get the confirmation tomorrow and you're faced with an imminent threat, I'll be more useful if I'm close at hand. How long will we have today?'

'We've got two hours at the end of the afternoon, but there'll be some guys who'll want to stay and have a drink. That's usually the best time to talk to them, less formal, more personal approach with your feelings about them, especially Ibrahim.'

'Same the world over. Right, I've got a flight at twelve-thirty. With the time difference I'll be with you before three this afternoon.'

Kellerman took a series of photographs of his incident wall chart. He couldn't carry all his files with him and they might help to jog his memory for this afternoon's talk. He confirmed with Eric Schuster he was leaving then drove home for lunch with Monika and to pack a case. He had plenty of work on his plate, but he knew the department liked international cooperation and, on this occasion, they might get some serious brownie points.

Vrhnika Asylum Centre, Western Slovenia

'I have all the papers here for your signature.' Alice Newman ushered them into her office. It was empty; their VIP visitors had left that morning to get on with other pressing but perhaps less enjoyable tasks. She opened a bulky file and started explaining the documents to them one by one.

Fifteen minutes later, Hema signed the last sheet and handed it across the desk. 'What happens now?'

'I'm sending everything by courier to Mr Bissel at the Ljubljana IMO office for the official signing and stamping and they'll be forwarded to London on tonight's flight. The Home Office will process them tomorrow and issue the necessary asylum approval, I've already seen the text on an email. That should be done by Friday at the latest, so I've arranged flights for you on Saturday.'

'We'll be in London on Saturday?' Hema couldn't believe that everything would happen so quickly, that they were so close to freedom. Her children exchanged excited glances.

'There's a flight leaving at 10:45 in the morning. I took the liberty of booking your seats, you're all together in rows four and five. I hope that's alright with you.'

'That's wonderful news, thank you, Alice.' She gave a worried frown. 'But we haven't received visas or any travel documents yet.'

'And we don't know anyone there. How will we find our way? Where do we go?' Aisha nervously took her mother's hand.

'There's no need to worry. I know this is all new and scary for you after everything you've been through, but everything's been planned. I'll be taking you to the airport myself and someone will meet you when you get off the flight in London. They'll have your UK asylum papers to take you through immigration. Then you'll be picked up and driven to your new home. I promise you won't have any surprises or delays.'

Hema nodded gratefully, 'I'm sorry, but everything was such a surprise yesterday, I didn't ask the right questions. I wasn't thinking of all the things we'll need in the UK. My children need a home, a proper roof over their heads.' She paused, feeling embarrassed, 'We don't have a lot of money. I don't know how long it will last and what will happen when it's gone.'

'That's what the sponsorship is about, Hema. Sir Patrick has guaranteed that you won't be a charge on the state. I don't know the details, but he will provide you with a home and an income for a period of time, until you or your children can find jobs and make your own way. He's arranged everything so your life in England will be as trouble-free as possible. He understands what you've been through and this is his way of helping you to start a new life.'

The Al-Douri family walked back to their tent, still trying to cope with the kind-heartedness and humanity of their benefactor.

Malik summed up their thoughts. 'Isn't it great to know there are still some good people left in the world?'

Guildford, England

Sami walked to the apartment building with her shopping bag. Ibrahim had finished the last box of TATP that morning so she didn't have to worry about buying any more ingredients, but she'd gone for a few last-minute items to get through until Saturday. As she went into the driveway, she looked nervously up at the second-floor window. There was no one there and she breathed a sigh of relief.

'Hiya, Sarah.' He was coming out the door towards her.

'Oh, hello Craig.'

She made to go past him and he said, 'Is that your partner, the guy with the stubble beard?'

She gave a forced laugh, 'No, it's me father, what do you think?'

'My mum hasn't got a partner, since he left us, my dad I mean.'

He was standing in her path and she said, 'I'm sorry, I'm in a bit of a hurry.'

'She hardly ever goes out now. I'm going to the shops to get some stuff for supper. I have to do everything, she just sits around watching telly.'

She walked around him, 'That's a shame. I've got to get on with things. See you, Craig.'

Sami went around the corner of the apartment building and put the key in the door to number one. Her fingers were trembling so much she could hardly find the lock. She said nothing to Ibrahim.

London, England

'We're expecting the DNA result from RAID in Paris tomorrow and I believe we'll get confirmation that Ibrahim bin Omar al-Ahmad and an unidentified English woman arrived in Torquay two weeks ago.' Max Kellerman looked around at the thirty or so anti-terrorism officers seated in front of him in in the conference room in New Scotland Yard. 'I don't think they're here for a seaside holiday. He's a dangerous man who killed his family while planning an atrocity in my country and he's managed to escape detection for almost two months. I hope I've given you a clear summary and I'm at your disposal if I can be of any further assistance.'

It had been several years since Max had spoken in public in English, but he was quite happy with his performance. Now, the British policemen crowded around him to shake hands and ask last minute questions. It was six-thirty and most of them were off duty and happy to chat informally with a foreign counterpart. He was staying at a London club not far from there where DCI Dewar was a member, and in view of the discrepancy between his travel budget and London hotel prices, he was happy to take advantage of the offer. When Dewar invited them for a drink at the club, several officers were keen to accept, and they walked along the Embankment in the evening sunshine to the terrace bar.

'How come you got landed with this business, you're not a part of BFE+, the anti-terrorist outfit, are you?' The speaker was Detective Inspector Arnold Bellowes, a Met veteran, now a Special Operations Branch Officer with SO15, Counter Terrorism Command.

Max explained the background to his involvement in the case. 'I didn't think I'd still be on it after almost two months,' he finished.

'I know what you mean. You get trapped in their world and get to know them better than anybody; the way they think, they plan, they act.'

'You've had cases like that?'

'Sure, a few.' He took a swig of his whiskey and soda. 'We've still got plenty like that. There's a group in the Aldershot area, that's west of London, near where I live. I've been looking at them for almost a year. It started with a complaint from a woman who said two young guys were preaching hatred in the local kids' park. You know, buying them sweets and cokes and radicalising them against the British.'

'I've never heard of that before.'

'Me neither. Anyway, I organised surveillance on these guys for a few months; where they lived, where they went, who they met, until I knew them better than their parents. That's not difficult these days. We're sure they're members of the *al-Muhajiroun* extremist group and they go to a nearby mosque where the Imam's known for his extremist views. He stops short of inciting violence in public, but we know he has private sessions with impressionable young people and we've seen these two going in there. So, we put one of our Muslim undercover men in the mosque to get friendly with them. We've got their homes, phones and laptops monitored, but with WhatsApp, they can get away with murder, literally. Anyway, we know they watch radical, murderous stuff online, executions and speeches by ISIL warlords, and they talk a lot about helping the jihadist cause with some kind of direct action in the UK.'

'And this has been going on for a year? Why haven't you taken them into custody for supporting or inciting terrorism, or whatever you call it here?'

'You know the answer to that, Max. Until these guys try something and we have proof of it, we can't touch them. We've foiled hundreds of plots over the last couple of years, but it's always at the last minute, when we've got definite proof of a specific threat to a specific target. The Human Rights Act and European free movement laws are not designed to make our jobs easier, it's the same in your country and all over Europe. The top brass is terrified of overstepping the mark and being accused of racism or panic, or simply doing their job properly. Since Cameron agreed to abolish control orders to keep Nick Clegg happy, we've had our hands tied. And they should never have watered down the police 'Stop and Search' powers; it's just catering to the 'don't offend potential criminals' lobby. Believe me, a lot more plots are going to be missed and innocent people killed before common sense prevails.'

Kellerman frowned, 'That's why DCI Dewar's afraid to do anything about Ibrahim bin Omar al-Ahmad and the woman until we've got positive proof they were on that boat. I just hope we have time to find them before they get their plans in place, whatever they are.'

Mosul, Iraq

'It must be the gearbox, I can't get the jib to lift at all. Crappy pre-war equipment. It's never been used for twenty years. No wonder it's fucked.'

Karl was becoming more and more exasperated. First the cannon hadn't arrived on time, then it had taken a day for the incompetent 'engineers' to install and stabilise it, and now that the munitions were finally there, the crane had broken down on the first lift. *At this rate*, he thought, *the Iraqi army will be able to help me load the Saladin when they retake Mosul.*

'Can you fix it or not?'

'I have no idea, but I don't expect so. If it's a busted part, I wouldn't know where to find a replacement. It's a mechanical crane, they don't make them anymore, just hydraulics.' The man climbed down to the quay. 'Do you want me to take it to pieces? It's rusty and corroded, so it'll take hours and then probably a waste of time if I can't fix it.'

'Forget it. I'll find a solution.'

The man wandered off and Karl pondered the situation. It was Wednesday night and they'd loaded nothing except the cannon and shells. He called one of the men who'd helped him in organising the distribution of the booby-trap vehicles in Mosul. 'Can you get hold of a pick-up with a crane on it?'

He promised to find something by the next morning and Karl called the supreme commander. 'We're going to be two days late.' He waited for the predictable response.

'You should have tested the crane before you moved the boat there. It's not fucking rocket science.' Abdullah was enjoying his moment of revenge.

He ignored the jibe – it didn't deserve a response. 'I'll ride down to Qayyarah to see what the situation is. I doubt they've got the bridge finished yet. If I leave on Friday night I should still be in time.' *In time for what?* He asked himself. *In time to be blown to smithereens in a pointless gesture of defiance?*

'If you don't leave on Friday, you'll never leave.' The phone went silent.

Now what did he mean by that? Maybe he'll have me boiled in oil and served for the commanders' dinner or chewed to death by goats in the market square.

He went to get his motorcycle to ride through the desert to Qayyarah. It was a warm, sultry night and the air outside of Mosul smelled sweeter.

FIFTY-SEVEN

Max Kellerman rushed into Callum Dewar's office. 'It's them,' he exclaimed. 'The DNA is ninety-nine percent identical with Ibrahim's family. I knew it had to be him.'

'I see.' The DCI cursed silently. 'Have you interrogated the boat's owners again?'

'I've asked Pascale Letouffe in Rennes to do that. But it'll take time and we don't have much. They crossed over on June 3rd, so they've been here three weeks and we don't know where or what they're doing. But I'm sure he's planning the same thing as he did in Cologne.'

'OK, OK. Calm down Max. I'll get a bulletin out to the whole force and we'll have a briefing session with SO15 and make a TV announcement this morning. You were right and I'm glad you're here to help coordinate things. Can you stay around until we get some traction?'

'I already called Lieutenant Schuster in Düsseldorf. They want me to see it through.'

'That's perfect.' He picked up his phone. 'Get me Commander Armstrong please, it's a priority call.'

When his boss came on the line, he gave a brief summary of the news, then said, 'Right away, sir.' Dewar got up from his desk, 'Come and meet the commander, Max. He's keen to hear your story.'

Guildford, England

Ibrahim switched on the BBC midday news and was astonished to see Max Kellerman again. 'Sami, we've got a problem.'

She ran into the living room in time to see their faces on the screen, the photofit image of her and two photos of Ibrahim, with and without the beard. Another man was with the German, Detective Chief Inspector Dewar, a senior English police officer.

Her heart beat faster and her mouth went dry as he said, 'Our security forces have established that the two fugitives crossed the Channel from France three weeks ago and landed in Torquay. Their present whereabouts and the woman's identity are unknown. The man, Ibrahim bin Omar al-Ahmad, who may be travelling under the name of Ali el Zafar, is a known ISIL fanatic who carried out a terrorist attack in Germany several months ago.'

She shivered when he continued, 'The woman calls herself Sarah and speaks English with an upper-class accent. We believe they may have come to the UK to carry out another attack. If you have seen or see either of these persons and know where they might be, you should immediately call the number on the screen below or go to your nearest police station. Do not approach them, they are dangerous.'

Sami sat on the settee, trying to calm her racing heart and trembling hands. 'I wonder how they know for sure we're in England?'

'I don't know, but it took them a long time. And those

pictures don't look like us anymore. And nobody knows we're in Guildford, so we won't be recognised.'

Sami could see Craig Hill at his bedroom window. She laughed, a sharp, brittle sound he didn't recognise. 'Sure and all, that's true enough.'

He looked worriedly at her. 'Are you alright? You seem very nervous these last few days.'

'I'm fine, but I think we should cancel the trip to Gatwick tomorrow. No sense in taking risks if we don't need to. I remember everything from my visit, don't worry. We'll stay in and make sure we're ready for Saturday?'

'Are you sure you're OK?'

'I told you, I'm fine,' she snapped, 'I just don't want to screw things up at the last minute. I'll call the car rental guy and cancel Friday. It won't be a problem. I'll walk along and get a couple of pizzas for supper. There's no reason for you to go out, that photo's too good for my liking.'

'Alright, Sami. I just don't want you to get nervous when there's only two days to go. I'm sure there's no risk of being seen.'

She sighed. 'Sorry, Ibrahim. I'm a bit tired, that's all. You're right, nobody's going to recognise us before Saturday, then it'll be too late.'

The press conference was on every hourly news bulletin and appeared in the evening newspapers, then again the next morning and continuously throughout the day. Fortunately, Craig Hill spent his time on social media and playing computer games and his mother watched nothing but soaps and, in any case, had never seen either of them.

Mosul, Iraq

'Where the fuck are the gunner and the loaders you promised me?'

Karl was overseeing a gang of workers who were loading the Saladin with two tons of explosives and he wasn't happy. The crane on the pick-up truck was in fact a small winch, which couldn't lift heavily loaded pallets. None of the crew promised to him by Abdullah had arrived yet and he had conscripted four men, two of whom were transferring the explosives from the pallets onto a platform which the winch lifted up to the deck of the Saladin. The other two men then carried the munitions along and laid them out in what had previously been the passenger lounge, on the second deck, under the cannon. Slowly but surely, rows of deadly piles of explosives were filling the room, but too slowly for his liking.

2000 kilos of explosives had been dumped on the quay and the winch could safely lift no more than 100 kg. Twenty loads were needed to transfer the material, but that wasn't the problem. The men couldn't carry more than 20 kg at a time without risking blowing up the whole load of munitions and the ferry boat with it, and they couldn't work non-stop; they had to rest and eat. Karl had made his calculations and knew it would take all night to load the boat, ready to sail the next morning.

But that wasn't the problem either. He still didn't have a gunner for the cannon, nor any ammunition loaders. He needed experienced men; the gun was a complicated piece of artillery and could either be an asset or a liability. It would most likely be needed during the trip down the Tigris, to warn away enemy reconnaissance aircraft and drones, although he knew they would stay safely out of range. But psychologically it might help them to get through to the pontoon bridge; it could make the difference between success and failure.

He'd seen the previous night that the bridge wasn't finished. If he could get down there by tomorrow, he might stand a chance of preventing it, but he couldn't leave without a crew. Although he was pleased to have the opportunity to insult the supreme commander, as always, his mind was set on accomplishing this task to the best of his ability. It would probably fail and he would likely not survive, but he would give it his best shot and put his faith in Allah.

His boss was saying, 'We've got a shortage of gunners. There's six Iraqi attacks going on around Qayyarah and they're getting close to Hamam Alil. You're lucky to be out of it.'

They're getting ready to move as soon as that bridge is in place, he realised, thinking of his men in Qayyarah, some of whom had been at his side for months, even years. *Whatever we do it's too little, too late. Even this idiot Abdullah must see that.*

'I'll get you some men by morning, you'll be able to leave tomorrow night, that's what you told me, right?'

'That's including the mechanic, pilot and guards?'

'I'll do my best.'

Karl always asked for more men than he needed, so he could settle for less. But he had to have at least a couple of experienced cannon operators. 'Make sure they know what they're doing, that gun could make or break the operation.'

'The gunner will be trained, don't worry. And don't forget we're moving out to Raqqa next week. You'd better be back for that, we need as many commanders as possible to build a new caliphate presence out of Syria.'

Karl laughed out loud. 'What in Allah's name are you talking about? I won't survive this operation, it's a suicide mission and you know, because you planned it.'

'You mean you can't get off that ferry boat before it's blown up? I never took you for stupid, Karl. There's no need to be killed with the other men, they're dispensable, you're not, you're a senior commander.'

'You're telling me to chicken out of this mission so I can come back to Mosul and flee the city with the rest of you cowardly shits while our men are dying around us for our cause?' Karl finally lost his cool. 'The only reason I would consider trying to survive this operation would be to come back to Mosul and cut your fucking balls off with a chainsaw. Get me that gunner in the morning then piss off to Raqqa. Whatever happens, I won't be going.'

FIFTY-EIGHT

'Pascale Letouffe just called me from Rennes. Miguel's ex-wife has confessed. She admitted Miguel and Eladio left St. Malo at between one and two on Thursday afternoon, but she says she doesn't know where they were going. That means they had plenty of time to pick up our fugitives somewhere around Lannion before starting their crossing. It all ties in, finally, exactly what I expected,' Max Kellerman said, triumphantly.

'And the brothers?'

'Nothing yet, but they've been called in for further questioning and they'll fall apart when they hear this from Letouffe.'

Dewar's phone rang. 'Yes sir, good morning, sir.' He stood up at his desk. 'I understand, sir. We'll be there in good time.'

He put the phone down and said to Max, 'The PM's called a Cobra meeting for ten this morning. My commander had a meeting with him yesterday.' He frowned, 'They're really worried about your man now, everybody's running scared, wondering where he's going to strike. We're going along to Downing Street. You can give them this latest news there yourself. Did you bring a uniform? Not for me or the meeting, it's for the reporters outside. The way the Brexit vote went yesterday, there'll be dozens of them there. Got to look the part in the photographs.' Max had wondered why Dewar was wearing his dress uniform; now he understood it was just a public relations thing.

'I'll go to the club and change.' The German went out, leaving the DCI with his paperwork. He didn't envy him the additional problems that Brexit would likely create for him and his people. *Another complication in an already over-complicated world.*

Callum Dewar's mind was not on Brexit; he was worrying about Ibrahim bin Omar al-Ahmad. He'd refused to make a priority case out of Kellerman's theories and the German had been right on the button. The fugitives had been in the UK now for three weeks. If something happened, he'd be like a rabbit in the headlights, nowhere to run. He also knew that there were two Cobra sessions that morning. He wasn't the only man who had top-level concerns to worry about; there was enough trouble around for everyone to share.

Mosul, Iraq

The gunner promised by Abdullah had arrived at midday with three guards and a mechanic, who said he could double as pilot. Karl had tried in vain to find Wadi, who had helped him to get the engine functioning, but he'd been sent down to Qayyarah to work on suicide vehicles and he didn't even know if he was still alive; the death toll of ISIL men in the battle hotspots was rising exponentially.

I can manage with a crew of five, he decided. *As long as the gunner and mechanic know what they're doing.* He immediately put them through their paces, first the gunner, firing test rounds and teaching the guards to reload the cannon. The mechanic managed to start the Saladin's engines and pronounced the vessel fit to undertake the voyage. The men were experienced, competent, and ready to die for the caliphate, well-suited to the assignment. *That's a surprise,* Karl reflected. *At least three things Abdullah's got right since he was appointed in my place.*

He returned to the problem of the loading. They were running late again; one of the men he'd conscripted had dropped a load on his foot the previous night. It hadn't caused an explosion, but another loader had to take him to the clinic and the incident had cost several hours of valuable time. They were still winching and carrying on the explosives and armaments and it looked like it would go on into the night.

Karl called Abdullah. 'We're still a day late. We'll have to go tomorrow night.'

'You told me you'd be ready to leave tonight.'

'I was wrong.' He didn't waste his words on a mealy-mouthed excuse. If the commander didn't understand by now how their untrained cannon fodder could screw up even the simplest tasks then he never would.

'When will you be loaded?'

'Probably by midnight.'

'Then don't wait. Leave as soon as you're loaded.'

'That means we'll be approaching the bridge in daylight hours. We'll be sitting ducks.'

'You heard what I said, you leave as soon as the boat's loaded. Midnight or morning, it makes no difference, they'll be waiting for you. The bridge is a target and it will be well protected.' The phone went dead.

So, whether we blow the bridge or get blown up by the infidels, it's heads Abdullah wins, tails I lose. Still, I'm glad I got the opportunity to tell him what I think about him and his cronies. It'll soon be time to make my peace with Allah. He walked over to the dockside and looked down at the filthy water. Dozens of rats were scurrying around in the detritus that had accumulated in the scum along the edge of the dock. *That's what I'll be doing tomorrow. Feeding the rats or the fish.*

The deadline made him think of Ibrahim and Sami again. It was June 24th and they were due to fulfil their destiny on the 25th. He texted, '*Qad yakun allah maeak ghadaan, may Allah be with you tomorrow*'.

Guildford, England

'There's a text from Karl.' Ibrahim had just heard the 'ping' on his mobile.

'Oh yes? I bet it's short, he doesn't waste words. What's it say?'

'Look.' He showed her the Arabic script. 'Do you know what it means?'

'Not really, apart from it's about Allah. Most things are, in ISIL.'

'He says, "*Qad yakun allah maeak ghadaan*".'

'May Allah be with you tomorrow. Thanks Karl, and the same to you, to be sure.' She gave a brittle laugh. 'I think we all need Allah to look after us right at the minute.' She went into the bathroom and closed the door behind her.

Sami's in a very strange mood these days, thought Ibrahim. He texted back, *'Shukraan w bialmithl lak,* thanks and the same to you'.

FIFTY-NINE

Friday, 24th June 2016
Guildford, England

'That's it. We're finished.' Ibrahim hoisted the case down from the table and laid it alongside the other on the living room floor. It was hot in the flat and he had taken off his tee-shirt, the sweat running down his face and upper body. Before laying the last layer of shrapnel, his final task had been to programme the two Sony detonator phones to work from his mobile and connect them to the toasters before the final wrapping of tissue paper. He weighed the cases on the bathroom scale and they were just under 16 kilos, *perfect*.

He ran the kitchen tap and rinsed his face and under his arms. Sami handed him a towel and he dried himself off. 'Thanks Sami, that was a big job and I couldn't have done it without you. I'm glad Karl sent you to be my partner.'

'Sure and all, you're welcome. It was very instructive. Not that I expect to ever be doing it again.' She gave a forced laugh.

'I think we have to celebrate tonight. I'll get something for supper. What would you like?'

'Now isn't that a daft question? Fish and chips of course, with extra chips. And maybe a bottle of wine?'

Ibrahim was surprised. They had never drunk alcohol together and he didn't know she liked wine. He had only drunk it when his father had been alive and hadn't particularly enjoyed it. 'What kind do you want?'

'Anything white, as long as it's cold. There's a wine shop near the chippy, ask them to take it out the fridge.'

He put on his hoodie and went to the door.

She thought of Craig Hill, as she always did when one of them had to go out. It was almost dark, so she was less worried. 'Keep your head down, today's not the time to get seen.'

'I know. It's the day before tomorrow. *Inshallah*.'

London, England

'How did you enjoy your trip to Downing Street?'

'A little scary as you say over here, but very interesting. There were a lot of smart people in the room, despite what they might think on the other side of the Channel.' Max Kellerman was in DCI Dewar's office, still wearing his dress uniform.

Dewar decided to ignore the last remark; discussing Brexit was bad enough between the English, never mind with the Germans. 'I thought it went well, under the circumstances.'

'You mean David Cameron resigning an hour after our meeting? I didn't take it personally, if that's what you mean.'

'We can't let political changes get in the way of our job.' He checked the time. 'We've got a briefing with my people in ten minutes, then another TV press conference. It'll have to be a good one to compete with Brexit and the PM's resignation. Come on, we'd better get moving.'

Guildford, England

Sami and Ibrahim watched DCI Callum Dewar and Major Max Kellerman on the eight o'clock BBC news. It came on after the announcement that the Prime Minister had resigned and there was nothing new, except a reward of fifty thousand pounds was offered for information leading to the capture of either of them and the Cobra Committee had raised the terrorist attack threat warning to 'Severe'.

'What does that mean?'

'It's like this Brexit vote, it means they're shitting in their pants and haven't got a clue what's going on or what's going to happen.' Sami laughed, 'Maybe that fella Cameron resigned 'cos he knows what we're going to do and he doesn't want to take the blame.'

She swallowed her last drop of Chardonnay and lay back against the settee cushion. Neither of them was used to drinking and they had finished the bottle between them. 'I'm feeling a bit tipsy,' she said.

He didn't understand the word and said, 'I'll run a bath for you. It's the last time I'll get to do it.' He stood up.

'Not now.' Unsteadily, she got to her feet and grabbed his hand. 'Come with me,' she said, leading him into her bedroom. 'Here.' She undid his shirt and pulled it off, then his trousers and pants. He immediately had an erection.

'Sami, I made a promise to Allah that I wouldn't be weak again. I can't ...'

'Shut up and come here.' She led him to the bed and made him lie on his back, then she stripped off her clothes. Climbing up beside him she straddled his body and took his organ in her hands, lifted up on her knees to position herself above him, then pushed down to take him inside her.

He gasped, 'Sami. Why are you doing this? I thought you didn't really like me.'

She pushed slowly up and down, grasping his sides with her knees and he gasped again.

'You told me we have to celebrate, that's what we're doing. Lie still and enjoy it, it's your last chance of a fuck this side of paradise.'

SIXTY

Saturday, 25th June 2016
Mosul, Iraq

'We're ready to go. Do you have any last-minute instructions?'

'Just blow the fucking bridge up, that's all.' The supreme commander sounded drunk, not for the first time.

'Thank you, sir, very useful advice, as always. We'll do our best.' Since Abdullah wasn't nearby as a target, Karl spat on the deck of the ferry boat in disgust.

He gave the order, the mechanic/pilot engaged gears and the *Saladin* pulled away from the dock, passing under the Iron Bridge and heading down the Tigris from the al-Nasser neighbourhood in the old town towards Al Qayyarah, eighty kilometres away. His phone said it was 4:30 am. That meant they'd arrive at the pontoon bridge sometime after midday. *If we make it that far,* he said to himself. He estimated his chances of getting near the bridge at close to zero and of blowing it up, at even less.

The continuous flashes from the explosions of the allied missiles and bombs landing on Mosul lit up the night sky as they pulled away. It had been like that every night for the last few weeks; the infidels were softening up the ISIL resistance from the air. Soon they would start their ground attacks and Allah help those still trapped in the city. There would be no escape for fighters and civilians alike, the ISIL commanders would see to that.

Except, of course, for those cowardly bastards who'll escape to Raqqa and leave the rest of our men behind to die. He was reconciled to not being part of that glorious last stand but would always be proud of helping to take Mosul for his caliphate.

The ferry boat reached its cruising speed of 5 knots, about 10 km/hour, and Karl went down to the lower deck, lay on a blanket and fell asleep. He'd been up for 24 hours straight and he'd need to have his wits about him before too long.

London, England

Max Kellerman couldn't sleep. His mind was going around and around in circles, trying to work out where Ibrahim bin Omar al-Ahmad was hiding, who the blonde woman was and what they were going to do. Everything he'd been able to discover about the terrorists and their journey through France to the UK still gave him no idea of their plans. Since they'd landed in Torquay, more than three weeks ago, they had completely disappeared – not a single sighting of them despite all the police announcements on TV. *What have they been doing all this time and where? They must be preparing an attack of some kind, it doesn't make any sense otherwise.*

He remembered his conversation with DI Arnold Bellowes, who had been following suspected terrorists for a year, waiting for them to do something so he could act; 'And when they finally do act, it's too late, all you can do is pick up the pieces afterwards.'

Is it going to be the same with these two? He asked

himself. *Are they playing a long game here, waiting until we get tired and sloppy, then act while we're asleep?*

No, they took a lot of chances to get here, on trains and a midnight run across the Channel. Ibrahim obviously went down from Germany to France to meet the woman and then come back to the UK. They're here on a mission and they've had three weeks to prepare for it; they'll execute it before long.

His last thought before sleep finally came, was, *fifty thousand pounds is a lot of money. Anyone watching TV is bound to pay attention to that. And someone, somewhere, must have seen them. We just need one person to see the announcement and the reward and put two and two together. We just need a little bit of luck.*

Tigris River, en route to Al Qayyarah, Iraq

It was 9:30 am and the *Saladin* had just passed Hammam al-Alil, thirty-five kilometres from Mosul, another forty-five to run to the pontoon bridge. Karl had slept for five hours and woke up feeling refreshed and optimistic, only to be told the engine was continuously overheating. The pilot had been obliged to reduce their cruising speed to 4 knots, just 7.5 km/hour. They'd arrive at the pontoon bridge at three-thirty in the afternoon travelling like a snail, a perfect target for the Iraqi defence and allied aircraft missiles.

He said his prayers then ate a sandwich and fruit with a glass of milk. The sun was already burning hot and there was no sound but the rhythmic, quiet throb of the boat's diesel engines. The silence was surreal compared with the cacophony of sound he'd become accustomed to in Mosul and every other battleground where he'd spent most of his adult life. On either side of the river, the desert stretched away in the haze with nothing in sight but occasional huts or tents, tiny dots in the distance. They were on an eastern bend of the river and through his binoculars he could just make out the Mar Benham Monastery at Al Khidhir, a small town about ten kilometres away to the east.

If only it could always be like this, he said to himself. *If only Allah could give us back our lands as they were, without huge buildings, without infidels, without battles. Inshallah, if only.*

He went to sit in the shade under a canopy with his binoculars, his eyes and ears peeled for the sight or sound of aircraft.

Guildford, England

There had been a thunderstorm in the night and it was cooler, but sunny and bright when Sami parked the silver Citroen Picasso in front of the apartment building at ten o'clock. It was on a yellow line, but they would only take a minute or two to load the suitcases onto the back seat. She had taken the time to adjust the mirrors and familiarise herself with the dashboard controls before driving away from the rental office. The roads were still wet and she had driven very slowly, unnecessarily changing gear and stopping and starting several times to get the feel of the car, to avoid any problems on their journey.

Ibrahim was at the door waiting; he'd been praying

while she was out and felt calm and resolved. He had on a pair of torn jeans and a white shirt, like those he'd worn for the Kalk attack, determined that this time it would bring him luck. Sami was also in jeans and open sandals; her colourful shirt spelled 'holidays'. He carried both cases out and carefully loaded them side by side on the back seat, pushing the passenger seat back to wedge them in place. When she saw him climb into the car, she locked the door, taped the key into the post box, then went to get in beside him.

'Hiya, Sarah.' Craig Hill had come out of the main entrance and hurried up to walk alongside her.

'Hi, Craig, sorry, I'm in a rush.' She tried to get past him, but he went to the car with her.

'Is that your car?' He waved to Ibrahim in the passenger seat, then saw the cases, 'You going on holidays?'

She thought quickly, 'I wish. We've found another flat, so we're leaving. It's been nice knowing you.'

'That's a shame. Well, bye, Sarah, I might see you around sometime.'

Sami climbed into the driver's seat and started the engine. Her foot slipped off the clutch pedal and the car stalled. Craig Hill was still standing there, watching. She took a deep breath and started the engine again, engaged first gear and pulled smoothly away. In the rear-view mirror, she saw him waving as they drove around the corner.

'Who was that?'

'Just a kid who lives upstairs. I've seen him a couple of times going shopping. Anyway, I've got no feckin' idea where we're going, so before we get lost, start reading the directions please.'

'Sorry.' *She's started swearing again, that's not a good sign.* He looked at her printed instructions. 'You have to take the next right turn and follow the signs for the A25 going east to Dorking then Reigate, then we go south on the A217 straight to the airport.' She had chosen the slightly longer route to stick to the smaller roads and stay off the motorways where there might be traffic controls or delays.

'OK, we're on our way to Gatwick Airport on a nice Saturday in June. Lucky us.'

Over Germany, en route to London

'Would you like anything to eat or drink?' The cabin attendant's name tag said Anita, and she was friendly and attentive. She'd fussed over the Al-Douri family when they boarded the flight and made sure they were comfortably seated one row behind the other. Hema wondered if Paddy Carr's influence extended to airline staff but decided she was just well trained. She ordered some snacks and paid in euros.

'Are you going home, or on a visit?' Anita asked.

Before she could answer, Hamid said, 'Both. We're visiting our new home.'

She avoided any political comments. 'You'll love it. England in June is marvellous. I hope you have a great trip.'

SIXTY-ONE

They passed Al Kuwayr, off to the east of the river, twenty-two kilometres from Al Qayyarah, just after midday. The sun was at its zenith and the deck of the boat was burning, like walking on hot coals. Makeshift canopies had been erected by the crew to protect themselves, but the heat was stifling and exhausting.

Karl walked to the stern of the boat, where the cannon had been installed on the upper deck; it was a Russian made ZU-23-2 light anti-aircraft weapon. Its twin barrels fired four hundred rounds/minute and could reach helicopters or low-flying strike aircraft at up to six or seven thousand feet altitude. A tarpaulin covered it in attempt at camouflage, but he knew it wouldn't fool the high-performance cameras of a professional reconnaissance plane or drone.

Karl called the gunner over. 'Fire a few test rounds. Make sure it's ready to perform.'

The silence was suddenly shattered by the loud staccato rattle of the cannon. He covered his ears until the firing ceased. 'OK, it's all we've got, so we'd better hope you can hit something with it, or we're toast.'

He went back to sit in the shade, his binoculars scouring the sky. They were sailing into the danger zone and he expected to be spotted very soon.

Guildford, England

Craig Hill came back home with the shopping at eleven-fifteen. His mother was still in bed and he went to his room to play his latest console game, *Special Forces 'Kill' Battalion*, where his record was ninety-five kills. Just before midday, when he hadn't improved his score, he went into the living room. His mother was nowhere to be seen; he'd have to fix something for himself. In the kitchenette, he put cornflakes and milk into a dish and went into the living room.

'Oh, hello Mum.' She was sitting on the sofa, lighting up her first cigarette of the day. He sat beside her and she switched on the television. The TV was on Channel 4, where she'd been watching a particularly bloodthirsty vampire movie before going to bed, drunk on cider, the only beverage she could afford in the quantities she needed.

'Great, they'll have the trials for tomorrow's British GP.'

'I'm not watchin' any motor racing, bursts your bloody ear drums it does.' She was about to switch channels when a news flash came up on the hour. 'What's happened now? More bloody politics I suppose. It makes you sick, all those poncy bastards in the government screwing everybody's life up.' She took a deep drag and watched the set.

In full dress uniform, Max Kellerman was standing alongside DCI Dewar, who was saying, '... suspected terrorist attack in the UK. Ibrahim bin Omar al-Ahmad, who may be using the name of Ali el Zafar, is a German national and a known ISIL fanatic who carried out a terrorist attack in Germany several months ago. The woman calls herself Sarah and speaks English with an upper-class accent.'

Full face images of the terrorists came up on the screen and Craig stared and blurted out, 'Look, I know him. That's him. That's the guy from downstairs with Sarah. Listen.' He took the remote from her and increased the volume. Dewar's voice was warning the public to be vigilant.

'That's definitely them. Her name's Sarah, the drawing doesn't look much like her and he's got his head shaved now, but I recognise them for sure. I just saw them outside, she said they were leaving.'

'Don't be stupid, Craig. It's them computer games messin' your head up. Put something else on, the news drives me crazy, whole bloody world's gone down the loo.'

Dewar was now saying, '... a reward of fifty thousand pounds ...'

'Did you hear that, Mum? Fifty thousand pounds reward.'

Now she was paying attention. 'Write that number down. Quick, before it's gone off. Bugger, it's finished. Did you get it?'

'I put it in my mobile, it's easier.'

'Well, what you waitin' for? Ring the number. Tell them what you seen. Fifty thousand quid, I don't believe it.' She switched off the TV. 'Go on, call them now. I'll make some tea, you tell them what you seen.'

'She's very nice, you know. She stopped and talked to me sometimes. I think she might be Irish. She's pretty as well. It's probably a mistake, she wouldn't do anything like that. I don't think it's worth calling, they won't believe me anyway, I'm just a kid.'

'Give me that bloody mobile here. I'll call them and you tell them what you seen or I'll give you a good hiding like your dad used to.' She grabbed the phone and pressed the call button.

Guildford, England

The apartment building in Watson Avenue was now cordoned off. The other residents had been taken to a nearby hotel and a forensic search was going on in flat number one. DI Arnold Bellowes had driven over from his home in Farnham, six miles away, and was onsite within fifteen minutes with the forensic team.

'The kitchen's full of bomb building material. Chemicals, cosmetic products, nuts and bolts, the lot, and there's traces of TATP in the sink. It's Ibrahim alright, the exact same process that Max described to us. Craig Hill, the kid who called in, confirmed the pictures and told us they left with two suitcases, so it looks like they're going after two targets,' Bellowes was reporting to DCI Dewar and Max Kellerman at Scotland Yard.

'But nothing to indicate where?'

'Nothing in the flat so far. The car's a silver five-door Citroen Picasso, Craig saw them loading the cases on the back seat and he recognised the two arrows design on the rear as they drove away. He's a smart kid, very observant, it's a 2014 car, but he didn't get the full number plate.'

'Does he know how long they've been there?'

'A couple of weeks. He's spoken to her a few times and says she's very pleasant, but I asked him about the posh accent and he said she didn't have one. More like an Irish one, he said. She's also no longer blonde, she's got short dark hair.'

'An Irish accent? OK, noted. What about al-Ahmad?'

'He only saw him once before today. He's shaved his head and his beard and got just stubble now, but he recognised him immediately.'

'No chance of a name, I suppose?'

'She was called Sarah, which checks out. He said there was a name on the post box one day, a German name he thought, but it was taken down.'

'Right. I'll organise controls on the motorways and all the junctions in a radius of fifty miles. We'll get an updated sketch and photo done and an urgent alert sent out on TV and to all our services. We'll advise Number Ten and get the threat level raised to 'Critical'. Every security officer available will be called in to police the area within hours.'

'They won't have time,' Kellerman interjected. 'These bombs are going to be used very soon, I'm certain of it. What high density centres are there around there?'

Bellowes answered, 'There's some quite large towns, like Reading, Maidenhead, Slough and Guildford itself. Aldershot, near where I live, is a garrison town, full of servicemen, so that's a possible target. And there's two airports, Farnborough and Gatwick, within thirty miles, both very busy on a Saturday in June.'

'Did Craig Hill describe the suitcases they were carrying?' Max asked.

'Hang on, I'll go and see. He's still outside, watching everything and taking photos. I bet he'll put it all up on Facebook.'

A moment later, he said, 'Medium size, made from some kind of material, canvas or similar. They must be old, maybe second hand, not the modern hard-shell type.'

'Colour?'

'One was a red and blue pattern, like a Scottish tartan, but he doesn't remember the other. What are you thinking?'

'The only place you'd take suitcases would be a railway or bus station or an airport, otherwise you'd stand out and be noticed.'

Dewar said, 'I'll get extra security organised at the airports and other points of transport and a helicopter scouting the area. Better have a marksman on board just in case. I have to go now to get on with this. See what else you can find on site and liaise with Max, he's staying here with me.'

SIXTY-TWO

North Terminal, Gatwick Airport, England
Saturday, June 25th 2016

'This is feckin' ridiculous, we've been in this queue for a half an hour. We'll miss our twelve o'clock slot at this rate.' The Citroen was stuck in traffic on the entrance road into the North Terminal. Driving slowly and carefully, Sami had covered the 34-mile journey in just over an hour, but it was now ten to twelve and they were within sight of the parking building, about two hundred metres away.

'Don't worry. It's going faster now, we'll get there in time.' *Sami's swearing a lot again. She's nervous and frightened and she can't admit it, Karl wouldn't approve*, Ibrahim realised.

'Finally.' The traffic started moving again and they arrived at the entrance just a minute before time. Sami took the confirmation form with the bar code, pressed it onto the reader and the arm came up. Slot number seventy-eight was next to the wall at the back of the lot and she pulled into it with a sigh of relief. 'Sorry, Ibrahim, I was a bit irritable there.'

'It's OK, I'm sorry you had to drive, it was easy for me.' He climbed out of the car, reaching into his pocket for the coins. 'I'll get two *wagens*.'

I'm not the only one who's nervous, Sami thought. *It's not often he forgets his English.*

He brought the trollies to the side of the car by the

wall where they were out of sight and lifted a case onto each one. 'OK, lock the car and we're ready to go.'

She put the keys into her bag and they walked out of the car park. In their summer clothing, chatting like carefree holidaymakers, they were indistinguishable from the crowds around them. The escalator to departures was directly across from the entrance, and they pushed the trolleys through the hall and stood at the side of the staircase, away from the flow of people going past them to catch flights.

'The shuttle's just over there. You go through that tunnel and follow signs for South Terminal. When you get off, you'll see another sign for trains.'

'OK.' He checked the time on his mobile. 'It's ten past twelve and it takes about ten minutes to get there. I'll make the call at half past twelve to be safe. You can walk around so you don't get noticed and come to stand at the escalator at exactly twelve-thirty. Is that alright?'

She shivered. 'Sure, and that's fine. I'll be ready.'

He took her hands and kissed her on the forehead as he'd done the first time they'd met in Palermo. 'Goodbye, Sami, it was great to know you. Thanks for helping me to make up for the last time. Karl would be proud of you and so would Baki.'

'Goodbye, Ibrahim.' She tried to say something funny but couldn't get the words out; there was a lump in her throat. Tears ran down her face as he pushed the trolley away towards the shuttle. She wiped them away. *Mustn't look miserable, I'm supposed to be going on holiday.*

Tigris River, en route to Al Qayyarah, Iraq

Karl heard the buzz of the drone before he could pick it out with his binoculars. He ran up to the top deck and ordered the gunner to try to take it out, knowing it was nigh on impossible. The remote surveillance device was too small and too high to be hit except by accident. He guessed it was a *NATO UAV*, which could fly at up to 10,000 feet altitude, with a range of 50 km. They were now only 10 km from the floating bridge, so it was clearly a part of their defence system. It stayed over the ferry boat for fifteen minutes, ignoring the chatter of the cannon and the shells exploding around it, but never near enough to harm it. He watched through the binoculars as it flew away, looking as small as a bee buzzing back to its hive.

Karl put his men on alert; the information from the drone would have been received and processed by the Iraqis and their allies, and they could expect a visit very soon. He ordered the pilot to make maximum speed. If the engine exploded it wouldn't change much and if it didn't they would be slightly less vulnerable, but only slightly. At 6 knots, 11 km/hour, they sailed towards the bridge, *probably the largest and most pointless suicide mission ever attempted*, he thought.

North Terminal, Gatwick Airport, England

Malik saw him first, as they pushed their baggage trollies through from the arrivals hall. 'It's Tony, Tony Miller. He's come to meet us.'

The Australian waved and rushed over to them, wrapping his arms around each of the family in turn. He held Hema for a long moment, comforting her sobbing body as she tried to come to terms with everything that had happened since the last time they'd seen him.

'It's all right, Hema. You're safe now, all five of you. You've done brilliantly, just as Faqir did, he would have been proud of you.'

'I'll leave you here, Madame Al-Douri. Good luck and I hope you enjoy living in our country.' The immigration officer shook hands with all of them and walked off.

Tony took the trolley from Aisha. 'Follow me. We're going to the other terminal to meet Paddy and Nancy. Their flight arrived a few minutes ago, so the timing is perfect.'

They walked to the shuttle train, the children chattering away as they regaled him with stories from their journey. The compartment was crowded, and a young Arab-looking man moved his trolley aside to give them space. Tony thanked him and glanced at the bag on the trolley; it was an old, battered soft-top case, made from cheap tartan canvas. The man had a shaved head and stubble beard and was wearing a smart white shirt and torn jeans.

No one has a case like that anymore, especially a young with-it kid like that. He'd have a hard-shell case. Looks better and lasts longer. He observed him discreetly. The man was obsessed with his mobile, checking it incessantly as they sped along. *He's not doing anything with it, just looking at it every few seconds.*

The shuttle deposited them at the South Terminal and he watched the man push his trolley to the ticket counter near the station entrance. Tony escorted Hema's family to the other side of the hall, as far away from the ticket machines as possible. He looked over towards the counter, where there was a long queue of passengers. The man was there, but he wasn't queuing. He was standing in the middle of the crowded hall, still consulting his mobile, looking at it every few seconds, then around him at the surrounding crowd.

He looks nervous, his eyes are flickering and he's fidgeting, like he's waiting for something to happen. Let's see what's going down here.

'Just wait here, while I go to find Paddy and Nancy.' Tony pushed his way through the crowd to the counter. He looked around in every direction. The man was no longer there – he had disappeared.

Behind him, he heard Hamid's voice, 'Sir Patrick, Lady Nancy!'

North Terminal, Gatwick Airport, England

Sami looked at her mobile; it was 12:28. She pushed her trolley slowly back to the escalator and stood there looking at the phone, as if she was reading a message. It was 12:29 and she closed her eyes, trying to control her trembling body, tears running down her cheeks, counting down the seconds in her head. Around her she could hear the excited chatter of holidaymakers as they passed to go up to the departure hall, laughing and happy to be going off to some exotic, sunny destination; the high spot of their year, the moment they'd been saving and waiting for. The moment that for some of them would be the last they'd ever experience.

Fifty-eight, fifty-nine, sixty. She closed her eyes even

tighter. *Dear Mother Mary and Jesus. Forgive me for my sins.*

'Sami.'

'Ibrahim?' He was standing in front of her, tears welling up in his eyes.

'What's wrong? What are you doing here?' She looked around in case anyone was watching them, but the crowds were ignoring them, intent on getting to their flights on time.

He came up and put his arms around her tremulous frame, whispered, 'I don't want you to die, Sami. I don't want anyone to die. My family is gone and I can't bring them back like this. I love you, Sami. I want to stay with you and love you as long as I live.'

She pulled him close and kissed him on the lips, gently and softly. 'I've wanted to do that for a while. I haven't done it since I lost Baki. He wouldn't mind.'

A middle-aged couple passed and the woman said, 'Off on honeymoon then?'

Sami gave a nervous laugh. 'Something like that.' Then quietly, to Ibrahim, 'We have to get out of here. What should we do?'

'We'll go back to the car. Then we have to find a place to dump the cases, like a river or a lake, where they won't explode. Come on, just walk out naturally, like we came in.'

South Terminal, Gatwick Airport, England

'Sir Patrick, Lady Carr, I don't know what to say, we're living in a dream world and it's all because of you.'

Hema had finally stopped crying and they were

following Tony and the family out of the airport. Nancy hugged her again, 'We were so worried about you all until we got Hamid's message. It was always our intention to help you get out of Slovenia, but we didn't know if you'd make it that far and we couldn't interfere until you were properly registered there.'

Paddy Carr said, 'You see, Hema, everything that happened before that had to be done without our involvement, or our integrity would have been compromised. And that would have been very bad for us and disastrous for you. But because of Faqir's cleverness in keeping you out of the system in Turkey and then throughout your journey, the Slovenian registration came up clean, so we had a legitimate basis to request UK asylum.'

'And that's why you sent us there, every step of Tony's instructions was planned to get us to an EU country. You organised it perfectly, we can never repay what you've done for us.'

'Let's say it was a combined effort. The only mistake we made was in counting on the contact in Montenegro. I can't tell you how sorry we are about that. These people come and go and it's impossible to know who's still there, who's honest and who's not. We made a mistake and we were devastated to learn the consequences of that mistake.'

'Sir Patrick, in the end, Faqir and I would have settled for our children reaching freedom and safety. We would both have given our lives for that.'

A smart black people carrier was parked at the kerb and the driver got out and opened the rear door. Tony gave up looking around for the young Arab man and helped him to load the bags. Malik turned to Hema. 'We know where we're going, Mama.'

'Tell me, where are we going?'

'To Brighton, on the south coast near the sea.'

Paddy Carr laughed, 'You're quite right, Malik, that's your new home. We'll be there in less than an hour.'

SIXTY-THREE

North Terminal, Gatwick Airport, England
Saturday, June 25th 2016

Sami put away the trolleys while Ibrahim loaded the suitcases back on the rear seat. They were driving slowly towards the exit gate when a young male attendant approached them. She wound the window down and said, 'Yes, can I help you?' In her posh voice.

'I just want to make sure your ticket is still valid, how long have you been here?'

'Less than an hour, I think it's still OK.'

'Here. Give it to me and I'll make sure.' He pressed the bar code onto the reader and the arm came up. 'Great, have a safe journey.'

'Thanks very much.' Sami drove carefully through the barrier and put on the right turn signal. Seeing she was nervous, he walked out ahead of the car to stop the oncoming traffic then waved them out. She nodded gratefully to him and drove off along the access road until she saw a sign for the A217 going back north towards Reigate. There was very little traffic going away from the airport.

'Do you know where you're going?'

'You want a lake, you said. There's a bloody great big one we passed before Reigate, on the right beside a church called Saint Mary the Virgin. It's only six miles.'

'Did you remember every place we passed?'

'It's a catholic church, of course I'd remember it.

Anyway, I was trying to keep my mind off why we were coming here.'

He put his hand over hers on the wheel. 'We'll make it. We've still got almost a thousand pounds left. When we get rid of the cases we'll drive to a pub or some place and work out where to go to be safe.'

'As long as we don't have fish and chips again. I'm getting a bit tired of them.'

Gatwick Airport, England

The Citroen had just driven off when the airport police arrived with barriers to close the access roads at the South and North Terminals. They checked the car occupants against the pictures they'd received from Scotland Yard and scrutinised their documents. Queues of hundreds of cars formed at both points and people started to become angry. It was likely that a lot of flights would be missed that Saturday.

The attendant in the North Terminal short-term parking came out to watch the confusion. An armed policeman in a yellow hi-vis jacket walked over to him armed with the pictures. 'Have you seen either of these two people?'

DI Arnold Bellowes was driving at sixty-five along the A25 going east from Guildford to Reigate, lights flashing and siren blaring. He'd just received news that the fugitives had driven away from Gatwick on the North Terminal access road. The witness confirmed that the cases were still in the car. As usual on a Saturday at this time, the M25 was completely blocked, and he guessed they'd take the Reigate road. If he was lucky, he could get there before them. He'd asked Kellerman to set up road checks around the town, but he didn't know how quickly it would be done. He kept his eyes peeled for a silver Citroen Picasso coming towards him.

As they left Reigate on the A25 going west, Sami saw in the rear-view mirror the blue flashing lights of a police car arrive at the interchange with the A217. She knew why it was there, but she said nothing to Ibrahim. She continued to drive carefully; it was only two miles to the church, she could make it. A few minutes later, she saw the sign she was looking for, Saint Mary the Virgin Church. The lake was beyond the church, a narrow lane going down alongside it. She slowed down, turned left onto the lane and drove slowly along a line of trees, looking for a point where they could get close to the water.

DI Bellowes' blue lights were still flashing, but he'd switched his siren off. He was stuck behind a lorry on the Reigate Road as it curved to go through the village. Directly ahead, he saw the silver Citroen coming towards him and turning off to the left. He flashed the oncoming traffic and cut across the road to follow it into the lane then stopped in the narrow passageway, closing off the exit. On his satnav he saw that the lane continued around and beyond the lake for about a mile, then joined up with several small roads in a residential area.

He called Max Kellerman and explained the situation. 'Pauper's Lane it's called, only wide enough for a single vehicle and one direction going from this end. I think something's gone wrong and they're going to dump the cases here, maybe in the lake. First, I need a car to block the other end of the lane, where it joins Flashford Road. I hope to hell there's no other cars further down, but it's really just a farm track, so we might be lucky. There's a couple of buildings off the track, we'll need to get them evacuated. They'll have to go out the back, across the fields, away from the lake. Get the helicopter here right away. Sorry?' He listened for a moment, 'It's at Gatwick? Good, that's just a couple of minutes. With a shooter? Great, it's too dangerous to follow them on this narrow lane, so we'll have to take them out from above. If we get them blocked in from the other end, they can't go anywhere. It's just a matter of time before it's over.'

A23, en route to Brighton, England

'The house you'll be staying in belongs to us, so there's no question of paying rent. It's on a quiet road, large enough for your family and it's got a lovely garden.' The Carrs were sitting on either side of Hema on the back seat.

'My daughter used to enjoy gardening,' Nancy said quietly.

'Did she live there?' Hema hesitated, then she said, 'We know about the accident and we're all dreadfully sorry for your loss.'

'We've all lost family, it's part of life. Yes, it was her house. They moved in after their first child. You'll like it, they were very happy there.'

'Where do you live?'

'In a small village called Itchenor. It's an hour's drive away. We keep the boat in Chichester Marina, which is right next door.'

They were quiet for a while, then Sir Patrick Carr said, 'When you get settled in, with the children at school and everything sorted out, would it be alright if we came to visit you sometimes? Just to see how you are, have a coffee and a chat.'

Hema took their hands in hers. 'My dear friends, it's your house. You can come as soon and as often as you like and stay for as long as you please.'

SIXTY-FOUR

Bucklebridge, England
Saturday, June 25th 2016

The Right Honourable Bernard Wilberforce had lived in Wilberforce House all his life, as had his ancestors all the way back to his great-great-grandparents who had bought the five-acre triangle of land between Pauper's Lane and Bridge Road and built the original farm and outbuildings in the nineteenth century. The property had been modified and extended many times over the years, including substantial renovations after bomb damage in WW2, but he had refused to move out, before, during and after the air attacks. An ex-magistrate, councillor and MP for his local constituency for forty years, he was now seventy-eight years old. Sadly, his son had forsaken his farming vocation and moved to Reigate, where he managed a real estate agency. Having lost his wife a couple of years previously, he lived alone, a local girl coming in three times a week to 'do' for him.

Well-respected in the town and known for his eccentric ways, Wilberforce had a number of unusual hobbies, notably collecting antique tractors, of which he had fourteen. This was the reason for the number of outbuildings, which were used to house the beautiful old machines. Wilberforce no longer owned a car, using a taxi service for his infrequent trips into town, but he still enjoyed going for a pint and a game of dominoes at the Cross Keys, a half mile up Pauper's Lane, turn left and the same distance down Bridge Road, about ten minutes by tractor. Since both roads were narrow and little used, the local constabulary turned a blind eye to this habit, so long as he didn't venture onto the main road, which he never did.

At exactly one o'clock, Wilberforce drove his royal blue 1945 Fordson Major e27n tractor out of the gateway and turned left onto Paupers Lane to drive to the Cross Keys. He stopped immediately at the sight of a silver coloured car parked on the lane directly in front of him. A man and woman were standing at the open rear door.

'Good morning,' he called from his perch two metres from the ground.

'Good morning,' Sami replied, in her posh accent. 'Are we in your way?'

'If you could just pull in towards the bank, I can get by.' He gestured to the grassy track that ran down to the water. 'Sorry to be a nuisance, but this old girl doesn't like going backwards anymore, got a cog loose, a bit like me. So she can only march onwards, like the Christian Soldiers.'

'Not a problem, I'll move the car.' Ibrahim shut the back door and she climbed in and drove off the lane onto the bank, just a few yards from the lake. Wilberforce thanked her and waved as he drove slowly around the bend towards Reigate Road.

Ibrahim opened the rear door again. 'What did he mean, "*the Christian Soldiers*"?'

Sami laughed. 'It's an old English hymn. He wasn't

talking about you, don't worry.' She got out and came around the rear of the car to help him.

'Be careful, it's very slippery.' He reached in for a suitcase then closed the door again. 'You'll have to pull the car back, I'm standing in a muddy pool. If I slip, I'll drop the case.' He walked to the side where the grass was less slippery.

'It's that thunderstorm last night, it must have been pouring here.' Sami climbed back into the Citroen and engaged reverse. Her shoes were wet and slick and her foot slipped off the clutch. The car stalled and jumped forward. It was now only a yard from the water. She started the engine again and revved it up, slowly letting the clutch out in reverse. The car didn't move; the front-drive wheels spun around on the muddy surface, unable to gain any traction on the upslope.

'Hell's feckin' bells. I don't believe it.' She opened her window to look down and revved up again, but the tyres dug deeper into the mud.

'Wait, I'll push you.' Ibrahim went to the front of the car, standing at the water's edge. 'Try again.' He gripped the bumper and pushed the bonnet with his shoulder as she revved the engine, but the wheels spun around with no effect, except to cover his legs with mud. 'It's no good. My feet are slipping all the time and the car's rocking too much. If we're not careful it'll disturb the cases and we'll be blown up.'

He came back to the driver's door, looking around. 'Can you hear that noise?'

She switched off the motor, looked out the window at the sky. 'Shite! It's up there. Look.'

A police helicopter was circling overhead, a powerful searchlight shining down from it. An amplified voice shouted, 'Move away from the car and lie face down on the ground with your arms and legs out wide.'

Now they could see the outline of an officer leaning from the open doorway, aiming a rifle down at them.

'Quick, get back in the car.' Sami put her window back up as Ibrahim slid into the passenger's seat.

He pulled her to him, kissed her on the lips. 'I'm sorry, Sami, I've messed it up again. We're trapped and they'll shoot us if we get out. My family died and now we're going to die, all for nothing. Just me trying to prove what a great warrior I am. How stupid I was, thinking I could change something. I love you and now I'll lose you. I'm sorry I made a mess of it.'

'Sure, and it's not your fault. The whole feckin' world's a mess. Nothing we can do about it, we tried to make a change, but no bugger really wants a change. They just want money, or power, or five minutes of glory on the telly or on Facebook.'

'What are we going to do?'

'Might as well go out with a splash and a bang.' Sami put the car in gear and drove into the water's edge, the tyres engaging on the downslope. Carefully she advanced until the Citroen was sitting in the lake. 'The car hire company's going to be seriously pissed about this.'

Tears came to his eyes. 'You always make a joke of everything. Even now.'

'What's the point of complaining? It's not going to change anything.'

He kissed her again, took out his mobile and put in the password. 'Do you want me to make the call?'

She put her arms around him and buried her face in his neck, her shaking body clinging to him as if she would never let go. 'Make the feckin' call. I love you, Ibrahim.' She tried not to think of Karl, or Baki. She tried to think of her mother.

He pressed the number.

Tigris River, near Al Qayyarah, Iraq

The noise was different this time, a deeper, more distant roar, not just the buzz of a drone. The French Air Force *Dassau Rafale* fighter plane came out of the sun at almost 40,000 feet altitude. Karl couldn't yet see it, but he raced to the top deck, where the gunner was already blazing away blindly into the sky. The Thales *SPECTRA* defensive-aid system, protecting the aircraft against airborne and ground threats, hardly registered the pop-pop of the cannon shells exploding 30,000 feet below it.

The delta wing warplane was armed with four Sagem *AASM* 'Hammer' air-to-surface 250 kg laser-guided bombs and had taken off from the French carrier, *Charles de Gaulle*, sailing five hundred kilometres away off the coast of Syria. Its Damocles XF electro-optical/laser designation pod was fed the position data calculated from the drone surveillance and advised the pilot when he was over the target. He checked the coordinates and released one missile. He had such confidence in his equipment, he wasn't going to waste any more. He didn't even look down to see the enormous blue and red cloud; he watched it on his console.

A moment before the *Saladin* disappeared in a huge geyser of heat, gases and water, Karl remembered his premonition, *the largest and most pointless suicide mission ever attempted.* His last thought was, *I hope Sami and Ibrahim have more success. Inshallah. Allahu Akbar.*

London, England

DI Bellowes was in Callum Dewar's office in New Scotland Yard with Max Kellerman for their debriefing session.

'Well done to both of you. That would have been the worst terrorist atrocity in UK history. Forensics reckon there was at least sixty pounds of TATP in those cases. The 'copter was at 300 feet and it was blown around like a toy, almost lost the rifleman out the door. The car park attendant said they had two trolleys with a case on each, so they were probably targeting both terminals. With the crowds at Gatwick today, it would have been a bloodbath. And thank God there was no one in the vicinity of the explosion, the petrol tank burned for an hour, nothing left of the car. It's a miracle we managed to escape the attack, you did a great job.'

'Thanks, Callum, but we didn't escape it, it escaped us. When Ibrahim and the woman left Gatwick, we assumed something must had gone wrong with the devices or the triggering. The explosion at the lake shows we were wrong. For some reason, they changed their minds and didn't trigger them at the airport. We'll never know why, but they blew themselves up instead.'

'That old codger on the tractor told me the bank was

very muddy and the shooter said it looked like Ibrahim was trying to push the car away from the lake. I wonder if that was what happened, they got stuck and couldn't get away, so they decided to commit suicide.'

'It still doesn't explain why they left the airport without carrying out the attack. That's what I don't understand, after travelling across Europe and then weeks of work to build the bombs. Very strange.'

'And I guess we'll also never know who the woman was,' Bellowes added. 'We found nothing at the flat, no ID, no prints we could identify. Apart from the remnants of the bomb- making material, just ordinary stuff you'd find in anybody's home. Pizza boxes, newspaper wrappings from fish and chips, empty coke bottles and tins. There was an empty bottle of bath essence and a couple of cosmetic items, a man's razor. Oh, and an empty Chardonnay bottle. It could have been my flat in Farnham, just ordinary, nothing special.'

'Forensics are going through the airport CCTV system now. It'll probably show us how it went down and we might get a good enough picture of the woman to ID her, but I wouldn't put money on it, unless she's been in trouble before. If we get an engine or chassis number off the car we might find something out, I assume it was hired locally, but even so, there's a lot we'll never know, and the British public will know even less, as it should be.' Dewar cleared his throat. 'Now, about the reward for Craig Hill.'

Max shook his head. 'I know, you want us to pay half. You'll have to talk to my boss about that, it's above my pay grade.'

•••

An hour later, Max Kellerman was in Dewar's staff car on his way to Heathrow. Monika was delighted he was coming home and the case was finally closed. Max knew he should be elated, but he wasn't. He felt somehow despondent, as if he'd lost a friend, or at least someone he'd gotten to know. He thought back to his visit to Kalk in May. *Was it only two months ago? It seems like a lifetime. I wonder what really happened this morning. Who was the woman and where did she come from? Why did they commit suicide instead of murder?*

He sat back in the seat and closed his eyes. *Goodbye, Ibrahim. It was interesting knowing you.*

SIXTY-FIVE

Brighton, England
September 2016

'Come through to the garden. The children are at the beach, they always are, when they're not at school, or doing jobs around the house. They'll be back soon and we can have lunch.'

It was a warm, sunny day, Sir Patrick and Lady Nancy followed Hema out onto the terrace where they sat talking and enjoying the peaceful morning.

'I see you've been busy. Everything looks lovely.' Nancy got up to inspect the flower beds and plants. 'This is new. What is it?'

'It's a miniature date palm. They grow in Iraq. It was Faqir's favourite plant, we had some in the restaurant. They don't need much looking after and they always look fresh and green and the fruit is sweet. It reminds me of him, I hope you don't mind.'

THE END

Acknowledgements

Kerry-Jane Lowery, Marjorie Lowery, Mike Jeffries and Nick Street, for honest criticism and ferocious editing.

My publisher, Matthew Smith for continuing to bring my stories to a growing audience.

Christopher is a Geordie, born in the northeast of England, who graduated in finance and economics after reluctantly giving up career choices in professional golf and rock & roll. He is a real estate and telecoms entrepreneur and has created several successful companies around the world. Chris was inspired to write his debut novel, *The Angolan Clan*, after the Revolution of the Carnations forced him to flee Portugal in 1975 with his family. He followed *The Angolan Clan* with two further titles in the African Diamonds thriller trilogy – *The Rwandan Hostage* and *The Dark Web*.

He and his wife live between Geneva and Marbella.

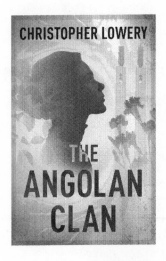

CHRISTOPHER LOWERY

THE
ANGOLAN
CLAN

CHRISTOPHER LOWERY

THE
RWANDAN
HOSTAGE

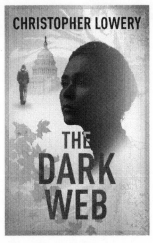

CHRISTOPHER LOWERY

THE
DARK
WEB

Have you discovered the thrilling African Diamonds trilogy from author Christopher Lowery?

The Angolan Clan takes the reader on a heart-stopping roller coaster ride, from past to present and back again. It is a deadly intercontinental treasure hunt laced with secrets, deceit and murder. The prize is a fortune in Angolan diamonds...or death at the hands of a pathological killer. The perfect read for fans of Frederick Forsyth, Wilbur Smith, Gerald Seymour and Clive Cussler.

Set against a European-African backdrop, the fast-paced plot twists and turns in a gripping series of events and action. *The Rwandan Hostage* is a compelling international mystery that will enthral all thriller fans, in the best traditions of Gerald Seymour, Frederick Forsyth and Richard North Patterson.

Christopher Lowery delivers a gripping final chapter in the bestselling African Diamonds trilogy, with *The Dark Web*, a thriller that is powerfully resonant of today's global dangers, hidden behind the ever-changing technological landscape.

AVAILABLE FROM AMAZON
AND ALL GOOD BOOKSHOPS

Urbane Publications is dedicated to
developing new author voices, and publishing
fiction and non-fiction that challenges,
thrills and fascinates.
From page-turning novels to innovative
reference books, our goal is to publish what
YOU want to read.

Find out more at
urbanepublications.com